The Irish Clans is an epic story immersed in the tumultuous Irish revolutionary period of 1915 through 1923, while the world is embroiled in the Great War and its aftermath. The once mighty McCarthy and O'Donnell Clans, overthrown in ancient times, are not extinct. They are linked on two continents by a medieval pact entwining military history and religious mythology. Divine intervention plays a pivotal role in unearthing the secrets of the Clans' treasure and heroic exploits. The patriotism and passion of Celtic heritage lies at the heart of this intriguing story.

Other novels in the series:

A tragedy at sea sets in motion the search for life's true treasures, both in 1915 Ireland, when the funeral of Fenian Rossa fans the flames of revolution, and in America, where the clans begin a journey toward their destiny in Searchers, the first book of the series.
Published March 2016

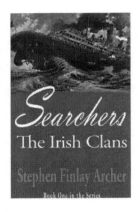

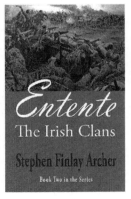

The mysteries of an ancient Clans Pact deepen beneath the horrors of WWI as Irish Rebels march toward revolution in Entente, the second book in the series.
Published May 2017

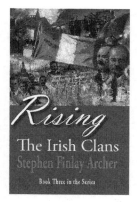

Irish Republican martyrs rise against overpowering British forces to spark the revolution in the 1916 Easter Rising, while the Clans search for unity and treasure to honor the Clans Pact of their ancestors in Rising the third book in the series.
Published January 2019.

The fortunes of the O'Donnell Clan are explored in Revolution, fifth book in the series, set in the midst of the Irish Revolution's upheaval, leading to the Anglo-Irish Treaty of 1921.

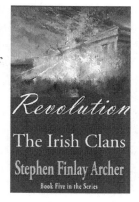

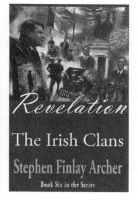

The Clans, while supporting the Irish Civil War in 1922-1923, seek to unravel and unearth an ancient religious mystery that has confounded civilization for centuries in Revelation, the sixth book in the series.

TESTIMONIALS

Searchers, Entente and Rising

Enthusiastic Reader

Searchers and Entente: *I am thoroughly enjoying your books! I'm on page 101 of Entente and holding my breath. I love the suspense and tension that you've created and I'm learning so much about my heritage--English, Irish, etc. I even have some German thrown in.*

I wanted to let you know that I was staying in Yosemite recently at the Wawona hotel and as I was checking out I happened to have Searchers with me because I'd been reading it at breakfast. A man who was also checking out recognized the cover and, with great enthusiasm, he told me that he had read your book and was now finishing Book II. I asked him where he bought the books and he said, Angels Camp, the Arts Emporium. Another man overheard us and said he was reading Searchers now and he had also bought his book at the Emporium. You are famous!!

Congratulations on such a wonderful achievement. I'll be on to book III soon. Linda Field

Amazon Five Star Review ★★★★★

Rising: Book Three: <u>**Excellent Irish History and story**</u>
March 4, 2019

I have read all three books published in this series now. This book has a lot of history and is a fascinating look into what happened during the Rising. Mr. Archer is a master of detail and research.

The story is interesting and is moving the main characters closer together. I just received this book and read right away. Can't wait for book four in the series! Thank you Mr. Archer for the wonderful read.

2019 Fiction BookLife Prize Critique, Rising: Book Three
(Overall 8.75/10)

Plot: *Archer's novel is well plotted throughout. The novel is clearly written, giving the reader an engaging storyline to follow and the great gift of knowledge of a period in Irish history that is not abundant in historical fiction. (9)*

Prose/Style: *Overall, the prose is well crafted, providing the reader with a mixture of a love story, brutal battles, and the search for a lost sibling. The novel felt authentic and true to the time period. (8)*

Originality: *Archer's exemplary novel is filled with original details and touches. The characters and subplots give the story extra flair and add even more strength to the novel. (10)*

Character Development: *The main characters of the novel are well-developed and easy for the reader to connect with. Morgan and Tadgh will have the reader rooting for a happily-ever-after ending, and readers will be rapt while following the adventures of Collin trying to find his long-lost sister. (8)*

McCarthy Gold

The Irish Clans

Book Four in the Series

Stephen Finlay Archer

Manzanita Writers Press
Angels Camp, California

McCarthy Gold: The Irish Clans
Book Four in the Series

Copyright © 2020 by Stephen Finlay Archer
All rights reserved.

ISBN: 978-0-9986910-4-6
Library of Congress Control Number: 2019917525
Publisher: Manzanita Writers Press
www.manzapress.com

Cover design: Stephen Archer
Book Layout design: Joyce Dedini
McCarthy Gold Cover credits:
> Front cover:
>> John Quider (American, 1801-1881). *The Money Diggers,* 1832. Oil on canvas, 15 15/16 x 20 15/16. Brooklyn Museum, Gift of Mr. and Mrs. Alastair Bradley Martin, 48.171
> Back cover:
>> *O'Donnell Claddagh Locket* by Stephen Archer,
>> Partial Folio of the *Book of MacCarthaigh Reagh (Lismore),* © Devonshire Collection, Chatsworth. Reproduced by permission of Chatsworth Settlement Trustees.

Searchers: Book One front cover:
> *The Sinking of the Lusitania,* courtesy of the Everett Collection
Entente: Book Two front cover:
> *Canadians at Ypres, The Belgian Front 1915,* painting by William Barnes Wollen, courtesy of the Princess Patricia's Canadian Light Infantry Museum
Rising: Book Three front cover:
> *Montage of the Irish Easter Rising 1916,* painting by Norman Teeling
Revolution: Book Five front cover:
> *The Burning of the Customs House,* painting by Norman Teeling
Revelation: Book Six front cover:
> *Montage of the Irish Civil War,* painting by Norman Teeling

This is a work of fiction. Any resemblance of my fictional characters to real persons, living or dead, is purely coincidental. The depictions of historical persons in these novels are not coincidental, and to the best of my knowledge, are historically sound. Some historical aspects have been augmented or adjusted for dramatic purposes.

AUTHOR'S NOTE

The front cover image on this novel is one in a series of paintings by John Quidor created in 1832 to illustrate the short stories of the famous American author, Washington Irving.[1,2] This painting, titled *The Money Diggers*,[1,1] which I feel is apropos of my novel, depicts Irving's story "Adventure of a Black Fisherman," part of his *Tales of a Traveler* series of short stories and essays written in 1824 under the pseudonym of Geoffrey Crayon, Gent, while he resided in Germany and Paris. Part Four of this series, which contained this story along with four others including "Kidd the Pirate" and "The Devil and Tom Walker," was titled "The Money Diggers."

The story of Captain Kidd, who supposedly buried his ill-gotten treasure somewhere along the East Coast of America just prior to his capture, became known after his subsequent execution in 1701 in London, England. As a result, a new illicit profession of charlatans grew up in northeastern America, called money diggers, professing to know where treasure was buried through the use of divining rods or seer-stones. These con men convinced citizens to pay money to go on such treasure hunts. These adventures would never result in finding any pirate booty, although the swindler would come away with his marks' money after they had supposedly been driven off the scent by the devil or his conspirators.

One example of the many tales of these practices was the true story of Ransford Rogers, documented and published in 1792[1,3] in "The Account of the Beginning, Transactions and Discovery of Ransford Rogers," who seduced many by pretended Hobgoblins and Apparitions, and therefore extorted money from their pockets in the County of Morris in the State of New Jersey,.

Another is the true story of Joseph Smith, the Mormon prophet who, on March 20, 1826, four years before publishing the *Book of Mormon*, was tried in court and found guilty for deceiving Josiah Stowel in Palmyra, New York into believing that he could locate hidden treasure through divination: by peering at a stone in a hat.

He had learned this trade from his father. Joseph employed the same process to translate the *Book of Mormon*.[1.4]

These stories were the grist of Irving's mill for such stories as can be found in "The Money Diggers."

Time, nature as well as human vanity and avarice have ways of obfuscating the history of man's actions. "To the victor go the spoils" only applies if those riches are found by the conqueror. Even with modern technology, the hunt for true historical knowledge is often mysterious and elusive. This applies to the location of purposefully buried treasure or inadvertently sunken treasure ships.

At least ten million dollars have been spent by hunters seeking Captain Kidd's treasure under the sands of tiny Oak Island in Mahone Bay off southern Nova Scotia.[1.5] Men have died in the search and the rising ocean levels threaten all who search in the booby-trapped, timber-lined shaft reaching deep underground. This is but one possible location for this trove of wealth. And this is just one notorious pirate who may have buried his booty to avoid its confiscation through the ages.

There are other theories as to what is buried in the Oak Island "Money Pit." In 1758 the British attacked and captured the French fortress at Louisburg on Cape Breton Island, a strategic part of Nova Scotia north of Oak Island that controlled the entrance to the St. Lawrence river, and therefore Canada, from British ships coming up the eastern American seaboard. This occurred a year before the British commander Wolfe defeated the French under Montcalm on the Plains of Abraham outside Quebec City to take ownership of Canada. It is speculated that the French moved their treasures from Louisburg to the pit in Oak Island before surrendering the fort to their British enemy. I note the parallel between this possible explanation and the theories that surround the disappearance of McCarthy gold at the time that Blarney Castle was under siege from the British Lord Broghill in 1646.

Another theory about what is buried under Oak Island's sands is associated with the Knights Templar. At the time that the last Grand Master, Jacques de Molay and his knights were being arrested on Friday, October 13, 1307, by the soldiers of Frances's King Phillipe IV in Paris, Molay's admiral, Roger Bonnechance, known as Jolly Roger, was believed to have sailed from the French Templar port of La Rochelle with much of their monetary and religious riches, headed for a safe haven, first in Portugal, and then Scotland. It is purported that they found their way to Henry Sinclair of Roslin and thence to Robert the Bruce the Scottish Leader in the fight against Britain, where they were reported to have fought at his side in the victorious Battle of Bannockburn in 1314. Interestingly, eighty-four years later, Henry I Sinclair, Earl of Orkney, Baron of Roslin is said to have travelled to the Orkney Islands and then on to the New World in Nova Scotia using maps that may have come from the Phoenicians. This was almost a hundred years before Columbus reached the Caribbean. Some treasure hunters have therefore surmised that the Oak Island Money Pit contains the Templar treasure. But that's a story for another day.

Treasures are out there for honest men of means and purpose to find. Stories like these stagger our minds and fuel our imagination.

Parallel to the Oak Island saga, but closer to our story, Sir James St. John Jeffreyes, governor of Cork City after he purchased the damaged Blarney Castle in the early 1700s, spent a fortune unsuccessfully dragging the nearby lake in search of the 'McCarthy Gold Plate'. Unfortunately for him, he had no knowledge of the Clans Pact nor of any of the clues devised by Clan Chieftains Red Hugh O'Donnell and Florence MacCarthaigh back in 1600.

Our Clans adventurers are not using divining rods nor seer-stones in their noble quest for the Clans Pact treasures, and they are not carrying out illicit searches to steal unsuspecting citizens' money, but they are being attacked by hobgoblins in the name of the devilish Head Sergeant Darcy Boyle and his underlings. These blaggards intend to shadow our protagonists' efforts to find the elusive booty and take it for themselves, as pirates of old used to do, following the adage "a dead man tells no tales." Will our adventurers find the McCarthy Gold supposedly hidden when Barney Castle was being besieged in 1646? Or will Boyle and his men find our heroes first and kill them off.

I hope my story will captivate you just as much as Washington Irving's "Adventure of the Black Fisherman" has delighted his audiences over the nearly two centuries since 1824. Happy reading.

INSPIRATION

"The Pillar Towers of Ireland" [4.1]

. . . Where blazed the sacred fire, rung out the vesper bell,
Where the fugitive found shelter, became the hermit's cell;
And hope hung out its symbol to the innocent and good,
For the cross o'er the moss of the pointed summit stood.

There may it stand for ever, while that symbol doth impart
To the mind one glorious vision, or one proud throb to the heart;
While the breast needeth rest may these gray old temples last,
Bright prophets of the future, as preachers of the past!

by Denis Florence MacCarthy (1817-1882)

DEDICATION

A wife and mother does her best,
Through life's travails with little rest,
No time for self from dawn to night,
Yet in her toil she does delight
To see her kin, both lad and lassie,
Grow strong and just, her legacy.

Shaina O'Donnell, Biddy O'Donnell, Lil Finlay, Lady Charlotte Perceval and now Morgan and even Kathy O'Donnell, were all brave women in turbulent times, matriarchs of their own domain just before the dawn of emancipation.

I would like to add another mother to that list who appears in these novels, albeit at the age of one year at the outset of the story. That is my mother Dorothy Archer, Dot, whose kind, caring effervescence and moral values nurtured me in my youth and guide me still. I have placed her face to represent Shaina in the O'Donnell locket.

There is one more mother to whom I dedicate this novel, Suzanne Murphy, my romance editor at the Manzanita Writers Press. Suzanne recently passed away suddenly, a great sorrow to us all at the Manzanita Writers Press. She had the spirit of a goddess, strong, honorable, witty, and wise, the epitome of bravery in an unfair life on earth. Now she soars with the angels, already with her wings, as strong on the outside as her soul on the inside.

I dedicate this novel to them all, and most importantly to my loving wife Kathy who is the protector of our family and the nurturer of my heart and soul in a wonderful yet challenging world that these strong women, except she and Suzanne, could never have imagined.

ACKNOWLEDGEMENTS

Once again, the author is indebted to Manzanita Writers Press of Angels Camp, California, for its tireless support in editing, producing, and marketing of these novels. Of particular note are its founding director and creative editor Monika Rose, and editor Suzanne Murphy, as well as book designer Joyce Dedini and eBook designer Jennifer Hoffman, who took me under their wing to wrestle my manuscripts into shape. Thank you, ladies!

There are a number of readers who have given me constructive feedback for *McCarthy Gold*, including Bob Kolakowski, Kathy Archer, Joy Roberts, Michael Murray,, and Victoria Bors. Thank you all.

The image of one folio from the magnificent *Book of MacCarthaigh Riabhach* (*Reagh*) (also known as *The Book of Lismore*), which is presented in the historical background section[2] is reproduced by permission of Chatsworth Settlement Trustees. © Devonshire Collection, Chatsworth. Thank you.

I would like to express my appreciation to Roderick Perceval, the current head of the Perceval family of noble lineage going back to the Knights of the Round Table, and to his lovely wife Helena, for their support. Their wonderful historic Temple House country manor and retreat[3] figures into the narrative and setting in Chapters Five and Six. The site can be found nestled in a pastoral and idyllic thousand-acre setting, just twenty miles south of Sligo, Ireland. Kathy and I visited in 2014 and eagerly look forward to staying in their splendid manor on a future visit to the Emerald Isle, perhaps when the last book of The Irish Clans, Revelation is launched.

I wish to thank Roderick's father, Sandy Perceval, for his expert review of my writings about his heritage, including his assistance in recreating a more accurate picture of what life was like in the Temple House demesne in 1916.

Most of all, I wish to express my undying love and appreciation to the woman who, for more than thirty years has been the wind beneath my wings, my darling wife Kathy. She has wholeheartedly

Acknowledgements

supported this new journey in our lives, even though it wasn't in our plans when we retired from the aerospace business more than a decade ago. It is she who wisely recommended that I finish writing the entire Irish Clans series of novels rather than focus on marketing. My readers, who have been requesting the release of Book Four *McCarthy Gold* can thank Kathy for her gentle nudging.

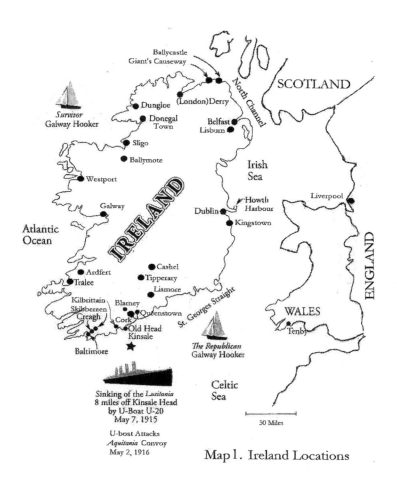

Map 1. Ireland Locations

CONTENTS

Contents

Chapter One
Boyle

*C*ollin O'Donnell leaped through the driving rain, his fingertips raking across the wicker of McCarthy's motorcycle sidecar. But he couldn't hold on and instead fell outstretched into the mud. Looking up, he saw Boyle's assailants hunched over to present a minimal target area.

From behind him, the gunfire hammered Collin's eardrums, bullets whizzing past the fleeing motorcycle riders. Moments later, the duo disappeared around the corner of St. Catherine's Church, with the guard running after them in vain.

"Shite, they're gone," Collin told Maureen back at the hospital lobby, soaked to the skin. At least the pelting rain had washed most of the mud off. She tried to dry him off with a towel after he lurched through the front door.

Realizing that he had lost his quarry, Collin blurted, "I hope to hell that Boyle's not dead," and raced toward the stairs with Maureen in his wake.

When they reached Room 312, Collin saw two doctors working on the body of the RIC head constable, one pumping his chest while the other blew into his mouth.

"Is he dead?" Collin asked Nurse Emma who stood by to assist.

"He wasn't breathing when I got to him. Then he started for a few minutes when I worked on him, but he's stopped again. They're forcing air into him now. It doesn't look good, I'm afraid. It's a last-ditch effort at this point, which could damage that repaired artery again. You'll have to wait out in the corridor."

Collin remembered being told about his own similar brush with death back in Toronto after the warehouse fire. That seemed an eternity ago. So many things had happened since. Hadn't there been some new shock equipment they had used on him to bring him back to life? He wished that his friend Sam could be here with him now. Whether Boyle died or not, Sam would know what to do.

As they waited, and watched the proceedings through the corridor window, Collin brought Maureen up to date on what had happened.

"You think that your sister is associated with these police killers?"

Collin wasn't about to tell her that Boyle had killed his father in cold blood when he was a boy. Or that he had shouted out to McCarthy to kill Boyle. "Yes, I'm sure of it now." He left it at that. Any attempt to justify McCarthy's actions would only elicit questions that he wasn't prepared to answer.

Maureen continued drying him off with the towel.

Collin held out his hand, showing her the split fingernails embedded with wicker splinters. "I was *this close* to catching them." His index finger and thumb nearly touched.

Suddenly, the man's legs twitched on the hospital bed. Collin heard a weak cough. The doctors continued their ministrations for a minute until they were satisfied that Head Constable Boyle was breathing on his own.

While checking Boyle's pulse, one of the doctors commented, "I'm amazed that we saved him. His heart artery could have ruptured and he may have brain damage after this time without breathing. How long has it been, nurse?"

Emma consulted her watch. "Twenty minutes now, but he was breathing despite his comatose state for about ten of them before you arrived, Doctor."

"Looks like you saved him, Collin," Maureen said, scribbling in her notebook.

"But he's in pretty bad shape." The nurse stepped to the doorway, as she made notes in his chart. "I heard that the assailants pushed on his chest pretty hard."

If the two medical personnel had any serious concerns about brain damage, those thoughts must have quickly evaporated.

Boyle came to and growled, "They almost killed me. Get out of my room, the lot of you."

Minutes later, from the nurses' station, Collin could still hear Boyle shouting obscenities down the hall. The security guard returned and called District Inspector Kearney, who questioned whether Collin had visited the head constable as his first visitor, just prior to the murder attempt.

When Kearney arrived, he vouched for the reporter. But the security guard said he had heard someone yell out, "Kill the bastard!" just before he entered the room and asked whether it had been Collin. Kearney offered that it was likely the smaller assailant, the same one who held down Boyle's feet. They all donned surgical masks, per the insistence of the duty nurse at the station, before setting off for room 312.

"I'd like to see the head constable for myself," Kearney said, as he headed down the corridor with the others in tow.

Upon reaching Boyle's room, Kearney entered while the others stood in the doorway. Boyle immediately started bellowing objections at this intrusion. The RIC officer tried to calm the patient down.

Meantime, the security guard asked, "Let me see your press pass, son. I should have gotten it when you came in."

Collin presented it to him.

"Let *me* see that press card," Boyle croaked, holding out his hand.

Collin decided, if the assault hadn't damaged his da's killer's throat, then surely all his yelling had.

The guard stepped forward to the bedside. Collin followed and tried to yank the card back, but it was too late. The security guard handed it to the patient. Collin could see the flicker of recognition sweep over Boyle's face as he turned to eye the reporter with a wicked stare.

"Take off that mask Mr. O'Donnell," Boyle said. "Let me see what a Canadian newspaper man looks like."

Nurse Emma objected and Collin let it be.

Boyle's hand shook uncontrollably in giving the card back to the guard. A spasm of wheezing coughs wracked the man's chest.

Nurse Emma shooed them out of the room. "You'll have to leave my patient now, gentlemen. He's had quite a shock on top of his serious condition, and we don't know the extent of his injuries."

After they left, Boyle couldn't believe the good fortune that had fallen into his lap once again. It was surely Divine Providence. The wife and children had disappeared right after he had tortured and killed the father. He had done some research and learned that an O'Donnell family with son Collin and daughter Claire had landed at Ellis Island in June 1905. It had been eleven years ago, right after the interrogation. But he remembered it with vivid clarity. *And didn't that invalid Jordan say he was looking for someone named Claire?* Finian O'Donnell had claimed he knew nothing of the treasure and had died without confessing anything of interest. When his son had tried to fight for him, the elder O'Donnell had called out, "No, Collin," just before Boyle had batted him away. Then when Boyle's attention had focused on the father, the mother had whisked the son and daughter out of sight. He had searched high and low for the heir with no success. Now it appeared that the heir had come right to him. Incredible.

So. It's the sister who's in cahoots with the McCarthy descendant! She doesn't have amnesia. She dropped out of sight so that they could combine their forces to find the Clans fortunes. And now the brother is trying to join them. He presumed that they had an O'Donnell copy of the Clans Pact.

Now, if his luck held, and when he got out of this infernal place, he would track O'Donnell down and apprehend the whole lot of them together after they made progress in their search. Then he'd force them to divulge their secrets.

Boyle was shaking, and not so much from the damned cold. He weakly tried to pull the covers up around his shoulders. Maybe his heart wasn't pumping blood properly. He realized that his recent thoughts had stemmed from a memory of his father's harsh voice driving him on, as usual. But what really disturbed him was the vision that had consumed his being while he'd lain unconscious. It was his mother pleading with him from some unearthly place not to follow his father's commandments, but to change his ways before it was too late. *Too late for what?* Then her voice had been snuffed out with his memory of her gruesome death at the hands of his wicked father.

Chapter Two
Sam's Plan

Monday, June 12, 1916
Barrow House, Barrow Bay, Ireland

*T*adgh McCarthy and his younger brother Aidan escaped undetected and made their way back to Barrow House.

"Did you see that mad fellow chasing after us with the security guard?" Aidan asked, once they were safely inside the Collis's home.

"Yeah, but I was more worried about the guard's bullets."

"The man yelled after us. I think he was trying to call out somebody's name, but his voice didn't carry through the downpour. He was the same fellow who surprised us when we were in the room with Boyle. Why would he do that, Tadgh?"

"Do what?"

"Chase after us. Unless he was a plain-clothes policeman. He sure seemed desperate to catch us."

"I'd be more interested to know if Boyle is dead right now."

"His feet stopped twitching before we left, Tadgh."

"Damn him. We only needed a few seconds more. What was he yelling about in Boyle's room?"

"He was screaming out 'McCarthy, they're coming. Kill the bastard!' Maybe he knew we wanted Boyle dead." Aidan looked at his brother quizzically.

Tadgh shook his head to try to clear it—*a mystery, to be sure.*

They stayed the night with Maurice and Martha and briefed them on the awful events.

On Tuesday morning at breakfast, Maurice told them, "Dr. O'Callihan checked and unfortunately, Head Constable Boyle is

27

still alive, although somewhat the worse for wear. He's madder than a hornet at the lack of security, so the RIC is going to guard him as long as he is still in the hospital."

Aidan looked up from his bacon and eggs. "Bollocks, Tadgh. We just needed a minute longer."

Tadgh had to devise another approach for executing the murderous villain, but he could not come up with a plan that would keep his promise to Morgan for a safe return. It was risky enough without a guard at his room.

"That guy who came in, I wonder who he was," Aidan said.

Tadgh had been thinking about that very question all night long. He had heard the man's yelling in the hospital room and he thought that the voice was familiar. Then he remembered. It was the same voice he had heard, although muffled, when he and Morgan hid out at O'Casey's house. Afterward, Sean had called him Collin, a Canadian newspaperman, likely the long-lost brother, the one who wrote that personal article in the *Southern Star*. He wished he could be sure.

Why would Collin want Boyle dead? He might have learned that Boyle identified his sister as a German spy and accomplice to murder. Killing Boyle wouldn't stop the RIC from hunting her down. On the contrary, they would come after them all the more vigorously for killing their precious head constable.

And why did he come back? He's the one I bumped into when he was leaving. But he came back in a rush. Did he recognize me somehow, even with the disguise? He couldn't have, could he? I've never seen him before. Tadgh turned his attention to more pressing business. "We're going to have to find another time and place to get this job done, Aidan. We'll need to shadow Boyle after he is out of hospital and back at work, but we have to bide our time. A promise made to Morgan is a promise kept, so we head back home today."

♣ ♣ ♣ ♣

Collin was sure that Boyle had recognized him. *I'll track Claire down by following this murdering scum when he gets out of hospital.* He needed to stay away from Boyle, not trusting himself to keep from killing the scoundrel while he was immobilized. The best place for him would be with Jack in Queenstown. Boyle would come after him, just like he had come after his own father. So be it. Man to man. He'd been in worse fights before and won.

One thing was certain. He had been right all along. Claire was alive and in the company of Tadgh McCarthy and his brother who were out to kill Boyle since the villain wanted them dead. How Claire got involved with this treasure hunter McCarthy, how he knew about the O'Donnell Treasure that Boyle was after, and how they came to be pursued by this monster, were all still mysteries, but she probably had her memory back by now if Boyle was after another O'Donnell. Forget the dangers of the revolution, this whole family situation was disturbing. He couldn't leave Ireland with his sister in peril.

Arriving back in Queenstown the next afternoon, Collin shared with Jack that he was convinced the girl Boyle was searching for was likely Claire.

"How do you know this, Collin?"

"Someday I'll share that with you, Jack. For now, let's leave it that. I'm sure that I can't travel back to Canada on the *Aquitania* on Thursday."

Jack reached for a pen and paper on his desk. "So Boyle knows more than he's been letting on for the last year, then. How can I help you continue the search? We can't leave Claire to the likes of Boyle."

"You can take your time on finding me a berth home. Surely there's some reason you can conjure up during wartime, Jack."

"It's an empty ship, Collin. But we have had some delays in getting her fit up at the John Brown and Company yards. I could have her ship out to Quebec directly from Scotland. There wouldn't be time to get you there before she sails."

"I like your creativity, Jack."

"It's in my interest for you to continue your search for Claire now, isn't it?"

Collin used the office telephone to call Mr. Healy, who, to the Canadian newspaperman's surprise, took the call.

The Irish Times publisher did not have good news. "I have been trying to reach you, young man. Your boss, John Ross, sent me a telegram yesterday saying that I am to send you home on Thursday. Your assignment here is complete, and they need you back in Canada."

Sam and Kathy may have had a hand in that decision, Collin thought. "I understand, sir. But I finally have news about my sister." Collin told him what had transpired, leaving out the facts that Boyle had murdered Collin's Da and avoiding any mention of treasure. "So you see, sir, I now have real proof that my sister is alive and in great danger, and I think I can find her by following Boyle when he is released. And besides, I'm told that the *Aquitania* is shipping directly from its repair docks in Scotland before I can get there."

"I see, but you have no confirmation that the girl is named Claire O'Donnell, only the vague hope of a naval officer and the sighting of a man and woman entering a house in Mountjoy Square."

"You are right sir, but everything I've discovered points to that. Try to convince Mr. Robertson to keep me here at least until the Royal Commission report is released on the twenty-sixth. And if nothing comes of my search, Jack Jordan says that I could be on the next ship to Canada on July thirteenth."

Healy was silent for a moment. "I'll do my best lad, but I can't promise."

Collin couldn't afford to lose his job or his marriage. Now came the hard part—wording his status the right way. He spent the rest of the evening composing various versions of a telegram for Kathy. Finally, on Wednesday morning, he wrote the lengthy message he would have preferred to send as a letter, but he would get it to her quicker by telegram, regardless of the extra cost. He read his draft one more time.

Dearest Kathy and Liam. Stop. I interviewed the RIC Head Constable Boyle who says he saw the fugitive girl I think is Claire. Stop. Incredibly, he's the villain who murdered my da and caused us to flee to America. Stop. I believe this proves that the girl he seeks is Claire. Stop. I am following close on her trail, so I cannot come home yet. Stop. Troop ship sailing directly from Scotland this week, not available in Liverpool until July thirteenth. Stop. Please understand. Stop. Love, Collin. Stop.

Boyle roared like a caged tiger. "I am not going to lie here and wait for another attack. I demand release."

"He is disturbing all the other patients on his floor and we have done all we can do for him," the chief surgeon later argued to the medical board. "The recent attack does not seem to have re-injured his artery. He can recuperate at home if he chooses not to heed our warnings. He's a damn nuisance. I say we let him go."

They consulted District Inspector Maloney, who said Boyle should not come back to work until he was fully recovered. When the medical staff released the patient that Thursday, June fifteenth, they all sighed in relief.

Boyle was feeling better, even though his chest still hurt if he took a deep breath. He decided to fake continued injuries to avoid having to take orders from that imbecile Maloney. He would get medical leave pay and could devote full time to pursue his goal in life—revenge. Although he gave Gordo's death more than a passing thought, underlings were dispensable. He had already recruited Harry Simpson, another RIC constable, to replace the deceased assistant. Harry arrived at the hospital in a RIC lorry at ten o'clock the morning of his release and transported Boyle home to Cork City.

I don't know how this mousey, thin, bespectacled constable ever made the force but at least he's corruptible, Boyle thought as they passed by Skibbereen on the way to Cork. When they arrived at Boyle's flat, Simpson was briefed on Boyle's plans. The doctors had forbidden Boyle anything stronger than tea, so Simpson got the constable settled and set the kettle on the range.

"They almost killed you on Monday, I'm told, sir."

"Dammit, yes, but I had control of the situation at all times. I know the younger brother was shot in the left leg, but he didn't show up in any hospital in Kerry, at least according to Kearney. You know those local RIC bastards. They're no damn good, the lot of them. Either the brother took him, or he was harbored by some citizen there until they came for me."

Simpson found a teapot and two cups. "What about the Irish Volunteers themselves, sir?"

"Their leader, Austin Stack, was arrested and detained on Easter Saturday night, before the Rising. I don't think they would have taken McCarthy in."

"Do you know where these brothers live?"

"The younger brother lived here in Cork. I had staked out his digs and he hadn't returned. But the older brother, Tadgh, I have no idea where he lives. I just know that I have chased him and his damned motorcycle all over Dublin. The crippled manager of the Cunard office in Queenstown said he saw the brothers on a similar motorcycle and a Galway hooker fishing vessel with a unique gray main sail."

"Not much to go on, is it?" The constable hunted in a drawer for a tea infuser and a tablespoon.

"Your predecessor wasn't very savvy," Boyle sneered. "I trust you will be better at it than he was." *After all, I'm not going to do the legwork*, he thought.

"So you believe that these brothers are German spies, do you?"

"Absolutely. They've got to be stopped," Boyle exclaimed. He slammed his fist on the table. "They killed at least three of my men in cold blood."

"So are we going back to Tralee, then?"

"A waste of time. They were only there to meet that traitor Casement and to make sure that the arms got delivered. My guess is they are long gone from County Kerry after their attack on me this week."

Simpson thought differently about what had caused Aidan's wound and the recent attempt on his life, given Boyle's account. Yet he wasn't about to challenge this angry curmudgeon. "So where do we go from here, boss?"

Boyle had given this as much thought as he could muster. "We let the brother do the work and then we strike."

"What brother?" Simpson stopped spooning loose tea leaves into the infuser and looked up.

"The girl's brother, Collin O'Donnell, a Canadian journalist searching for her. He was there Monday in my hospital room asking questions. After the attack on me, I overheard O'Donnell call the woman with him Maureen. Maybe she's a colleague. You go to Dublin, find out her last name, and where she works and lives. Start with *The Irish Times*. Then there's the Cunard manager in Queenstown. He seems anxious to find the girl and he must have been the agent who booked passage for the O'Donnell lad. He won't be far from the journalist. First we need to scare these searchers into action."

"Why would these people be able to find them if all the resources of the RIC haven't been able to do it?" Simpson asked, wary of his new boss's wrath.

"Hell, I found them and got two bullets for the effort." Boyle rubbed his chest. "They dropped out of sight since the Rising was put down—until this last Monday. The girl's brother was raised in Ireland. So the girl must be from Ireland, too. It's not clear to me that she ever lost her memory, so she may go back to where she was born, looking for her brother."

Boyle knew precisely where she was from, Donegal Town, but he wasn't sharing that juicy piece of information with Simpson.

"Even if she doesn't go home, the brother may still find a way to lead us to her."

"How do we scare them into action, then?"

"I think we need to pay the Cunard manager a little visit when you get back from Dublin."

Boyle wasn't sure that he was ready for a physical confrontation quite yet, but he was feeling stronger. His father would have egged him on, at gunpoint if need be, but his mother would have coaxed him to take it easy until he had fully recuperated. When he thought about it, he greatly preferred his Ma's support, God bless her. Why had he just stood by on the terrible night that his father killed her? He still feared the wrath of his father haunting him from the grave.

Collin's telegram had arrived at Number Ten Balsam on Wednesday, before Sam and Kathy got home from school. When he saw it on the hall table, Sam tucked it into his waistcoat pocket so Kathy wouldn't find it. He read the message later in his studio while he lit and puffed on his pipe. This would never do. He slipped into the kitchen so he could talk to Lil about the contents. When Kathy came down the stairs and asked Lil if a telegram had come in response to her ultimatum, Sam shook his head at his wife, and Lil said, "Not yet, dear." All through dinner Kathy lamented the lack of response to her telegram, especially since the *Aquitania* was expected to sail the next day. Sam and Lil stayed mum, trying to divert the conversation with talk of the little girls' affairs.

But little girls have big ears. "Auntie Kaffie, when will Unca Collie be home?" Norah asked, during dessert of rice pudding.

"Yes, Auntie, when?" Dot chimed in, getting up from the table and tugging her skirt.

"I don't know, girls. If he's on the boat that sails tomorrow, he would be home in eight days, I think."

"But he's been gone too long."

"Yes, Norah. Agreed."

"Maybe he'll bring us something nice like the dollies at Christmas," Norah brightened.

"A pretty one." Dot went looking for her dolly near the hearth.

"He has a lot on his mind, girls. I don't want you to be disappointed." Kathy sighed and began to clear the table.

Later that evening behind closed bedroom doors, Lil combed out her hair at the vanity while Sam laid out his clothes for the next day. Lil chastised him, "Why didn't you give it to her? She has a right to know. The man is not coming home. It's as simple as that."

"Not that simple. Collin has definite leads, and he is certain that Claire is alive."

"I don't read it that way, Sam. He is still wishing, and he's putting himself in grave danger. If they find out he's the brother of a presumed German spy, he could easily be thrown in jail like the other thirty-five hundred detainees he's been reporting on. He could have gotten himself killed when he found the man who killed his da. And what about this reporter Maureen O'Sullivan who Kathy thinks is flirting with Collin because they're working together? It's unforgivable that he's left his new bride and baby in the lurch to run off on this wild goose chase."

"I think that the situation has changed, *astore*."

"Don't you '*astore*' me. You men always stick together." Lil hit a snag with her comb, and waited, suspended.

Sam buttoned his pajama shirt slowly, fumbling with the last one, and then faced her in the mirror. "Do you think that Kathy should file for divorce since Collin won't be on the *Aquitania* tomorrow, Lil?"

"She has a legal right to do so."

"That's not what I asked. *Should* she, is what I said. Your opinion?"

"That's *her* decision." Lil turned away from him and opened a drawer in the bureau.

"I want your opinion, my love."

She sat still for a moment, then stared at her husband who was watching her in the mirror. "If it were me, I would go after you before I would do that. But you would never do what Collin has done."

Sam took the comb which Lil was now brandishing high above her head. "That's right, and that's my opinion, too."

"What?"

"That she should go after him before filing for divorce." Sam carefully held her hair above the snag and gently teased the knot out of his wife's hair before handing the comb back.

"She couldn't possibly go across that ocean by herself in the middle of the war, even if she were willing to do so, which I am sure she isn't."

Sam raised his eyebrows. "So, should we just let her throw her life away in divorce?"

"Not her fault, is it?"

"Forgetting blame, do they truly love each other?"

"Why, yes, I think so, except for this one insurmountable problem."

"A major issue, I grant you, which they've had ever since I met Collin. He's got to resolve his guilt or the marriage is over anyway, Lil."

"So, what would you propose, mister mediator?"

"I propose that you sit down here on the bed. Take your sweater off and let me rub your shoulders." Sam grinned.

"Don't you dare try to sweet talk me, Samuel Finlay. What do you have in mind?"

Standing square behind her, Sam massaged Lil's shoulders. "I think we should try to convince Kathy to go after him, with me as chaperone, dear. You could look after baby Liam for her, and I could visit my father whom I haven't seen since he married his Russian wife."

Lil turned and stared wide-eyed at her husband. "Are you daft, man? Leave school and head into danger? They sink troop ships you know. I can't go along with that idea."

"I checked with that Cunard agent Jordan and the *Aquitania* will be turning around after this voyage and heading back to Europe on June twenty-eighth, which is five days after school lets out for the summer recess. I think this is the only way to save their marriage, my love. Kathy already has the divorce papers prepared."

"I'm not for it, Sam."

"She's your best friend, and Collin is like a young brother to me."

Lil remembered that Collin's need for a mentor had helped Sam deal with the loss of his own brother. He would defend him, she knew.

"You owe it to her, Lil, even though she can't see her way clearly."

Lil thought a few moments longer about what her husband said, wondering what she would do if the situation had been reversed. She hesitated, then bit her lip. "I suppose I could handle all the children. It's only one more after all, and it will be summer. I'm already doing it, really."

"Will you take it on?" Sam's voice grew eager.

"For how long?" Lil asked.

"Jordan says the next westbound ship would be out of Liverpool on July thirteenth, which would get us home on the twenty-first, more than a month before school starts."

"So you would be gone twenty-four days."

"Twenty-five, if you count the one-day train ride to Montreal. The *Aquitania* sails from there at this time of year," Sam shrugged.

"It would get mopey Kathy out of my house for a time."

"Yes, there's that too, astore."

"What about the money, Sam? How would we pay for all that, and Kathy, too?"

"I'll talk to Mr. Jordan. Surely, he can just add us to the manifest at no cost under the circumstances. It's not a luxury cruise for heaven's sake. He wants Claire found. And we would stay with my father and his new Russian wife."

"I still don't know about this, but I appreciate the fact that you talked with me before suggesting it to Kathy. Let me sleep on it, and I'll tell you in the morning."

"Fair enough, astore. Now get out of those clothes and let's get into bed."

"All right, but no romance tonight, *creena*."

When he awoke in the morning, Sam found a note on Lil's pillow. She had already gone down to make breakfast.

I trust your judgment. Bring yourselves back safely or I'll die a lonely death! She had drawn a big red heart as an exclamation mark.

Sam mused while shaving. *Good. That's half the battle.*

The other half awaited him at the bottom of the stairs. Kathy waved the divorce papers in his face. "He had better be on that ship today, Sam. I am not bluffing about this. My solicitor has contacted his counterpart in Dublin, and they are just waiting for my decision."

"Now, hold your horses, Kathy. Let's have some breakfast and talk about it first."

"I'm not hungry, and I have to get to school."

"It'll just take a minute."

Kathy allowed herself to be led into the kitchen where the children were already eating their meal at the breakfast table.

"As my mother always said, you can't march on an empty stomach, or was that my father?" Sam cocked his head, trying to remember.

"Sam's right, dear. This is a big decision day." Lil set a plate of egg-on-toast on the table for Kathy. "Sam and I have an idea that he will talk to you about on the way to work."

"What is it?" Kathy's eyes narrowed. "What do you know?"

"Not in front of the children, dear. It will be all right."

After she kissed the baby goodbye, Kathy climbed into the car for the ride to school.

"What do you have in mind, Sam?"

He reached into an inside breast pocket. "Read this first."

Kathy opened the telegram. "What? This came yesterday. And you read my mail without telling me?" She flipped the page open, glaring at Sam.

Sam dodged in and out of the morning traffic. "I wanted to come up with a plan before worrying you, lass," was all he could come up with.

Kathy turned her attention to reading the contents. "All right, if that's how he wants it, I'm going ahead with my plans."

"Now, hear me out. You've got nothing to lose if you just listen to me, Kathy."

With the windshield wipers slapping time in the rain, Sam outlined his plan, carefully pointing out all the good parts of the O'Donnell marriage. "So, you can see that your marriage would not work out if you forced him home empty-handed. You know it, and I know it. My plan gives us all a chance for success and happiness down the road."

"If he finds Claire."

"Or if he proves that this girl is not Claire and that she did not survive the sinking of the *Lusitania*, yes."

"And you say that Lil would care for Liam while we are gone?"

"Yes, that's right. We discussed it last night."

Kathy stared straight ahead, mulling over Sam's plan.

"It helps me too, Kathy. I will get to see my father in Lisburn again after seven years apart."

"And we would set a deadline to return no later than July thirteenth?"

"No later." Sam knew that he was stretching when making that commitment.

"And I can bring my divorce papers in case Collin is not willing to return by then or has taken up with this Maureen O'Sullivan."

"Yes, bring the papers, but these thoughts you have about the O'Sullivan woman are way off base. I know Collin's character and I think you do, too."

Kathy shook her head. "I can't leave Liam at his tender age, even in Lil's care. But I'll consider your proposal today and talk to my solicitor."

Sam knew that taking wee Liam to Ireland was out of the question, but he let that sleeping dog lie. "All right, if you agree not to send the Dublin solicitor approval to proceed."

"I promise."

Just as Sam pulled up to Kingston Road School, the rain stopped, and the sun came out. Sam went around the car to open Kathy's door. "Have a wonderful day, my dear. I think this will be a grand day for a decision."

Kathy agonized all that morning at school. As the afternoon dragged on, Kathy gave the students a fun project to do to give herself time to think. Her students must have realized that she was hurting. One of them brought her an orange. As she peeled it, she thought of her father Ryan and his love of oranges. She had kept him out of her adult life, yet she now realized that everything she did was subconsciously influenced by what she thought her father would think about it. He had changed. His breakdown at the church just before her wedding service had been the turning point, and Mother had been the catalyst by taking a stand against his authoritarian behavior.

Divorce would be a terrible decision, not only for herself, but for her parents and the O'Sullivan name. But Collin had truly abandoned her and baby Liam with no commitment to return. And then there were the joint newspaper reports with that Maureen woman. Kathy had seen a picture of them together in their byline in the paper when they covered the executions at the jail. She was a looker. Kathy had her answer.

When Sam arrived after school to pick her up, he was anxious to know her decision regarding his proposal. "Have you talked to your solicitor yet, lass?"

"Of course not, Sam. I've been teaching all day. I need you to drive me to my parents' home in Rosedale."

On the way there, Kathy explained that she needed to talk to them.

Finally. She's going to deal with her demons. "Your father's a changed man, you know. I've hesitated to suggest that you talk to him because of your feelings, but I certainly agree you should talk to both of them."

"Depending on how it goes, you may need to drive me home, Sam. Or I may stay the night."

They arrived at Number Two-Thirteen Elm Street, and Sam stopped the Model T they called *Tin Lillie* at the curb. "I'll just wait here until you let me know."

Kathy leaned over and kissed his cheek before getting out of the sedan. "Thank you, Sam, for everything."

There it was. The recognition of all the years that Sam had substituted for her father, been a mentor to both her and to her husband, Collin, and had done a marvelous job of both. Now she was taking a step forward with her family. Kathy knew it, and she was glad Sam was happy with this development in their relationship. She waved back to him from the front porch when Fiona O'Sullivan opened the door.

Kathy's mother looked out at Sam in his automobile and then back to her daughter. "Is everything all right, Kathleen? You look a fright. What's wrong?"

"I need to talk to you and Father."

"Of course, dear. Your father is still at the university, but he'll be home soon. Can you stay the night?"

"We'll see."

Twenty minutes later, Ryan O'Sullivan drove up in his maroon Packard Twin Six touring car and parked it in the driveway. When he got out, he recognized Sam's car from Kathy's wedding and went to talk with him at the curb. "Nice rig, young man," he said, eyeing the *Lillie*.

"I brought your daughter, Mr. O'Sullivan. She is inside and needs to talk with you."

Ryan grew uneasy at the seriousness in the younger man's tone. "Won't you come in, Sam? Have a drink?"

"I think it best that you all work this out amongst yourselves. I'll wait out here to see if she needs me to drive her home."

"As you wish. I'll try not to take too much of your time."

Sam hoped that they wouldn't rush the visit, but he wanted to get home just the same. Lil would be wondering what was keeping him.

When Ryan entered the parlor, his daughter and wife were in somber conversation sitting side-by-side on the chesterfield. He set down his briefcase on the sideboard and situated himself on an up-holstered chair opposite the two.

Fiona rested her hand on top of her daughter's. "Kathy was just telling me that Collin has been gone since the time we were together at Liam's christening on Easter Monday."

"*Gone where* for almost two months, lass?"

"Europe, Father."

"To the Front?" Ryan's voice rose in alarm.

"No. On a wild goose chase to Ireland looking for his dead sister."

"I don't understand."

Kathy started to cry. "He abandoned me and little Liam, and he decided he won't be coming home."

Ryan pulled his chair closer to his daughter, took her shaking hands in earnest, ready to be of help this time—unlike the past fifteen years of estrangement. His daughter's tears dripped onto his hand.

Fiona took out her lace handkerchief. "Here, use this, Kathleen. We can work this out, together as a family."

Ryan clasped her hands tighter, and the floodgates opened. All those years of standoffish isolation now broken by one gesture.

Kathy and her father both rose and threw their arms around each other, holding tight. "Oh, Daddy," she sobbed, "I don't know what to do."

It had been a long time since Ryan had heard the word *Daddy*.

Tears welled up in his eyes as he patted her shoulder to comfort her. "Did you and Collin have a fight?"

"Yes. A terrible one the night of Liam's christening when he said he had to leave. I begged him not to go, but he wouldn't listen. He left and I told him never to come back."

After a moment, Ryan eased his daughter away, taking the handkerchief and dabbing at her eyes. "What did Collin say to that?"

"He said, 'Don't be daft, woman'. But he's the one who's off the beam, searching for a ghost he'll never find. He puts his dead sister ahead of me and his son."

Ryan remembered with appreciation how Collin had handled the sticky situation he had created himself at his daughter's wedding. He didn't want to drive her away again. "You have every right to be angry, Kathleen. What Collin is doing is wrong, but he's a smart lad. He'll come to his senses, if you let him."

"You don't know how guilty he feels about his sister, Father. You don't know him like I do. He'll never give up."

"Do you love him?"

"I don't know anymore. I need a husband and Liam needs a father."

Fiona spoke up for the first time. "Of course you do."

Ryan interjected, "Many wives have to cope without their husbands during this dreadful war."

"Yes, Father, but they know their husbands will come home when it's over."

"If they live so long, lass."

"You're not helping, Ryan," Fiona scolded.

"I'm just stating a fact."

"I've had papers drawn up."

Ryan stared at his daughter. "What kind of papers?"

Fiona looked stricken. "Oh, dear."

"Divorce papers, Father. I was going to send them to Collin in Ireland."

"On what basis, lass?"

"Abandonment."

"I know I have caused you that kind of grief before, for which I am truly ashamed, but it's a mite early for that with Collin, isn't it? He's only been gone two months."

This admission set off another round of crying. Fiona fidgeted with her pearl necklace. "Our family will never live it down."

"Now, now, Mother. It hasn't come to that yet."

Ryan went to the sideboard and poured sherry for all three of them. After he delivered the drinks and coaxed his distraught daughter to take a sip, he said, "If you want my advice, there's only one thing to do."

Kathy cradled the glass. "Yes, Daddy. What is it?"

"You've got to go after him, Kathleen. The sooner the better."

Fiona stood up, frowning. "You can't mean that, Ryan." She set her glass down firmly on the table. "Traipsing across the ocean to who knows where, in the middle of a war? And with a new baby?" Her arms crossed in front of her.

Ryan raised his glass as in salute. "We could keep wee Liam with us, Fiona. It will be fine."

"Sam has recommended the same thing. If I were to go, I wouldn't be alone. Sam has offered to go with me to find Collin in Ireland." Kathy took another sip and wrinkled her nose. She got up, crossed to where her father was standing, and threw her arms around him. "Would you really be willing to take care of Liam for me, Daddy?"

"Yes, of course we would, Kathleen, wouldn't we, Mother."

Fiona beamed. "I could manage and so could your father. I still remember how to take care of a baby."

"I appreciate that, Daddy, but Lil has already been caring for Liam while I have been teaching, and, well, she is still nursing wee Ernie. But you could visit and help her."

Ryan thought for a minute, then brightened. "I could go with you to Ireland, daughter. My college teaching is ending for the summer."

"Just the fact that you offered means all the world to me, Daddy." She smiled and took his hand again. "And I appreciate your advice, really I do. If I go, then I think it best that Sam take me because he knows Collin really well and can help convince him of his foolishness."

"As you wish, Kathleen. Your mother and I will assist you in any way we can. And if you do decide to divorce, we will respect your choice, won't we, Fiona."

Fiona lowered her head and averted her husband's stare. "*If* it comes to that," she sighed, and leaned back against the cushion, "but I will be praying every night that you two will reconcile."

Kathy looked up at her father. "You would support me, even if it came to a separation?"

"Of course, lass." He reached out and drew her back in. "I don't want you to be stubborn like I was with you and your mother when you were a child. I was wrong and it took a separation for me to see that I had to change. You have been estranged from Collin for a different reason. Use this time to reflect on how you might change to better your marriage, Daughter. He's a good man at heart."

Kathy stopped short of expressing her worries about Maureen and her involvement with her husband. "It's not his heart I'm most worried about, it's his compulsion to find his long-lost sister even though we all know she died during the *Lusitania* sinking. He's obsessed with finding a ghost."

"I still say, go to him to sort this out, Kathleen. You owe him and Liam that."

"All right, Daddy. I'll go meet with Collin, join him in his search, and convince him to come home. Just knowing that you and Mother both love me, come what may, means the world."

Fiona stood up and put her arms around the both of them. "Just make sure you bring him home. He's a good boy, you know." She clapped her hands. "Now why don't we all have supper and you can stay the night, just like old times."

"I can drive you to school in the morning, Daughter." Ryan beamed. "Let me tell Sam so he can go home to his family."

Sam was staring at the hands on his watch when Ryan walked up to *Lillie* and opened the driver's door.

"Will Kathy be out soon? I need to be going."

"She's going to stay the night, Sam. She told us what is happening with Collin and she was pretty upset."

Sam got out of the car and put one foot up on the running board to retie his shoe. "What was the outcome?"

"We support her, but we hope she doesn't file for divorce." Ryan rubbed the back of his neck.

"Lil and I are with you there. I don't think it will come to that."

"Sam, I told her that she needs to find Collin. She said you had already offered to take her to Ireland. That's very kind of you."

"I have a strong interest in seeing this matter resolved happily, Ryan. Besides, this trip will give me a chance to check on my father for the first time in seven years, up near Belfast. He's married a Russian woman, of all things."

Ryan reached out to shake Sam's hand. "Kathleen will tell you tomorrow what she decided, but my guess is that she will most likely accept your invitation. Thank you for your interest in my daughter's well-being." He paused. "I would like to pay for your trip."

Sam shook his head. "I hope that won't be necessary, Mr. O'Sullivan. The passage is likely paid for by an interested party in Ireland, and we will stay with my father, but I certainly appreciate the offer."

"Then I've three requests, please. Keep us informed by telegram, won't you?"

"What are the other two requests?"

"Keep her safe. I have not been a very good father in the past, but your Collin has opened my eyes. I've reunited with my daughter, and I want to make sure she is happy and comes home safely, no matter what happens."

"I understand perfectly. Don't worry. I won't let anything bad happen to Kathy. And the third?"

"Baby Liam. Fiona and I would like to look after him."

Sam scratched his chin, remembering his promise to Kathy that he and Lil would care for the boy. "Why don't we share the duties? Lil will keep him. She's handling three children now, so she has a routine. You and Fiona can come over whenever you want to see the tyke. I'm sure she would love the extra help."

Ryan nodded. "You're a grand chap to do this, Sam. Kathleen's a lucky girl to have such dear friends."

"We all do our part in this life, don't we? Tell Fiona that everything's going to work out for the best."

"I will, thank you. I'll take her to school tomorrow if you'll pick her up afterwards as usual."

As Sam drove off, he hoped Lil would understand why he was so late for supper. Now, at least Kathy's family had a plan.

The next day on the way home after school for the weekend, Kathy gave Sam her answer. "I am willing to go to Ireland with you, Sam, but I will serve the divorce papers if Collin refuses to return on July thirteenth, or if I find out that he is entangled with that floozy, Maureen. The solicitor thinks that I should meet him face to face before I take such a far-reaching step as divorce."

"I am glad you are willing to listen to what Collin and the solicitor have to say, lass. I will contact Mr. Jordan and my father to set our travel plans."

The next morning, Saturday, Sam met with Jim Fletcher at the *Tely*. He told the news editor about the contents of Collin's letter. "I know that we have been urging you to order Collin back home, but we have a change of plans, Jim, so we'd like you to keep him there."

"It's not as easy as that, Sam. The other journalists are upset about this, and I've been prodding Mr. Robertson to get him home."

"But he won't come, not now, so he says," Sam replied. "He'll end up losing his job. Is that what you want, Jim?"

"No, of course not. He's a good reporter, but—"

"But nothing, Jim. You've got to convince Robertson to keep him there until the July thirteenth sailing."

"I'll let you know, Sam. If it wasn't you asking, I wouldn't do this. You know that."

"I do. And Jim?"

"Eh?"

"Thanks."

Sam made another stop before going to Riverdale to mark his school papers for the year, this time at the University of Toronto Faculty of Medicine. There he received good news from his inquiries.

Collin got a telephone call from Mr. Healy Saturday morning at the Cunard office while Jack was out inspecting the docks.

"Mr. Robertson is quite upset that you didn't make the sailing last Thursday, Collin. Apparently, the other journalists are not happy about your special travel treatment. He started the conversation by saying he is about to fire you."

"I'm not going home yet, sir. I can't. The ship sailed from Scotland and I couldn't have gotten there in time even if I wanted to, which I didn't."

"Even if it means losing your job, boy?"

"That's not the worst of it, sir. My wife is threatening divorce. But I'm not giving up my search, not when I now know Claire's in danger."

"That's what I hoped you'd say, Collin. A great newspaperman never gives up on an important story, no matter the risks. I've spoken up on your behalf, lad. Mr. Robertson has reluctantly agreed to keep you here until the next ship sails west on July thirteenth. But here's the catch. I shared with him privately that the Allies are about to launch a major offensive on the continent on July first. The

Somme Offensive, they're calling it. It's hush-hush. You are to go to the war office on my behalf in London where they will brief you so that we can be ready to report out the day it starts. This will give our paper and yours the scoop of the war and should assure you of a prominent position with the *Tely*. What do you say, lad?"

"I say that's bloody marvelous, sir. Thank you. How did you hear about it, if I might be askin'?"

"I have my sources, lad."

Collin knew to stop probing. "How many days would I be in London?"

"I would say seven days, and if you leave on Monday, you should be back in Queenstown by the twenty-sixth."

"I appreciate this offer, sir." Collin's features clouded. "Only problem is, that will delay my private investigation."

"It's that or be fired, lad. I need your answer now. What's it to be?"

"Yes, of course," Collin answered, but then asked, "Isn't that the day the Royal Commission report comes out, sir?"

"Oh, yes. That's right. You could stay over in London and go to the press briefing. Kill two birds with one stone. That would mean I wouldn't have to send Miss O'Sullivan back there again. Good thinking, son. Then you'd get back on the twenty-eighth."

"That sounds fine to me, Mr. Healy. I think I can get Jack Jordan to arrange my transportation."

"Splendid, Collin. Then it's settled. Do a good job, lad."

"Yes, sir, I will."

When Jack Jordan returned to the Cunard office, he carried a telegram. Collin was waiting for him at the door.

"I've news, Jack."

"Me, too. I think you're going to like mine but let me hear your news first."

Collin briefed him on his conversation with Healy. "Can you arrange transportation to Portsmouth for me early next week?"

"Consider it done. I have a ship leaving for that port on Monday morning. Here, I have a telegram for you. Read it."

Collin took the paper from Jack, and he pored over it.

Mr. Jordan. Stop. Please arrange transport for myself and Kathy O'Donnell on *Aquitania* return trip from Montreal June 28. Stop. Will visit my father in Lisburn where Collin can reunite with his wife. Stop. Critical that we all return on your next sailing of July 13 from Liverpool. Stop. This is the only way to avoid marital grief. Stop. Thank you. Stop. Sam. Stop.

"I can certainly squeeze them in at no cost to them, Collin. Isn't that great news?"

Collin could see that this could help sort out his problem with Kathy, but he certainly wasn't going to commit to a July thirteenth return, especially since he had to postpone his search for nine days to go to London. "Yes. Great news." He clapped Jack on the back and stuffed the telegram in his pocket. "You're a grand friend. I couldn't be doing all this without you."

Chapter Three
Unlocking The Key

Friday, June 23, 1916
Boyle's Rooms, Cork City, Ireland

"**D**ammit, he was** supposed to be back at work by now," Boyle yelled into the telephone. "I need to talk with him, right away."

"I am sorry, Head Constable, but Mr. Jordan is making great progress in his reconstruction aid sessions and they want to keep him two days longer," Simone, the receptionist at the Cunard office, explained. "I can make an appointment for you to see him next Monday, sir."

Constable Simpson stepped in and accepted the appointment since Boyle was too wound up to speak civilly.

At four in the afternoon on Monday, Boyle and his lackey arrived at the Cunard office in Queenstown. They found Jack Jordan seated in a wheelchair behind his desk.

"I told you he was a cripple," Boyle muttered under his breath to Simpson.

"Good afternoon, officers," Jack greeted them, as he stood up and walked evenly over to them, aided by his cane.

"I see you are making some progress," Boyle conceded, shaking his hand, almost pulling Jack off balance.

"Any news of Claire's whereabouts?"

"I caught her near Tralee, but she eluded me. The men with her killed my deputy and shot me. There is no question. She is at the least an accomplice to murder."

"She certainly did not appear to be the murdering type to me."

"Well, she is. I need your help in finding her."

51

"How can I assist you?"

"I think you arranged for her brother Collin to come to Ireland. You know he came to visit me during my convalescence and caused quite a stir in the hospital. I'm willing to give her a fair chance to exonerate herself, if he can reason with her."

Jack knew that Boyle would certainly *not* give the girl a fair chance if he caught her again.

"What makes you think it was this Collin who visited you?"

"Don't play games with the law, sir. You'll lose. I repeat my question."

"If it were indeed Collin, what makes you think he can find her, constable?"

"Head constable to you. If he's Irish, she's Irish. She might return to the place of her birth, and he might find her there. I don't know."

"If she has regained her memory that is, constable."

Boyle turned his head sharply. "I know he's around here some place. Just tell him this for me. I'll go easy on her if *he* finds her, but if *I* find her first, all bets are off. You got that?"

"Yes. I got that."

"Make it happen, Jordan." Boyle turned on his heel and strode from the room, dragging Constable Simpson behind him.

Jack concluded that he would tell Collin, but he had no intention of ever talking to that bully Boyle again. He would stay well away from that blaggard.

"Kathy, are you packed yet, dear?" Lil glanced at the disarray in her friend's room.

"No, Lil. I'm not sure that I want to go after all."

"Nonsense, girl. It's a grand adventure, so it is. Now select from these." Lil opened Kathy's closet door and pulled out one of her most alluring outfits. "How about this little black and white velvet number?" *Slim pickings*, Lil thought.

Kathy shrugged. "What if he doesn't agree to come home, if he hates me for demanding it?"

"You can't have it both ways, girl. If you don't go, you'll just make matters worse. Is that what you want?"

"I can't bear to leave Liam."

"He'll be fine with me. I'll take extra care of him, you know that."

"I know he'll be fine. I just don't know how to manage without him."

"You'll have Sam. He's a good substitute."

"Of course. I love him to bits, and I trust him and his judgment."

"Then go and bring your man home. Aren't you the gal who is convinced that there is a solution to any problem?"

"Other people's problems," Kathy replied. Opening her valise, she threw the divorce papers in first.

"All right then, dear. Let's get you packed. Where are your underthings?"

Sam came home that evening with good news. "Jack Jordan has organized our ship travel, including Liverpool to Belfast and back, and it won't cost us a cent."

"How did he manage that?" Lil ladled chicken soup into bowls for dinner. "Sit down, everyone."

"I think that the publisher of *The Irish Times* might have had something to do with it. Are you going to see us off at Union Station tomorrow? We don't want a repeat of Collin's departure now, do we. So we'll have to leave early."

"Of course, Sam, we'll all go, won't we, girls?"

"Yes, Mommy. We'll all go on the big ship." Norah shook with excitement.

"No, girls. We're just going to the train station to say goodbye."

"If we can cram everyone and everything into the car," Kathy said, crumbling a cracker into her soup.

That evening, after the children and Kathy had finally all dropped off to sleep, Sam surprised Lil. While she had been reading a story to the children, he prepared their master bedroom for a farewell romantic evening. He had bought an RCA Victor Victrola gramophone with the latest Columbia two-sided phonograph recordings of Lil's favorite music a week earlier and stored them out of sight in his studio. This device now came with an electric motor to regulate the speed of its turntable. Sam was astonished at the inventiveness of the modernized world as he set this contraption up on the nightstand on Lil's side of the bed. The champagne, which he had also hidden in his studio, was not vintage but the best he could buy during wartime. Now it was chilling in a bucket of chipped ice on a stand near the bed.

When Lil finally appeared, shoulders drooping from the strains of the day and impending departure of her loved ones, she was met with strains of "Clair de Lune" and the pleasant vision of a partially clad husband lounging on the bed.

"Oh, Sam. I'm bushed. But this music, it's delightful. And where did you get this marvelous new RCA Victor?"

"At Eaton's, love. Come with me to the bathroom, astore. I've a bath drawn."

Twenty minutes later, Lil was in a much better mood.

"Could you wash the back of my arms, please dear? I think you missed them."

"All right, then. That's sorted. Stand up and I'll dry you off, my love."

Standing in the bathwater during the toweling, Lil exclaimed, "Give me that towel, Samuel. I can dry those parts of me myself. What would the children think if they came in right now?"

Sam opened the soft cotton towel and kissed her left nipple. "That's why I locked the door, my sweet." He handed a robe to her as she stepped from the tub. She slipped into it and pulled the tie tight before turning and kissing Sam squarely on the mouth, a lingering exploration with her tongue.

"You really know how to treat a girl, creena."

When they returned to their bedroom, Lil heard that the music had ended. "Play that tune once more, darling. It's one of my favorites."

As the music started up, Lil took Sam's hand and pulled him into a dance. There wasn't much room between the bed and the wall, but they made do, twirling in a tight circle, bodies sliding together.

"Would you like some bubbly, my love? It should be chilled by now."

"Mmmm. That would be lovely. How thoughtful of you, dear, but just one glass, as I'm still nursing."

Although the music didn't disturb wee Ernie in his bassinette under the window, he cried out when Sam popped the cork. Lil crossed the room to comfort her son, and then she soothed him back to sleep.

Taking the glass offered her, she sat on the bed to sip the effervescent wine. "We're all going to miss you terribly, you know. I can understand Kathy's agony."

Sam sat down beside Lil and held her close. "You're a grand lass to sacrifice for your best friend. I can promise you I will keep us safe and we will return on the thirteenth from Liverpool, astore."

"You'd better or I'll be the one off to the solicitor, if you're not careful."

Sam raised his eyebrows.

"Just clowning. I know you'll do your best and I trust your instincts, Sam."

"And I love you too, Lil."

"This champagne is going to my head. I'm not used to it."

"All the better to seduce you with, astore. Lie back now." Sam turned down the comforter, lit the tapers on his bedside table, and turned off the overhead light.

"You know what we said, my love, about the size of our family. But we should be safe tonight."

"That's what I wanted to hear." Sam opened Lil's robe.

"Here, let me loosen your belt for you. I can see that it is straining under the force of your love," Lil teased.

Moments later, both Finlays were naked and intertwined. When they came up for air after a prolonged kiss, Sam said, "I love your breasts when you are nursing." He cupped her right breast and squeezed.

"Go gently there, my sweet."

"Can I help?" He awkwardly tried to suckle and milk trickled down his chin.

"Let's save it for the little one."

"I have another spot I wish to explore then," Sam said, letting his tongue travel down from her breast to her navel and below.

"That's tender in a different way, creena, a much nicer way. Don't stop, my love." Her eyes closed.

There was a pattern to their lovemaking and they fell into the rhythm of it smoothly and sensuously. Lil's moaning woke Ernie again, who started bawling. It was time for a feeding, so Lil couldn't relax in the afterglow of their lovemaking. Children came first.

In the next bedroom, Kathy fretted, lying in bed and clutching Liam to her bosom.

Despite careful planning, everyone struggled the next morning to prepare, look presentable, and get to the station on time. On the platform, Sam gave Lil a long and lingering kiss. "I love you, astore."

"I love you more. Keep everyone safe."

Then Sam patted Ernie's cheek and bent down, kissing Norah and Dot. "You take care of Mommy for me while Aunt Kathy and I are gone, all right, girls?"

Never having experienced their father leaving on a trip before, the two daughters were grabbing his trouser legs and holding on tight.

Dot looked up with saucer eyes. "Are you going to bring Unca Collie back with you, Daddy?"

"Yes, Dorothy, we'll try."

"Hooray," Norah said, taking her father's hand. "I can help. I'm going too, and that's that."

"I know you want to go with us, Norah, but I really need you to stay here and look after Mommy for me. There's no space on the big boat for girls, I'm afraid."

Sam peeled the girls away from his legs and they clutched their mother, instead. Dot started sobbing.

Sam was having difficulty holding back his emotions. "It will be all right, girls. I will be home soon."

Kathy started crying when Lil took her baby from her.

"Go on, dear. Get on board. Liam will be fine. The train won't wait for you, you know." Lil embraced her tightly with one arm while Kathy kissed her child once more. "Bring your husband home to his little boy. You're the only one that can do it, girl."

Sam reached down and gently coaxed the reluctant mother up the steps and into the 10:40 express to Montreal, waving to his family as he went.

"Goodbye, Auntie Kaffie, bye Daddy," the girls cried, tears rolling down their faces.

The Finlay family waved, as the train pulled out heading east that June twenty-seventh morning. Lil's heart sank as she ushered the children down the steps to the terminal rotunda and home. She hadn't been separated from Sam, ever, and a gaping hole opened inside of her.

The next day at four in the afternoon, Collin stepped off the freighter onto the docks at Queenstown, Ireland, returning from London. Jack met him at the Cunard office.

"Successful trip?"

"Yes, quite. I have to finish my reports to the papers, so I'll need to go up to Dublin tomorrow. Any more insults from our friend Boyle?"

"I couldn't reach you, Collin. He paid me a visit with one of his goons, demanding that I tell you to find Claire and have her surrender before he finds her, or else. I played dumb, of course. He said he knows that you are her brother and that you were the reporter in the hospital. How does he know that?"

Collin had seen the flash of recognition and now knew Boyle would be tracking him. How stupid to expose his hand clumsily like this. So be it. He now had to answer his friend's question. "Sit down Jack. You're going to be shocked with what I have to say, so you will."

The Cunard manager plopped down in the office swivel that had recently replaced his wheelchair while Collin leaned over the desk, fists down.

"Boyle's the bastard who killed my da and drove us out of Ireland, Jack. I recognized him in the hospital and he saw my press card and obviously recognized me He thinks that the girl he is searching for is my sister and I think he's right."

"My God, Collin. Why did he kill your da? Was he a fugitive?"

Collin wasn't sure. *Some absurdity about a treasure?* "It was a family feud, I think, between the O'Donnells and the Boyles, one that goes way back in history. My da was an honest cobbler, Jack."

"But how does he know you have a sister?"

"We were all nearby before he killed da, ma, Claire and me. Ma and I saw him killed.

"How awful for you. And he's still after her because of the feud and not just as a supposed German spy? How odd."

"Yes, Jack, it is. But he can be helpful in finding Claire if we play our cards right, don't you see? He obviously doesn't know where she is."

"I guess so. I see now that Boyle's a very dangerous man, Collin. He seems like a blowhard, but he's likely squirreled away somewhere now with lots of armed bodyguards to protect him."

"Big man when he has a gun pointed at you."

"The goon that came with him has been hanging around since the visit, you know."

"Describe him for me."

"Mouse of a guy, thin, horn-rimmed glasses."

"I think that Boyle and the mouse will not attack until they find Claire and her rebel friend, Jack. Let's be observant of being tracked and stay in touch."

"All right, but you be careful, Collin. Sam and your wife will be departing Montreal in about six hours, Collin."

"Remind me when they will get to the Finlay residence in Lisburn."

"They get into Liverpool next Tuesday, the fourth, and they'll be in Belfast the next day."

"That doesn't give me much time, does it? I'm thinking I should go back and talk with Sean O'Casey."

"I have to stay on duty here in Queenstown, Collin, and I'll be needing the Cunard car here as well."

"Understood. Jack, you have done more than I could have imagined. Thank you."

As he was dropping Collin off at the train station in Cork City early the next morning, Jack said, "Find her, friend, for both our sakes."

Collin arrived at Dublin's Kingsbridge railway station at two in the afternoon. He admired the Italian palazzo design and wondered how this majestic edifice had escaped the fighting at Phoenix Park. He had an appointment with Mr. Healy and Maureen at four o'clock at *The Irish Times* building. Except for the bombed-out sections of the city, Dublin seemed to be returning to normal. He could see big rats scurrying up from the river as he picked his way eastward along the River Liffey, past the destruction of the Four Courts.

He arrived at the executive office at Thirty-One Westmoreland Street. The receptionist ushered him up to the publisher's walnut-lined office. Maureen was already there, looking vivacious in a red skirt and matching shirtwaist. Collin wondered whether this was the color that women wore to exert whatever power society would allow them.

Mr. Healy stood up from behind his massive desk and motioned to Collin. "O'Donnell, come and sit down at the table, son. You look parched, the both of you. Jameson, or tea?"

"I'll have tea, sir," Maureen said, smoothing her skirt to cover her shapely calves. "May I pour?"

"If you like, lass, but Collin, here, looks like he could use a stiffer drink."

Collin came to the sideboard to accept the liquor. "Yes, sir, that would be grand."

"Sit down, sit down, lad. We've got to talk. What have you learned at the Commission?"

Collin took a sip from his glass and savored it in his mouth before answering. "The commission basically criticized Birrell, Nathan and Chamberlain for being too lenient before the Rising. Lord Wimborne has been exonerated, as have the police and military forces. The report states that the main cause of the rebellion appears to be that lawlessness was allowed to go unchecked, and that Ireland for several years past has been administered on the principle that it is safer and more expedient to leave the law in abeyance if collision with any faction of the Irish people could thereby be avoided."

The publisher leaned forward, resting his glass on the shiny desk. "Was there a root cause stated?"

Collin took another sip of his Jameson and sat down in a now-familiar soft leather chair. "The lack of certainty as to whether Home Rule would ever be implemented, and if so, in what form, sir. This was exacerbated by the arming of the Ulster Volunteer Force in the north with the intent of stopping Home Rule, if it were to be imposed."

"I see." Healy tipped his chair back, tapping the fingertips of both hands together. "What did you learn of the upcoming Somme Offensive?"

Collin pulled his chair closer to Healy's massive mahogany desk and spoke in subdued tones. "The military leaders were reticent to inform me of the details of this offensive for good reason. But I dug deeper. Based on agreements reached at Chantilly last December, there will be a major push by the British and French forces along the Somme River against the German Second Army. For the first time, we will employ the Mark I tanks and aircraft squadrons to try to break the deadlock of the trenches. We are not sure what chemical weapons the enemy will employ. Combined casualties are expected to exceed one million."

Maureen spilled her tea on her lap. "My God, Collin. A disastrous loss of life." She quickly jumped up and grabbed a towel off the sideboard to mop up.

"Like cannon fodder, lass," Collin agreed, drumming his fingers on the desktop. "But we need more new weapons like the tank."

"Good work, lad," Mr. Healy complimented him. "Write it up, and we will hold the story until they start the offensive. Now, what about your sister?"

"Well, I've been gone for eight days and my wife will be joining me, or divorcing me, I don't know which, on July fifth near Belfast. The RIC Head Constable Boyle, at the center of the claims of German spies, is now tracking my whereabouts. I don't have a direct link to Claire, so I had better get busy."

"I would like Miss O'Sullivan to go with you this week, Collin." Maureen smiled demurely as she blotted her skirt.

Collin took this as the signal to depart and put his empty glass on the sideboard. "Ah, I work better alone, sir, so I do."

"Just the same, I want Miss O'Sullivan with you. Understood?" Collin understood all right. Healy wanted Collin's personal business splashed all over his newspaper. Collin rose from his chair, ears reddening, and wanted to respond to Maureen's boss. But he thought the better of it. After all, the man was paying his way. "Certainly, Mr. Healy."

"Well, get on with it, lad. The time bomb is ticking."

Collin held the door for Maureen. "Yes, sir. In more ways than one."

"We're going back to visit Sean O'Casey, Maureen," Collin said, as they left the newspaper office. "I think that the woman we saw entering O'Casey's during the raids may have been my sister."

"What? How could that be? It seems an impossible coincidence."

"Impossible or not, I think that I may be right on this."

Minutes later, they were outside Number Thirty-Five Mountjoy Square South, Collin knocking on the green door.

"No one is home, I'm afraid," Maureen observed, peering through the cut-glass window.

At her suggestion, they looked for O'Casey at four local pubs but saw no sign of the playwright.

"Shall we go back to the Shelbourne and have dinner, Collin?" He frowned with annoyance, and she quickly added, "Nothing more than a journalistic repast."

Over dinner, they discussed the situation in more depth. Maureen was curious about Boyle's part in the story. "Aren't you afraid that Boyle will arrest you, or worse?"

"I'm not worried about him, Maureen. I look forward to having him try, so that I can have revenge."

"Revenge for what?"

I should not have said that! "Let's just leave it at that, revenge. He's an evil man."

"An evil man with the law on his side."

"He may be a policeman, but he's a lawless one, for all that."

"Then you're going to have to prove it."

"We'll see, lass." Collin revisited the scene in the hospital in his mind and thought about Boyle's crafty way of operating.

"I wanted to talk to you about the other night, Collin."

"We're not going up to my room, Maureen."

"No. no. You've got the wrong idea, and I don't blame you for what you're thinking. If you can resist your physical needs because of a stronger love bond, then I can, too. I'm going to change my ways and be true to my young man, Duncan. You may remember him, the one who's at the Front."

"That's grand, Maureen. I can tell you that there was a time not so long ago when I might have reacted differently. But I've grown stronger because of my wife."

"I understand that and thank you for being the gentleman you are."

"Good. Let's meet here at eight-thirty tomorrow morning, and we will go back and talk with O'Casey."

After Maureen left, Collin had a Guinness and then trudged back to check one thing on the street behind Sean's home. O'Casey still wasn't back yet.

Around nine o'clock on Friday, O'Casey answered the door to find Collin and Maureen standing expectantly on his doorstep.

"Journalists, right? The raiders."

"That's right, Mr. O'Casey," Collin said, reaching out to shake the playwright's hand.

Sean took the hand warmly. "Come in and sit down, both of you. I can't turn away fellow writers who wield the pen rather than the sword. I've been reading your joint reports in *The Times*. Competent writing, I must say, not that I agree with most of it."

Maureen sat down on the parlor chesterfield. "What can I say? My *Irish Times* takes a Unionist view, although Collin, here, is a persuasive colleague."

"Aye. Then I got hold of a few of your earlier *Toronto Evening Telegram* articles, lad. Playwriting friend of mine in Canada sent them to me. Your writing about the mood of the people is insightful, more in depth, lad. More to my liking."

"Good words, coming from you, sir. Thank you."

"Sit down, for heaven's sake you two," Sean said, settling into his favorite wingchair. "Can I offer you tea?"

Collin remained standing. "Thank you, but no."

"How can I help you, then?"

"I am wondering if you can tell me more about the woman who ran into your home ahead of the military search."

Sean peered at Collin who was staring straight into his eyes. "Why do you ask?"

"Last evening I spoke to the two neighbors you mentioned. The husband said that his wife Marg hasn't been limping lately."

"I see. Quite observant of you, Collin. isn't it? I guess that's a trait of a good reporter, or writer of any sort."

"Yes, sir. I saw an unusual motorcycle and sidecar on your property."

"Have you ever told a lie to protect a good friend who has done no wrong, lad?"

"Collin hesitated, then answered truthfully. "Yes. I just did, two weeks ago, and to protect myself, actually."

"Well, I don't slip very often, but I did with you. I was protecting my friend and fellow playwright."

"Tadgh McCarthy, sir. Am I right?"

"You overheard?"

Maureen stared at Collin with a look of wonder in her eyes.

"Yes, although I just remembered the name recently when it came up elsewhere." Collin paused. "You see, it is crucial that I find the woman who was with him. The one with the limp. I believe that she is my long-lost sister I told you about. I was responsible for her many years ago when she was abducted in America, and I must find her now. Her life depends upon it."

"I see. It sounds to me that your life depends upon it, too."

"Yes, sir. You're dead right. Well, can you tell me where they

are now, where they live?" Collin pressed, pulling out his notebook.

"I'm afraid not, lad. Tadgh was driven out of Dublin in 1914
because of a play he wrote, and he lives somewhere to the southwest,
as far as I know."

"Can you tell me her name, then?"

"I don't actually know it, Collin. And maybe she doesn't either,
according to her story."

"Amnesia, maybe?"

"That's what she said. If I did know her name and told you,
then I would be breaking a promise that I made to Tadgh. I can
tell you that Tadgh saved her from dying at sea and nursed her
back to health. I believe he loves her, and he has saved her more
than once during our recent political upheaval."

"That may be, but she is in grave danger still, perhaps more so
than ever. Is there anything else that you can remember? Anything
that doesn't break your promise?" Collin paused, ready to write.

"No, son. I don't think so, I'm afraid."

"Then why was she limping?"

"I understand that she was shot trying to save a wounded soldier
in the killing zone down at St. Stephen's Green during the Rising.
Tadgh risked his life to cross British lines to bring her to hospital.
What he did saved her."

"I see. Well, thank you, Mr. O'Casey, for being candid with
us. If you think of anything else, I will be staying at the Shelbourne
Hotel for the next few days."

"Aye, lad. I will tell Tadgh what we discussed if he contacts me,
and I will ask him to contact you at the Shelbourne."

"This conversation is off the record, Mr. O'Casey, and you may
be sure neither Miss O'Sullivan nor I will mention it." Maureen
nodded her head in agreement, and the reporters got up to leave.
"By the way, where did you hide them?"

"You want me to give away my hiding place, lad?"

Collin reddened in embarrassment. "No, of course not."

"Right there beside where you were sitting. Behind the grate of the radiator window seat."

Collin looked. "That can't be, surely. You couldn't fit a cat in there."

"It was a tight squeeze, I'll warrant you."

The reporters were out the door, starting down the walk when Sean called after them, "I just remembered. They had one visitor when they were here." That was an understatement. "Oddly, he had your last name. It was a young Irishman, a student at St. Patrick up Drumcondra, I think, called Peader."

Collin spun around. "Peader O'Donnell?"

"Yes, that's him, I think. Does that ring a bell?"

Collin stood there, rooted, his mouth opening and closing like a fish.

An hour later, as they sat in the front lounge of the Shelbourne, Collin confided in Maureen. "My God. Sean had the key to the puzzle all along."

"What key, Collin? Who is this Peader O'Donnell?"

"He's my cousin. His family used to live near Dungloe just north of where I was born in Donegal Town. We used to play as boys, before . . . before my da was murdered by Boyle and we had to flee to America."

"What?"

"It has been a revealing two weeks, eh, Maureen?"

"And I thought your guess about your sister being the limping girl was amazing."

"Yah, don't I know it."

St. Patrick's School was closed when Collin and Maureen went to Drumcondra the next day. A sign on the door stated graduation had been the previous Thursday.

"Maybe they are just closed for the weekend, Collin. We can ask back on Monday."

"That's all I can hope for. I checked with the telephone operator at the Shelbourne last night, and she told me no O'Donnells have telephones in Dungloe. It's a pretty remote area, and she said that storms usually take down the telegraph lines there. I've tried to send a telegram, but there's no guarantee that it will get through. Even mail service is spotty since the Rising."

On Monday morning, July third, the Shelbourne operator got Collin's call through to the summer class receptionist at St. Patrick's.

"Yes, we get the students' plans after school lets out, so the parents will know when they will return home. It's our responsibility, you know," the voice on the other end told him.

"Good, tell me the plans for Peader O'Donnell, please? I am Peader's cousin, Collin O'Donnell."

"Can you come here to the school in a couple of hours and show me your identification, please? I will go to the records room for the information you want."

When Collin arrived, the receptionist told him, "It says here that Mr. O'Donnell is taking an excursion with some student friends to the Giant's Causeway and will arrive home tomorrow."

"Thank you, ma'am."

There was no point in going to Dungloe until Peader was home. He might not even know where Claire was now anyway, but it was the best lead he had.

When Maureen called later, Collin filled her in. "Wednesday, I'm going to Lisburn where Sam's father lives. My wife and friend Sam should have arrived by then."

"Do you want me to go with you? Mr. Healy would want it."

"I don't think that's wise, Maureen. I don't know what trouble I may run into there. It's personal."

"I understand, I don't want to intrude. But if your wife, as you told me, is concerned about your . . . ah . . . work with me, then I could dispel her fears on that count. I will wait in the wings, so to speak, if that would help."

"I guess it would help if you drove me there. I should not use your company car after that, and you won't be able to come with me beyond Lisburn."

"Why not?"

"Because it is not *The Irish Times'* business."

"Remember that Mr. Healy is paying your way here, partly because of your human-interest story."

"Yes, and I will write it up with you when it is resolved."

"Fine then, Collin. I'll pick you up at eleven on Wednesday at the Shelbourne."

"All right. That will give me time to finish my reports from my London assignment."

Collin was excited yet anxious. Kathy was coming all this way to do what, hand him divorce papers? *I'm not going to let that happen.*

Chapter Four
Showdown

Tuesday, July 4, 1916
Celtic Sea, South of Ireland

*F*inding their assigned berths and eating location on the massive *Aquitania* liner had been the first of the challenges that Sam and Kathy faced, but gradually they settled in and made friends with a few of the six thousand Canadian soldiers on board. The radioman had his own berth near the wireless room, and he gave it up to allow Kathy privacy. By the sixth and final day at sea, they had fallen into the routine. The soldiers had conducted a modest ceremony to mark Dominion Day on July first, and now it was Independence Day in the United States. Sam got the feeling after talking to some of the soldiers that they wished that their neighbors to the south would enter the war and help liberate the Allied forces before it was too late.

Compared to the thousands of nervous troops on board, Sam and Kathy had it easy. Corporal Robert Johnson had been assigned to make them as comfortable as possible.

"How many crossings have you made on the *Aquitania*, Corporal?" Sam asked as they ate their powdered egg breakfast down on C deck.

"I've been ferrying these young men for two years now, sir. That's thirty-one crossings so far, including on the HMS *Olympic* that we call 'Old Reliable'. It's not easy conditioning these troops for battle on the way overseas. As you can see, the men are determined to do their duty in stopping the Kaiser but they fear what lies ahead for them in the trenches of France."

"I wonder if that comes from the stories we've published in our Toronto paper about the atrocities caused by chemical warfare at

Ypres, Corporal," Sam said, spearing a forkful of eggs.

"What's really got them spooked is the report relayed from the Front two days ago about the Somme offensive. We heard that about sixty thousand Triple Alliance casualties were reported on the first day alone."

"Your last name is O'Donnell, isn't it, ma'am," the corporal commented as he rose to check on his men. "We had a young gentleman by that name on board some two months back. Any relation?"

"He's my husband, sir. We're going to bring him home."

"Are you now? He talked about you all the way over, as I recall."

"Did he?"

"Like most of the men who miss their loved ones terribly. But he has the chance to go home unlike the rest of this lot."

Sam turned from his eggs and asked, "How dangerous was the U-boat attack on that trip, Corporal?

"Dangerous enough. But the convoy saved us once again."

Kathy looked stricken. "Let's hope we won't need them on this trip, then."

"They're here if need be, lass. We'll be all right. Don't you worry."

"Easier said than done, sir."

"All these risks are relative, ma'am," the corporal said, sweeping his arm around toward the soldiers eating their breakfast.

This made the upcoming reconciliation with Collin pale by comparison.

On their way out of the mouth of the St. Lawrence, and now, as they passed by the southern coast of Ireland, they had been on high alert for the possibility of *Unterseeboot* attack, they called them U-boats. All on board kept life vests at the ready, and the troops frequently mustered for submarine watch. At least on this occasion, they had a destroyer escort.

After breakfast, Sam and Kathy took a stroll on deck to view the Irish coast off the port side. Kathy seemed to be increasingly agitated, and Sam wanted to help her stay calm.

"I think you made the right decision to leave wee Liam with Lil, Kathy. His health would have been at risk in this dangerous environment."

"Yes, but I miss him something terrible."

"You need to make your case without him, and Collin would be upset if you had brought his son into this strained situation."

"Now you're worrying me."

"The real danger is with your marriage, isn't it, lass. And you're taking the grand initiative to fix it." In truth, he didn't know if she was only coming all this way to serve Collin with divorce papers.

Kathy looked away, then back to Sam. "Is Mr. Jordan going to accompany us to Lisburn, Sam?"

"Probably not, but he seems very excited about the prospect of finding Claire, to be sure."

"You know what I think, Sam? Maybe a romantic interest, there. Call it female intuition."

"Listen to me, Kathy. These stories are probably just a figment of Mr. Jordan's imagination. But what if Claire is alive and actually is the woman that Mr. Jordan has seen? What if Collin and Jack find her? Then Collin will likely have a difficult time convincing her to come home to Canada with us, won't he? She may be committed to her new rebel life, likely with her own romantic interest by now."

"I suppose you are right, Sam, but this is beside the point, I assure you. We won't even bring Collin home unless he's changed his tune, which I don't expect."

"Now here's something I've been thinking about. Claire is a nurse, right? A kind of Florence Nightingale, if I remember what you and Collin told me."

"That's right. We found out that she taught herself nursing skills at the factory and orphanage and then went into training briefly in New York before leaving for Europe on the Lusitania."

"So, she appears to be motivated to help people and save lives. I read that the University of Toronto started accepting women to become doctors in 1906. This was revolutionary and they are leaders in the world for giving women this opportunity. That all came about because Dr. Emily Stowe, the first Canadian woman licensed to practice medicine, standing up for women's rights, crusaded to open a woman's medical college a few years earlier. Then, in 1909, prominent Toronto women opened the Women's College Hospital, which is now staffed by women."

"How does that help us?"

"Toronto is one of the few places where Claire would be accepted to study to become a doctor and to have a modern women's hospital to practice in. I have spoken with the university medical board director who said she would be an excellent candidate with her dedication to the sick and her nursing background."

"So this could be the carrot to convince her to leave Ireland, if she is still alive?"

"Yes. We must tell Collin."

"If we even get that far with him, Sam." Kathy tapped her purse.

Sam knew the contents. "Can I not convince you to just throw that overboard?"

"Not on your life." Kathy clutched the purse to her chest in case Sam tried to execute his suggestion.

"Does the ocean seem rougher to you today?" she asked as they passed by eight miles offshore from Fenit's Light.

"I don't think so, why?"

"Because I've felt sick to my stomach this morning. I guess sea travel doesn't agree with me."

"Many people experience seasickness. It's common. I will bring you some saltine crackers. That may help. Besides, we should be docked in Liverpool overnight. Maybe you should go below and rest."

"No, thank you. I feel worse in close quarters. I'll take this ocean sea air anytime."

"Fine, look at the horizon, then."

"Oh, what a lovely sailboat." Kathy pointed toward the coast at a vessel headed out to sea.

Sam squinted. "I'd say it looks like a hooker. That's a type of fishing boat usually found in Galway Bay. I remember them from my youth."

As the boat sailed into clear view, Kathy said, "I think I see a fisherman waving to us, or maybe that's my imagination."

Aidan saw the impressive four-stack ocean liner among the other convoy ships offshore to the south. The zigzag black stripe painted along its hull identified it as a troop carrier. He waved at it in passing.

Tadgh and Morgan had headed out for Meenmore very early that morning on the Kerry, giving Aidan the run of the Creagh house in their absence. He accepted the responsibility that came with it. The sea air made his leg feel much better. Maybe it was the salt spray shower he was getting. *I guess I finally have my sea legs back.*

Aidan had watched as Tadgh carefully tied the family Bible and some other documents in an oilskin cloth before they left. Morgan had been assigned custodian of these treasures, which she held close to her in the wicker sidecar. Aidan didn't know why they were biking three hundred miles to meet with the man they called Comrade Peader, a man who, to his knowledge, they had only met with a couple of times in Dublin.

"Let me talk with him," Boyle ordered, when the Cunard receptionist told him that her manager was busy.

"He can call you back tomorrow," she answered in a frosty tone.

"Tomorrow's not good enough. This is the police."

"Just a minute, then."

The receptionist stepped into the boss's office. "Jack, that awful policeman you don't want to talk to is on the telephone. I told him you were busy but he insists on speaking with you." The woman left and closed the door behind her.

The Cunard manager drummed his fingers on the desk and then reluctantly picked up the receiver. "This is Jack Jordan. What can I do for you?"

"You know bloody well what you can do for me, Jordan!" Boyle screamed into the telephone. "Why didn't you get back to me? Did you see the brother and tell him? It's July fourth already."

"I haven't seen him."

At his end, Boyle knew Jordan was lying. His man Simpson, who was standing beside him, had seen them together several days ago. Unfortunately, he had not followed O'Donnell. "That's not good enough, Jordan," Boyle growled. "This is a murder investigation, and you need to get him my message."

"I'll let you know," Jack answered curtly, then hung up.

"Goddammit! No one hangs up on Darcy Boyle!" the head constable barked.

"Calm down, sir," Simpson said. "Doesn't it seem to you that Jordan is trying to keep us out of the picture?"

"I want you to go to Dublin and follow that reporter Maureen and report back to me if she contacts our suspect. Then follow him this time. Got it?"

"Yes, sir." Constable Simpson turned smartly and scurried out of Boyle's flat as quickly as his legs would carry him. Like Gordo before him, he didn't trust his boss, not one iota.

On Wednesday morning, July fifth, at eleven sharp, Maureen rolled up in *The Irish Times* sedan to the front entrance of the Shelbourne Hotel on St. Stephen's Green North. Collin was standing at the curb, valise in hand. "Good morning," she called out, "Are you planning to leave for good?"

"Not sure, Maureen. That depends on what happens later today. I might be coming back to Dublin for good, but I hope not."

The trip to Lisburn, a linen industry town on the southwest outskirts of Belfast, took three hours. The weather was dismal, made even more so when it started to rain an hour from their destination. Maureen's mood seemed as glum as the weather, so Collin attempted to distract her in light conversation. "Did you know that linen mills in the western end of Belfast on Falls Road and adjacent Lisburn employed forty percent of the workers of the Belfast area in their heyday? I understand there is early Irish literature that speaks of linen being used in the eighth century where the country's climate was conducive to growing flax."

"You know more about this than I do, Collin."

"My friend Sam once told me that his father, John Finlay, was a bleacher at the Bessbrook Spinning Company southwest of Lisburn."

"He must be a Protestant, then." Maureen appeared more interested in people and religion than the history of the linen industry.

"I think you are right, Maureen. Apparently, the Finlay name was Scottish, a Sept of the Farquarson Clan. They settled in the Belfast area as part of Queen Elizabeth's plantation program in the 1590s. Sam's father went to Russia to check out a local grass as a substitute for flax in the linen process. The grass sample didn't work out, but John found and married his second wife there and brought her to his home in Ireland. The Russian political unrest between the Tsar and his government over high food prices, fuel shortages, and crippling losses on the Eastern Front of the Great War is becoming acute."

"Out of the fat and into the fire of war, so to speak."

"Good point, Maureen."

"What happened to his first wife?"

"Sam's mother, Elizabeth, died just before he immigrated to Canada. His middle name is her maiden one, Stevenson."

They had reached the road into town, so Maureen asked, "What street are we looking for?"

"Sam sent it in a telegram. Just a minute. Here it is, Number Eighty-Five, Longstone Street."

They hunted and found the address just a half mile from the Lisburn Market Square.

"I think it best that you stay in the automobile, Maureen, until I need you." Collin said, exiting the car without waiting for an answer. In the rain, he walked cautiously to the front door, as if expecting a herd of charging elephants to come stampeding out of the ramshackle tenement. This was a workman's home, to be sure.

"It's now or never," he muttered to himself, as he grasped the doorknocker and sounded his arrival.

"It will be all right," Maureen called out from the car.

Collin stood there dripping as an older man with gnarled hands opened the door. There was something about his pointed nose and sunken eyes that reminded him of Sam, but with unkempt whiskers. "Collin, is that you, lad?"

"Yes sir, in the flesh."

"Come in, come in, my boy."

Inside the small vestibule with its faded flowered wallpaper, a stern, stocky woman took his dripping raincoat. "It's still nippy out when the nor'easter blows, isn't it."

"Yes, ma'am. Thank you."

"This is my wife Riah, Collin. Your name's O'Donnell, isn't it?"

"Do come in," the woman smiled, and led him through to the parlor. The room was empty, but Collin saw a painting resting on a table. He wasn't surprised to see it was a portrait of Sam, Lil, and the three children, as lifelike as could be—Sam's gift to his father, most likely.

Collin pointed towards the painting, "I see that Sam and my Kathy have arrived."

"My son and Kathy are upstairs unpacking. They only just beat you here by an hour. The rain and all. Come in and sit down. Riah will get you tea, and I'll let them know that you are here."

Kathy peered through the curtains of the front bedroom window. She could barely make out the woman sitting in the car that had just pulled up. "My God, I think he's brought that reporter girl with him, Sam. He'll probably tell me off and leave with her."

"Nonsense, Kathy. Get a grip on your emotions." Sam spoke to her from the doorway.

"You're right, Sam. I am just scared of the outcome."

"Be positive, lass. Now is the moment that you've been waiting for. It will work out. Just let him say his piece first." Sam prayed that this meeting would go well for everyone's sake. "I'll go down and talk to Collin, then ask the folks to give you some privacy with him. All right?"

"Fine. Come back and get me then."

Sam descended the stairs and saw Collin standing in the parlor with his back to him, eyeing the family painting. "There you are, my boy."

Collin spun around. "You're a sight for sore eyes, boss." Collin advanced and enthusiastically shook Sam's hand.

"We've missed you, lad."

"I've missed you all, too, don't ya know."

"You look none the worse for wear, Collin," Sam said, stepping back to have a good look at his protégé. "Are you ready to reconcile with Kathy? It won't be easy."

Riah came in with the tea tray and set the table with cups, a plate of biscuits, and an enormous teapot before retreating to the kitchen with her husband.

"Yes, with a lot of apprehension."

"It will be all right if you just speak from your heart, lad. I'll go bring her down."

Collin clenched and unclenched his fists, then paced. He hadn't felt this anxious since he and Kathy were trapped on Governor Lippitt's front porch by the devil Fredricson.

Kathy came down the stairs followed by Sam. She was dressed in somber gray, an angry frown on her face. Collin stepped forward to embrace her, but she side-stepped him, putting the table between them. Sam sat down in a corner chair.

"I see you brought your girl, Collin." Kathy spoke in a frosty tone.

"No, that's not right, darlin'. Please, let me explain."

"Don't you dare call me darlin', you, you, deserter!"

So that's how it's going to be, then. "Kathy, I love you and Liam more than anything else in the world."

"How could you? You abandoned us. I can never forgive you for that." Kathy started to cry.

Collin took a handkerchief from his pocket and held it out to her across the table. Kathy batted it away.

"I am here now, for you."

"But I had to leave the baby and come all this way across the ocean in the middle of a war to even talk with you. You wouldn't come to me. Do you know how hard it was for me to leave Liam? He's only four months old."

"I can only imagine, Kathy, and am so glad that you came. It pained me to leave you when the soldiers heard you calling me on the train platform. I almost pulled the cord to stop the train."

"So why didn't you?"

"I knew that you would be safe in Toronto with Sam and Lil, and Claire must be saved."

"Claire, Claire, It's always Claire first, me second. And she's probably not even alive anymore."

"She is alive, Kathy. I've proof, and I know how to find her. It is so exciting."

"Stop talking about Claire."

"You remember our adventures in New York and Rhode Island together, hunting to find her. Well, we can finish the search now and bring her home with us."

"I've heard that before, ad nauseam. Are you going to come

home with Sam and me on the next ship even if you don't find Claire by then?"

"But we can find her by then. I know it." Collin inched closer to her.

"Don't you take another step. I will repeat my question. Are you going to come home, stop this ridiculous obsession about your lost sister, and put your family first?"

"We will find her, darlin'."

Kathy pulled the packet of legal papers from under the waistband of her skirt and threw it down on the table between them. "I guess the answer is no. I can't live like this, Collin. Why don't you just leave with your new girlfriend—but take these papers with you."

Collin saw the word "Divorce" on the cover of her document. "No. I won't leave, and you can burn those papers. I love you, don't ya know."

"Actions speak louder than words, Collin. Much louder." Kathy turned on her heel and marched back up the stairs.

Collin started after her, but Sam jumped up and stopped him. "Let her go for the moment, Collin."

"But I love her, Sam."

"You didn't say what she needed to hear, boy."

"We will find Claire in time."

"That's not the point, lad. This is your moment of reckoning. You've been driven to find your lost sister, so much so that you've abandoned your family in the pursuit of her. If you want Kathy back, then you have to commit in your heart to put Kathy and Liam first forever, forsaking all others as you said in your marriage vows. If you can't do that, then you've lost her and Liam. It's as simple as that. Come now, lad, what will you choose?"

Collin stood in front of his mentor, silent.

"Then we've come all this way in vain. You've lost them both."

"No. No, Sam. I won't allow that."

"It's not up to you, lad. The courts don't look favorably on divorce, but they look even less favorably on abandonment."

Collin started up the stairs again. "But I didn't abandon—"

Sam grabbed his arm. "Yes, you did. You've had more than two months to think about this. And you're damned lucky that Kathy agreed to make this trip for the sake of your marriage. What's it going to be, Collin?"

Collin firmly pushed his friend's arm aside. "Sam, I am very grateful to you for bringing Kathy all this way. She could not have done it on her own. I won't lose her. I will commit to going home with you both on the thirteenth, whether or not we find Claire."

"I'm sure you're saying that because you believe you can find her in time. How, I don't know. But you are willing to make this commitment. What about the rest?"

"The rest?"

"Putting Claire out of your mind and focusing on your family in Canada, now and forever?"

"It's not that easy, Sam!"

"Life's not that easy, now is it? Do you think that the six thousand soldiers on that ship didn't make hard decisions they would have to live or die with?"

"I suppose I see your point."

"We have talked about this so many times, lad. You remember our discussion just before we beached that salmon in Lake Ontario?"

"Yes, boss, I remember. Saved my wedding, so it did."

"It wasn't your fault, just like it wasn't my fault with my brother Liam. Coming back to this house stirs up very painful memories, but I couldn't let the past ruin my future. You need to do the same, in your heart, once and for all."

"I can't."

"You must," Sam paused, still blocking the stairs and biting his lip in frustration. He took a different tack. "Look at it this way. If you are right and she's alive, she would be a resourceful woman now, not the dependent youngster that you remember. She would have survived horrendous things, including the sinking of the *Lusitania*.

If she is alive, then she is in the company of a resourceful, capable Irishman. They may be in danger, yet they are undoubtedly caring for each other. Doesn't she deserve her chance in life for happiness and success without your interference. Can't you live with that?"

Collin stayed silent for several moments, before finally replying, "Yes. I guess I can. If you put it that way."

"You have to put it that way, Collin, in your brain and in your heart."

"All right, Sam. I will. And I mean it."

Sam clapped Collin on the shoulder and gripped his hand. "I'll hold you to that promise, lad. Now get up the stairs, take that girl of yours in your arms, and pledge yourself to her, body and soul."

When Collin was halfway up the stairs, Sam added, "Not a word about Claire or Maureen now."

Kathy was lying face down on the bed crying softly when Collin entered her room.

"Kathy…"

"Get out!"

"No. I'm not leaving you again." Collin moved to the bed and sat down on the edge beside her. "I was very wrong, and I am so sorry for causing you this anguish. I see now that I have put my guilt first, and you and Liam second. I will come home with you and Sam on the thirteenth, no matter what. Also, I promise to let Claire go and have her own life without me if we don't find her, and to put her out of my thoughts. I vow to keep you and Liam and our life together as most important in my heart. Kathy, you are the love of my life, and I want only you, always. Please let me look at your lovely face, lass."

Kathy turned on her side toward him with tear-stained cheeks. "Can you do that, Collin, really?"

Collin answered without hesitation. "Yes, my love, I can and I will."

"I want to believe you, but I don't. You're obsessed."

Collin moved closer and gently caressed Kathy's arm. He wanted to kiss her but that might be an intrusion at such a sensitive moment, so he just put his hand on her back and rubbed gently. She flinched and moved away.

Collin inched closer to her on the bed. "I want to tell you again why I have to do this, Kathy. There's something I haven't told you, about what happened when my Ma was raped and murdered on the Toronto waterfront. Something deeply personal."

Kathy turned toward him. "What?"

Collin took his locket from under his shirt and Kathy held it in her hand, still draped around his neck. "The image in here is all I have left of her, lass. When she gave it to me and before she uttered those few baffling words, she knew she was dying. She begged me to promise her that I would never stop searching for her baby girl Claire. It was her last request in this life. I swore that I would find Claire and protect her, and then my mother died right there in my arms. They tried to bring her back, but she was gone."

"My God, Collin. I had no idea. A sacred vow to your mother. The last thing you got to say to her." The locket warmed in her hand. His revelation changed everything. Kathy thought about what a burden that would be on a loving son. What if she had to make such a crucial request of Liam someday knowing she would never see him again in this life? How it would affect his life forever. She hoped she would never have to do such a thing. But what if they had a daughter and some monster took her away?

"But why didn't you tell me this before?"

"I always felt responsible since I left Claire alone on the day of her abduction when I was in charge. I didn't need to explain any other justification for my actions and I am embarrassed to say that I have not fulfilled my Ma's dying request."

Collin cradled her hands in his, the locket enclosed in the safety of their new union. "I love you more than anything in the world, Kathy. As long as we're together, we can do anything and everything."

"You're not just saying that?"

Collin kissed her hard on the mouth. "I've missed you and Liam terribly." Tears flowed down his cheeks. "I want to spend my life making it up to the both of you."

"Oh, Collin. I love you so much, too. I want to believe you." Kathy sat up on the bed.

Collin fixed his eyes on Kathy's swollen cheeks, realizing that this was a pivotal moment in their relationship. "As you said, actions speak louder than words. I don't expect you to trust me until I can prove my commitment to our life together. Can you give me that chance?" he pleaded.

"Yes, I can and will do that, but only until the next boat sails." Kathy touched his arm, opening her heart once more.

"That's all I ask, my love." He drew her into a loving embrace, and they remained close for some time.

Collin reluctantly broke away and said, "They're waiting for us downstairs."

They freshened up. Kathy touched up her face with powder.

Collin hesitated, then said, "Now, Kathy, dear, I really want you to meet the reporter who has helped me to write my stories of the Rising."

Kathy made a face.

"Darling, I want to prove to you that we are only colleagues and nothing more. She drove me up here from Dublin in her company car."

"I saw her out there." Kathy touched up her lips. "I don't know, Collin. I look a mess."

"You look wonderful. Let's go, now." Collin led her down the stairs. He could see the relieved look on Sam's face when they reached the parlor. "Have a seat darlin', and I'll go get my colleague, Miss O'Sullivan."

When Collin disappeared out the front door, Sam turned to Kathy, "Everything all right, lass?"

"Oh Sam, he said all the right things without being asked. If only he could live up to them. I believe that's how he feels now, but—"

"But nothing, lass. I spoke to him too. I think that he's seen the light. Trust your husband's word."

"I will, Sam. I do."

"Good, Kathy. Your marriage must be built on trust."

Kathy nodded just as Collin returned with Maureen. The room's atmosphere crackled with tension. Sam stepped forward to put everyone at ease. He asked Maureen if he could take her coat and offered her a seat.

"Thank you, sir." Maureen shrugged off her coat.

With a hand at his wife's elbow, Collin spoke evenly, "Kathy and Sam, let me introduce Miss Maureen O'Sullivan, my colleague from *The Irish Times*. Maureen, this is my wonderful wife Kathleen and this is my best friend and mentor, Samuel Stevenson Finlay."

"Pleased to meet you, Miss O'Sullivan," Sam said, extending his hand to her.

"Likewise, sir." Maureen turned her attention to Kathy and offered her hand. Her voice was shy and respectful. "Mrs. O'Donnell. I am so glad to finally meet you. Collin is so lucky to have a wife who is willing to come all this way to show her love for him. You are a brave lady, indeed, to cross the ocean in a time of war to join him. He has spoken so highly of you. It is a privilege to have you here."

Kathy stepped forward. "Thank you." She paused awkwardly. "I must admit that I was jealous of you. Your names were together in the articles."

"There's nothing to worry about. I have a betrothed who is at the Front in France at the moment. I can assure you that I am as committed to him as Collin is to you, Mrs. O'Donnell."

"Thank you for your honesty. I am relieved, I must say. Call me Kathy, please."

"War separates lovers, Kathy, and we must keep our love strong during these terrible times. I'm glad that you two are reunited."

"Did Collin tell you that my maiden name was O'Sullivan?"

Maureen was shocked. "No, what a coincidence that we both have the same last name."

Sam and Collin stood by while the two women discussed their heritage and where they were born and raised in Ireland. Then it was the men's turn to be shocked.

"I have an uncle who was a welder at Harland and Wolff up here in Belfast," Maureen shared. "We never met him and his family since we lived in Tipperary. I think his name was—

Kathy finished her sentence, "Ryan?"

"Yes, I think it was. The story goes that he was qualified to be a history professor but there weren't jobs in that field for him in Belfast, so he and his family emigrated somewhere. Wait. How did you know my uncle's first name?"

"He's my father, Maureen. You just described my father."

Maureen's mouth dropped open in surprise.

"My goodness, dear girl, don't you see that we're cousins?" The two women fell into each other's arms, laughing through tears. They sank onto the chesterfield overwhelmed with this revelation and turn of events.

Collin looked at Sam in disbelief. "This is bizarre. I wouldn't have figured this outcome to this afternoon's reconciliation, not in a million years."

"Aye, lad. Do ya believe in Divine intervention now?"

Finally, they settled down to their new understanding of their familial connection. John and Riah, having heard this dialog from the wings, came into the parlor and invited them all to high tea before Maureen left. They wouldn't take no for an answer.

Collin sat next to Kathy at the kitchen table for tea, her leg against his, under the table. He could see the tension between Sam and his father. Nothing was said, but their body language spoke volumes. It surprised him to see Sam, usually so warm and convivial, so impatient with the old man. It must have been difficult for his mentor to come back to this home and its memories.

It was up to Sam to broach the subject that was on everyone's mind. A shame to spoil such a wonderful reunion, but time was of the essence. Neither Kathy nor Collin would take the initiative. "Why do you think that you can find Claire in the next eight days, Collin?"

Even though Kathy seemed to have overcome her jealousy of Maureen, Collin decided not to give her any credit in the process of discovery. They had brought up the possibility of this discussion on the ride up from Dublin. He also wasn't going to go into the details of the risks involved, yet.

"Strangely enough, I have been within thirty feet of Claire without seeing her or realizing it. She is alive and in the company of Tadgh McCarthy. I know his name but not where he lives. He is a resourceful man of about my age."

"How do you know this?" Kathy was taking an interest.

Collin glanced at her. *She actually wants to be part of this. That's my girl.* "I actually bumped into McCarthy on another occasion three weeks ago, literally. I chased him and another man and saw them flee on his motorcycle, the one that Jack Jordan had seen earlier when he was sure he had seen Claire."

"But how do you know it was her, my love?"

Good, she is coming around. She called me love. "Because I have it from a reliable source that my cousin, Peader O'Donnell, has been meeting with this Tadgh McCarthy and my sister. It's got to be her, Peader's cousin."

Sam dunked a biscuit into his tea. "What reliable source, if I may ask?"

"Sean O'Casey. You know, the budding playwright."

Sam's eyes opened wide and he smiled. "I've heard of that writer. You have been a busy lad, Collin."

"There's much more. We can talk about it later. Tomorrow we must go to Peader's home in Dungloe. It's about thirty-five miles north of where I was born in Donegal Town. He must know where she is. I have to talk with him in person."

Collin was astonished when Kathy blurted out, "I wish that I'd have been here to help you search, Collin, like in New York. I should have trusted that you knew what you were doing."

Maureen got up from the table. "Now I must be going. I have a three-hour drive ahead of me in the rain." She grasped Kathy's hands and kissed her cheek. "This has been a lovely reunion, dear cousin Kathy. We have much to talk about, but you and Collin have a crucial search ahead of you right now, and I must be getting back." She thanked the Finlays for tea and made ready to leave.

Sam got Maureen's coat from the rack in the vestibule, and Collin said to her, "I'll see you out."

"It's still raining. You don't need to walk me to the car, Collin."

"Nonsense." Collin picked up an umbrella from the stand and opened the door, "Let's go."

When Maureen was safely seated in the automobile, Collin said, "Thank you for your help, Maureen. It made a difference."

"Oh, Collin, can you imagine? Your wife is my cousin—I'm still shaking. To come all this way, she's a woman of great courage."

"Yes, she is. I will call you when we get back from Donegal to update you on my search and to write our report."

"That's fine, Collin. I understand the need for you to do this with your family now that they are here."

Collin gave her hand a squeeze. "I appreciate your understanding. Drive safe in this weather." He closed the door and waved as she drove off down Longstone Street. Then he turned and whistled as he headed back to the Finlay home where the love of his life awaited him.

Twenty feet away, a thin man with horn-rim glasses stood in the shadow of a stout oak tree, smiling in the dark rain.

When Collin returned to the vestibule, he couldn't help overhearing a heated discussion between Sam and his father while Riah fussed in the kitchen.

"I had to go. You know that, father."

"You left me and your brother Harry here alone just after your mother died, bless her soul."

"I had to follow the love of my life when her parents emigrated to Canada. I explained all that."

"The homeland wasn't good enough for you?"

"I love my family more than anything else, and this is no place to live any kind of decent life. There's no peace here. Please, I have enough money, father, for you and Riah to move to Toronto. It would be a lot safer, don't ya know?"

"I don't want to leave my home, my people, son."

"There's a storm coming. This Rising is only the start. Lil and I would feel so much better if you would come to Canada. There are great opportunities there."

"How many times do I have to tell you, Samuel, I will not move."

Collin stood still, unsure if he wanted to hear more but knowing this was exactly the argument he would use with Claire when he found her. *She has to listen and come away from this dangerous place.*

"Father, I am quite tired from our travels and the stress of today. Let's discuss this tomorrow, please. Collin and Kathy will be going on to Donegal, and I will stay here to have a good visit with you two. Is that all right?"

"It's fine with me, son," the older man sighed, adding, "You're a sight for sore eyes after being away for five years and more."

"Thank you, Father. Good night."

Collin discreetly entered the parlor and followed Sam up the narrow stairs. Just before heading off to his bedroom, Sam said, "We both have our crosses to bear. I'm proud of you for coming to your senses today. Now, don't let Kathy down again."

"Thank you, Sam. I won't. Good night to you."

"Good night, my lad."

Collin closed the door softly. Kathy was already in bed, sound asleep. Collin undressed and climbed under the comforter. It seemed like an eternity since he and his wife had shared the same bed, and he shivered at the sight of her form beneath the covers. He lay there, breathing shallowly so as not to disturb her. Yet, in the fever of his desire, he finally reached out to draw her into his embrace.

Without hesitation, she turned her body to him and showered his face and neck with kisses that grew insistent with her own need. Her hands stole to his hips and pressed him into her body.

He let go of any thought or words and instead made her know the depth of his love physically as he pushed into her core. He was tangled in the thrusting that made her breath stutter when she begged him to go deeper. His body responded so naturally to her quickening movement that his climax came on as she rode her own waves of pleasure.

For a moment they were suspended in complete union and knew nothing else but their love for each other. As their hearts slowed, Collin slowly rocked Kathy while she brought her hands to his face and breathed her kisses into his mouth. He was about to withdraw to rest against her when she grasped him and brought him back to life.

He was powerless to refuse her and groaned his enjoyment as she reawakened him. His hands moved to stroke her breasts with increasing pressure and when he could stand it no longer, he lifted her and gasped to find she was ready again for him with her sweet wetness. A second time he touched her, even deeper than before. This time the force of this mounting bliss took her breath away, and she wrapped her arms around him more tightly as his frenzy heightened.

He broke in her with wave upon wave of exquisite pleasure, and they drove each other on until they were completely spent. When they at last came to rest, Collin fell asleep still entwined in Kathy's body and her sweetness. "Mmm," Kathy sighed, and snuggled further into him.

Chapter Five
Ballymote

Wednesday, July 5, 1916
Road Trip from Home to Ballymote

*T*adgh and Morgan had spent two wild days of riding through hauntingly beautiful terrain. They had passed through Limerick and stayed in Galway the first night. The next afternoon just eleven miles shy of Sligo, Tadgh took a four-mile detour and stopped at a small country market town.

"Well now, lass. This is Ballymote,"[3] he exclaimed, stopping at the north end of the main street.

"Tadgh, what are those ruins?" Morgan cried, as she leapt out of the sidecar and made her way through the weeds to a faded wooden sign staked into the ground near the entrance to a broken-down stone monastery. She slowly read it and said, "This was a Franciscan Friary. I wonder if that's where the *Book of Ballymote* that Professor Lawlor referred to was written."

"Pardon me."

Morgan heard an unfamiliar voice. She turned and saw a grizzled old man standing nearby. He smiled and tipped his hat. Morgan relaxed a little. The old man seemed no threat. She took him for a local.

"I couldn't help noticing your interest in that dilapidated edifice. I take it you're not from around here?"

Both Tadgh and Morgan nodded.

The local pointed down the road. "Don't miss the Castle at the south end of town, folks. They say that O'Donnell mustered his forces there before he marched on Kinsale."

"Red Hugh O'Donnell?" Morgan's face tightened.

"The very same, lass. Alas, our last spiritual leader."

91

"A religious man, then?"

"A spiritual leader who fought for our Gaelic freedom, meting out justice for all men, including his enemies."

"Did he, now?" Tadgh was interested. "Why did he rally his troops here, do ya think?"

"It's told that the British were closing in on Donegal Town, so he set a torch to his own castle there. This was the last-ditch battle to be fought before oppression."

"Yes, but why here?"

"They say that the special book had something to do with why he acquired this castle."

"What book was that, if I might be after askin'?"

"Why, the *Book of Ballymote* that the O'Donnell's grandfather bought for one hundred and twenty milch cows. The one they say held the secret, lad."

Morgan leaned forward, right up to the old man's face. "What secret was that?" She and Tadgh might finally be getting closer to answering the questions they had been wrestling with for so long.

"No one knows. It wouldn't be a secret if we knew, now would it, lass?"

"So how'd you know it held a secret, then?"

"It was told many years ago by the *seanachai*." The old man glanced at Morgan's quizzical expression and winked. "A rural storyteller, lass. One who roams from town to town recounting our history. Almost extinct as a breed these days."

"I've been told that Ballymote was a Hospitaller site in those days."

"Aye, lad. This monastery and the castle out by the lake. Helped the Templars get to freedom in Scotland, so they say."

"Seanachai story, then?"

"'Tis the truth of it, lad."

"Do you know where we can find this wise man, then?"

"Dead and gone these many years now, poor fellow."

"Is there a new seanachai, now?"

"I heard tell there's one down in Galway, but he moves around, nomad-like. Haven't seen him in these parts." Tadgh and Morgan exchanged disappointed looks, but they thanked the old man and headed for the town's castle.

"This certainly must have been a formidable fortress in its day," Morgan said, as they walked about the internal square courtyard of the castle. "Those remaining walls must be forty feet high. You can just imagine the gathering of Red Hugh's forces here."

"Desperate times, to be sure, lass."

On their way back to the Sligo Road, they spotted a country estate on a lake and drove to it. Traveling through the property's gates, they rode down a lane fenced with cattle fields on both sides. The lane took them up a hill to a stately gunpowder-grey manor house befitting nobility.

Morgan saw it first from her perch in the sidecar. "Stop, Tadgh. There, down by the lake on the left. Ruins. There's a plaque."

He brought the Kerry to a halt near the monument and they got off to read the sign—

> *'Here, on the Temple House[3] estate, are the ruins of the old house which was given to the Knights Hospitaller in the fourteenth century.'*

"Tadgh, this was the way station for the escaping Knights Templar heading north after the purge in the early 1300s. It's just like Maurice and the old man described. Do you think that some of the Templars remained in Ireland?"

"Never heard it, lass, but that doesn't mean it didn't happen. We've got to get our hands on that *Book of Ballymote*, right enough."

They returned to the motorcycle and continued up to the porte-cochere of the manor house to the right, on the hill.

"Maybe the lord of the manor can shed some light," Morgan offered, jumping from the sidecar before Tadgh had even come to a full stop. She ran up the steps of the Doric-columned mansion and thumped the massive bronze knocker on the large, oaken front door. She turned with satisfaction just as Tadgh parked the Kerry opposite the entrance under the portico, leaving its engine idling.

"Leave go, girl. We'd best be on our way."

"Tadgh, hurry up."

He sighed, turned off the engine, and joined her.

The door cracked open, and a portly gentleman in evening jacket, ribbed black trousers, and spats leaned his head out the door.

"Good afternoon. May I help you?"

"We're travelers in search of answers to ancient riddles, sir." Morgan offered her hand.

The full-throated sound of a woman boomed from the home's interior. "Who is it, Arthur?"

"A nice young couple on an abominable motorcycle, ma'am. You might want to come and see for yourself."

A regal silver-haired woman appeared behind Arthur. She stepped in front of her butler and opened the door wider. Her dark eyes glittered. "Arthur, what delightful company. My dears, have you come to visit me today?"

"Excuse us for the intrusion, madam, but my friend Tadgh and I are very interested in the history of your property, especially regarding the Knights Templar and Hospitallers."

The woman closely scrutinized first Morgan and then Tadgh and his motorcycle before speaking. "What do you have to say for yourself, young man?"

"We are Republicans, ma'am. The history of the Clans is very important to us."

"And what is your name?"

"Tadgh McCarthy, ma'am, of the MacCarthaigh Reagh Clan from Munster. And this is my betrothed Morgan."

The woman's face brightened with an amused grin. She opened her front door wide and stepped out onto the porch. "My, you don't say. Republicans. Charlotte Perceval, here, of the O'Hara Clan, matron of this estate these forty years." She shook the hand that Morgan offered. "Come in, come in. You must be exhausted, by the look of ye both, and it's time for tea."

Morgan needed no further invitation. Tadgh reluctantly followed her through the entrance way, the butler closing the heavy door after him. Morgan allowed herself to be escorted by the prim and proper lady back into the high-ceilinged expansive vestibule.

Morgan took it all in, the yellowing family portraits and animal heads mounted on the walls, silver candelabra on beautifully ornate tables, and elegant inlaid marble flooring. "You have a wonderful home here, Mrs. Perceval."

"Two hundred and fifty years of Percevals have lived here, more or less. You accumulate a lot of history in that time," she answered, as she led them into a cavernous drawing room, inviting them to sit on an ancient-looking English divan.

"What a magnificent chesterfield, Madam." Morgan hesitated, afraid to sit in her disheveled state.

"Please, do sit."

Morgan reluctantly situated herself. "This is a lovely piece."

"Why yes, it is, made by Johnson & Jeane in London in 1865, specifically for the Big House." Mrs. Perceval rang a silver bell, and Arthur appeared from a green baize side door.

"Tea for three, Arthur," Mrs. Perceval requested, in a pleasant voice, and the butler turned quickly on his heel, disappearing through the doorway.

The early summer air had been crisp during their afternoon ride and Morgan was still shivering.

"Perhaps you'd be more comfortable in the chintz chair by the fire, lass," Mrs. Perceval said. "I'll have Arthur stoke it for us."

Morgan looked at the white marble fireplace with framing Corinthian columns and ornate brass hearth rail on the wall opposite the windows. All the furniture was arranged around it. She got up and walked to the hearth, raising her hands, palms outward to feel the radiant heat. The glow of the red-hot logs was a cheery sight, drawing her in.

"What's your name, lass?"

Morgan saw her windswept face in the massive mirror above the fireplace. Grimacing, she turned away from the sight to face her hostess, running her fingers through her tousled locks and answered unsteadily. "Morgan, madam, and soon to be Morgan McCarthy."

The woman's eyes squinted as she stared at her visitor. "By your voice, I would say you come from a different land."

"That may very well be. I do not know my identity."

Mrs. Perceval's eyes widened. "You don't know—? Well, what is your story, then?"

"I was aboard the *Lusitania* when it was sunk last year, and I have had amnesia ever since. Tadgh found me clinging to life at sea. He saved me and nursed me back to health. Cunard officials don't know who I am either, ma'am."

"You poor dear. Don't know your family. I hope you regain your memory soon."

"It's been over a year now since the sinking. A little has come back about that nightmare, but I can't remember anything before that, I'm afraid."

"You will, soon enough. Mark my words. Now then, why are you two traipsing so far from home, may I ask? And on a rickety motorcycle, no less."

Tadgh leaned across Morgan to answer for her. "We're en route to visit our good friend and compatriot Peader O'Donnell in Meenmore, ma'am. But we came down through Ballymote because we wanted to see the place where Red Hugh O'Donnell mustered his troops before their valiant march to Kinsale."

The woman's eyebrows rose. "I see."

"Isn't Perceval an English surname, ma'am?"

"We Percevals go way back in mythology to the King Arthur's Court, it's true, but we really came to Ireland from Normandy with Strongbow in the 1100s. I was an O'Hara of Annaghmore before my marriage, one of the old Irish families. We're Irish now, through and through, and though we are Protestant, I am inclined to sympathize with your cause for freedom from tyranny, God help me."

"There's a story, isn't there," Tadgh remembered, "about Perceval of the Holy Grail?"

Mrs. Perceval's gaze swung around and locked on her visitor. "It was written by Chrétien de Troyes in Flanders, I believe, back in the twelfth century during the time of the Knights Templar and the Crusades. That's part of our family mythology, and the origin of our association with Arthur and his court dating back to the sixth century."

The butler opened the door and carried in an enormous silver tray with matching teapot and service. Morgan excused herself, and at the woman's direction, located a washroom. There she pulled her windswept black curls into a tidy knot to make herself as presentable as possible to the lady of the house. The dirt from her face turned the white washcloth gray as she applied the fragrant soap. When she returned, the butler had added logs to the fire and was pouring the tea.

The matron of the Big House then urged them to partake of the small triangular sandwiches and freshly baked cakes that Arthur brought to the table. The woman smiled with pleasure as her famished guests fell to the meal. She sipped from her own cup.

"Was this, then, a Knights Templar castle back during the Crusades, Mrs. Perceval?" Morgan asked, between mouthfuls. "We saw the ruins down by the lake."

"Yes, indeed it was. We understand they built it in 1216 and folks lived there until my ancestor, Colonel Perceval, started building a smaller portion of this home with its entrance facing the ruins and lake back in 1825."

"So was it a Perceval who built the castle?"

"No, our family only started living here in 1665, Tadgh."

"After Red Hugh left for Kinsale, then."

"That's right. Sixty-four years later, to be precise. But he left from the castle in the village, the one he had acquired two years earlier."

"What happened here after the Knights Templar were disbanded in the early 1300s, do ya know?"

"This castle by the lake and its lands were turned over to the Knights Hospitaller."

"We had heard that down in Fenit, near Ardfert," Tadgh commented.

"Oh, you did, did you. Yes, young man, I can tell you that Ardfert and Ballymote were the two Irish monasteries that took in the fleeing Knights Templar. They were heading for safe haven in Scotland after de Molay and his knights were executed in Paris. And, of course, they were welcomed at the Templar castle on our estate. Our ancestors spoke of the journey from Newport in County Mayo to this place, and then on to Temple Patrick. The Templars helped Robert the Bruce at Bannockburn in 1314, so I'm told."

"Amazing history of these grounds, Mrs. Perceval," Morgan said, shaking her head in wonderment.

"Yes, it is, lass. We are very proud of our heritage. That's why we have stayed through the centuries."

"Do you think the Templars had a hand in writing the *Book of Ballymote*?" Morgan asked.

"I don't know. So you've heard of our magnificent book then, have you, Morgan?"

"Yes, ma'am. A man in town told us that it contains an important secret."

"Old wives' tale, I'm sure. No truth to it, as far as I know. But those O'Donnells wanted it for something back in the 1500s. It might have something to do with why Red Hugh chose Ballymote for his gathering point. They say that he had joined the Hospitallers after he acquired the castle to restore that Order in these parts."

Morgan held her cup in her hands without sipping from it. "What do you mean by *restore*, ma'am?"

"Once the Templars had passed through Ballymote on their

way to Rosslyn in Scotland, the Knights Hospitallers sold the castle to the McDonaghs in 1360. When the crown took over the church lands, the O'Hara's reacquired it as it had been built on O'Hara territory."

"We heard that the Fitzmaurices of Ardfert were Red Hugh's allies."

"Well, that would fit with what we already know, wouldn't it now, Morgan?"

"Yes, indeed it would."

Tadgh nodded at Morgan and stood up. "We'd better be going, ma'am. Sure it was a true Hospitaller welcome you've given us, for certain."

Morgan looked pleadingly at her betrothed. She liked this self-assured woman and loved her home. She'd never seen such elegance as far as she knew.

Charlotte saw the look. "It'll be dark soon and you've at least eighty rugged miles to go to Dungloe, as you've told me your destination. I'll not hear of you leaving tonight. I don't get many visitors, and certainly not such delightful ones as you, though you are Republicans. So it's settled. You will be my guests tonight. Tomorrow, after a good night's rest and a good breakfast, you can be on your way. Surely your good friend would understand."

It was two against one, and Tadgh had to admit that it was now getting late in the day. This stop hadn't helped. He shrugged his shoulders to show his reluctance to stay in this uncomfortable environment overnight, but he didn't open his mouth.

"Come on, you two. I'll show you to your rooms," Mrs. Perceval stood and took Morgan's hand. "You can refresh yourself, and I wager you will enjoy a little tour of this big old hulk of a manor. You can look around to your heart's delight in all the corners, and I'll tell you such interesting old stories. And we'll have a lovely dinner. Come, then."

"Thank you very much," Morgan said, smiling wide like a Cheshire cat.

She looked pleadingly towards Tadgh who said, "We'll just be needing one room, ma'am," as he turned and nodded wearily, following behind while they returned to the immense forty-foot-high vestibule with its leaded glass ceiling.

Morgan looked at Charlotte who appeared momentarily taken aback and said, "Perhaps tonight we should honor our host's wishes."

Tadgh glared and repeated, "We'll just need one room, thanks."

Charlotte looked askance and started to ascend the grand staircase like a duchess, beckoning her guests upward.

Such opulence, Morgan thought, as she looked up at centuries of gilded family pictures ringing the second-floor stairwell inside arched plaster reliefs. Some looked so regal, others in full battle gear, so military. The children all looked angelic. She didn't even know who her family was or have even one picture of them, and here there were twelve or more generations of Percevals all in a row. By the time they had reached the second floor of the manor, Morgan resolved that she and Tadgh would make as good a family as all the people of the Perceval family over the ages put together. They'd have their own angelic children. Just the same, the history of the place was impressive, as was its current matron.

Charlotte steered them into the beautiful blue bedroom overlooking the ruins and the lake, saying, "There are two single beds in this room that can be separated for privacy." The message was clear. Then she reminded them, "Dinner will be at eight in the main dining room."

Thanking her, Morgan closed the hardwood door.

"Hardy woman there, don't you think, Tadgh?"

"To be sure, lass. But I wanted to get on our way."

"Oh, Tadgh. Thank you for agreeing to stay. I don't get to talk to many women, you know. Not since poor Constance." She clasped her hands around Tadgh's neck and brushed his mouth with her lips.

"Yes, well. Let's try to clean up as best we can. By the look of those candlesticks on the bureau, we'll have candlelight after the sun goes down.

"But what is that light fixture in the center of the ceiling, Tadgh? It looks like a chandelier."

"I didn't notice until you mentioned it. It must be a gasolier."

"A what?"

"A gas operated chandelier. It's a portmanteau word."

"Let's leave it off this evening. Candlelight will be very romantic. I am sure I'll be at your mercy, if you think to have your way with me."

"It's a good thing it's a Protestant household right enough 'cause I'm mad in lust for you, lass." Tadgh bent down to taste her lips again.

Dinner in the main dining room was like something from a dream. The mahogany table could easily seat twenty-four, and fine silver candelabra reflected the candlelight. From the double height windows, Morgan could see a winding gravel path led down to the lake, now enshrouded by a mist settling in amidst the purples of twilight. Green and white plush rugs, soft underfoot, complemented the tile patterns inside the rose marble fireplace surround. Although it was early July, a fire burned cheerily in that central fireplace, logs piled high.

Bone china inscribed with the family crest and crystal goblets for wine and water were arranged at one end of the table. Morgan had never seen so much silver in one place before. The gilded wall mirrors and sparkling white table linens added splendor to the setting. It all seemed so elegant and Morgan loved it.

Charlotte introduced her daughter-in-law Eleanora Margaret, whom she called Nora, and the matron's three-year-old grandson Ascelin. The other dinner guest that evening was Nora's best friend who they called Lady Gaga, the wife of Henry Gore-Booth of neighboring Lissadell.

Morgan could sense that Tadgh would have preferred his foxhole on St. Stephen's Green to this gaggle of women in these sumptuous surroundings. Poor boy. A nanny came in, curtsied and took young Ascelin from his mother before retiring, but not before Nora kissed him goodnight.

Dinner arrived as soon as everyone was seated.

Morgan saw that Tadgh was eyeing and then fiddling with the array of silver utensils in front of him before he finally chose the correct larger spoon for his soup. *At least he's not completely unrefined.*

The soup course was followed by wild salmon, pike from the lake, and roast beef from their herd. Carrots, potatoes, and leeks from the garden completed the main course. Tadgh's disposition changed for the better.

"So tell me, Tadgh. Being Republicans, were you and Morgan in Dublin during the Rising?" Charlotte asked. "We get so little news out here in the country."

All the ladies at the table leaned forward to hear his response. Except Morgan, who sat back to take it all in.

"Well, now, ma'am. We were there, yes."

"Oh, Tadgh, go gently." Morgan's voice was tremulous from the memory of the conflict.

He stole a look at her furrowed brow and decided to leave out the gory details in front of these refined ladies. "The damn British—*pardon me*—forces overran the city and left it in ruins with their artillery against our antiquated guns and pitchforks."

"*Our* Tadgh?" chorused Lady Gaga and Nora.

"Yes, *our*. The brave men of the Irish Volunteers. Valiant men of strong Irish principles, willing to lay down their lives for the hope of freedom."

"Religious freedom?" Nora asked, laying down her forkful of salmon.

"That's just a part of it. The British took our lands, our homes, our cattle and horses, our way of life, and finally our food, and left us to die like vermin in the ditch, so they did."

"That's a gross exaggeration, surely," Lady Gaga replied, wrinkling her nose.

Morgan stayed silent. Tadgh could handle his own battle. She was curious to see how he dealt with women of breeding.

"I was born in Skibbereen, ma'am. We lost ten thousand in the Great Hunger while the overlords stole our food to feed their own bellies in England and abroad. And that's not an exaggeration, to be sure. We were desperate tenants on what had once been our own land."

Gaga stopped eating. "But you lost your lands when the British conquered you. To the victor go the spoils, as they say."

Morgan could see that Tadgh was about to explode. His lips pressed tightly together, and white- knuckled fingers clenched the knife and fork.

Charlotte jumped into the fray. "Let me remind you, young ladies, that we lost our Perceval demesne here after the Great Hunger. Nora, your husband's great-grandmother Jane died when she went out nursing the dying tenants, and we had to sell when the inheritance tax took effect. I can appreciate Tadgh's opinion. I surely can. I may have a different religion but we are all one under God. What's fair is fair, and what's evil is evil."

"But you're an O'Hara, are you not," Lady Gaga came back quickly. "This was your family's land when we conquered you in 1602. Yet your line survived and you have now recaptured what was yours once, albeit through marriage. I don't think you accomplished this without stepping on quite a few toes."

Now it was Nora's turn to get prickly. "Really, Gaga. Mother is right. Neither the Percevals nor the O'Haras have been ruthless tyrants, like Mr. McCarthy describes. Why, my son's grandfather Alexander Perceval, the Hong Kong taipan, who we call the *Chinaman*, used his fortune to buy back our estate and expand this manor. He spent a million pounds, I was told. He brought back many of the tenants who had been cruelly displaced and gave them back their homes, health and dignity as well, didn't he, Charlotte?"

"Yes, dear, he did back in 1860. Alexander was a very good man. God rest his soul."

Nora couldn't let that lie without discussing her own MacDowel family. "And you know my father is a surgeon in Sligo, Gaga. He has two offices there, one to tend to nationalists and the other to treat unionists. He is fair to all."

Gaga was turning a bright shade of crimson but fortunately kept her mouth shut.

Nora looked pale in comparison. "Mother, if the British took away the O'Hara lands long ago and mistreated the tenants during the Famine, then why has my Ascelin gone away to fight for them in the Great War? We argued about it before he left. I am very frightened for my husband."

The exchange fascinated Morgan. Charlotte had taken the discussion in a direction entirely away from religion to humanity and thereby defused the attack on her guest. Further, she was testing her daughter-in-law to see what her principles were. An amazing woman. Morgan couldn't wait to hear what she would say next.

Charlotte waggled her fork in the direction of her daughter-in-law to gain her attention. "Your husband believes that the Germans and their allies are terrible men bent on conquering and ruling the world, not just Britain and Europe. And that includes Ireland as well. They must be stopped."

"And I'm sure that your ancestors felt the same way when the British conquered them back in 1602, ma'am."

"Touché, Tadgh!" Charlotte exclaimed, a mischievous sparkle in her eyes.

Lady Gaga spoke again. "It's not the same thing, surely."

"How is it different, young lady?" Charlotte shot back, her eyes turning to daggers.

"Well, we're British, of course."

"You may be British, young lady, but we're Irish first and proud of it."

Morgan could see that Gaga had come to the end of her debating skills and the glower on Charlotte's countenance could have dropped a charging bull in its tracks. Nora fidgeted with the stem of her water goblet, and she was tearful, undoubtedly thinking of her husband in the dank muddy trenches of France.

"You have a lovely home here, Mrs. Perceval," Morgan said, in an attempt to lighten their talk. "I can see so many Oriental touches and knickknacks perhaps brought back by the *Chinaman*. Was he Chinese?" It was all she could think of to divert the conversation.

Charlotte's demeanor changed like a chameleon as she turned to respond to her guest. "Heavens no, dear. He was a Perceval, as Nora mentioned. His portrait is there over the fireplace. Our ancestors came from Normandy, as I told you earlier. So we're all French, actually. He was a tea merchant, and a very successful one at that."

Nora took this opportunity to excuse herself and Gaga from the dinner table. Charlotte waved them away and resumed her conversation with Morgan.

"While we're looking around this room, do you see that portrait on the wall between the windows?" Charlotte continued. "It's of my grandmother Jane. I have a letter she wrote while she was dying of 'famine fever' in 1847, in which she begged her children to take care of the tenant families between her death and her funeral."

Morgan was impressed. *They're both fine women. The one on the wall and the one seated beside me are two peas in a pod. I'm so glad we came here today.* These two were the real role models for modern women who, like herself, believed in saving and not taking lives.

"May I offer you a whiskey in the drawing room, Tadgh, and a cigar, perhaps, if you would retire to the billiard room?" Charlotte asked, as she got up from the dinner table.

"Yes, thank you for the whiskey, ma'am, and for the offer of a cigar, but I don't smoke. I'm sorry to hear that you lost your husband."

"Yes, back in '87. Ascelin, Nora's husband, was only two years old then."

"Who runs your estate?" Morgan asked, when they had settled in the drawing room.

"Why, I do, Morgan, all these thirty years."

Amazing. So much to learn from this woman of substance. Too bad we have to leave right away.

"Do you side with the Unionists in this part of the country, Mrs. Perceval?" Tadgh asked, when they were sipping their whiskey.

"I'm not in favor of violence nor of Mr. Carson's Ulster Volunteers, if that's what you mean, Tadgh. And I do favor the rights of the common man, sir, as I mentioned before."

"Well, at least we can agree on that," Tadgh said, and raised his glass to toast his hostess.

"I think that our northwestern counties would have a hard time deciding which way to vote if it comes to Home Rule. You do know that Britain will never give up Ulster, don't you, Tadgh?"

He rubbed his forehead and sighed. "The brain knows but the heart rebels, so it does. What about the poor Catholics left there?"

"That die was cast at the Battle of Kinsale, and when the Earls fled in 1607. That's when we O'Haras lost our lands. But we won them back, not by battle but through love. As you can plainly see, I am here in a magnificent home far more beautiful than my ancestral abode that lies down by the lake in ruins caused by the British invader."

"To be here, you had to marry the enemy."

"My husband was a wonderful man who believed in humanity and justice for all. He was certainly not my enemy. Don't let your hatred get the better of you, Tadgh. We must change with the times. What if Morgan is British? Would she be your enemy, then?"

"Morgan is not British. She came from America."

"There are millions of British emigrants in America."

"Morgan is not British. That's absurd. I'll hear none of it."

"Have it your way, Tadgh. However this fight goes, there will be troubles in our land for a long time to come, maybe forever. You mark my words."

"We in the south are committed to restoring all of Ireland to Gaelic life, liberty, and pursuit of happiness, to borrow an American phrase."

"A noble cause, Tadgh, but one I fear is doomed."

"We will not fail. Not while there is breath in my body, ma'am."

"We'll see how you feel if and when the time comes for that choice," Charlotte commented, tipping her head toward Morgan.

"Where Tadgh goes, I go, ma'am, but I agree with you. A solution without violence would be much preferable to one that's bloody and prolonged."

"That's right, Morgan. Now I must bid good evening to you both. Shall we breakfast together before you continue your journey?"

Tadgh thumped his empty whiskey glass down on the oak sideboard. "We'll see you in the morning, then, Mrs. Perceval. We've a long day ahead of us tomorrow."

Morgan put down her glass. "Thank you for your gracious hospitality and for the wonderful dinner."

"You're most welcome Morgan, and you Tadgh, as well. Well, good night, then."

"Yes, thank you ma'am for dinner," Tadgh mumbled. Taking Morgan's arm, he lifted her up out of the settee and turned her towards the foyer.

"Irish breakfast will be in the small dining room at eight o'clock," Charlotte called out after them. "Sleep tight."

Looking over her shoulder and smiling at her hostess, Morgan added, "and don't let the bedbugs bite."

"We have none of those here, my lass," Charlotte called out, flashing a sly smile. "Anyway, Tadgh will take good care of you, I'm sure."

Tadgh stomped up the massive white marble staircase, gripping Morgan's arm.

"Ouch! Tadgh, You're hurting me."

"I'm tired, and we need to get to bed," he groused, as they rushed along the plush red-carpeted second-story corridor.

This was a new side of him, one she had seen only once before, on the night before the Rising started. Maybe having to drive the motorcycle so far in the last two days was working on him.

Tadgh turned the oversized porcelain doorknob to the blue room and threw open the heavy door. Pulling Morgan inwards, he closed it with a thud.

"Really, Tadgh. Calm down, love."

"That woman sounds just like Sean O'Casey, and you agreed with her. She doesn't understand the problem. She's burying her head in the sand, to be sure. Millions died you know."

"So you've said, Tadgh, and I believe you. But don't let your hatred destroy your love. Look at how you are treating me now."

"Protestants."

"Charlotte was not speaking with you from her religious teachings, Tadgh, but from her heart and her loving experience. Just like us, my love."

"Well she's very well off, and that's the truth of it. She didn't know the death of millions at the hands of her husband's people."

"But she was taught by her husband's grandmother, a woman who gave her life to help the sick and dying tenants on her land in the Great Hunger. Now that's love as Jesus taught us all, whether Catholic or Protestant."

"I'll give you that, Morgan. Now let's get to bed." Tadgh stripped off his clothes, then threw down the bed comforter and slid inside the white linen sheets.

Morgan removed the last of her undergarments, looking closely at the purple bruise that was forming on her upper arm from where Tadgh had grabbed her. Then she pushed the beds together.

Tadgh had turned on his side away from her, already fast asleep, snoring.

"I guess lovemaking is not in the plan, my love," Morgan whispered.

Morgan used the basin, cloth, and pitcher of water to sponge the remaining road grime off her face and arms before she propped the big feather pillow up against the polished oak headboard and slid under the starched sheets beside him. Sitting back, she reached over and stroked the matted curls on the back of his sweaty neck.

Charlotte's words struck a chord within her. Maybe it was just how women think, different than hotheaded men. Nurturers versus warriors. This was the first time that she had had meaningful conversation with another woman in her whole life as far as she knew. It was marvelous. Oh, she had talked briefly to Constance at St. Stephen's Green and with Deirdre at the Temple Bar Pub, but that was different.

Suddenly she felt hollow inside. Not so much alone, but lonely. What happened to her parents, her friends, her other lovers, if she had any? Were they alive or dead? Were they still looking for her? She loved Tadgh, but this new life of hers had turned violent and dangerous. She felt a stabbing pain in her leg, a reminder of what she had endured. A phrase jumped into her head. *'Forgive us our trespasses as we forgive those who trespass against us.' The Lord said. How did I know that?*

For the first time, she prayed. *Lord, I am lost. Help me now to learn who I was and to guide Tadgh along the path that you have shown us through your life here on earth. In Jesus' name. Amen.*

Morgan's racing mind calmed then, and she felt relieved of a burden that she hadn't realized she was carrying. She'd been so caught up in helping the man she loved that she hadn't given a thought to her own needs. She didn't know why but she trusted in the Lord, just as she trusted Tadgh.

The darkened room around her looked beautiful in the dancing candlelight. The canopy over the four-poster was stitched in intricate gold-colored thread patterns, and tassels dangled. The elaborate woman's dressing table and chair and the wardrobe all matched the curved style and materials of the oak bed frame. Plush carpeted flooring matched the blue sash draperies, framing windows that looked out on the lake. She quickly realized that they must be directly above the main dining room. This was a mansion and a life that she could quickly learn to love, but it wasn't Tadgh's way of life.

She sighed and knew she would always share his destiny and life after they were married.

Morgan kissed Tadgh's neck and mumbled, "Where you go, my love, I go," just before she nodded off to sleep. It had been quite a day, to be sure.

Morgan awoke in a sweat. She had been under water and the huge squid had her in its tentacles dragging her below the surface. Her breath came in gulps and her heart pounded in her ears. *Where am I?* She recognized the snores to her left. Tadgh. *What time was it?*

She wondered if the squid in her dream, which was holding her down and suffocating her could be the manifestation of Tadgh's anger at her having a non-violent public opinion of the fight for freedom.

The evening tapers had snuffed out. At first the room was completely dark. Morgan listened intently, her sense of hearing acute to the groans and creaks of her surroundings. The windowpanes rattled, their lead pointing likely missing in some spots. *Windy out there.*

The full moon burst from behind a cloud and illuminated the large oak tree just outside the window. The shadows danced on the wall opposite the bed, like the giant squid arms rising from the depths to attack her, At least that's what she thought in her sleepy condition.

That's when she heard the whinny of a horse, faint at first and then louder. Sliding out of bed, Morgan tiptoed to the window and opened the sash. The full moon shimmered off the lake beyond the ruins, two hundred yards from her window, illuminating the pearled sky and its mosaic of gilt-rimmed clouds. She thought it made the ruins, now standing stark against the moonlight, much more ominous than in the day's light.

There was no horse to be seen in the pasture, but she could hear one, nonetheless, snorting. A mist came up off the lake and began to encircle the castle ruins. It was then that she saw a rider and horse emerge from behind the main ruin through the mist. The ghostly figure and beast were dressed for battle. The rider wore full mail armor, and a helmet and face piece obscured his countenance. The lance balanced on his right arm and red cross shield indicated that he meant to joust or attack.

Morgan was frozen in fascination. She shivered, and the back of her neck tingled. She leaned over the sash, straining to get a clearer view.

I can see the wall of the ruin through the horseman. Is it just an apparition?

The horse turned toward the house and stopped in its tracks. The horseman raised the lance and waved it towards her. Morgan scrambled to the bed and roused Tadgh. "Get up my love. Get up!"

"What? Can't you see it's not morning yet? Get back into bed."

"No, no. Come to the window—right now."

She pulled Tadgh out of bed and pushed him over to the window. "Look. Out by the ruins." Her voice was hoarse with fright.

"What? Moonlight is all I see. Can I just get back to bed?"

"You mean to tell me that you can't see them?"

"See what? The ruins?"

"No, the crusader knight on his horse."

Tadgh shook his head and shot her a strange look.

"I tell you he was there a minute ago."

The mist had gone and with it the knight on his horse. Dawn was just creeping over the eastern horizon to their left.

"He was there. Honestly," Morgan exclaimed, turning to see Tadgh crawling back into bed.

"I need more sleep," Tadgh complained, pulling the covers up to his chin. He immediately dozed off again.

Morgan, resting on the one-sided fainting couch under the window, continued to hold vigil over the pastoral scene. This was the first time in her memory that she had seen a vision. What did it mean? Who was he? Whatever it was, it was gone.

Exhausted, Morgan finally dozed off, imagining many of the Perceval women before her, curled up on that very couch, as the sun slowly rose to bathe the Temple House demesne in its awakening glow. She wondered how many had seen the noble horseman on his splendid steed. She could faintly hear the crowing of the cock and the lowing of the cattle as they heralded in yet another day in the seven-hundred-year-old life of the Templar manor grounds.

Chapter Six
Donegal

Thursday, July 6, 1916
Temple House, Ballymote, Ireland

*T*adgh found Morgan there on the divan, curled up like a tabby cat. She looked beautifully peaceful. The clock on the bedside table showed that it was late, seven-thirty. Crossing to the washstand, he poured cold water from the pitcher and splashed some on his face and neck.

His first thought was that they needed to get out of this Protestant mansion as soon as possible. He was still angry at the way Morgan had taken sides as usual against the Cause, and therefore against him, the night before. *She shouldn't publicize her passivism,* he grumbled to himself. Damn women. He quickly brushed down his clothes and pulled them on. *Was that a dream or did she drag me out of bed to see—what was it—a ghost?*

"Morgan?" Tadgh coaxed, giving her shoulder a gentle squeeze. "Morgan? You must get up and get dressed."

Morgan jolted awake. "Did you see them?" she asked, rubbing her eyes, looking out the window. "The horse and rider?"

Tadgh then remembered the conversation. *A crusader.* "No, there was nothing out there earlier. C'mon now, we have to be on our way."

"They were there, Tadgh, as plain as day. A horse and rider. I saw them. He signaled to me with his coat of arms, the red cross on the shield."

"Did he, now? You've been dreaming of Templars, that's all."

"No, Tadgh. I know what I saw."

"Let's sort this later. Now please get dressed."

As they were walking down the guest wing corridor, Nora came

113

bounding up the stairs.

"There you are, you two. Breakfast is ready and Gaga's gone home."

"Good morning, Nora," Morgan said, happy to see a female face.

Tadgh brushed past Nora and hurried down the wide staircase. Morgan took Nora's arm, and they started down together. "It was so nice of you and your mother-in-law to put us up for the night. Thank you."

"No bother. Your beau is a bit prickly."

Morgan stopped and turned to her companion. "He's been through a lot, Nora. We both have."

The younger Perceval disengaged her arm and put her hands up to her cheeks. "I'm afraid of his kind. What's the world coming to?"

Morgan took Nora's hands and pulled them away from her face. "He's a good man. He has strong beliefs about his way of life and freedom." She pointed to one of the Perceval military portraits on the stairwell. "Stern—just like your ancestors. Who is *this*?"

"I have no idea. Ascelin told me once."

Morgan took her hand and started down the stairs again, but Nora held her back, her eyes pleading. "I just want us to stay free of danger and war."

"I'm not sure that we can stop it, dear," Morgan said, and the two walked down to the small dining room. "Be vigilant, Nora."

"There you are." Charlotte greeted the women from her place at the head of the breakfast table. "Tadgh, here, has already started eating."

The kitchen cook was just putting more Irish breakfast victuals on the sideboard.

Charlotte waved her arm in that direction. "Help yourselves to the fried eggs, girls. Did you sleep well, Morgan?"

Morgan filled a plate with eggs, black pudding, bacon, and dry toast, and sat down next to her hostess. "Yes, thank you so much for your hospitality." She hesitated, knowing what she wanted to ask Charlotte, but reticent to do so. "You know, I saw something curious last night out the window. Tadgh thinks it's my imagination, but I'm sure there was a rider and horse out there at the ruins. It was misty, but the rider was dressed as a knight, and he held his shield as if he saw me, too. Was I dreaming?"

As Morgan spoke, Charlotte's eyes widened, and her fork stopped midair. "Well, girl, I should have known you would see him."

"Why, what do you mean?"

"The ghost of the knight Sir Owain is what you saw. The story has long been in the family. Sir Owain made a pilgrimage to Ireland, seeking the entrance to purgatory. He came up the Templar path through Ardfert and Ballymote and on his return stopped here at the castle. He was sore afraid of what he had seen, as it says of the shepherds on Christ's birth night in Luke 2, Verse 9. He met a maiden here who soothed his troubles, and they fell in love. Out of a sense of duty, he returned to Europe, leaving the heartbroken girl behind. They say he regretted this mistake for the rest of his life, and he's returned from the grave to look for his true love."

"Do you mean others have seen him?"

"Only those like you, lass. Those who are lost, themselves."

"Morgan is not lost, ma'am. She is with me," Tadgh protested.

"Yes, Tadgh, but she has lost her memories, her past. The spirit knows this. She must have been thinking about it last night." Arthur appeared and poured out tea for Morgan.

"I was. I was. My God, I was."

Charlotte nibbled on her piece of toast. "Sir Owain appears when a change is about to happen. I saw the apparition myself just before my husband died. But that was a long time ago."

Tadgh didn't like where this conversation was going. It was bad enough that she was a Protestant pacifist. Now she was filling Morgan's head with fanciful ideas. "Have you finished your breakfast, Morgan? We really must be going. We're expected."

"In a minute, love. This is all very strange because I'm not at all frightened by seeing a ghost. What's the change coming, I wonder?"

Charlotte reached out and grasped Morgan's hand, patting it with her other palm. "It's as if you were destined to come here to stay with us, Morgan. You'll have to let me know what happens to you both." She handed Morgan her calling card with her address.

Nora could keep quiet no longer. "Mother, with all the talk of revolution last night, I told Morgan that I am worried about war here, at Temple House."

"It will come. You will need to decide which side you are on. Ireland or England," Tadgh said with conviction, finishing the last rasher of bacon on his plate.

"I pray it will become a negotiation, not a battle, Tadgh."

"I sincerely expect it will be much more than that, Mrs. Perceval."

"There. You see, Mother? With Ascelin away at the war and all."

Charlotte frowned at Tadgh. "We'll manage, Nora. You hush now."

"Maybe that's why Sir Owain is here—change, meaning the rebellion," Tadgh replied. "Morgan did say that he was dressed for battle."

"Perhaps. But I think he may indicate a change ahead for Morgan, since he appeared to her."

Tadgh grunted and turned away, mumbling.

"Please be vigilant, ma'am," Morgan said, finishing up her breakfast. "You and your family. Tadgh is right. War is coming."

"I will look after my own, young lady."

With that, breakfast was over. They thanked their hostess and said their goodbyes. Tadgh ushered Morgan out as quickly as possible.

"Please come back and visit again when you can," Charlotte called after them as Tadgh gunned the Kerry back down the half-mile drive. Morgan looked back longingly at the gray mansion receding into the distance and waved to its mistress. She was sure she saw Sir Owain watching from behind the ruins.

Morgan sat lost in thought as they traveled, and Tadgh let her be as he pushed the Kerry to its limit. Finally, she spoke up over the roar of the engine, "I've been thinking, Tadgh, about Ballymote. The book. We need to ask Peader about it."

"Aye, lass. It's a puzzle for certain. We're only about fifty miles south of Donegal Town now. Wait until you see the coastline at Ballyshannon. I've been told that it's beautiful and this is a fine bright morning. We missed it when we passed by in the *Survivor*."

"I feel as if we've been put through the wringer," Morgan lamented, as they finally entered the outskirts of Donegal Town just before noon.

"Just think how Red Hugh's soldiers must have felt when they made that trek on foot in the fall and winter of 1601, lass. Back then, they had to fight the British at Kinsale almost as soon as they arrived that January."

"No wonder they lost the battle, Tadgh."

"They didn't just lose the battle. They lost their birthright, their culture, and their country, or what was left of it. With that kind of valor, how can we do anything less than give our all to regain these treasures? There'll be no negotiations, lass."

"How much farther do we have to go today?" she asked, shifting in her seat to give her leg some relief.

"It's about thirty-five miles to Meenmore, if you'll recall."

"We came by boat the last time. That's different."

"You're right. So, in one more hour we should be at Peader's, just in time for dinner."

They entered central Donegal Town before crossing the Eske River. Morgan could have reached out and touched the brick building that had been her da's cobbler shop in The Diamond had she been able to remember it. As it was, the back of her neck tingled again, and she thought that strange. "I've been here before. I can sense it, but I can't put my finger on it." A partly ruined castle appeared on their right.

"The feeling has to do with something that we passed, or maybe that bridge over the river. The more I try, the murkier my thoughts become."

"Look on the bright side, lass. You're probably Irish. And some memories are starting to cross into your conscious mind. That's progress, right?" But he wasn't at all sure that he wanted her to remember. He loved her just as she was now. And the discussion about Sir Owain bothered him. *Damn. It was only an old wives' tale.*

"I suppose so. But it's maddening just the same."

Simpson reported to Boyle early Thursday morning. "I overheard. O'Donnell's plan to go to Donegal, boss. Collin met up with his wife yesterday too. She must have come over from Canada."

If he was looking for some praise from his boss, Simpson didn't know him very well yet.

"I knew it. They're going home. That cripple Jordan tried to pull a fast one. That damn liar. We'll have to take care of him later, Simpson. He can't run very fast with that cane." Boyle knew exactly where he had killed the father. *We'll go there first.* "We may not get McCarthy, but we'll get O'Donnell."

"I thought we were just using O'Donnell to get to the murderer McCarthy."

Glowering, Boyle ordered, "Get my police van ready for a long trip. We're going to Donegal Town, and we're leaving in an hour."

When Peader got home from school, his mother had a barrage of questions for him.

"These friends of yours are not followers of Larkin, are they, son?"

Peader answered very carefully. "Let's just say that they are committed to the betterment of the common Irish man and woman."

"But they are Republicans. They said so."

"Like meself, they are very interested in our Gaelic heritage."

"I want you to very careful of the like, son."

On Thursday July sixth, Peader admonished his brothers and sisters. "Now, all you lot, I want you to be polite to my friends. They'll be here shortly."

Just before noon Peader's eldest sister, who had been looking through the parlor window for what seemed like hours, announced, "They're here." She needn't have bothered since they all heard the motorcycle drive up.

After introductions to the children were made, Peader took Tadgh and Morgan into the parlor and shut the door. "You've come a ways, then?"

"Almost three days' travel. We had an interesting stay last night in Ballymote, which we will tell you about later."

"Ma stayed home today because you were coming. She told me of your earlier visit."

"She is a fine woman, Peader," Morgan said, warmth in her voice.

"I know that, Morgan, even more now since I've been away at school having to fend for myself."

A few minutes later, one of the children knocked on the door, letting them know that an early tea was ready. The topics of conversation in the dining room, led by mother Biddy O'Donnell, ranged from classical music to the recent treatise by German Albert Einstein on the general theory of relativity. Clearly, here was a family with intellectual curiosity, certainly not what Tadgh expected from a rural family in a Gaeltacht area. He noticed the expanse of books lining the dining room shelves and reproductions of paintings by the Masters on the walls that he had missed on his first visit. Tadgh felt much more comfortable in this country home than in the extravagant manor they'd stayed in the night before.

"So, what do you think about how our women are faring in this modern industrial era, Morgan?" Mrs. O'Donnell asked, out of the blue, during a dessert of custard and berries.

Morgan replied," Oppressed, repressed, and undervalued."

Tadgh wondered whether Morgan's life before he knew her had been far from happy. Perhaps an overbearing father. Maybe that is why the amnesia persisted, blocking that early life from her consciousness. "Aroon, I hope you're not referring to me, there."

He noticed Mrs. O'Donnell nodding, as if she approved.

Morgan continued, "Of course, I'm speaking in general. As for myself, I am engaged to the most wonderful man who cares for me, and shares with me as an equal. In fact, he has asked me to marry him on his birthday, August fifteenth, and I have agreed to his proposal."

Tadgh relaxed and smiled knowingly.

He turned to Peader seated next to him. "I'd be honored if you would be a groomsman at our wedding, if ya please?"

"It would be my pleasure, Tadgh," Peader responded, clapping him on the back.

Despite her exhaustion from the rigors of travel, Morgan said, "Let me help you with the dishes." Mrs. O'Donnell gratefully accepted.

As she passed her son on the way to the kitchen, Biddy murmured, "There's something about this girl, Peader. She's one of us."

Tadgh saw Peader's smile. His mother's opinion was still an important part of the lad's psyche.

"Can we go somewhere where we can talk privately, Peader?"

"Of course, Tadgh. This way."

Once they were behind closed doors in Peader's room, Tadgh filled him in on their Clans Pact adventures since they had last seen him in Howth.

"Jaysus, Tadgh. You were lucky to get out of Howth Harbour alive, weren't ya, now."

"My guerrilla training paid off on that occasion, to be sure."

Tadgh undid the string that bound the oilskin on his historical research package and spread its contents on the bed. He briefly related the results of his discussion with Morgan in Mountjoy Square Park. "We think that Florence confided in McCarthy Mor to protect the *Book of MacCarthaigh Reagh*² and to hide the treasures of both Clans in a location he chose."

"That makes sense, Tadgh, especially with your story about the disappearance of the 'McCarthy Gold' from Blarney."

"Right you are. I had nearly forgotten about that historical piece of the puzzle."

"All we have to do is find and follow all the clues to determine if your theory is true, my friend." Peader got up and paced the length of his room.

Tadgh coaxed him to pay attention. "Come back here, comrade. Now look at the circled headers in the Psalms of my family Bible. D'you recognize them?"

"They're the end folios of *an Cathach*. My God, Tadgh! You were right when we talked back at Boland's Bakery. At least one of your ancestors understood the significance of those passages."

"It must have been Florence."

They heard a soft knock at the door, and Morgan entered the room. "Where are you in the explanation?" she asked, as she shut the door and sat on the bed.

"Just talking about the circles in our Bible, lass."

That got Morgan's attention. "Those circles had to have been put there by Florence himself. It stands to reason that only he and Red Hugh presumably knew the significance of the truncation, right?"

"That's what we've just concluded, lass."

Peader pointed to the worn title page. "But Tadgh, you said that Florence was arrested and put in the Tower of London six months before the Battle of Kinsale in 1601 and that this Douvay-Rheims translation was not published until 1610."

"Wait a minute," Tadgh said, turning to the inscription on the inside frontispiece where it was written, "'Herein lies the salvation of all mankind, signed and sealed by Florence MacCarthaigh, dated 1627, London.' From my research, I read that Florence was set free from that imprisonment in 1626 to write his histories as long as he provided sureties that he would stay in that city and never return to Ireland. I am reasonably sure that he stayed there until his death in 1640."

"So, my love, Florence must have acquired the Bible while in prison," Morgan surmised.

"Or later, when he was living in London. Then he kept it with him and marked it up himself," Tadgh guessed.

"Then how did you come to have the Bible, Tadgh, if he never returned to Kilbrittain or Ireland, then?" Peader asked.

"It came back from Europe with some of my ancestors when they returned to Wales from the continent. My pa didn't have it, but he thought it was still there. I did some investigating and found it with relatives in Tenby." He turned to Morgan. "It was with me on *The Republican* when I rescued you, mavourneen."

"Another fact is that the *Cumdach* and *an Cathach* were in the hands of the O'Donnells from the seventeenth century to the present, and not available to the Boyles, according to Professor Lawlor," Peader noted.

"So, the bottom line is that we don't think Boyle or any other McCarthy ancestor except Florence knew about the truncation of *an Cathach* as a clue."

"That's right, Morgan, and we now believe that the McCarthy clans eventually joined forces to hide their combined treasures. That would have occurred when the thieving British closed in on them during the Confederate Wars of the 1640s, when Florence would have already been dead. By the way, Peader reminded me about the 'McCarthy Gold' historical story. That is another reason to think that Florence confided in the McCarthy Mor once before he was incarcerated in 1601 to set the stage, and again, during his exile in London after his release in 1626 to plan the hiding if the McCarthys were threatened."

"My God, Tadgh. That's right." Morgan got up off the bed and gazed out the window for a moment before turning back to the men. "But how do we know that the treasure hasn't already been found?"

"That is a good question. Obviously, the Boyles haven't been successful or the head constable would not be killing McCarthys at will. And I doubt that McCarthys have found it, either."

Before she could open her mouth with another question, Tadgh went on, "If it had been found in the MacCarthaigh Reagh Clan line after the British captured Kilbrittain Castle, then I would no longer have my locket."

"The locket could just be a family heirloom passed down like a matriarchal cameo, couldn't it?"

Tadgh stroked his moustache. "I don't think so, Morgan. My pa would not have been so secretive when he passed it on to me, his first born, if the treasure had already been found by our ancestors."

Peader had been re-examining the Clans Pact and laid it back down on the bed. "If, as we suspect, the treasure was hidden by the McCarthy Mor line at the time of the siege on Blarney Castle, then they knew its location. What if they came back to claim it?"

Tadgh thought about it. "We don't know whether a member of that Sept of my clan may have recovered it, but there has never been a resurgence of wealth in that branch of the family, as far as I know. I believe that the treasure has not been found unless it has been inadvertently exposed. Of course, that may be wishful thinking on my part."

"And we're no closer to finding it either, I might add," Morgan said.

Tadgh wiped his brow. "Alas, 'tis true. We're missing something."

"Or many things, my friend. We have no idea how convoluted the trail is, do we." Peader resumed his pacing.

The logic was hurting Tadgh's head, so he changed the conversation. "What about Boyle? He's still alive and presumably will be looking for us. He has killed on numerous occasions, and he won't let a bullet wound or a smothering attempt stop him."

"We have to plan on the likelihood that the monster is a serious threat," Morgan added.

"You're right, aroon. He will be out of hospital soon, if he isn't already. I aim to kill him as soon as we return to Creagh."

"You'll do nothing of the kind, Tadgh McCarthy, unless he threatens us again. I need you alive, my love."

"Mark my words, Morgan. Boyle will be dead before we're wed."

"But we won't wed if *you're* dead, mavourneen."

"How will he find you?" Peader asked, continuing his pacing.

"We'll find him and finish him off, once and for all," Tadgh replied, knowing secretly that Boyle would have to contact Jack Jordan. The Cunard manager would be under surveillance now that he had undoubtedly brought Collin to Ireland. Tadgh's hatred of the villain who killed his parents shut out the words of his betrothed.

"Did you tell Peader about the other circled Psalm?" Morgan asked Tadgh, opening the Bible to that location for Peader to see.

Tadgh described their findings regarding Psalm 68, Verse 26, the verse almost exactly halfway between the other two.

"What does it say?"

Tadgh consulted the page. "*Praise God in the great congregation. Praise the Lord in the Assembly of Israel.*"

Peader stopped pacing to look at the Bible. "How clever you two are. So now we know that there are three passages that could mean something, but we have no idea what they are trying to tell us."

"I've been thinking about those verses," Morgan said, flipping her dark curls away from her eyes and checking the Bible. "Here's what I think. Psalm 30, Verse 10 is—*Hear, O Lord, and have mercy upon me. Lord, be thou my helper.* That could be referring to a period or location where The Lord helped one of the Clans." She turned to pages farther ahead in the book. "Psalm 105 Verse, 13 reads, *When they went from one nation to another, from one kingdom to another people.* That could be referring to the time when the O'Donnell or the MacCarthy Clan settled in Ireland, coming from somewhere else."

Then she flipped back and jabbed her finger down on the page. "I'm stumped when it comes to the content of Psalm 68, Verse 26. I'm not sure at all where the Assembly of Israel might have figured in the Irish Clans."

Tadgh stood up and wearily walked to the window before turning back to comment, "Those are interesting interpretations, Morgan, but I think we are still missing some critical pieces of information. Nothing is clear yet."

Morgan spoke up. "I think that we need a rest, Tadgh. All this is hurting my brain, I can't keep my eyes open, and my back is aching."

Peader understood immediately and put on his host manners. "Please, let me show you to your room. By the way, this Saturday the eighth, the traditional Orangemen's Parade will be held in Donegal Town. It brings in William of Orange's followers from all over the northwest. For some reason they hold it there on the Saturday before the traditional twelfth of July. The Catholic families traditionally protest, so you might join us in peaceful demonstration, if you've a mind to."

Morgan and Tadgh nodded their acceptance.

That night in their Spartan room when Tadgh was trying to get to sleep, his mind churned, observing that Morgan had been unusually quiet and withdrawn when they were alone.

He was going to wake her to find out why but decided the better of it. *Let her be. Let's see if tomorrow will bring more answers to the riddles. She's asleep already anyway, probably dreaming about that damned knight. We never should have gone to Ballymote.* Unlike his girl, he was unable to nod off until just before sunrise.

Chapter Seven
Searching For Claire

Friday, July 7, 1916
Meenmore, Ireland

*D*awn found the mist still clinging to Dungloe Lough as they rose to meet what promised to become a gloomy day. Standing at the window, Tadgh felt the chill both from outside and within the bedroom. Morgan was still ignoring his attempts at conversation.

"So, let's talk about this weddin' you're gonna have a month from now, lass," Biddy said to Morgan during Friday morning's breakfast. "Have you considered what style of dress you want to have?"

"I haven't had time to consider the wedding at all," Morgan replied, sincerely touched by the woman's sudden interest in her affairs.

"We have some of the best dressmakers here in Dungloe, dear. The cloth industry is my business, don't ya know? I'd like to take you down to my shop this afternoon and show you some fabrics. We have a beautiful medieval weddin' gown with mock pearls sewn in at the bodice. I think that it would look lovely on you."

Tadgh saw that Morgan was looking inquisitively at him. Peader's ma hastily added," It would give this old lady great pleasure to gift this garment to you, Morgan."

"Well now, ma'am. That's very kind of you, but we couldn't possibly accept that much generosity," Tadgh commented despite Morgan's pleading eyes.

"Nonsense, dear fellow, I didn't offer it to you, and I don't think that you would look good in that style of dress anyway."

Peader gave Tadgh a look as if to say, "She's made up her mind. Stop trying to change it."

Directly after lunch the two women headed off downtown on foot, leaving the men to address the political turmoil on their own.

♣   ♣   ♣   ♣

Collin and Kathy stood on the platform at the Dungloe Road station after disembarking from their adventurous train ride from Lisburn. "Collin, where to next?"

"I remember this place from when I was last here, my love, even though I was only thirteen. It's only a mile or so to the town."

"A mile? I'm not ready for that. My stomach has been upset all morning."

"It's just a pleasant outing for the feet, as they say here, Kathy. And it's such a soft day at that." At his words, a gentle rain began to fall. "Here, let me hold the umbrella for you." Hefting the beaten leather suitcase, Collin guided Kathy down into the town.

Half an hour later, they stopped, and Collin looked at his watch, "Down Lower Main Street over there we can find a pub and get lunch if they're still serving at three o'clock. They should be able to tell us where my aunt and Peader live, if they still live around here. I'm sure you'll feel better when we can get some hot soup into you, darlin'. The train ride was very drafty and bumpy, wasn't it?"

They found Main Street across the Dungloe River Bridge. "This is certainly wild country, I'll grant you that," Kathy exclaimed. "But it is very beautiful in a rugged sort of way. I'm just happy to finally see the area where you were born."

"I was actually born thirty-five miles southeast of here, in Donegal Town."

Just before they reached Doherty's Restaurant, they passed a clothing store with fashionable women's apparel in the window. A Celtic ivory satin wedding dress caught Kathy's eye, a medieval-style garment.

"Collin, can you get us a table? I just want to take a look in this store for a minute."

"Not too long, my dear. I'm starving, and you need to eat. Just looking, I hope," he added, as he strode off to the pub.

Before she entered the quaint little shop, Kathy brushed off the wetness from her coat and shook her hair while she took in her surroundings. A multitude of brightly colored bolts of cloth on display first caught her eye. In the far corner, a woman sat at an old-fashioned loom intertwining fabric of golds with blues and oranges. *Magnificent*, she thought to herself. *Such a different process than the mass production sweatshop we saw on Rhode Island on our first trip together.*

A shop matron was showing a young woman the same wedding dress that Kathy had seen in the window display.

The woman turned to Kathy. "May I help you, lass?"

"What a lovely dress. Was it made locally?" Kathy asked, as she stepped forward.

"Right here in this shop, dear. But I think it may be taken," the saleslady said, as she motioned towards her other young customer.

"It's so soft," The bride-to-be ran her hand down the garment. "I've never seen one so beautiful before."

"You'll be the most beautiful bride," Kathy told her, seeing that the young woman had her heart set on the gown. "He'll be the luckiest man in the world."

"Thanks. I think I am the luckiest girl in the world. My name is Morgan." She offered her hand.

"And I'm Kathy, honored to make your acquaintance," Kathy replied, shaking the woman's hand.

"And I'm Brigid, known as Biddy to my friends, at your service."

Morgan twirled in the air with her arms extended. "We were in a fancy manor home just yesterday. I can imagine descending its magnificent staircase in this dress to the oohs and ahs of assembled guests, accompanied by flutes and violins playing the wedding march."

"That's a wonderful vision, Morgan, if we lived in a different time with different means."

"A girl can dream, can't she?"

Kathy immediately liked this woman. "Of course you can, and anyway this splendid dress is real, and you'd look regal in it."

Biddy loved the compliment and showed Kathy the dress. "Here, feel the fabric. I tailored the gown and its train in ivory satin, with ivory chiffon for the sleeves. Do you see the clasp with the Celtic knot design and linked rope belt with tassels?"

Kathy ran her fingers over the satin as the tailor draped it over her arm. "It is lovely. The material reminds me of my own wedding gown."

Biddy held the dress up to Morgan, eyeing the fit. "Are you visiting the area, Kathy?"

"My husband Collin and I are just arrived on the train from Lisburn, ma'am. Which reminds me, he is waiting in the restaurant next door. So, I'd better go," Kathy said, checking her watch. "I just popped in to see that dress. It is so nice to meet you both. Best wishes on your nuptials, Morgan."

As she was leaving, Kathy heard the saleslady ask Morgan if she had time for a fitting. *She's going to take it,* Kathy thought. *She'll dazzle her beau in that gown.*

"I have good news, dear," Collin exclaimed when Kathy joined him in the restaurant. "My aunt still lives in the area, in Meenmore just a mile north of town, according to the waiter. He gave me her address. And he said that she is the manager of the store you just visited."

"Maybe she's the seamstress I just met. We could stop by there after lunch."

"The waiter says she doesn't normally work on Fridays. I think we should press on to her home as soon as we have eaten. I'm eager to see if Peader is there and whether Claire has contacted him."

♣ ♣ ♣ ♣

"Tadgh, I can't believe who has come to visit," Peader announced, as Collin and Kathy came trudging up the walk an hour later.

"Who is it, comrade?" Tadgh asked, as he looked out the window at the weary travelers.

"It's been eleven years, but I do believe it's my cousin Collin with a lovely colleen in tow. He's filled out a lot, not the scrawny boy I remember, but I'd know that face anywhere."

Tadgh looked closely. *Is that the lad who was visiting Boyle and then came back to spoil his execution? Damn, it is. What's he doing here?*

"He and I are cousins about the same age, and boyhood pals. He had a younger sister, but I don't really remember her, except by name. When his father was murdered eleven years ago, my Aunt Shaina was so terrified, she immediately took the two children to America, I always thought that she must have witnessed the killing and feared for the lives of her family. It's the last that I heard from any of them, that's certain."

Tadgh pulled Peader back from the door. "Introduce me as a friend if you must, but not by name. And don't talk about Morgan."

"Why?"

"Just do it, comrade."

Opening the door, Peader called out, "Collin O'Donnell, you are a sight for sore eyes."

Collin looked up, and seeing a familiar but older face, called back, "Peader, is that you, cousin?"

Tadgh and Kathy watched while the two young men embraced.

"I'm so glad to find you, cousin. I didn't know if you would still be here. You've moved since I was last in Dungloe with my folks and my letters to you were returned. Peader, let me introduce you to my wife, Kathleen."

"Pleased to meet you, Kathleen," Peader responded. "Come in, come in, the both of you."

He hugged her welcome, then took her coat.

"Call me Kathy, please."

"Right then, Kathy. Where are you coming from, Collin? Last

131

thing we heard was that your family became Yanks."

"It's a long story, Peader. But we live in Canada now, in Toronto. It's a great new country, so it is."

Tadgh stepped in before Peader could make an introduction to save him from having to lie. "Pleased to meet you. I'm a friend from Dublin visiting for a few days." Remembering the butler at Temple House, he blurted out, "Just call me Arthur."

Peader's mouth dropped open, but he didn't utter a sound.

Tadgh shook hands with the newcomers. *Grand. I guess he doesn't recognize me because of my doctor getup from the hospital.*

Peader waved them into the parlor. "Let me get you something to drink. You folks look exhausted. Please make yourself comfortable. He offered Kathy and Collin a seat on the chesterfield by the front window, then went to the sideboard to prepare a refreshment. "I'm curious—why have you come all this way to find us?" He brought them each a glass of lemonade. Kathy asked for tea, instead, and he started for the kitchen to put the kettle on.

"Can you help me, uh . . . Arthur," he asked as he disappeared through the door, Tadgh in tow.

"What's going on here?" he asked when they were out of earshot.

'Nothing you need worry about, Peader. Let's get the tea."

When they returned with the teapot and a tin of tea, Collin asked him, "Is your mother in good health and living here with you?"

"Yes, she'll be back later this afternoon. And your sister? Claire, wasn't it? Where is she?" Peader handed Kathy a steaming cup. "Milk and sugar?"

"Yes, please."

Peader put the creamer and sugar bowl on the table in front of her.

Collin's face clouded over. "That's why we're here, Peader. I think you met her in Dublin, in the company of an Irishman named Tadgh McCarthy. We are hoping that she has come to see you recently and that you recognized each other. Most importantly we need to know where we can find her."

Peader shot a look at Tadgh and was about to respond when McCarthy shook his head. Peader got the message. He hesitated and then spoke. "I know, Collin, but I'm sorry, the woman you are talking about is not named Claire. Your sister has not come here, as far as I know, but then I don't really remember her anyway. Didn't she go to America with you when you emigrated?"

Collin's face turned ashen, and his hand shook, almost spilling his drink. "It has to be her, Peader."

Kathy gripped his hand.

"We can ask Ma about her when she gets back. I was away at college until the end of June. Did Claire also live in Canada?"

"No, cousin, she came from New York last year in May, we believe." Collin fumbled for words.

Kathy came to his aid. "We now know that Claire was a passenger on the *Lusitania*. At first, we were told that she was lost at sea. Then one of the surviving ship's officers, Mr. Jack Jordan who helped her on board during the sinking, said she came to the Cunard office in Queenstown about a month after the disaster and met with one of his men. She told him that she had amnesia. Jack only glimpsed the young woman from a distance, leaving on a motorcycle with a man who we now know is Tadgh McCarthy. He thought he recognized her as the young woman Claire, the one whom he had helped escape the *Lusitania* disaster.

"Jack couldn't stop them because he was in a wheelchair," Kathy continued. "We understand that you know McCarthy and the girl. Collin was hoping that she would have regained her memory and realized that you are cousins or that you would have recognized her. That's why we're here."

"Well, now. I can see how painful this is for both of you," Tadgh interjected. "If Collin's sister had regained her memory, wouldn't she have contacted you immediately?" A sense of unease crept over him.

Kathy curled her hands around the teacup without lifting it. "Collin and Claire were separated years ago in New York. She had no way of knowing that he had moved to Canada and our attempts to find her led to our discovery that she was onboard the doomed ship."

"What about your ma, Collin?" Peader asked.

"She's dead, Peader." Collin looked away. "Killed by a dock-worker on Toronto's waterfront several years ago."

"My God, Collin! Did they catch the murderer?"

"He's dead too, Peader. It was self-defense on my part, to be sure."

Kathy leaned forward. "Collin saved my honor in the process. The man was after me, and I could have been killed, or worse."

Tadgh wanted to know more about Claire. "Dear Lord, it sounds like you have had a very rough time of it since your family left Ireland. What happened in New York to separate your sister from your family?"

Collin took over the explanation. "She was abducted when she was thirteen and forced into slave labor in a Rhode Island textile mill, working there until she was twenty. She not only survived her ordeal, but she became a nightingale nurse for the rest of the abducted and abused children. Finally, she managed to escape with the help of an orderly and fled back to New York to start training as a registered nurse. This orderly brought her with him to England on the *Lusitania* to support the war effort. There may have been a romantic involvement because Jack said she was calling out the orderly's name when the ship went down. He drowned, but we're convinced she survived and is now this woman with McCarthy, Peader."

A lot of things were falling into place for Tadgh, but he needed confirmation. His chest tightened, and dread settled over his heart. He sat down in the chair opposite Collin. "How do you know all this?"

"Last summer we spent two weeks in New York and Rhode Island uncovering the child labor racket and exposing the perpetrators at great risk to life and limb."

There was no question now in Tadgh's mind that Morgan was indeed Claire. He got up and turned to face the front window, needing time to think. *My God. They are going to take her away from me.* And then a twinge of remorse for his selfishness set in. *What a tortured life she had been forced to live. Yet she has been so strong and resourceful.* These terrible truths made him love her more fiercely and want to protect and keep her even more.

Tadgh's mind raced as he noticed Peader's worry lines form. *What will happen when she recognizes her brother. I shouldn't have been so hard on her recently. And what an unbelievable coincidence that we would all show up together in Meenmore. Or was it the same Divine destiny that brought us together with Peader for the first time at an Stad more than a year ago?*

"Arthur?"

Tadgh turned to see Peader taking Kathy's now-empty cup. Seeing how distraught she was, their host started to speak. "The truth of the matter—"

Tadgh cut him off. "This sounds like an incredible journey of trial and tribulation for you, Collin, and your whole family, to be sure. I just wish we could help you." He tried to sound as if he meant it. "Where will you go next?"

Collin avoided the question. "Do you know where we can find McCarthy and the girl, Peader?"

An uncomfortable silence followed Collin's question. Tadgh stared hard at his friend. After a few moments, he spoke. "Perhaps they would have gone to your old home because they didn't know that you had moved."

Collin looked crestfallen. "We were so hoping that she would have come here, that you would know how to reach them, Peader. We should go to Donegal Town, I suppose. There may be friends who have seen her. If she isn't there, we will go to Queenstown and meet with Jack. He may have seen her again or perhaps traced the motorcycle and sidecar she was riding in."

Tadgh remembered that his Kerry, that very motorcycle Collin was talking about, was visible behind the house. He would have to hide it because Collin might have seen the motorcycle in the back garden of Sean's home and then again near the hospital in Tralee. He would make the connection, but maybe he already had, and that's why he rushed back into the hospital.

Now it was Peader's turn to stare at Tadgh. "I want you to stay here at least overnight tonight, cousin. Things might look quite different by the morning."

Tadgh knew what Peader was doing, and he didn't like it. Morgan would be back soon, and he didn't want Collin and Kathy to meet her. Part of him knew it would be right for Morgan to meet her family. But he needed her more than Collin did. His stomach churned.

Collin calculated his schedule. "We have to be back on the *Aquitania* in Liverpool six days from today after the ship provisions for the return trip to Montreal. We've got a lot of territory to cover if Claire is not here."

Kathy grasped Collin's hand and looked plaintively into his eyes. "Can't we stay at least tonight to rest up, love? My stomach is quite unsettled."

"If you folks would like to remain here in the parlor, Arthur and I will refresh your drinks and bring out something from the larder." Without giving Tadgh an opportunity to protest, Peader grabbed his elbow and pulled him into the kitchen, closing the door behind him.

Alone in the kitchen, he dropped the cups on the table, grabbed Tadgh by the lapels and shook him hard. "What has gotten into you? Why didn't you tell him about Morgan now you know that she has been my cousin Claire, all this time?" he demanded. "I'm thinking about what's best for her right now."

Tadgh batted Peader's arms away and took a step back before speaking. "Calm down, Peader." He stared down his compatriot. "I do have her best interests at heart. Her name is Morgan, she loves me, and doesn't appear to be worried about finding out her past. She may leave me if she finds out who she really is. I couldn't bear to lose her."

Peader slapped his forehead with his right hand and rolled his eyes as they stood face to face. "Don't be daft, lad. Think of it another way, Tadgh. What happens if you pull this off, and then she recalls things on her own in future? She says that she sometimes remembers bits and pieces. If she contacts her brother and finds out that you lied to them and kept it from her, that could certainly drive her away from you. Don't start your marriage with a lie, and don't underestimate her love for you, comrade."

Tadgh let that sink in for a minute. "But she might never remember."

"I have been sheltered, but you are a neophyte when it comes to women, Tadgh. I think you owe it to Morgan and all her relatives, but what you do is up to you. I won't interfere but I won't lie for you again either. Why did you name yourself Arthur, anyway?"

"My middle name, and I hate it."

When they returned with a refreshment tray, Collin was pacing the length of the room. "I notice that there is a motorcycle parked out there, Peader," he said, staring intently at Tadgh. "I'll wager it's the one that I saw in Sean O'Casey's backyard, and again in Tralee, isn't it, Arthur? Or should I say *Tadgh*?"

A coldness crept into Tadgh, and he steeled himself.

"You are lying to us. Did you come alone? Or did she accompany you?"

Tadgh could see Collin's eyes glower and his hands clench. "I came with my fiancée, Morgan," Tadgh answered truthfully. He was caught.

"That must the same Morgan who I met in the clothing shop," Kathy interrupted, standing to move between the two men. "She's lovely. You're a lucky man."

"I'd like to stay lucky." Tadgh muttered, avoiding Collin's glare.

"How long have you known this Morgan, Tadgh, or Arthur, or whatever your name is?"

Tadgh hesitated, then spoke, "It's been a little over a year now since we met." He dreaded the next question.

"How did you two meet?"

Damn. When will this all end? "At sea. We met at sea," he stammered.

"On the day that the *Lusitania* was sunk?"

Tadgh could only nod his head.

Peader had had enough and blurted, "He rescued her and brought her back from near death. If it weren't for Tadgh's care, she'd be dead and gone, that's certain."

Collin eyed his cousin. "You were willing to go along with this villain, trying to keep me from my long-lost sister. How could you turn on kin like that? We'll wait here for her to return with Aunt Biddy. Then she's coming with us back to Canada where she belongs. We won't stay under your roof, Peader."

Tadgh moved between his nemesis and Peader. "Look here, Collin, Morgan may not be your sister. You don't know that for a certainty. There were at least eight hundred women on board the *Lusitania* that day. Morgan has amnesia, so she doesn't know her name or history. I don't want her hurt needlessly. You appear to be relying on the memory of a ship's officer who would have been under extreme duress when the ship was going down."

"If Morgan, as you call her, doesn't recognize me, then we will take her to meet Jack Jordan, the ship's officer, so he can identify her properly. He seems eager to do so."

Tadgh gripped Collin's right shoulder and squeezed hard. "Hear me now. Morgan's not going back to Canada or anywhere else with you, Collin. We love each other, and we're going to be married this August."

Collin pushed Tadgh's hand away and balled his fists. "You hear me, you liar and German spy, so I'm told. You've implicated my sister Claire in your deadly revolution, and I'm going to rescue her. So, don't get in my way."

Peader got between them. "Calm down, lads. First, let's see if Morgan recognizes Collin. If she does, then surely she alone should decide her fate."

Collin elbowed Peader aside. "Morgan is Claire, of that I am certain now. She's coming with me, even if she doesn't remember me. We will bring her memory back." He glared at Tadgh.

"No! I forbid it!" Tadgh unleashed his right fist and caught Collin in the ribs.

Collin coiled, raised his fists and struck Tadgh with a lightning left to the nose.

Peader shouted, "If you insist on killing each other, take your fight outside! There'll be no fisticuffs in this house!"

"A duel then, in the yard."

Kathy grabbed her husband's arm. "No, Collin. This is ridiculous. I won't have it. Wait for Claire to come and then decide."

"Stop interfering, Kathleen. We're having this out now, once and for all, before Claire arrives."

Tadgh wiped his bloody nose with his sleeve, then pulled out his Luger and checked the ammunition clip. "Pistols?"

"Aha. I see that you have a German weapon, Tadgh. Still the spy, eh? Peader, do you have a pistol?"

"No, Collin, I don't. And there will be no duel. Both of you, calm down."

"Bare knuckles, no holds barred, then, Tadgh."

The two men jostled their way into the yard, shoving as they went, and the others followed.

Kathy screamed, "No! Don't do this. You promised you'd never fight like this again."

"Stay out of this, woman! This blaggard isn't going to give up any other way."

Tadgh pulled off his sweater and threw it down. "Fine with me, Collin. Let's go." He spit on his hands.

Peader jumped in between them. "You're both too angry and not thinking clearly."

Collin threw his coat over the porch railing after they stepped outside the front door. Despite Kathy's protests, Peader held her back so she wouldn't get in the way. Both men were white hot and there was every possibility they could injure her.

The two men circled each other on the grassy area hidden from the street. With his military training and a height advantage of three inches, Tadgh was confident he could whip this challenger with one hand tied behind his back.

That's when Collin knifed in and hit him with a right uppercut that rattled his teeth and followed with a series of body blows that pummeled his chest. Then, just as quickly, Collin danced away as Tadgh swung.

Tadgh shook it off. *Damn, the kid's good.* "I see you've been in some scrapes before, Collin," he growled.

"I've had my share," Collin grunted, standing his ground. "Claire's coming to Canada."

"Over my dead body."

"So be it, you bastard."

Tadgh lurched forward and grabbed Collin in a headlock with his left arm, nearly lifting him off the grass. Tadgh pounded Collin's face, and blood spurted from the man's nose.

It was Collin's turn to be surprised. He pummeled Tadgh's stomach, then watched him double over.

Tadgh's stomach spasmed as Collin broke free of the lock.

This guy knows how to attack a vulnerable spot and damage it. Collin paid no attention to the cut under his left eye as he moved in on his foe once again. This time he went after the kidneys with a series of staccato blows that would have felled a horse. All the while, he ducked and evaded Tadgh's attacks, which only delivered glancing blows to the top of his head.

Tadgh wheezed now, trying to catch his breath. He thought of going for the knife in his boot. Not yet. *That will be my last resort only.*

When Collin danced away again, Tadgh threw caution to the wind. Just as he had been taught during bayonet training, he lunged straight ahead at his evasive assailant and timed a roundhouse punch perfectly to Collin's left cheek, splitting the skin open and knocking him to the ground. Then he pounced on him before he could get up and started pounding him in the chest.

Blood flowed freely from Collin's face. Kathy cried out and struggled against Peader's restraint.

Collin kicked upward, and his foot caught Tadgh in the groin, temporarily doubling him up and distracting him. Collin rolled out from under and kicked upwards again. This time his boot landed squarely under Tadgh's chin. In an instant, Collin was up and moving away, but slower than before.

Tadgh was bleeding at the mouth, having severely bitten through his tongue and lip.

Collin saw his adversary stretch upright in obvious pain. Before he could regain his composure, Collin flashed in and landed a staggering uppercut. Then he grabbed him in a clinch and hammered at his kidneys, again and again.

With one last burst of strength, Tadgh thrust his arms up under the circle of Collin's grasp, breaking free and throwing him back against a mighty elm in the lawn. The sound of Collin's head hitting the tree trunk was like a ripe melon cracking open. Dazed, he dropped to his knees and held his head in bruised and swollen hands.

Tadgh hunched over, gasping for breath. His stomach and kidneys were on fire. He couldn't stop the spasms.

Collin got up, shaking his head to get the sweat out of his eyes, and lurched forward to finish Tadgh off. He remembered the man he had killed by mistake in that fight in Brooklyn. *This* man he aimed to kill.

Collin grunted as he lunged and caught Tadgh with another left uppercut, and then followed with a right roundhouse, followed by a kick striking Tadgh's midsection. Tadgh went down, hitting his head on the cement sidewalk with a dull thud. Collin stumbled forward and fell beside him, spent.

Tadgh couldn't catch his breath, and his head pounded with pain. He slowly rolled over to face his foe, but his eyes could not focus properly. *Should I use the knife?* No. What he had been taught in these circumstances of hand-to-hand combat where weapons were

141

unavailable, was to twist the enemy's head until it snapped the spine. Tadgh struggled to stand, grabbing Collin's head, and slammed his knee down on his foe's chest. He couldn't get a good grip on Collin's neck, slippery with blood.

Collin squirmed under Tadgh's weight but was unable to break free. "You bastard," he wheezed, as Tadgh's hands tightened on his throat. "She'll never stay with you now."

"No!" Peader yelled, as he rushed forward to stop them. Kathy followed him, wailing.

Tadgh hesitated, his hands holding Collin's life in the balance. *What would Morgan think of me?*

Then he heard new voices. Recognizing them, he looked up, blood stinging his eyes, to see Aunt Biddy and Morgan emerge from behind the street hedge and turn, arm in arm, onto the walkway, laughing.

Chapter Eight
Claire's Choice

Friday, July 7, 1916
O'Donnell Residence, Meenmore, Ireland

*T*adgh saw the sunny expression on Biddy's face turn to shock as she screamed out, "God in heaven. What's the meaning of this?"

Morgan rushed past her. "Tadgh, let go. What's gotten into you? You'll kill the man!"

Still wheezing, Tadgh realized that he'd gone far enough and loosened his grip on Collin's throat. The jig was up.

Peader pushed Tadgh away from his cousin, and Tadgh lost his balance and fell. "I tried to stop them, Ma."

Morgan glowered at Tadgh while she bent over and examined his mouth for broken teeth. Then she looked at Kathy who was tending to Collin's face, dabbing at it with a handkerchief. She asked, "Kathy, what's going on here?"

Collin shifted, wincing as Kathy rubbed his cheek and neck with her handkerchief. When he attempted to get up to go after Tadgh, Peader had to restrain him.

Having recovered his breath, it was now Tadgh's turn to be surprised. "Morgan, you know this woman?"

"It's Kathy. We met briefly at Aunt Biddy's dress shop just to-day." Morgan turned to Kathy. "Why are *you* here?"

Biddy couldn't take her eyes off Collin's bruised face.

"This is cousin Collin, Mama," Peader said, lifting him up to face his aunt.

"Yes, I see it now, Shaina's son. Where in the world did you come from?"

Collin tried to answer her, but his jaw was swollen, and all he could muster was a weak grimace as he was lifted from the concrete with difficulty.

Tadgh had to think fast. Morgan should not have seen him with his hands on her brother's neck. What could he possibly say?

Tadgh struggled to his feet with Morgan's help. He limped toward Collin and raised his bloody hands, showing empty palms. As Peader moved to intervene, Collin beckoned with both hands, as if to say they were not through.

Tadgh extended his hands, and grinned. "You pack a hell of a wallop, lad, I'll grant you that."

Collin accepted Tadgh's offering with a bloody handshake. "You've fought once or twice in your day, I reckon." He paused, nursing a bruised knuckle. "She's coming with me, Tadgh."

"We'll see about that, Collin. Nothing's changed. I beat you, fair and square."

"I wasn't done yet. This fight's not over."

"There'll be no more fighting!" Morgan exclaimed, stepping forward to hold her man back. "Will someone please answer my question?"

Tadgh coughed to clear his throat and put a bloody hand on her arm. "We were having a friendly sparring match, is all, aroon."

"It didn't look like that to me, Tadgh McCarthy. You were about to strangle this man. I saw you!"

Tadgh stood there grinning like an idiot.

Kathy turned to Morgan, "Collin is my husband, Morgan. We are the O'Donnells from Canada."

"All the way from Canada in the middle of a war? Why, for heaven's sake?"

Collin worked his jaw with his right hand and blurted, "We came to find you, Claire. You are my sister, an O'Donnell. We have come to take you home."

Morgan's jaw dropped as she stood rooted, staring at Collin and then Kathy. "I'm afraid that I have never seen your faces before today."

Tadgh quickly interrupted. "Morgan and I are going to be married this August, and we are staying here to free Ireland."

Morgan clapped her hands to her cheeks, her green eyes staring, her mouth open. "You're my brother? And an O'Donnell. That's Peader's last name, and Biddy's. After all this time of seeking my identity, have I found my family?" She turned to stare at Peader, her arms uplifted, pleading. "We're related, then?" Her heart stirred at the possibility of finding family.

Peader stepped forward and put his arm around Morgan's shoulder. "I'm as shocked as you are, Morgan." He hesitated, then whispered, "Claire."

"We believe you are family," Kathy went on. "Can you remember anything about your past at all?"

"No, Kathy, I'm afraid I can't. Not before the sinking. I've given up trying to remember, really."

"Claire, do you recognize the child in this photograph?" Collin asked, hobbling over and retrieving his coat from the porch railing. He reached into its upper pocket, pulling out a heavily creased photograph. "Here, Claire, this is you at eleven years old." He placed the photograph into her hand, and Tadgh joined her as they peered closely.

Morgan responded after a time, "I am sorry, Collin, but I do not recognize the girl in this photograph any more than I recognize you." She looked up at him.

Collin's face crumpled at her words.

Morgan saw Collin staring blankly at her, as if he were trying to remember something.

"You are very beautiful, Claire. You certainly have blossomed since that scrawny girl in my photograph that I used to tease."

Biddy interrupted the conversation. "Come in the house and sit down, for heaven's sake, everyone." She placed her fists squarely on her hips and sternly eyed both Tadgh and Collin as though they were a couple of little boys caught being naughty. Then stamping her right foot impatiently, she said, "You two ragamuffins clean yourselves up out back at the wash basin before coming inside." Turning to Peader, she murmured, "I told you she was *our kind* of people." She examined the photograph, and then looked at Morgan. "This photo is little Claire, all right. Who'd have thought you would grow up to be this splendid woman."

Tadgh said, "That's not clear yet, Mrs. O'Donnell."

"Oh, yes, Tadgh. This is Claire O'Donnell, all right." She touched the image and stared at Morgan.

"It is not at all clear that Morgan is that girl, ma'am," Tadgh firmly replied, and grabbed Morgan's hand.

When Tadgh and Collin finished washing and came inside, Biddy bade them to sit at the kitchen table. Then she brought out the first aid kit to patch up their wounds. Morgan checked its contents, nodding approvingly, and started working on Tadgh while Biddy tended to Collin's head.

Kathy sat next to her husband, cradling her abdomen. She asked Morgan, "What if I told you that a manager from the *Lusitania* said he helped you to a lifeboat on the day your ship sank and he knew your first name?"

Morgan's eyes widened. "I sort of remember someone helping me get off the ship."

"He recognized you as the woman who had come to the Cunard office a month after the sinking, claiming to have amnesia," Kathy said.

"I did go to the Cunard office, but how do you know that this person you call Claire is me?"

"Because Jack Jordan said he saw you riding off on a motorcycle like the one right out there," Collin replied, pointing out the back window. "Does that name sound familiar to you?"

Morgan looked at Tadgh with questioning eyes.

"Jordan could have been wrong if he only saw a glimpse of her at the time, don't ya know?" Tadgh replied, gingerly massaging his kidney area. "There must have been several Claires on board the ship."

"But only one had a companion on board named Byron Harrison," Collin said, working his jaw from side to side, hoping to trigger her memory. "Does that name ring a bell for you, Claire? He was a nurse on board."

"Call me Morgan, as that's my name. And I've never heard of a Byron."

Peader observed something that the others hadn't seen. "What keepsake is attached to the chain around your neck, Collin?"

Morgan could see that Tadgh was upset about this new line of questioning, as he sputtered, "Who cares about that? It's Morgan who is important here, not some amulet."

"I agree. Don't change the subject," Collin said, his fingers tingling with a pugilist's memory.

"Let me see," Peader insisted, grabbing hold of the chain.

Collin relented. "It's my family locket, if you must know."

"Show it to us, please."

When Collin pulled the locket up from under his shirt and showed it to the group, Tadgh, Morgan, and Peader looked at each other in disbelief.

"That's a nice piece of ancient jewelry you have there, to be sure, Collin," Peader remarked, pointing at the locket.

Morgan cried, "Show them your locket, Tadgh."

He pulled out his own locket and held it out in his palm.

Peader whistled. "Isn't that a Claddagh ring design?"

Morgan stood next to Collin to study his pendant, leaning toward him. "This is just like yours, mavourneen. They are a matched pair!"

Collin was speechless and stared at McCarthy's locket. He lifted his own locket and examined it as if for the first time. "Mine is a family heirloom passed down by my ma. It has been in my family forever. Where did you get yours?" he asked, still holding Morgan fast and reaching out to touch the matching locket.

"My pa gave it to me just before he died, so he did," Tadgh answered, his fingers trembling.

Collin studied Tadgh's battered face. There had to be a connection, but what did it mean? Two lockets with the same design. Then he had an idea. "I want you to look at the picture that is inside my locket, Claire," he said, opening the ancient mechanism and leaning toward her, their heads nearly touching.

Morgan peered at a photograph of a woman who had some of her own features. The same dark hair and flashing eyes. Something about the arch of her brow. Then, a kaleidoscope of images flooded her brain.

"Ma!" she cried, tears rolling down her face. Her hands shook as she pulled at the locket, the chain digging into Collin's bruised neck. "It's my ma!" she cried, over and over again.

Tadgh could see Collin and Kathy crying now for joy. They stood up, moved to encircle Morgan and held her in their arms. A wretched shudder ran through his body, as he was shut out of the circle, abandoned.

"I need to sit down," Morgan said, holding her head in her hands. "This is all too much for me."

Collin guided her to a kitchen chair and sat beside her.

Biddy brought her a glass of water and Morgan looked up into familiar eyes. "I remember you now, Auntie. You were thinner, then, and your hair was black, just like my ma's."

Biddy grabbed her niece's hand. "And with ringlets, like yours. We all were younger then Claire." She sighed. "I didn't recognize you, either, a grown woman. But I see it now in your green eyes. What a blessing for your memory to be coming back."

Tadgh muttered something unintelligible and frowned from the other side of the table.

"You mentioned a name a few minutes ago. Byron. I vaguely remember that name. He was handsome, I recall." She paused and looked out the window. "On the ship, with the babies. Now, I remember." Her eyes glistened. "I don't remember how I met him, though. Where is he now?"

Tadgh stewed in his own juices. He hated thinking about her in the arms of another man.

"I'm sorry, dear. He was reported drowned trying to save the babies," Collin answered softly.

"I remember that we kissed just after the ship was torpedoed," Morgan whispered. "I loved him."

Morgan sagged against her brother's arm. He held her tight. "Oh, I remember the babies. I had two."

Tadgh turned away. He wondered if the babies were her own.

Morgan continued, "But a crazy woman stole one. What happened to them, where did they go. Where were they taken?"

"They drowned, I'm afraid."

"Oh, no! Gone!" Morgan gasped and started to cry. "They weren't any of my babies. I remember now."

Tadgh's eyes glistened and looked up at her.

Morgan's tortured eyes looked again on the picture in her brother's locket. "And Ma? Oh, Collin, tell me she is still alive. I looked all over for you in New York."

"We know that. After you disappeared, we searched for you in New York, too, for more than a year. The situation with Ma got so dangerous that we had to try to escape."

Wiping her cheeks with her sleeve, Morgan nodded her head showing that she understood.

"We went to Toronto in Canada where we thought we would be safe. Ma was murdered there a few years back," Collin said tenderly, holding his sister as her tears once again began to flow. He took the chain off his neck and handed the locket to her.

Morgan kissed the picture of her mother and held the locket to her cheek. "I missed you both so much," she paused, remembering the years she spent in the factory coming back to her in a flood of images. "I tried to find you," she cried. "I didn't have a chance to say goodbye to Ma."

"I avenged her death, Claire, and killed the man who murdered her. I was powerless to save her. Or you. It wasn't safe for us then, even in Toronto."

Kathy handed Morgan her handkerchief. "Collin saved me from being raped by that same monster."

Morgan grabbed for Kathy's hand with one hand and dabbed her eyes with the other. "Oh, no. Who was he?"

"A sailor who was working for Enrico, sister."

"God, Enrico!" A vicious face appeared in Morgan's mind and she shuddered. "He's the one who abducted me." She covered her mouth with the handkerchief to stop herself from screaming out in horror at the memory.

Collin held her close and whispered, "Enrico's dead, and the children have been released from the orphanage. Your friend Lucy remembered you well and hoped you were still alive."

"Lucy! I remember now, the abduction, the orphans, the factory."

"Kathy and I, we went looking for you there last year. We know now what happened. I'm so sorry that I wasn't there to save you, dearest sister."

"Don't even think that way. You could have been abducted yourself or worse, killed."

"Finally," Kathy murmured, too softly to be heard. "From Claire's mouth."

Tadgh looked at Morgan and her brother from across the table with a newfound respect. *What she has endured and what Collin and his wife have been through to find her. The whole family's lifelong nightmare so like my own.*

Kathy blurted out, "It is so wonderful to have found you, alive and well after all this time, Claire." She brushed the hair from her sister-in-law's eyes. Kathy saw Collin's swollen left eye water. The tears slid down over his cut-up cheek. But he didn't, maybe couldn't, speak. Her thoughts went back to Lil's wedding night just over five years earlier when Collin had first confessed his guilt and shame about his long-lost sister. How wonderful it must be for him to have his family reunited.

Biddy, witnessing this turn of events, stepped forward and

touched Morgan's arm. "Well, now that you've learned who you are, niece, how about we have some tea. Peader, get the biscuits down from the pantry."

Kathy helped Morgan to her feet and guided her to the padded rocker in the corner by the stove. "Why don't you sit here, my dear. This has come as a great shock to all of us, Claire."

Tadgh could take it no more. He walked up to the two, and announced firmly, "Her name is Morgan."

Morgan realized that she had been completely ignoring the man she loved and stood up, grabbing his hand.

"Oh, Kathy, please let me formally introduce you to the man who saved me, the man I love, and who I will marry in August," she said happily, as she stood up again next to Tadgh, and hugged him tightly. Her eyes twinkled as she glanced over at her aunt. "The wedding dress is going to be altered."

Kathy stood up from the table and stared at Tadgh. "The man who almost killed my husband and your brother."

Tadgh held Morgan tight. "He would have killed me if I hadn't gotten the better of him first."

Collin took his wife's hand and then started toward Tadgh, eyes blazing.

Morgan stood up and intervened, pulling Collin and Kathy away. "Stop, now. That's enough."

Tadgh backed away from her, eyes downcast, and said, "August may be too soon, Morgan, with the ongoing plans for the revolution and all. There's so much to do, and then there's Boyle."

Morgan felt a knife twisting in her heart. "But I'll be with you, mavourneen."

"Maybe. You have your family about you now." He turned away from her, and the group, and stared out the window.

Collin saw his advantage. "Now you are beginning to remember your past, dear Claire, you do understand you must come home to Canada with Kathy and me, away from the dangers of war-torn Ireland, and these rebels. I met that wicked man Tadgh referred to as Boyle, the same blaggard who killed our da, and he is still looking for us. We must take you where you'll be safe." He pointed toward Tadgh, who didn't turn around. "Claire, *he* can't keep you safe."

What Collin said about his father triggered something in Tadgh who pivoted to face Morgan's brother. "Boyle killed your pa, too?" It came back to him, now, in the hospital scene, with the head constable. He now knew why Collin had been at Boyle's bedside and why he had wanted the devil killed. Boyle was trying to kill McCarthys *and* O'Donnells.

"What do you mean, 'He killed your pa, too'?" Collin asked in amazement.

"He killed my parents in cold blood, Collin. My brother and I witnessed the evil act. It seems there is a connection between the two terrible events."

Morgan gasped. "Boyle killed our da?"

Collin put a protective arm around his sister. "Yes, Claire. You didn't see him like I did back then. He is definitely the killer, missing a little finger, same mean face with that tattoo. I recognized from when I was boy, so I knew it was him."

"Do you think he knows who I am, Collin?"

"He knows I have a younger sister, and yes, he now knows who you are."

Morgan turned to Tadgh. "Then he's been after the both of us, mavourneen." Her green eyes widened.

Tadgh pulled Collin's arm from his sister's shoulder, and Collin scowled at him as he said, "I don't think Boyle knows who you are, Morgan. Your Aunt Biddy and Peader, here, didn't even recognize you. But he might be suspicious if he recognized Collin at the hospital. Did he know you, Collin?"

"He heard my name, and I thought I saw a flicker of recognition in his evil eyes."

"Then surely he will be connecting the dots. We've got to be vigilant, all of us."

Collin looked at Tadgh knowingly and resumed his persuasive

speech to Claire. "Canada is a stable, secure land with great opportunities, Claire. You'll love it there with us."

Morgan reached for Tadgh's hand and he did not pull away this time.

Tadgh moved to face his foe once more. "As I have already told you, Morgan is staying here with me where we have created a life together. We love each other deeply, and we believe in the cause of liberating our country from the British oppressor."

"You have no right to put her life in danger like that, if you truly love her." Collin pushed between them again, meeting stiff resistance from Tadgh.

"All right, boys. Stop it." Morgan stepped between them again before any fists could fly again. "May I see the inside of your locket again, Collin?" She held it out to him to open.

Collin reached over and released the catch. "There you are." An odd tingling, like in the past, ran down the back of his neck. "It feels strange not to have it on my person. As if it has become a part of my flesh."

She opened the locket, and her gaze shifted from her mother's picture to the other side of the heirloom. "Look, Tadgh, there's a message in Collin's locket, just as in yours."

"I know the words must be important, but I was never able to translate the old Gaelic," her brother said.

"Tadgh, can you translate?" Morgan held the open locket in her palm. "The calligraphy looks similar to the writing in yours, maybe the same message."

Tadgh took the keepsake and squinted down at it while he opened his own locket, and then compared the two.

Morgan urged, "Collin, do you remember anything about what may have been said to you about the locket?"

"I'm not certain. When da gave it to our ma the day before he was killed, he must have known his life was in danger. She told me then that he had begged her to guard it for me with her life, that it was traditionally handed down to the eldest son of the family to be kept for future generations until the time came. Maybe the message relates to a family secret, like a motto. I can't remember..." His voice trailed off.

"Until the time comes. I was told that by my pa, the day before he and Mam were killed, and now I know what that meant," Tadgh said, as he peered down at the two lockets in his hands.

Collin was confused. "I can't tell you what that means, and I don't think my ma knew, either. It's all we have to remember our parents by, Claire. So, I keep it on my neck always."

"What does it say, Tadgh?" Morgan asked again.

"Well, then. It translates as *Seek ye the rock of ages*," Tadgh announced.

"What does that mean?" Collin looked around at quizzical faces. "What am I missing?"

"I'm not sure, but the fact that you have the family locket means that you are likely the rightful chieftain of the O'Donnell Clan, brother." Morgan looked to Tadgh to confirm her guess, and then to Peader, who nodded in agreement.

"Morgan is right, Collin. Seems that you have new O'Donnell Clan responsibilities here in Ireland. You really do not know the significance of that locket, do you?" Tadgh challenged, handing the piece back to its owner.

"Obviously not, but I presume *you* do," Collin sneered at Tadgh.

"Yes, we all do, and we'd like to tell you," Tadgh responded.

"We'll deal with that clan matter later," Collin said, hanging the locket back over his head.

Aunt Biddy, who been quietly listening to this fascinating story unfold while she stoked the fire in the stove to get the kettle of water boiling for tea, interrupted, "Well now, one thing's for sure. You don't have to go traipsing all over the country looking for each other no more. So, we can settle down, family-like, and enjoy a meal together. Peader, offer our family some drinks, for heaven's sake." She set a basket of biscuits down on the table and continued, "And I want to know by the end of the evening who will be the bridesmaids and ushers for this here weddin', so I can take some measurements." She grinned. "Tadgh, it's planned for August, is it?"

"It's set in stone, August fifteenth it is," Tadgh announced, more assuredly now.

Morgan grabbed his hand and squeezed.

Then, as Aunt Biddy turned toward the larder to get ingredients for supper, she gave one parting shot. "The weddin' reception will be here at our house, don't ya know—and I won't take no for an answer."

With all this talk of a wedding, Collin felt compelled to pursue his argument. "Begging your pardon, Aunt Biddy, but, as I've already said, Claire *will* come home to Canada with Kathy and me. There is something I want to know about you, Tadgh, since you claim to want my sister to stay with you in a dangerous situation. What do you do for a living, anyway?"

"I'm a fisherman by trade, so I am," Tadgh answered. *Never mind that I haven't caught any new fish of late. But Aidan has.*

"Really. Then why are you *both* fugitives from justice? Fishermen aren't generally lawbreakers, are they?" His eyes narrowed. "By the way, I was at Mr. O'Casey's home when they came for you."

Morgan's eyes opened wide. She was curious to know why Tadgh didn't appear as shocked as she was.

"Well, now." Tadgh stole a glance at Morgan. "Fugitives from injustice you mean," he answered without flinching. "The British are the villains and have been for centuries."

"You make my point for me, Tadgh. Claire needs to get away from this mayhem and come with us to Toronto where it's safe."

"There are some things in life that are more important than safety, Collin. I think that Morgan knows this, don't you, aroon?"

"Claire, there is a wonderful life awaiting you in Toronto." Collin proceeded to describe the medical opportunity that Sam had researched for Claire, and he noticed a glint of interest in her eyes as he spoke.

Tadgh could see that Morgan wavered and was considering her

options. "It's love that matters most, Collin." He glanced at Morgan.

"Boys, can we stop this bickering right now, please?" Morgan pleaded. She was terribly confused.

Collin continued, unabated. "It will be far safer for her in Canada and it is a beautiful place to live with our family. We have to be aboard the *Aquitania* in Liverpool on the thirteenth."

"Now just a minute—" Tadgh began, but Peader cut him off.

"This is getting us nowhere. It has been a great shock to everyone, to be sure. I am thinkin' it is Morgan or Claire's decision as to where she chooses to go. Let's hear it from her, when she's ready." He rubbed his hands together. "My idea is that we have supper and afterwards sit down to tell Collin and Kathy what we know about the lockets and the bigger adventure we have undertaken. Maybe then Collin will realize that Ireland has more to offer our Clans than just a dangerous revolution."

"Just, comrade?"

"All right, Tadgh. To some of us, the glorious revolution."

"To most true Irishmen, Peader."

"Yes, of course, Tadgh. Tomorrow, some of us are after going to the Orangemen's Parade in Donegal Town. You are all invited, so you are."

Morgan weighed in. "Thank you, Peader. I appreciate what you are doing. Tadgh, you are the love of my life. And yet I am so happy my memory is coming back and to be reunited with my brother and his wife. Miraculously, Sir Owain may have appeared to me for this very reason."

"Who is Sir Owain?" Collin asked, bewildered.

"We'll save that explanation for later, brother. Frankly, I am overwhelmed with your attention and concern for my well-being. It certainly makes me happy that you didn't kill each other over me." She turned towards Kathy. "I choose to think that two men who love me were fighting for me and not just against themselves."

Kathy said, "But that doesn't justify—"

"No, of course not." Morgan grasped the right hands of both

men and tried to bring them together for a more enthusiastic joining of hands and family. "I understand that Collin and Kathy have
to return to Canada shortly and need an answer from me on my
intentions, so here is my promise. When I come down to breakfast
tomorrow, having slept on it, you will have my answer. I will write
on a piece of paper the name you shall call me for the rest of my
life: Claire, if I choose to go to Canada with Collin, and Morgan if
I choose to stay in Ireland with Tadgh. In the meantime, let's get to
know each other much better over a wonderful meal prepared by
my lovely aunt. Please give me some time to think about all this.
Just let me say that I love you all and am most grateful to you."

Peader started to clap and they all joined in. "Well said. Can
we all agree we have other things to talk about and leave this young
woman in peace about this until tomorrow morning?"

Morgan gave Peader a hug. "Thank you for understanding."

Kathy leaned over and brushed a tear from Morgan's cheek. "I,
for one, will support your decision one hundred percent, Sis."

Morgan covered Kathy's hand with her own, murmuring, "Just
like Aidan."

Collin scowled at his wife, as Tadgh scowled at Collin.

Simpson was dog-tired. He had driven for seventeen hours to
get them to Donegal Town before sunset. Being cooped up with
Boyle that long seemed like an eternity in hell.

"Take that road over there," Boyle ordered as they approached
Donegal Castle from the south. "It leads east to Lough Eske."

They soon arrived at Castle Lough Eske where the infamous
Brookes of Donegal Castle infamy had resided until 1896.

"This is where I found the O'Donnells when they fled here
from their cobbler shop in town almost eleven years ago," Boyle
remembered. "They lived there until the family disappeared after I,
ah, questioned the father."

He remembered clearly the night that he had dragged Finian O'Donnell up the Road to Nowhere for seclusion, scaling Burns Mountain to the Peak of Banagher Hill. There he interrogated and then executed him, while his wife Shaina and son tried to save him. He would have killed the bitch and her brood, too, if they hadn't escaped into the woods. Finian O'Donnell, the father, would not divulge the secrets of the O'Donnell treasure, so he had to pay in his own way.

"How are the O'Donnells related to the German spies, boss? Has this espionage been going on for eleven years?"

Boyle answered without hesitation. "The O'Donnells organized the Flight of the Earls when my people crushed the Clans back in 1607. They took their compatriots the McCarthys with them and they fled to the continent, to Germany, who harbored the infidels. There has been a strong allegiance between these two families and the Germans ever since." *Pure bullshit.*

Simpson adjusted his grimy glasses. "Damn traitors."

"Go and ask at the Castle whether anyone has seen Collin O'Donnell or the sister in the last two days. They may have come here to find out what happened to their father."

Upon his return, Simpson relayed, "No one has seen anyone by that name, boss. But the caretaker suggested that they might go to the Orangemen's Parade in Donegal Town tomorrow. Ulster Volunteers and Donegal men and women come from near and far for this event every year."

Boyle thought his underling had heard wrong. "If the O'Donnells and McCarthys have reunited up here in Donegal, they may be attending this event. But why is the parade tomorrow? It has always been held on July twelfth to commemorate Protestant William's glorious victory over the Catholic masses at the Battle of the Boyne. That's not until next Wednesday."

"Not in these parts, boss. It's always on the Saturday before the twelfth in Donegal Town."

"Drive me back into town," Boyle snapped. "Someone may

have seen them there, maybe at the old cobbler's shop, or whatever it is called these days. They've got to be around here somewhere."

After supper, Kathy asked to be excused since her stomach was still giving her trouble. Morgan noticed that her face looked tired and pale from the exertions of the long day. She obviously wasn't feeling herself. "I'll be fine in the morning," she told her husband in a low voice before she mounted the stairs to the second guest room.

Morgan, Tadgh, Peader and Collin took their leave from the rest of the family to talk privately in Peader's bedroom. He brought out the Jameson and four glasses. They sat around a card table and Peader lit the tapers as dusk settled into the valley outside the window. The candlelight flickered off the beige walls, casting murky shadows as they took up the conversation from before supper in animated gestures and tones.

Tadgh opened the oilskin and laid its contents on the table, and then grabbed the Jameson, pouring a healthy measure into each glass. While he handed them around, he suggested, "Drink up. We're going to need this elixir. Especially you, Collin."

Peader spoke first, once more asking that they focus on the treasure's adventure and not on Morgan's decision. "Collin, I think that it's time to tell you what we know. Your locket message should really help us understand what our forefathers had in mind."

Collin took a swig from his glass and looked intently at his cousin. "What about our forefathers and treasure?"

Tadgh opened his oilskin and handed his copy of the Clans Pact, which he had translated into English to Morgan's brother. "Read this."

Collin's eyes widened as he scanned the crucial document. "My God. 1600. Can this be authentic?"

Morgan said, "We found it in an ancient box in the National Museum in Dublin based on the message in Tadgh's locket, and only because Peader knew the meaning."

"Seek ye the battler's box," Peader added, and then explained the meaning regarding the *Cumdach.*

Collin stood up from the table, clenching his left fist as he shook the Clans Pact with his right arm. "So this is the real thing, then."

"Yes, Collin," Tadgh said. "You and I, north and south are called together to our destiny by that sacred document."

Tadgh explained a brief history of the McCarthy Clan in Ireland, Peader presented the relevant O'Donnell Clan history, and Morgan added the information received from Professor Lawlor about *an Cathach* and its relevant Psalms.

At the end of these monologues, Peader summarized, "As I see it, you and Tadgh are the two remaining chieftains of the O'Donnell and McCarthy Clans. Call it destiny if you will, as Tadgh said, but you have been chosen at this point in history to work together to seek out and find the hidden treasures of the two families so that, finally, they may be used to support the liberation of the Irish nation from the British oppressor. The intertwined lockets prove it. Collin, can't you see that your sister is the link between the two clans? Imagine if she had not been on the *Lusitania*, if it had not been torpedoed, if Tadgh had not rescued her, and if you had not been driven by some strong force to find her."

Collin, overwhelmed with this flood of information, reluctantly agreed. "I see your point, Peader. I know we should be thankful to you, Tadgh. What a story. You say all this comes from the message in Tadgh's locket and leads to my Clan's relics. So now, where will the message in my locket lead us?"

Tadgh could see that Collin was already intrigued.

Morgan pushed the glass away from her place at the table. "You are right, Collin. We know that the messages were linked by Red Hugh and Florence to enforce future collaboration by our two great Clans, north and south. I think that the message 'Seek ye the rock of ages' in your locket should refer to the McCarthy relics or place of religious significance."

"There you go now, aroon. I should have known sooner. *The Rock of Cashel.* That's got to be it!"

"Please explain, Tadgh," Collin insisted, draining the contents of his glass in one gulp and reaching for the bottle.

"Easy, brother," Morgan urged. "That stuff is potent and you've had a long day."

"I need to drown the ringin' in my ears from Tadgh knocking me into the tree, so I do."

Tadgh drank from his glass and said, "Think about that verse at the end of *an Cathach.* What was it?"

Morgan picked up the Bible. "Psalm 105 Verse 13—*They went from one nation to another, from one kingdom to another people.*"

"Precisely," Tadgh said and then paused for effect. "Well?"

Collin repeated the history lesson. "As you described earlier, Tadgh, the Eoghanachta civilization founded the McCarthy dynasties after migrating to Ireland from Wales in the fifth century."

"And?" Tadgh waited for a response, sounding quite like Professor Lawlor again.

"And they settled on the Rock of Cashel!" Morgan answered, remembering what Tadgh had told her when they were running the guns to Dublin before Rossa's funeral. Her eyes widened in surprise "My God, they did remove folios from *an Cathach* as clues, didn't they? But where on that large rock, mavourneen?"

Tadgh shrugged and took another swig of Jameson. No one else had an answer. "There's one more piece of information that supports my thinking. What is it?"

Collin held up his hand. "Wait, didn't you say that the McCarthys of Muscry were the last to fall to Lord Broghill, who was a Boyle, in 1646? He laid siege to Blarney Castle from the Card Hill to the south. You said that the garrison fled through the Badger's Cave tunnels. One tunnel led southeast to Cork, a second led west towards Kerry, and the last led south past the lake. Then, I think you also said that Sir James St. John Jeffreyes later bought the property and spent a small fortune dragging the lake for 'McCarthy

Gold' to no avail. Well, if I remember my geography lesson correctly, Cashel is northeast of Blarney Castle. They did not go to the lake. They went in the one direction that the tunnels didn't go in, the one direction that nobody would expect. They must have taken the treasure north to Cashel."

Collin's recall of the story astounded them all. He had appeared to be nodding off during Tadgh's talk, understandable after his recent travel schedule and the brutal fight with Tadgh. Yet he heard and remembered every detail. When questioned, he merely shrugged and answered, "I'm a newspaperman."

"My brother's spot on. It's got to be Cashel."

"There has to be another clue, Morgan," Tadgh said quietly, leafing through his Bible, and they all agreed.

Peader filled his own glass, setting the Jameson bottle on the table beside him before responding, "It may as well be on the moon, for all the good it does us to know it is at the Rock of Cashel."

"If the modified end of *an Cathach* points to the McCarthy burial location, then surely the Psalm at the front should give a clue as to where the O'Donnell treasure is buried," Morgan reasoned, changing the subject for the moment. She sipped a little of her Jameson. "What does it say, exactly?"

"Psalm 30, verse 10 reads, *Hear, O Lord, and have mercy upon me. Lord, be thou my helper,*" Tadgh said.

"That's about as clear as mud, don't ye think," Peader mused, snatching the bottle back from Collin who was about to freshen his drink.

Morgan leaned forward, elbows on the table, and massaged her temples. "As Tadgh said, there have to be other clues."

"Didn't you say that there is another Psalm that was marked in your family Bible, Tadgh?"

"Yes, Collin. Psalm 68 verse 26. But it doesn't seem to provide a clue."

"Well, what does that verse say?"

Morgan consulted the Bible and read it aloud. "*Praise God in the great congregations; praise the Lord in the Assembly of Israel.*"

Collin drummed his fingers on the table. "Claire, isn't that Psalm about in the middle between the front and back of *an Cathach*?"

"Yes, that's right."

"Then I think we can safely assume that its message is meant to apply to both the McCarthy and the O'Donnell legacies."

"That makes sense, Collin, I guess, but what is its message? Where does the *Assembly of Israel* fit in?"

"I have no idea, Peader. But what if we are focusing on the wrong words? What if the message is in the first half of the verse?"

"You mean *Praise God in the great congregations?*" Morgan reread from the verses.

"That's it!" Tadgh exclaimed once more, "You're a wonder, Morgan. And what did Professor Lawlor suggest? Let's think."

After a few seconds of confused silence, Peader's face lit up, and he blurted out, "I see where you are going."

Tadgh smirked. "Can you tell us, cousin?"

"No, I'm baffled."

Peader explained. "Listen, Collin. I forgot to mention earlier. Professor Lawlor suggested that I evaluate the *Book of Ballymote*, which was in the possession of my ancestor and signatory of the Clans Pact, Red Hugh O'Donnell in 1600."

Tadgh quickly added, "And he told me to evaluate the *Book of Lismore*, or correctly the *Book of MacCarthaigh Reagh*, which was in the possession of my ancestor and signatory of the Clans Pact, Florence MacCarthaigh in 1600."

"Remember that old man in the square at Ballymote?" Morgan piped up.

A fine sweat had broken across Collin's brow in his efforts to put together the story. "Now I'm really confused. What man? Don't tell me it's Sir Owain."

"You're close, brother. The old man told us that there's a secret in the old *Book of Ballymote*."

"What secret? Out with it!"

Morgan responded, "He said, 'If I knew it wouldn't be a secret now, would it?'"

"Well, that's a big help."

Tadgh took a swig of his Jameson and winced as the amber liquid stung his swollen tongue. Then he finished his glass and held it out for his first refill. "Well, Collin, as we understand it, each of these books is a compendium of stories handed down, facts recorded, excerpts of important early religious and secular literature, and so on, assembled for the chieftains and their wives."

"Now I get it!" Morgan exclaimed, clapping Tadgh's shoulder. "Compendia—congregations. They are synonyms for the same thing. Praise God in the great compendia of the books of *Ballymote* and *MacCarthaigh Reagh*."

"Precisely, my dear." Tadgh absently rubbed the spot she had swatted on his shoulder, the site of his old bullet wound. "I'd wager that we've got to find the correct religious passage in each book to discover the next clues."

"Isn't this too contrived and convoluted?" Collin mused.

"It all seems to fit together somehow," Morgan answered, "And Florence's hand-drawn circles in his ancient Bible are the key. Since we seem to be on the right track regarding the McCarthy clues, then I suggest we concentrate on the *Book of MacCarthaigh Reagh* for the time being, mavourneen."

"Unless, of course, the clues are cross-linked again, aroon."

"You mean the *Book of Ballymote* for the McCarthys and the *Book of MacCarthaigh Reagh* for the O'Donnells?"

Collin smacked his forehead with the palm of his right hand, then winced. "It's hurting my brain. Maybe Sir Owain can tell us."

Morgan could see that the liquor and fatigue were affecting her brother. "C'mon, Collin. You were doing so well up until this point." She reached over to examine his raw left cheek and blackening eye, swollen nearly shut. "Let me clear up one mystery for you. Sir Owain was a medieval knight who haunts Temple House grounds near Ballymote. He has appeared to a few people over the ages who were in agony searching for lost souls. I saw him two nights ago and now you and Kathy have found me. Amazing, isn't it?"

"They've got you believing in ghosts, have they, Claire?"

"You decide, Collin. I know what I saw."

Tadgh rubbed his chin where it was cut. "I looked where she said and I didn't see anything."

"You wouldn't have, mavourneen, would you? You weren't in agony searching for a lost soul."

Peader put the bottle on the floor by the door. "All right, then. Let's not complicate the riddles any further than we have to for now and see where that leads us."

Maybe it was the Jameson talking, but Tadgh could see that the talk of the treasures and their clues had animated Collin. This was the leverage he needed to get Collin to agree to support their Clans Pact adventure if Morgan chose to stay in Ireland. If that's what she really wanted, of course.

"Trying to determine where the clues are in the McCarthy compendium is going to be quite difficult with the many segments to examine," Tadgh lamented, picking up the scrawled list the professor had given them from the documents on the table. "Not to mention the problem that Morgan and I are not welcome in Dublin at the moment where the copy of the book is located."

Peader looked at the Lawlor list. "Of course, we could always visit Lismore Castle where the original is kept. But I don't think the British supporters who own the document would be likely to show it to us at this stage. I certainly do not advocate another break-in."

"*Another* break-in? You've done this before?" Collin's eyes widened.

Tadgh quickly changed the subject. "Collin, didn't you say that your friend Sam, who escorted your wife from Canada, has stayed with his father in Lisburn near Belfast. You have to go back there before leaving for Canada, am I right?"

"That's correct. He is waiting there for us to go to Liverpool for the departure on the thirteenth."

"All right, then. I've got a plan for your consideration."

Collin finished the last of his Jameson. "My plan is to collect Sam and head for the boat."

Tadgh held up his hand. "Collin, we are a team here, and it's certain this whole affair has as much to do with you as it does with the rest of us. I just have a suggestion."

"Let's hear it, then."

"In Donegal Town, I guess a man could find a public telephone, is that so, Peader?"

"Yes, at a shop off the main square called the Diamond."

"When we get to town for the parade tomorrow, I will call the professor and ask him if we can have a look at the *Book of MacCarthaigh Reagh* in the next few days. Collin, do you think that you and Kathy could go to Dublin on your way to Lisburn and meet with Professor Lawlor? There are trains to Dublin and Belfast. I would introduce you as our colleagues over the telephone. Morgan and I could meet you in Lisburn."

Collin saw an opening. "Wouldn't it be better if we all went together, Tadgh?"

"As I said, I don't think that Dublin is a healthy place for Morgan and me just at the moment."

"Which again makes my point about coming to Canada."

"We agreed not to get on that subject tonight, Collin."

"Fine, Peader." He still wanted an answer to his question, so he persisted. "What about the break-in?"

"Nothing was stolen, and no one was hurt," Morgan commented.

"I get the picture." Collin still wasn't satisfied, but he let it go for the moment. "Yes, Kathy and I could meet with Professor Lawlor and then join you in Lisburn before we head back home."

Peader moderated. "Good. It's settled then. We're really making progress now that you and Kathy are here. Thank you."

"I'm tired, and I need rest," Morgan spoke up, quaffing the last of her Jameson. "But I am pleased that we could work together this evening rather than bickering over my fate. Thank you all."

With that, they agreed to call it a night. The Jameson bottle was empty anyway.

When they entered their assigned bedroom, Morgan closed the door. Tadgh started to open his mouth to speak and Morgan held up her hand to stop him.

"There are many competing thoughts swirling in my head right now, about my past, our time together, the Clans Pact riddles. But I need an answer to one burning question that's been bothering me all evening before I can try to figure out what to do."

"Just one question, aroon? I would have thought you have scads of them."

"Just one for tonight. Why weren't you surprised when my brother said he had been at Sean's house when we were hiding?"

Tadgh turned to the dark window, gazed out of it a few moments, then turned back before responding. He knew that his answer would be a watershed moment for his own moral life and likely for the longevity of his relationship with Morgan. Then he remembered what Peader had said to him in the kitchen earlier in the afternoon.

"I heard mumbled voices during the raid and asked Sean afterward if there were any non-raider people present. He mentioned that two newspaper reporters had accompanied the police. Before you came back here this afternoon, Collin introduced himself as a reporter and claimed that he had been at Sean's with the police that day."

"Is that all there is to it, Tadgh? I can ask Sean."

Tadgh fidgeted with the ends of his moustache. *It's now or never.*

Morgan crossed her arms and tapped her right foot on the floor. "I'm waiting for your answer."

"Sean said that this reporter mentioned that he was looking for his sister named Claire who was seen on the *Lusitania* and then again after the sinking by the Cunard manager."

Morgan's green eyes burned into him, scarring his soul. "What? And you didn't tell me?" She shook her head in disbelief. "How *could* you, Tadgh?"

He knew he was on thin ice. "I was afraid."

"Of what? Me knowing the truth about myself?"

"Yes. I was afraid that you had a family that would take you away from me. Look what's happened here today."

"I guess you don't give much credit to the strength of our love, then. Maybe you don't feel it like I do."

Tadgh stepped toward Morgan but she backed away around the bed.

"Quite the contrary, Morgan. It is because I love you so much that I couldn't survive if you left me. I thought I was fine by myself before God brought you to me and now, I am at a loss when you are out of my sight. I was so worried when you were shot."

"I want you to leave me alone tonight, Tadgh. I'm not sure who to trust anymore, other than my brother and his wife would have moved heaven and earth to find and protect me."

"Don't talk that way, aroon. Remember how we've survived together through thick and thin."

"Don't you '*aroon*' me Tadgh. Not tonight. Leave me alone to decide what to do."

"No, I won't leave you like this."

"You must. Now get out before I call on my brother to get you out. You'll have my answer in the morning."

Tadgh realized that anything he added would only make matters worse. He didn't blame her for her anger. But having lost both his parents in that horrific way had made him vulnerable. "I'll mind you, Morgan, but please remember that I did what I did out of love for you."

Skirting around Tadgh, Morgan went to the door and opened it for him to leave. "You'll have my answer in the morning. Now, get out!"

Saturday morning, both Tadgh and Collin were up early and in the kitchen, silently waiting for Morgan's decision. Tadgh's shoulder and stomach muscles ached from sleeping on the chesterfield, to which he had been relegated. Both men knew that it was the most important morning of all their lives. Tadgh agonized over Morgan's having seen him wringing Collin's neck, and having kept the truth about her identity from her.

He couldn't get one verse of Robert Service's poem, "The Rhyme of the Restless Ones" out of his head—

> *Oh, they shook us off and shipped us o'er the foam,*
> *To the larger lands that lure a man to roam;*
> *And we took the chance they gave*
> *Of a far and foreign grave,*
> *And we bade good-by for evermore to home.*

He hoped to hell that the poet wasn't right with those prophetic words. After all, Service had left his English home for Canada, hadn't he?

Gradually the rest of the family made their appearance, and Aunt Biddy heated a skillet to cook breakfast for the whole lot.

"Do you need to get an early start to Donegal Town?" Biddy asked, as she sliced the bacon and watched the kettle.

Peader checked his watch. "We have to leave no later than nine-thirty. The parade starts at noon." He glanced sharply in his guests' direction. "Tadgh? Collin? You are both very quiet this morning."

Neither man responded to his comment.

By eight o'clock, the other children were fed and had gone outside to play. Only Morgan and Kathy had yet to appear.

"Good morning, Kathy," Morgan said enthusiastically, when they passed each other in the upstairs hallway. She had just come out of the bathroom as Kathy was heading in.

"I don't feel very well again this morning," Kathy confided. "It's not like me to feel sick to my stomach."

"When was your last monthly courses, dear, if you don't mind my asking?" Morgan queried as she sat Kathy down on the commode.

"They're always spotty, about four days before we left Toronto. Let's see, that would be fifteen days ago."

"When was the last time you were close with Collin?"

"The only time in the last two and a half months was two nights ago. You don't think—" she blushed.

"I think that it's a definite possibility. Morning sickness happens immediately for some women."

"But I felt sick on the ship too, before that."

"That's different."

"I'm told you are a nurse, and you certainly took good care of Tadgh's injured head, Morgan."

"Yes I am, in training, and then in the battlefield of Belgium and Dublin."

"My God, Morgan, it's a wonder you survived! Wouldn't it be better to come back to Canada with us?"

"Come downstairs and you'll have my answer, dear. Now that you know me as a nurse, you can understand that I value the saving and nurturing of life highly. On the other hand, despite my better judgment, I love Tadgh and believe in his cause to free Ireland, even with all its killing and dangers. So you can see that I am forced to make the hardest decision of my life this morning."

"Yes, I see that, and I can plainly see the love that you feel for him. We all have our crosses to bear, yet I believe that God guides us at these crucial moments."

"With regards to your condition, would that be good news?"

"It's just so soon. My son Liam is only four months old." Kathy eyes glazed over for a moment before snapping back to engage Morgan face-to-face. "Collin will be thrilled. I'm sure of it."

"It's wonderful then, isn't it?" Morgan threw her arms around Kathy and stroked her hair, as a sister would do. She pulled Kathy to the bathroom mirror, and they both laughed. "Why, look, you're positively glowing, where a moment ago you looked green at the gills."

"Yes. Yes. It is grand news, especially if the baby were to be a girl." Kathy suddenly turned giddy.

The two descended the stairs and entered the kitchen with clasped hands and bright smiles. They both had exciting news. All activity and conversation stopped when they appeared. Morgan took the first steps, kissing Collin and Tadgh on their heads. Peader could see the folded piece of paper in her right hand.

"Before I give my answer this bright morning, I have a few words to say." She addressed both Collin and Tadgh directly. "I want both of you to know that I love you dearly. You have both risked everything to find me, to love me, to protect me, and to give me opportunity for a wonderful life. For these gifts I am extremely grateful to and proud of both of you! I couldn't ask for two better champions. I want you both to know that I intend to find ways to have both of you in my life, even if you reside an ocean away from each other. I feel twice blessed."

Having said her piece, she slowly put the folded paper on the kitchen table between them and stood back. Neither of the men initially had the courage to open the folded paper.

Tadgh put his right hand over the paper and spoke out. "Before we see your decision, I want to clear the air. Collin, yesterday I did everything short of outright lying to get you to leave before seeing Morgan. This was because I love her so much and would be devastated if we were separated. And while she did not remember her past, I knew that she loved me the same way. I feared what would happen if she remembered her life before we met. Last night I realized that I had been selfish and wrong. Love is only true if you give it away. I am prepared this morning, if Morgan chooses her past, to find a way to be part of her future, in Canada if necessary. I don't want to have to do it, but if I had to choose between Morgan and my commitment to helping free Ireland from the British oppressor, I would choose Morgan."

Morgan looked shocked, and Collin started to smile.

Finally, Peader leaned over, saying, "For heaven's sake, let's get beyond this." He lifted Tadgh's hand, opened the paper, and dropped it on the table as everyone gathered close to read it.

Chapter Nine
Decision

Saturday, July 8, 1916
O'Donnell Home, Meenmore, Ireland

Beaming, and straightening his full frame, Tadgh let the name roll off his lips. "Morgan!"

She looked at him and her eyes danced.

Collin scowled. "Morgan, indeed! And what will your life be like—running from the authorities, with a price on your head? With a man who cannot care for you?"

Morgan stepped toward Collin to calm him, but he put his hand up to stop her, avoiding her gaze. So she turned away and grabbed Tadgh's hand, taking her place beside him.

Collin spat out, "You're no fisherman, McCarthy. I know what you are all about."

"Oh, yes, I am a fisherman, with my own boat. But most importantly, I am a Republican Irish Volunteer. Morgan is, too."

Collin persisted. "That is a dangerous occupation. You were involved in the recent Rising in Dublin, weren't you?"

"Yes, Collin," Tadgh replied. "But we're safe at the moment."

Collin laughed bitterly. "But you are wanted by the authorities."

"British oppressors, you mean, holding our population hostage. We oppose them, and yes, they happen to be looking for us."

Collin turned to face his sister. "Claire, are you sure that you want to do this?"

"It's Morgan, now, and yes, I am sure," she answered, throwing her arm around Tadgh.

Tadgh moved opposite the Canadian, staring him down. "This is your fight too, Collin."

"I don't see that at all."

"You are now the leader of the O'Donnell Clan. Your ancestors fought and died for their freedom and ours, and they lost. We must carry on the fight. Are you going to let them down? We showed you the Clans Pact. You and I have been chosen to carry out this pact between our two kingdoms at this point in our country's history."

"The Clan system is dead, Tadgh. The world is different now. The old battles and ways have no place in our modern society."

"Tell that to the Irish men and women treated like vermin and exterminated by the British penal laws and to the millions who died in the Great Hunger," Tadgh retorted. "And don't forget the more than a million in Ireland alone who were forced from their homesteads to find work in the squalor of the modern cities."

Collin picked up his mug of tea, took a sip, then put it down. "Yes, I remember the plight of the Irish in Brooklyn." He reached out and sought his sister's hand, his eyes misting.

"I remember it now, as well." Morgan didn't pull away.

Tadgh pulled out a page of his scribbling from the night before. "Regarding the Great Hunger, my great-great uncle Denis Florence MacCarthy put it this way in his poem 'A Mystery'."[4.2] His voice rang clear in the small room as he read from his notes,

> *They are dying! they are dying! where the golden corn is growing,*
> *They are dying! they are dying! where the crowded herds are lowing;*
> *They are gasping for existence where the streams of life are flowing,*
> *And they perish of the plague where the breeze of health is blowing!"*

Collin picked up his mug and stared into it, lost in another thought. *What occurred in Brooklyn, not my fault, then.*

Tadgh read on,

> *"We have ploughed, we have sown*
> *But the crop was not our own;*
> *We have reaped, but harpy hands*
> *Swept the harvest from our lands;*

We were perishing for food,
When, lo! in pitying mood,
Our kindly rulers gave
The fat fluid of the slave,
While our corn filled the manger
Of the war-horse of the stranger!"

Collin blurted out, "God of mercy! Enough. You've made your point, Tadgh."

"Just one more important stanza, lad."

"No more," groaned Collin.

"One more important stanza," Tadgh continued,

"Do our numbers multiply
But to perish and to die?
Is this all our destiny below,
That our bodies, as they rot,
May fertilise the spot
Where the harvests of the stranger grow?"

Tadgh pounded the kitchen table with his fist. "The British enemy caused all this. And that damned Head Constable Boyle, the villain you wanted me to kill, is one of the worst of them!"

Collin jumped up from his seat, "Yes, and now I know that you were there, disguised as the doctor. I almost caught you then, you and your infernal motorcycle!"

"I honestly didn't know who you were then, but it makes sense now, Collin. We have common goals, don't ya see."

"You failed to kill Boyle."

Tadgh shot back, "Because you came back with the security guard a minute too soon."

He felt emboldened now that Morgan had chosen him. "I have skin in that game, lad." He resolved to say nothing about the encounter when Morgan was accosted and they were almost killed.

Collin pressed forward his face so close to Tadgh's that their noses almost touched. "That's what I'm worried about! I saw the rope and ring at Rahoneen Castle ruins."

How the hell does he know what I'm thinking? "Well, we survived that mess. That monster has been systematically torturing and murdering my kinfolk for the last thirty years." Tadgh filled him in on more details of how Boyle was on a hunt for the treasures, and now likely in possession of the McCarthy Clans Pact. He pointed out that Boyle was the current descendant of the seventeenth-century British devil, Richard Boyle. "I'm willing to bet that he already knew who you were when you met him in Tralee."

"You make my point for me, Tadgh. This is gettin' more bizarre and dangerous. Are you tryin' to tell me that Kathy and I may be in danger from the authorities, too?"

"No, not the authorities, at this point. The danger comes from the rogue Boyle and his underlings. We have to stop them before they kill us, just like they murdered our parents. Does Boyle know your travel plans?"

"No, not as far as I know. Jack Jordan said he didn't trust the man, so I'm sure he wouldn't have told Boyle anything."

"Well, I'd guess that he does know, Collin."

"All the more reason to get my wife and Claire—I mean, Morgan—safely home to Canada. Surely you can see that." Collin looked over at his stoic sister.

Then her countenance clouded with Tadgh's icy reply. "What makes you think that you'd be safe from Boyle in Canada? Look what happened to your poor Ma at the hands of a New York villain. We need you, Collin. You and I must finish this business together, here and now. So, are you in, or out?"

Kathy, with a radiant smile, and bursting at the seams, picked this moment to make her announcement, "I have good news for everyone. I think that I'm pregnant, and Morgan thinks so, too." She threw herself into her husband's arms and laughed.

Collin's face took on a sheepish grin. He covered his wife's neck and face with kisses and murmured into her ear, "That would be wonderful if it were true, darlin'. But how—?"

"These things happen for a reason, my love. I believe in fate," Kathy said, curling her arms around his neck. "It can happen so quickly."

"I think you should stay here with Aunt Biddy today and rest. Here, sit down."

"Really, Collin. I feel glorious, never better." Kathy's entire body glowed with beauty. She took her husband's hand and smiled at him, "And dear Collin, if this one is a girl, we will name her Claire, yes?"

He nodded. "That would be wonderful." He put his hand on her abdomen and smiled.

When Tadgh opened his mouth to question Collin on his response to the Boyle predicament, Morgan kissed him on the lips and murmured, "Not now."

Biddy, who had been watching this unfold with anticipation, turned from the kitchen sink. "Come and sit down, lass. Have some breakfast. You've got two mouths to feed, so to speak, at least you hope you do. You an' I will stay right here, and I will design a pattern for a special dress for your condition. That will give us some time to get to know each other."

"Yes, Aunt Biddy. That would be splendid."

"Good, then. Now, what breakfast can I make my new niece?"

Morgan asked for eggs, then went to Kathy and gave her a big hug, murmuring, "There, you see. All is right with the world."

Kathy pulled her close and said, "In your world too."

Once Biddy had satisfied their hunger, Morgan took Tadgh aside into their bedroom.

Once there, with the door closed, he tried to take her into his arms, saying, "I'm so relieved and happy, aroon, that you chose me. I thought, after last night—"

Morgan held him at arm's length, her green eyes locking onto his. "I love you dearly, Tadgh. My future is in your hands. But if you ever lie to me or withhold information from me again, I will be on the next boat to Canada without you. I won't brook anyone that I cannot trust. Do you understand?"

Tadgh dropped his arms and looked at his shoes before returning her gaze. "I feel so ashamed, Morgan. You are the only lass that I have known or wanted to know. I was afraid of losing you."

"Don't you know that true love conquers all? You have to be prepared to give it away, as you offered this morning, in order for it to freely come back to you. So. Can I trust you, Tadgh?"

Mean it! Tadgh told himself sternly. "Oh yes, my love."

"Good. Then come here and give me a kiss to seal our understanding."

Chapter Ten
Orangemen's Parade

Saturday, July 8, 1916
Donegal Town

*T*he Diamond in the center of Donegal Town was decorated in orange. Sunlit banners and bunting waved from the second-story shop balconies and hanging flowerpots full of marigolds draped storefront light standards. The crowds thronged the parade route starting at the Anglican Church of Ireland. They looped up Tirconaill Street, then around and back to Quay Street, coming to parade rest in front of the Hastings Hotel on the south side of Diamond Square.

"I always wondered why they didn't call it the Diamond Triangle," Collin remarked, noting the real shape of the open area. He had his eye on the Olde Castle Pub opposite on the north point and beyond it, the castle.

"That's why it's just The Diamond," Peader answered, "as otherwise it would be The Diamond Triangular Square. Now there's a trigonometric aberration that would have bamboozled even the brilliant mathematician Leonhard Euler."

While the brass band played *Rule Britannia*, the marching men, with their orange sashes, black bowler hats, and white gloves, rounded the corner of Quay Street and headed towards the hotel.

"It's too bad that Kathy has to miss these festivities because of her condition. It would never do to make her stand in this mass of people," Collin commented, shifting left and right to see through the crowd.

"Just look at all those colorful placards," Morgan said, standing on tiptoes.

Collin pushed forward in the throng at the south end of the

Diamond to take pictures with his Brownie for the *Tely* in Toronto. He turned back to Tadgh who had just come up behind him and asked, "Did you know that the Orange Order is quite active in Canada, also?"

Tadgh did not look amused. "Damned Protestants oppose Home Rule, comrade."

"Of course they do, Tadgh," said Peader with a note of sarcasm, standing beside Collin. "Otherwise, the center of the government would switch from Belfast to Dublin. I heard that at the end of the march, the Honorable Edward Carson, leader of the Ulster Unionist Party, is going to talk to the crowd over there from the balcony of the hotel."

Morgan, standing beside Tadgh asked, "Isn't he the one who organized the Ulster Volunteers and threatens armed insurrection if the British monarch signs the bill into law?"

"Yes, aroon. The very same bastard. He'd vote for conscription, too."

Peader looked back at Tadgh. "I hate it when he assumes that Donegal would support the rest of Ulster if push came to shove. Most of us are rural and Catholic and we are sympathetic to the South. We suffered through the Great Hunger like you did. And his position on trade unions and the status of women is archaic and bourgeois."

"You all really like him then, eh," Collin piped up, pulling his sister beside him to protect her from the crowd.

Tadgh put his arm around Morgan and drew her back to him.

The marchers abruptly halted in front of the hotel. There the Orangemen remained, standing at attention while an officious penguin-dressed stuffed shirt appeared at a makeshift podium on the balcony. Peader turned to Collin and whispered, "Sir Edward Carson doesn't really like the Orange Order, but these parades suit his purpose. Donegal is sitting on the fence and he needs us to get on his bandwagon, so he does."

"Fellow Ulster countrymen," Carson shouted, and the crowd quieted to listen. "I am here today to convince you to join our righteous Ulster Unionist Party. We must protect our northern birthright and our hard-earned industrial base." He paused and then added, "By force, if necessary."

Peader cried out, "Sir, what is your position on the vote for women?"

"Women should tend to their families and let the men handle business and politics," Carson replied.

"And how do you feel about preservation of the Gaelic way of life?" Peader prodded.

The penguin squawked, "Only where it supports our nation's union with the omnipotent United Kingdom of Great Britain."

That got the crowd's attention.

"And what do you say about the need for trade unions to represent the common worker in our country?"

The crowd hushed, waiting for a reply.

"Why are we not in uniform?" Constable Simpson asked. From their position under the Olde Castle Pub sign, he and Boyle searched the crowd for both McCarthy and O'Donnell.

"Because we are here on semi-private business," Boyle explained for the second time. Just as with Gordo, he wasn't going to share his true motives with an underling. This cretin would be disposable later. "As I told you before, these bastards are German spies. But they are not the masterminds. We need to find, but not spook, these minions so we can track them to their leaders." He had decided that the direct assault approach would not work. After the events at the hospital, he had changed his game plan to a cat and mouse strategy.

"Aha!" Boyle pointed, as the heckler in the crowd drew his attention. "Over there, Simpson, that small group of three men and a woman. That's them. I want you to get close enough to hear what they are saying. Then come back and tell me."

"Yes, boss." Harry Simpson obeyed and slid through the crowd until he was directly behind the group.

"Trade unions sap the strength of our industrial nation," the penguin answered. The glib remark seemed to anger the workers in the crowd. Tadgh could hear them grumble. He noticed that a small group of the Ulster Volunteer Force congregated just behind Carson. An officer, their leader perhaps, stepped up to Carson who was pointing at Peader in the crowd.

Tadgh stepped forward in front of his comrade. "Come on, Peader. That's enough now. You are going to get us in trouble. And we don't need that when we are so close to solving the riddles that will help our Cause."

Peader, incensed at the callousness of the speaker, growled at Tadgh, "Give me a few more minutes, and I'll have the crowd at his throat."

"In a few more minutes, those UVF goons will have you by the throat, don't ya know," Tadgh cautioned him. Then he added, "I contacted Lawlor from the hotel telephone, and he's agreed to let us look at the *Book of MacCarthaigh Reagh* on Monday."

"You seem to put your own interests and those of the bourgeois capitalist business owners over the needs of our impoverished and oppressed Irish men and women," Peader yelled out, waving his fist in the air.

Tadgh pulled his pacifist friend back into the crowd. *Damn. That's done it.* Before he could muzzle and hide his comrade, the UVF squad descended upon Peader, handcuffing and dragging him away. Tadgh wanted to run out and assist his friend, but it was useless to try to stop the armed mercenaries. The crowd roared at the goons when they saw their countryman being roughed up for asking pertinent questions. It puzzled Tadgh that the Orangemen remained standing in formation.

Collin and Morgan stood frozen in shock.

"Get back into the crowd," he urged his compatriots, pushing them backward. "The last thing we need is for you and me to end up jailed."

Tadgh stumbled into a slender, mutton-chopped young man behind him, knocking him down and cracking one of the lenses of his spectacles. But before he could help the man up, the stranger had bolted off into the crowd without saying a word.

"They're on to something, all right," Simpson reported, turning his glasses over to check the damage. "The leader said that they were close to solving the riddles that would help them with their cause. Presumably, that means German infiltration of our society."

Boyle let that remark go. Maybe Simpson was thinking along the right lines. "Did he say anything else?"

His underling relayed Tadgh's comment regarding his telephone conversation., then added, "Lawlor may also be a spy, referring to some code book."

Boyle's mind seethed with new thoughts. *Gotcha. They must be getting close now that the O'Donnell lad has joined them. And by refer-ring to the Book of MacCarthaigh Reagh, they must already know the story of its theft by my family and the subsequent change of name. Do they know about the Clans Pact already? Why would they be together if they didn't have a copy? And who and where is Lawlor? One thing's for certain, I'll do better following them than I ever did trying to beat it out of them, their parents, or their grandparents.* "When did he say?"

"Monday, boss."

Boyle also knew that this would pose a big problem. That loud-mouthed friend who was just arrested was part of their team. He remembered—the one he saw with McCarthy and the girl after the

Rossa funeral at O'Connell's Tower. They would never leave him in captivity. In trying to get him released, they would likely get themselves arrested. And that was unacceptable. *Damn, I hate to have to play this card.*

"Simpson, get into your uniform and go down to the gaol. Tell the UVF that the man they just arrested is a German spy you have been tracking for some months and that he is your prisoner. Tell them that you are to take him to Cork to stand trial. Give them Maloney's name if they need confirmation, and do not use my name. It is critical that these stupid local police leave him in your custody. After they release him to you, take him to Donegal Castle grounds. They should be deserted after the parade disperses. I can guarantee that his friends will try to free him and plan an escape. Pretend to interrogate him once they show up, let him go after a struggle and then follow them closely after they leave. If there's trouble, just know I won't be far behind you. Don't disappoint me, Simpson. Got it?"

"If it's so important, then why don't you do it, boss? It's more convincing if you do the talking."

Boyle had to think fast. If McCarthy or his girlfriend saw him, the cat and mouse game would be exposed. After he disposed of them once the treasures were found, he would not want anyone to be able to trace their disappearance back to him.

"Just do your job, man. I'll be nearby if you need me. And here, you'll be wanting this." Boyle took a folded paper from his waistcoat pocket. "I always carry a draft warrant for occasions like this. Take it and fill in the name. It always works better to send in the junior officer first and have the senior one in reserve to come in and show solidarity if necessary. And get your damned glasses fixed."

Simpson took the warrant, examined it, then folded it back up and inserted it in his coat breast pocket without asking questions.

Boyle was satisfied. Simpson had bought the story. *Good. He's controllable.*

184

Carson was mad as hell. The UVF had dispersed the crowd, but he never got a chance to finish his important speech. That heckler would pay for his disruption. But first he had to deal with the local town council. He observed with some satisfaction that the Orangemen had been disbanded along with the spectators.

"Well now. We're going to have to break him out," Tadgh announced later, as they sat in the Olde Castle Pub after the crowd had been sent packing. "Collin, they dragged Peader over to that old building beside the Church across the street. Do you happen to remember what that place is?"

"I was only twelve when we left, but I do remember that we had to make a report to the police on the circumstances of Da's death. We had to go inside that building. I think it was the courthouse. I remember it had temporary jail cells in the basement. They were holdin' a vagrant who they thought might have killed Da, but Ma said it wasn't him."

Tadgh asked, "Was your ma hurt when your da was murdered, lad?"

Collin scowled, the memory stabbing his heart like an icepick. Tadgh saw the reaction before Collin spoke and it reawakened old feelings. He wished he hadn't asked the question.

"Not physically. I was there near Castle Lough Eske when he attacked us and dragged my da up the Road to Nowhere. I saw his face, and I'll never forget the cruelty in that man's eyes. I should have tried to stop him, but Da said he could handle the situation. Then Boyle pulled out his gun and hit Da with it, hard across his face. So I stood in front of my ma to shield her and the devil demanded information about some ridiculous treasure. When Da just laughed at him, Boyle went into a frenzy and shot him through the mouth. He fell to the ground, dead."

Tadgh nodded, quietly listening.

Collin shuddered. "Ma wanted to run to Da but Boyle turned on us. I grabbed her hand and forced her back into the woods on a run. We rushed back to the Castle where Claire was being cared for and headed home. I never saw Da again. Ma was panicked. We all were. She took us to stay with Aunt Biddy that night until she could book us passage to America. We left Donegal Town two days later and have never been back, until now."

"Boyle must kill all of us to get at the treasure," Tadgh hissed. "He killed our parents and now he has to finish the job with us."

A realization hit both of them and bound them in the Clans Pact at that moment.

"As I told you, my brother and I saw Boyle and his men kill my parents in cold blood and then set fire to our home with us inside," Tadgh growled. The two men clapped each other's arms in the bond of shared grief. "What do you say now to joining me in ridding ourselves of this scum?"

"Into death, if it means I can avenge my da's murder after all these years."

"Good, Collin. We should get the chance again. I am certain that Boyle is out of hospital and on your trail now that he probably recognized you at the hospital. He might even think that you were behind the attempt on his life. But first I need you to help me get your cousin out of jail. No small task indeed."

"How, Tadgh?"

"This is what you must do, lad." Tadgh ticked off points on his fingers for Collin. "March into the jail, identify yourself as Peader's cousin, and demand to see him. Then, after you have confirmed that he's there, you must demand his release, since he didn't actually break any laws."

"How about disturbin' the peace?"

"Good enough for a trumped-up charge but probably not legally defendable during a public address. Peader didn't threaten or slander anyone and he made no attempt to stop the parade."

"You can use your newspaper credentials. Threaten to write a story about the injustice of it. I don't expect them to release him, but you can figure out the layout of the building and jail cells as well as finding out the number of UVF or police present. I am also sure that you can find a way to let Peader know that we are going to get him out. A cousin's a cousin, for all that."

"Why don't you come with me, Tadgh?"

"Don't forget, I'm a wanted man, Collin, maybe even up here in Donegal."

"We need to help him, Tadgh," Morgan urged as Collin got up to leave.

"I'll be all right, sis. Remember Brooklyn."

Morgan kissed Collin gently on the forehead. "Be careful, brother. The last thing we need is to have both cousins in gaol."

"All right, then. I'll be back in a few minutes with or without Peader." Collin walked off towards the steps of the courthouse.

"That's odd," Tadgh remarked as Collin disappeared into the courthouse. "Do you remember seeing that RIC constable that your brother just passed at the entrance to the jail in the crowd earlier?"

Morgan turned to look at the figure. "That's the mutton-chopped bean-pole guy you knocked down right after they grabbed Peader. But he wasn't in uniform then."

Tadgh was fairly certain that they were being watched. "Look around and see if you can spot Boyle."

The two looked the area over carefully but couldn't spot their nemesis.

A blind beggar at the side of the courthouse building stooped over his cane, tin cup in hand. Behind the tinted glasses, he was looking directly at them.

♣   ♣   ♣   ♣

"I demand to see my cousin," Collin insisted to the prison guard after he entered the courthouse. "I spoke to the officer at the duty desk."

"We cannot give you access until Lord Carson has decided what to do with the prisoner."

Collin schemed about how to get past this obstacle, then came up with an idea. "Can I post bail for my cousin, sir? Just pay you the fee and be done with it?"

"Is that a bribe?" The guard's eyes narrowed. "Didn't I tell you to wait? Maybe you'd like to be reunited with your traitorous cousin in his cell. That can be arranged."

"No, sir. I'll stay here if you don't mind."

"Suit yourself but leave me be."

At that moment, in walked a thin RIC constable, a burly guard accompanying him. The first guard pushed Collin out of his way to deal with these new officers, saying, "Who is this, George?"

"I'll take charge here, Henry. The judge says that we are to release the prisoner into the custody of Constable Simpson, here, from Cork. He has a warrant from his district inspector."

"Is that what Carson wants?" Henry replied.

"He's still tied up with the Town Council, and, as I say, Simpson, here, has a warrant. The judge thinks that espionage is a more serious charge than disturbing the peace."

Collin waited while Simpson and his escort descended to the gaol cells. When they returned, Peader was handcuffed to Simpson's wrist. Collin and Peader exchanged quizzical glances, and then Collin followed the procession into the sunlight. *At least he's out of gaol.*

"Will ya look at that," Tadgh gestured to Morgan when he saw Peader and then Collin emerge from the courthouse one after the other. From their vantage point at the north corner of the Diamond, they had a clear view of Tirconnail Road. They watched as the RIC constable led Peader across the street and into the castle grounds. Collin crossed over towards his comrades, shrugging his shoulders.

"What good fortune for us, mavourneen. Peader's out of gaol. It seems almost too good to be true," Morgan said.

"Well now, lass. I'm not so sure. It may be a setup. But one that we must walk into, don't ye know."

"What do you mean?"

"That mutton-chop may be replacing Gordon James. He'll be Boyle's man, then, if that's the case. We have to confirm that Boyle is out of hospital."

Collin interrupted, "Who is Gordon James, Tadgh?"

"He was Boyle's henchman who was there when Boyle murdered my parents, rest their souls."

"There was a short constable hanging around the place when my da was killed," Collin said.

"Perhaps the same one, lad. Gordo died near Tralee when we wounded Boyle."

"Did he, now."

Morgan turned to face Collin. "It was Tadgh's brother Aidan who killed the man before he could kill us, and then Aidan was seriously wounded in the gun battle."

Tadgh threw her a disparaging look. She immediately regretted saying that because it only added fuel to Collin's argument that she was in too much danger.

"I found out that the constable's name is Simpson. He said he had a warrant for espionage that trumped Carson's disturbance charge. What's the next step, Tadgh?" Collin asked eagerly.

"Let's follow Simpson. I'm guessing that they wouldn't be doing this unless Boyle's behind it. I think that he is changing his approach from frontal assault to track and pounce. If he's on the loose, he won't show his face here in Donegal Town to be sure. But right now, comrades, we need to go forward with this charade and free Peader from Simpson's grasp." As they headed for the castle, Tadgh was worried. *What had mutton chops overheard, if anything?*

♣ ♣ ♣ ♣

Tadgh saw that the castle grounds were surrounded by a twelve-foot-high battlements. He had heard stories about the glorious days of the O'Donnell Clan, when the square gate house tower entrance facing the Diamond was manned by armed guards controlling the massive wooden barrier that protected the castle keep from foreign invaders. Beyond these outer fortifications, lay an expansive courtyard, and behind it, the main castle tower with its one-story kitchen and hall. Since Red Hugh's time the gate had been generally left open to the public for use of the courtyard.

Today was no exception, although at this late hour with the sun dropping below the tree line, it was deserted, except for the wiry RIC constable and his prisoner, Peader, who were moving across the courtyard toward the main building.

Tadgh held his hand up for Collin and Morgan to wait when they reached the entrance. He crouched low and slipped through the gate house to assess the situation. He saw Peader off to his left between the hall ruins and the west battlement, through a copse of trees in the back of the courtyard. He was still handcuffed to the weasely RIC constable who had his back to the entrance. They were in animated conversation. Tadgh waved his team through the entrance and motioned them to stay low. Then he quietly moved towards the trees close enough to hear the conversation.

"What is your connection to the German army?" Simpson demanded, poking Peader in the chest.

Peader twisted his hands in their shackles. "Who are you? I don't know what you're talkin' about. Take these handcuffs off. I'm just a concerned local Donegal Irishman, that's for certain."

"That's not what this warrant says. I'm going to take you back to Cork to stand trial."

"I've never even been to Cork. Let me see that warrant."

Simpson unlocked the handcuffs then showed him the warrant that Boyle had prepared. He drew his Webley with his free hand. "District Inspector Maloney has authorized your incarceration."

Peader rubbed his wrists and took the document, scrutinizing Maloney's name and official signature. His own name looked forged, undoubtedly by this stupid constable.

Tadgh stepped into Peader's view and put his Luger to the back of Simpson's neck. Before he could fire the weapon, Simpson spun around, striking Tadgh's nose with the Webley and reopening the cut. While Tadgh was momentarily distracted, Simpson grabbed Peader in a choke hold, pressing the Webley to Peader's throat.

"This is my prisoner. Back off or I will shoot him."

Before Tadgh could move, Collin jumped from behind a tree and landed a jarring hook to the constable's right temple. He went down for the count without uttering another word.

"Thanks, Collin, me lad. I forgot to ask you yesterday. Where'd you learn to scrap like that?"

"Brooklyn streets. Survival skills, really. Gave it up. Had to." He looked at Tadgh, "Until yesterday, that is."

"Why? You're good at it."

"I accidently killed an opponent."

Tadgh rubbed his chin where Collin's roundhouse had struck home. "I can see where that could happen."

"Good thing you didn't forget, cousin," Peader joked, as Tadgh bent down and restrained Simpson's limp arms behind his back with his own handcuffs. "Let's get out of here before Carson calls the dogs on me."

"You all head to your automobile, Peader, just in case. I'll join you in a few minutes. I am not finished with Simpson, here."

After the others had left the castle grounds, Tadgh shook Simpson conscious. The man looked scared, his eyes blinking rapidly.

"Where's Boyle?" Tadgh demanded, putting his Luger to the constable's temple. He saw what he thought was a flicker of recognition behind the cracked spectacles. "So, you know Boyle then, do you?"

"Only by reputation. He's been incapacitated," Simpson stammered.

"Where is Boyle now? If you know what's good for you, don't lie to me."

"I . . . I don't know. I heard he was in hospital." The corners of the man's mouth drooped. "I take my orders from Inspector Maloney."

Tadgh didn't believe a word of it. "The truth, or I'll blow your head off."

"Just look at the warrant. It's signed by my boss."

Tadgh picked the paper up from the ground where Peader had dropped it during the scuffle. Why would Maloney have a warrant for Peader? It didn't make sense unless Peader had been identified with them in Dublin during the Rossa funeral escape. And why would Simpson come all the way to Donegal?

"I don't believe you."

"That is the truth. Kill me if you must. You've done it before to protect your German spying motives."

"I'm not a German spy, you imbecile."

"That's what Maloney told me." He nodded smugly. "And that's a Luger, isn't it?"

Even after Tadgh pistol-whipped Simpson repeatedly across the mouth, drawing blood, Simpson still wouldn't change his story. Tadgh shook his head in disgust. This man wasn't going to crack.

"You tell Boyle that I am coming for him. He's the traitor, not me, and he'll die for it."

Tadgh hit the man once more, this time with his fist, and knocked him to the ground. The man was out cold. Then Tadgh headed for the O'Donnell automobile.

From the gathering shadows of the castle ruins, Boyle witnessed the escape with pleasure. He had overheard the conversation. *Simpson's got some guts after all and he fears me more than anyone.*

The head constable's adrenalin flowed. The mice were on the run and they knew the cat was out to get them. Boyle couldn't wait to pounce when they found the cheese. His dead father would be so proud of his only son. When McCarthy rushed out of the castle grounds, Boyle followed, staying in the shadows. A block later, McCarthy jumped into an old sedan which roared out of sight before Boyle could identify it clearly. Damn. His own vehicle was five blocks away and its driver was lying senseless on the castle grounds.

The head constable returned to the copse of trees where Simpson was still lying motionless on the ground. He hoped that McCarthy hadn't killed him since he was running out of accomplices he could manipulate.

Then he flinched at the thought of his mother's scorn and the beating she took for it from her husband before she died. That image had haunted him ever since his time in the Tralee hospital. It was as if she called him from the grave to redeem the evil ways of his father and to join her in Paradise. Her voice was more insistent now and doubt crept into his brain, blurring his thoughts.

Darcy Boyle moaned, "Mother, don't keep hounding me." He spoke into the air, addressing her as if she stood right in front of him. "Father ordered on his deathbed that I must obey him. The treasure is rightfully ours, won in the heat of battle against the vermin MacCarthaigh rebels." His head filled with the voices of his ancestors including his English father, chiding him for his doubts and demanding his obedience.

Simpson groaned and raised his right hand slowly to touch his jaw.

Boyle reached down and grabbed the man's arm. "Get up, Simpson. There's work to be done." He saw the man stir and shake his head. *Damn. I wonder what the cretin heard me say.*

Chapter Eleven
Book of Lismore

Sunday, July 9, 1916
Meenmore, Ireland

*U*pstairs, **Morgan attended** to her sister-in-law, who sat up in bed, propped up by pillows. "I got these stomach salts yesterday at the chemist for you, dear. You were already asleep when we got back last night, and I didn't want to wake you. They should help settle your digestive upset." Morgan set the bottle on the table at Kathy's side and sat down on the edge of the bed.

Kathy reached for the bottle and a glass of water next to it, but Morgan swiftly rose and stopped her.

"Here now, let me do that." She measured a dose of the salts into the water and handed the glass to Kathy. "You just rest."

"You're a dear person, Morgan," Kathy murmured, "I am so lucky to know you. How did you come by the name Morgan, by the way?"

"Tadgh gave me the name when I couldn't remember anything. It means, 'from the sea' in Welsh, the language of Tadgh's ancient ancestral home. Even then, I knew that I was falling in love with him." She looked out the bedroom window and imagined the roiling sea in her mind. The past encroached on the present at moments like this. She turned back toward the room, smoothed a wrinkle in the quilt and said to Kathy. "The name Morgan fits me now."

"Then it's the perfect name for you, my dear." Kathy gazed into her new sister-in-law's inviting green eyes. "What have our men decided to do?"

Morgan fluffed the pillow behind Kathy's head, then crossed back to the window and opened it, letting in the morning breezes.

She took a deep breath of lilac scent from the garden before turning back around to face Kathy once more.

"We're going to seek an historical book. The men planned the trip on the way back from the castle last night. Tadgh and Peader met a Professor Lawlor at the Royal Irish Academy in Dublin this last April. Tomorrow, he's agreed to show us a copy of a very important book that was compiled for Tadgh's ancestors five centuries ago. The men think it holds a clue to solving the Clans Pact riddles. You, Collin, and Peader are going to meet with Lawlor because none of you are wanted by the authorities in that part of the country. They think that any policemen or soldiers who saw Tadgh and me in Dublin can't bother us anymore. But it's still too risky for us to go there right now."

Kathy sat bolt upright. "What do you mean by that? They can't bother you anymore?"

"They were killed in self-defense, or in the case of that devil Boyle, he's not likely to be in Dublin," Morgan answered, sitting down on the edge of the bed, her hands twisting in her lap.

Kathy propped her chin in her palms, her eyes wild. "Oh, dear. Then, what are you and Tadgh meaning to do?"

Morgan stared out the window from the bed and sighed deeply, then turned back to Kathy. "Before we left Donegal Town yesterday, Collin telephoned your friend Sam in Lisburn."

Kathy reached out and took Morgan's hand. "That man has been my rock I can tell you. Salt of the earth, Sam is."

Morgan gently settled Kathy back down onto the pillow. "There, dear, better?"

"Much, thank you."

"Tadgh and I arranged to go to Belfast today by retracing your steps on the Swilly railroad. After your meeting with the professor, you will join us in Lisburn. Then you will take the boat from Belfast to Liverpool in three days to catch the *Aquitania* when it sails back to America on Thursday. It all works out."

"It's just too bad that we won't meet Jack Jordan, though. He was instrumental in helping us come to Ireland to locate you."

"I remember this much, Kathy. Jack was the man who helped me get off the *Lusitania*. He was a handsome, robust fellow. The ship went down so fast, and he stayed behind after all the lifeboats were gone. I don't see how he could have survived."

"Apparently, he did, though. I understand from Collin that he was at first in a wheelchair from his injuries, but now he is up and about with a cane. They made him manager of the Cunard office in Queenstown."

"He wasn't there when I went to find out my real name."

"He must have been. He thought he saw you. Otherwise, we wouldn't be here right now. I think he has a fascination with finding you."

"What? How could that be?" Morgan asked, putting her hand to her mouth. "I only knew him for a couple of minutes."

"Well, you must have made quite an impression then. He's been tirelessly looking for you for over a year now."

Wheelchair. Wait. It dawned on Morgan that this man may have been the same man in the wheelchair who had tried to hail them as they sailed by the pier in Queenstown Harbour. He obviously had a hand in how Kathy and Collin learned she was possibly alive in Ireland. It all started to make some sense. "How are you feeling now, dear?"

"Much better, thanks to you."

"Well then, you rest a while before you have to be on your way, Kathy. I can tell that Collin's getting impatient to leave, but you have a little time."

Downstairs in the kitchen, Aunt Biddy said to Peader, "I guess I brought you up right," as she tidied up after breakfast. The cousins had explained how Peader stood up to Edward Carson. "Labor unions and women's rights. That's my boy. There ye go now. We'll beat the Unionist carpetbaggers yet, to use a Yankee term."

197

"I learned a lot in Dublin, Mother, especially during the Rising. I have a very different view of the urgency for reform there in the big city. The wickedness of the British." He shook his head in disgust.

Biddy's eyes blazed, capturing her son's attention. "Just so as you stay away from military action, son. We O'Donnells believe in a peaceful revolution."

"We'll have to do what's necessary when the time comes, Ma. It may be out of our control," Peader cautioned, reaching out to hold her hand.

Tadgh observed that Peader had become more aggressive since returning to his home turf. *Good, as long as it didn't get them all arrested.*

Collin started for the stairs. "I'd better tell Kathy it's time to go and bring her down here. Our train leaves at eleven and it takes an hour to get to the station."

Boyle realized that Simpson's cover had been compromised in the Donegal Town courthouse. It couldn't be helped. That previous evening he called his remaining Cork henchman Jackson from the Donegal hotel, and ordered him to go to the RIA in Dublin immediately, find out about Lawlor, and call him back at his Donegal hotel lobby.

"He's a professor who studies ancient Gaelic documents at the academy, boss," Jackson reported at ten o'clock the next morning after driving all night. They're open today and he's there working on Sunday, bloody academics."

"Where are you calling from?"

"The Castle RIC office, of course."

"Get out of there and wait for us at the Emory Arms in Temple Bar," Boyle instructed. "We'll be there this evening."

Boyle roused Simpson who was eating breakfast in the bar.

"We're going back to the Capital, now. Get a move on." He'd have to watch out for that bastard Chamberlain who had banned him from Dublin.

He verbally berated the weakling Simpson all the way back until they reached the third-rate Emory at eight o'clock.

Leroy Jackson, Gordo's henchman in the early days, was drinking in the bar. He was a bruiser. Standing six foot two, he had arms like nine-pound hammers and legs to match. A broken bottle during a barroom brawl had disfigured his upper lip, drawing it down into a permanent snarl. Both Gordo and Boyle had been surprised when this lout had passed the course to become an RIC officer, given his aggressive attitude and apparent slow wit. But Boyle needed the muscle.

Boyle gave the order to Jackson. "You and Simpson are to tail the people that visit Lawlor tomorrow and report back, nothing more. Do you understand?"

"Ya, all right." There was no sir coming from Jackson.

Boyle let the insubordination pass this time.

Professor Lawlor greeted the clans group at the front door of the RIA on Monday afternoon and enthusiastically shook hands all around. "Peader, isn't it? Welcome once again. Where's your mate McCarthy? Surely he would want to be here to look at his ancestors' document."

"Unfortunately, Tadgh will not be with us on this trip. Let me introduce my cousin, Collin O'Donnell, and his wife Kathy from America."

"What? Another O'Donnell? And a Yank at that."

"Canadian, sir," Collin said.

"Don't you mean that you want to view the *Book of Ballymote?*" The professor looked confused.

"Another time perhaps. Today it's the *Book of Lismore.*"

"Well, good, because that's the document that I have permission to bring to the reading room for you to examine, lad."

"I understand that it is just a copy."

"In fact, what you will be examining today is an unbound parchment English translation by Mr. Whitley Stokes that was produced in the late 1800s. I felt that it was important for you to have the English version."

As the professor walked them to the reading room, he explained, "When the original vellum book was found walled up in Lismore Castle in 1814, it was given to a local Cork historian named O'Flynn who split it up and sold folios off to collectors. So unfortunate. Most of the book was recovered and reassembled sometime later and returned to Lismore Castle, where it resides today. We have a Gaelic copy here at the academy locked up in the stacks."

Peader changed the subject. "How is the restoration of *an Cathach* coming along, sir?"

"Very slow progress, I'm afraid. But I haven't destroyed it so far."

"You wouldn't know by any chance whether there is a missing Psalm in the middle of the document, would you?" Peader asked.

"No, lad. I haven't managed to separate the folios yet. Well, here we are." Lawlor stopped in the reading room where Peader remembered that he had viewed St. Columba's Psalter on a previous occasion. Stokes' translation lay flat on a long viewing table for examination. "You will need to use these gloves to protect the document. You can copy the text, if you would like. Could you tell me what you are looking for so that I can assist you in your evaluation?"

"We are looking for some reference to a rock of ages," Collin replied.

"Oh, dear. I was hoping that you would be seeking something more specific. That's like looking for a needle in a haystack in this compendium. There are probably fifty references to old rocks in the original two hundred folio collection." He adjusted his spectacles. "This compendium contains histories of the Irish saints, like St. Patrick, St. Columba, and St. Brigid."

Peader donned the gloves and said, "Yes, we know, sir. Remember, you gave us a hand scribed list of contents when we were here before. It's quiet a complex book, to be sure."

Somewhat oblivious of Peader's statement, Lawlor leafed through the pages of Stoke's translation, stopping at various points. "Here, you can see we have a section on Sir Marco Polo and another on the Conquests of Charlemagne. Then at the back, the *Colloquy of the Ancients* section contains stories of the Ossian Fianna before and up to the time of St. Patrick. It also includes many poems from long ago," the professor said, pointing to the last section of the translation.

At that moment, Lawlor's graduate student Henry popped his head into the reading room. "We've hit a snag with *an Cathach*, sir. I recommend that you come to the restoration lab with me now, Professor."

Lawlor turned to leave. "Peader, you're in charge here, while I see to this problem. For heaven's sake, handle these documents carefully, and I will return shortly. You have use of the facilities as needed."

Once the two had left, Peader was in his scholarly element. "All right. We need to read the beginning, middle and ending pages of each of these sections of the book and then copy any passage that relates to a rock of some sort. We'll split up the task. Fortunately, this copy of the book is not bound, so we can each take a section and review it at the table. Keep the pages in order," he warned. They settled into the task, each poring over their section with a notepad beside them, only halting their efforts for an occasional visit to the lavatory.

Hours had passed, and Professor Lawlor had still not returned. Immersed in their task, they realized it was much later than the normal closing time of the Academy.

"We have over thirty pages of writing among us," Kathy lamented, rubbing her cramped fingers with her left hand and wriggled them to loosen them up. "I haven't worked this hard since I marked all my students' papers a month ago."

When Collin saw his wife curl her hair around her ears as she spoke, he knew what that gesture meant. "We'll be going home to Toronto soon, Kathy."

"Fine, love, but we still haven't examined the poems." Her scholarly curiosity had taken over.

"There's nothing here that looks promising," Peader remarked, skimming the poetry sections.

"And I'm certainly not the best judge of Irish history, myself." Kathy stood and arched her back. "So I erred on the side of copying most of the termination pages that I read."

"Maybe we're barkin' up the wrong tree," Collin wondered aloud, getting up to join his wife.

Peader looked up from his task in Collin's direction. "I've been thinking about that, cousin. What if our ancestors didn't cross-link the riddle in your locket to anything McCarthy, like they did in Tadgh's?"

"Or maybe the key McCarthy clue is in the O'Donnell compendium?" Collin added.

Kathy was trying to connect the dots. "Is that the *Book of Ballymote* that the professor referred to?"

"Yes, it's a similar compendium. When we were here in April, Professor Lawlor said there is a copy of that document here at the Academy as well." Peader pointed to the walls lined with floor-to-ceiling bookshelves.

Collin got up, stretched, and scanned the stacks. "If the rock of ages riddle really does refer to the Rock of Cashel, then the clues in these compendia, if there are any, may have nothin' to do with a rock of ages at all. Otherwise, that clue has a double meaning. And further, what if the translation changed the meaning of those words to something else, eh? What do you think, Peader?"

Still seated, with a finger holding his place on his page of the book, Peader responded. "Those are not comforting thoughts now, are they." He paused, looking down at his pencil that had shrunk down to a nub. "I think that it's time to go. I'm done with this nonsense."

Kathy put her hands on her hips. "Men. Why can't you keep a positive outlook? We may have already found what we need. Tadgh or Morgan will figure it out. The clue might be right under our noses. I think we've done all we can here today. Peader, you could come back if needed, but Collin and I will be leaving for Toronto in three days." She was happy to see Collin nod his agreement.

Professor Lawlor returned. "I am sorry I was kept so long. Have you found what you were looking for?"

Collin answered, "You were right, sir. It's like looking for a lost button in a peat bog."

"I'm afraid you're going to have to stop for tonight. The bog will still be here in the morning."

Peader laughed, then in earnest, said, "We had just come to the same conclusion. Professor, you might have been right this afternoon when you suggested that we O'Donnells should be examining the *Book of Ballymote*. Is there any chance that we could take a look at it tomorrow, sir?"

"I am afraid that won't be possible. It would take at least four days to get approval to review that volume. It is the original vellum. Maybe you could come back next week, once I get approval."

"We'll have to let you know," Peader answered glumly, standing up and shaking the professor's hand. "But we appreciate your assistance today, to be sure."

"Glad to help, Peader, lad."

As he ushered them to the front door, the professor commented. "By the way, it has been a very strange day. While I was in the restoration lab, we had another inquiry about the *Book of Lismore*. Two requests in one day—very unusual. To my knowledge, that has never happened before for an antiquated item like this. I told the man it was unavailable. By the looks of him, he wasn't a scholar." Lawlor's eyebrows raised, he peered at the group.

"Did he give his name?" Collin asked calmly, and they all turned to hear the response.

"No. He asked if anyone else had been here for the same purpose." Lawlor looked perplexed.

"What did you tell him?"

"I didn't like his looks, so I said no. He questioned my statement, shouting that I was a liar. But I stuck to my story," Lawlor beamed.

"Then what happened?"

"That's the other strange thing. The man rushed off without identifying himself when I wouldn't back down."

"If I might ask, sir, was he a slight man, with spectacles, heavy sideburns?"

"Not at all. He was a big, ugly brute of a man. Why?" Lawlor's eyes narrowed. "Is that important?"

"Maybe." Peader paused. "When was he here?"

"About three hours ago, I'd say." Lawlor stopped and frowned. "Say, are you three in any trouble?"

"No, I don't think so," Peader answered, shaking the professor's hand. "But just the same, we'd be obliged if you could show us out the back way." Peader tried to keep his tone light.

Lawlor looked at them over his pince-nez but did as he was asked.

As they exited through the worker's entrance, Peader said, "We'll let you know about whether we need to review *Ballymote* next week, sir. Thank you again for your time with us today."

"No bother, son. I'll be here as usual."

As they walked north, Collin said, "What happens next will be up to Tadgh, Morgan and you, Peader. I don't think we have been successful here today."

♣ ♣ ♣ ♣

Two figures waited in the dark for the trio. One covered the front entrance and the other the tradesmen's door. A simple warbler's call summoned the one in front when their subjects left the back door and headed up South Frederick Street towards College Park. They followed at a distance in silence until the three entered the Nassau Hotel. Then they stayed until it appeared that the prey had settled for the night.

"Come on, Simpson. Get moving. The boss is waiting." When the smaller constable hesitated, Jackson cuffed him across the head, sending his eyeglasses flying.

The three rogue policemen held a clandestine meeting at midnight in Boyle's seedy hotel room. After they made their report of the day's activities, the head constable addressed the other two. "You and I should not be seen by our targets, Simpson. We're identifiable," Boyle ordered, sneering. "Leroy, you will tail our friends from now on, reporting all movements back to me. Get back down to the Nassau Hotel now and stake it out. Got it?" He eyed his new subordinate, and when he shook Jackson's hand, his fingers were crushed in an iron grip. *Brute strength*, thought Boyle.

"Yes, boss." Leroy didn't like Boyle's demeanor, but he needed the work. He would play along for now and see how the grab played out. He wasn't buying the German spy ploy at all. He had worked for bastards like Boyle before and knew what that entailed. There was money involved. He could smell it. There could be a big stash in it for him if he played his cards right.

Chapter Twelve
Lia Fáil

Tuesday, July 11, 1916
Dublin, Ireland

*C*ollin reached Tadgh by telephone on Tuesday morning and got an earful. "By all that's holy, your friend's a gem, but his father is a character and his new Russian mother's a force to be reckoned with. Formidable woman, don't ya know. Anyway, they have put us up and not out."

Collin hoped that Sam's father and stepmother were not in earshot. "I hear ya."

Tadgh continued, "When are you coming to Lisburn?"

"We're on the Great Northern out of the Westland Row Station. Arriving about one thirty, give or take."

"Good. Well now, Collin. Were you successful at the RIA?"

Kathy also had her ear close to the telephone receiver. "Tell him, nothing that we recognize, but we copied quite a lot of the termination pages for him to look at," she whispered.

"I heard that," Tadgh said. "We'll look forward to your return then."

"By the way, Professor Lawlor turned away a man wanting see the document while we were there."

"As I suspected," Tadgh chuckled into the phone. "Mutton chops?"

"No, a brute of a man, I'm told."

"I'll bet he's another Boyle lackey. Did the professor tell him you were there?"

"No, he didn't, thankfully, but Boyle probably knows, anyway."

"No doubt of it. Mutton Chops must have overheard our conversation on the Diamond. We're going to have to deal with them when the time comes, Collin."

"Correction. *You* will have to take care of them."

"What happened to your promise, '*Into the death?*'"

"Kathy insists that we return to Canada on the *Aquitania* when it leaves Liverpool Thursday." Collin saw Kathy smile at his words.

"We'll see about that, lad. Just get here in one piece, or three pieces, actually."

♣ ♣ ♣ ♣

After the O'Donnells had entered their private compartment of the Lisburn train, Jackson slipped alone into the tiny room next door.

Kathy placed the lunch basket Collin had bought in the train station on the checked leatherette seat beside her as she sat down, facing forward. She knew that traveling backward would only cause her stomach discomfort to erupt once more.

Collin wrestled their valise onto the overhead brass rail above Kathy's head in the stuffy compartment. He and Peader sat opposite, heads against the faded wallpaper, only an inch away from where Jackson was holding a glass to the bulkhead.

The train lurched and started to roll north out of Westland Row Station, clacking as it started to cross the Loop Line bridge over the Liffey.

"Isn't that the customs house on the north side of the river?" Kathy exclaimed, pulling the musty velvet curtains back as she looked east.

"You're right, lass," Peader answered, looking to his left. "But how did you know?"

"I'm a schoolteacher. Magnificent building, isn't it."

"All of the import and export businesses in Dublin are handled there, Kathy," Peader said, turning back to face her.

"A book I read mentioned that it houses all the genealogical records for southern Ireland. I think that is just as important. I'm surprised it wasn't damaged in the insurrection," Kathy said.

"The rebels didn't hole up there, lass. They prize their history and wouldn't dare harm those records, now would they. But the gunboat *Helga* sat right there in the river and bombarded the rebel positions to the west."

Kathy looked out again, but they had left the river behind. "It must have been terrible. The Rising, I mean."

"I can attest to that fact," Peader said, wiping his brow.

Collin took the opening offered by the conversation of his companions.

"Tell me what you know of Tadgh and Claire's involvement in that tragedy, Peader."

"Morgan, dear," Kathy corrected. "Morgan."

"All right, Kathy—Tadgh and Morgan's involvement."

Peader knew that he was caught between allegiance to McCarthy and compassion for his cousin. He certainly didn't want to give Collin more ammunition to cause trouble. "I was in school in Drumcondra at the north end of the city during most of the Rising, but I understand that they both committed themselves to the Cause."

"Did they now."

"That's my understanding, Collin. Tadgh is a fierce protector of your sister of that you can be sure."

"Is that how she got shot, then?"

"Her obsession with saving lives caused that misfortune, I was told."

"How about some lunch, men?" Kathy asked, opening the basket. "Beer, anyone?"

On the way north, the trio discussed the fact that they had not found any link to Cashel in the *Book of Lismore*. At each crossing the train's whistle would temporarily drown out their conversation.

Collin wouldn't give up. "I think that we have come to a dead end, cousin. There's no proof that the rock of ages is Cashel. And now it's time for Kathy and me to go home. I will try one more time to get my sister to join us. It's too dangerous for her in Ireland with Tadgh."

"She made up her mind, dear. Love wins every time and she's head over heels," Kathy murmured as she sank back into the cracked upholstered seat, munching a slice of sugared Irish soda bread to settle her stomach.

"We'll see about that, love."

Kathy shot him a disapproving glare. *Men!*

In the next chamber, Leroy Jackson listened to the conversation in the adjoining compartment with his ear pressed to the glass. He could only make out some of the words being said. He wrote the word "*Cashel*" into his notebook. He concentrated hard because if he was any judge of the situation, there were riches to be had, and he would be one to have them. He wasn't going to miss out on this one opportunity for booty after a hard life of bad luck. Boyle would pay the price for his deception.

"Good afternoon, Mr. Finlay. This is my cousin Peader," Collin said, when the hunched-over linen designer answered his front door. "Thank you for hosting our friends in our absence."

"Had no choice, my boy, did I," John Finlay grumbled, ushering them into his spartan parlor. "But it's all right. Your friends are Republicans."

"But aren't you Protestant, sir?"

"Yes, but I've recently been to Russia. Linen design business, you know. I see the suffering there just like here. A man's got to have dignity and a livelihood. The Lord God loves all and especially the meek, don't he, though."

Morgan smiled. *He sounds just like Charlotte. There is some sanity in this crazy world.*

She got up from the sofa and hugged her new sister-in-law. "Come and sit down. You must be exhausted, Kathy. How's your tummy doing?"

"It's better. But the train ride you know."

"I'm sure that we can muster up some tea for you, can't we Mr. Finlay."

"I'll put the kettle on," John's wife Riah announced, as she bustled off to the kitchen.

Morgan turned back to her host who had sat down in his favorite armchair. "I agree with you entirely sir, about the meek, I mean."

"Do you, lass? I don't think that your once-in-a-lifetime here agrees with us."

"We just want justice and freedom for all Irish men and women," Tadgh exclaimed, taking Morgan's hand and squeezing it hard.

"It's not going to happen up here in Ulster, lad. Of that I can assure you."

"There's a fight comin', to be sure, sir."

Sam made his way down the stairs, pulling on the Prince Albert in his pipe. Kathy ran up and gave him a hug.

"I hear that you two have been gallivanting about in Dublin, lass. And you with another little one in tow, we hear." Sam gave Kathy a wink.

"We found her, Sam. Isn't she lovely?" Collin went over and put his arm around Morgan.

Sam puffed again as he brought Kathy back to the sofa. "Yes. That's grand, to be sure. After all this time and worry. We've had quite a chat up in your absence. Nightingale, she is. And Tadgh is quite the freedom fighter, I'll warrant you, as is his girl."

Morgan flushed. "Go on with you. I'm nothing of the sort really."

"You are too, my precious girl." Tadgh said, pulling Morgan away from her brother.

"Where are your manners? Introduce me to your cousin, Collin, my lad," Sam chided.

"This is Peader O'Donnell from Donegal. He's going to be a teacher, like Kathy."

Peader stepped forward and shook Sam's hand. "Glad to meet you and your family. Thank you for your hospitality."

"Come in and sit down," the elder Finlay said, ushering Peader into the parlor. The more the merrier, I guess, although I don't know where you're all going to sleep."

Sam turned to Collin. "Are you ready to head home then, lad? The boat won't wait for us, you know."

"Yes, Sam, after we have a discussion with our friends, here."

They all sat down in the parlor and drank cup after cup of strong Russian tea that the Mrs. Finlay insisted on pouring. Kathy could tell that Tadgh and Morgan were eager to find out what the three of them had determined from the *Book of Lismore*.

Finally, taking leave of their hosts, the five comrades found a bedroom where they could talk privately. Kathy was included for the first time, while Sam stayed behind with his parents.

Morgan went to the window and pulled back the dark crepe curtains, filling the room with waning sunlight. Opening the casement window, she smelled the honeysuckle from the garden as the fragrance wafted into the room.

Tadgh set out Lawlor's list of contents for the *Book of Lismore* on the bed for reference. "I think we need a name for our group."

Morgan turned toward him, her eyes sparkling at the thought of a team of both families. "How about the *adventurers?*"

They all agreed, and Morgan was pleased that they were all getting along.

Collin sat on the bed and pulled an oilskin sheaf from his inside jacket pocket. "Here are the notes we made during our examination." He offered Tadgh a number of papers. "Did you know that this book has more than thirty sections and almost two hundred folios?"

Tadgh picked up the notes with Morgan looking over his shoulder. The room fell silent as he read. Once in a while, she would point to some phrase as if confused by it. Finally, Tadgh said, "Well, now. I don't think our ancestors would have used the documents about foreign dignitaries like Marco Polo for such an important historic clue."

"We wondered whether they would have used the McCarthy book for O'Donnell clues, and vice versa," Collin offered. "That would mean that any clues for McCarthy would be found in the *Book of Ballymote*, which was not available to us while we were there."

Tadgh continued his line of reasoning. "I don't think so, Collin. I can see why our ancestors would cross-link the lockets to bring us together, but they were knowledgeable of the contents of their own compendia and would likely have imbedded clues in them for their own treasures."

He scanned the list of contents. "If it is here, it would have to be in the *Lives of the Saints* or the *Colloquy of the Ancients* sections, I would think."

A few minutes later, Tadgh put down all the papers except one that Kathy had scribed.

"You have a fine cursive hand, lass."

"Thanks. Schoolmarm life does it."

Tadgh rattled the page. "I keep coming back to this last page of the Colloquy of the Ancients. Remember the alpha and the omega reference from the Clans Pact?"

Kathy closed the window against the cool and now-damp twilight air and turned up the gaslight. "I read that last page carefully and nothing struck me as being significant."

"That's because you've never been told the story of *Lia Fáil*, the stone of destiny. Let me explain. It is partly described, as you wrote, near the end of the last folio of the whole book, where it says,

Conn of the Hundred Battles bed stone . . . and the Lia Fáil, or 'stone of destiny', that was there, were the two wonders of Tara . . . Ossian told Dermot, son of Cerbhall . . . when Ireland's monarch stepped onto it the stone would cry out under him, and her three arch-waves boom in answer: as the wave of Cleena, the wave of Ballintoy, and the wave of Loch Rury; when a provincial king went on it the flag would rumble . . ."

Tadgh cleared his throat, as his voice had turned husky. "This particular stone of destiny was located on the hill at Tara, the center of our Celtic civilization beginning in the pre-Christian period before St. Patrick. It isn't clear where the stone came from, but it was revered, and all the Irish High Kings were crowned upon it. As I have just read, this stone had magical powers to cry out thrice when the true High King stepped onto it and to rumble when a lesser King rose upon it. I suppose that is how they chose their Kings, at least in mythology."

"I see where you're going. 'Seek ye the rock of ages'," Morgan cried, taking Collin's locket from around his neck. "What a terrific choice that would be if our forefathers picked *Lia Fáil* as a talisman to signal the way to their treasures," she exclaimed, getting up from her squat position on the floor to sit next to Tadgh on the bed. "Imagine, a talking rock that heralded the King."

Peader picked up Kathy's notes and reread the passage. "I think that this could be their message from the McCarthy *congregation* found at the *omega* of the *Colloquy of the Ancients*. But what does it mean?"

"Of course, it could also be the bed stone for Conn of the Hundred Battles, which we learn was the second wonder of Tara, cousin."

"I don't think that's likely, Collin. Let's go to Tara and see what each of these wonders can tell us," Morgan suggested, her eyes shining.

Tadgh got up and turned to address his comrades. "It's not as easy as that, lass. There's more of the story to tell, so there is."

"Go on, mavourneen."

Tadgh took up the notes again. "Look here. At the very end of the *Colloquy*, the following is written before it is left unfinished,

> *Dermot, son of Cerbhall sought now: 'and who was it that lifted that flag, or that carried it away out of Ireland.' It was an oglaech of a great spirit that ruled over . . .* "

"How is that significant, my love?"

Tadgh smiled knowingly and then winced as his jaw joint cracked from its recent beating. "I know that it was the Irish King Fergus in the year five hundred who took the *Lia Fáil* to Pictland, now Scotland, when he went to conquer the Picts. By the way, Collin and Peader, Fergus came from O'Domnhaill ancestry. After that, the Scottish Kings were crowned upon this stone for centuries. They called it the 'Stone of Scone' there because of where it was located."

"Tadgh, do you think that Florence and Red Hugh removed the remaining pages of this *Colloquy* to point the way to Scotland or to the stone of destiny?" Peader's eyes went wide with his question.

"It wouldn't surprise me, given how we think they truncated *an Cathach*."

"Can we go to Scone and examine it there, mavourneen?" Morgan asked.

"Alas, no. In 1295, the English King Edward I defeated William Wallace outside Sterling Castle in Scotland and temporarily brought Scotland to heel. Edward is reported to have taken the Stone of Scone to London where it now lies as a seat for the throne of Edward the Confessor in Westminster Abbey. Do you want to tell them what it's used for, Morgan?"

"All the English kings and queens have been crowned on that throne since Edward I. Does it still cry out when the true monarch sits on it?"

"Right you are, but I haven't heard anything told of it making noise except when a portly king like Henry VIII would sit on that old wooden chair, and it was said to emit a creakin' sound," Tadgh laughed.

"So, we have to go to Westminster Abbey, then."

"Perhaps, Morgan. I'll have to think about that, but it doesn't make sense that our ancestors would use an English object as a talisman."

♣ ♣ ♣ ♣

Kathy knew that Collin's silence during their late supper meant that he was strategizing how he would convince Morgan to come home with them. Nothing she had said could dissuade him from that goal.

"I'm sad, too, that we will be separated so soon after our reunion," Morgan remarked.

"That's not why I'm pensive, sister."

Kathy saw that Morgan had just given him the opportunity to drive home his desires and shook her head at her husband.

He spoke anyway. "I know that you love Tadgh. But Ireland is a very violent country and likely to become even more dangerous in the near future. We saw the devastation in Dublin. Kathy and I have been searchin' for you for years because I love you so much."

"We both do," Kathy interjected, gripping Morgan's hand under the table.

Morgan turned and gave her a light kiss on the cheek.

Collin leaned toward Morgan from his place across the table. "We are so happy we found you alive after all this time. Canada is a wonderful fresh new country, full of opportunity for a fulfilling and secure life. Tadgh has said that he would move to Canada to be with you. This crusade that you all are on to find treasure, although exciting, seems to have stalled. Who knows whether you will ever be able to find any more clues? So, as your older brother, I must insist that you come to Canada with us tomorrow. I've telephoned Mr. Jordan and he has secured you a berth on the HMS

Aquitania." He paused for a response.

Tadgh opened his mouth to object, but Morgan held up her hand to cut him off.

"I understand your concerns, brother, but I thought I made myself clear three days ago. I don't want to force my man to leave the homeland that he is fighting for with all his being. That would destroy our relationship. And it's my fight, too, if only to reduce the bloodshed. Now that I have my memory back, thanks to you, my feelings make more sense. In a way, the abuse I suffered as a child mirrors the oppression that Irish people have endured, or succumbed to, over the centuries. Defeating these blaggards is like avenging my captivity. So I am going to stay here, and die if necessary, with my soon-to-be husband."

Tadgh rose and took her in his arms.

Collin's heart sank. It was not what he wanted to hear.

Kathy thought that her newly found sister had expressed herself very convincingly. "Bravo," she cried, only to receive an angry look from her husband.

Tadgh urged, "Come now, comrade. We all need you here with us to fulfill the destiny of our two great clans. Without your lightning right cross in Donegal, we couldn't have subdued mutton chops. There's no doubt of it. And who knows how important your experiences and thoughts will be as we proceed on our journey. Where would we be today without you and your locket? Please, stay with us."

It was clear to Sam that the two sides were deadlocked. Further discourse would result in hard feelings and that would be a disastrous end to this otherwise miraculous reunion.

At just the wrong moment, Sam's father broke the tense silence and spoke. "Lad, you can't leave Ireland. It's your home."

This was Sam's cue to speak. "I'm not sure what adventure you are undertaking, but there are responsibilities for Collin and Kathy back home. And, Collin, a woman named Maureen O'Sullivan came to the house while you were gone with a note from her boss, a Mr. Healy. The *Tely* has ordered you home now that the Rising Royal Commission has ended. You must return now, or you will lose your job, my boy. Surely this adventure can go on without you or wait until you can return."

"You heard what Sam said, Sister, so Kathy and I are leaving tomorrow to catch the boat home." Collin was still having trouble calling her Morgan. "If you stay here with Tadgh, you'll be dead within a year. That's what I fear." His eyes grew dark.

Tadgh started to respond, but Morgan shook her head at him. Their position had already been stated, and any more argument would just make matters worse. Supper was over, and everyone retired for the evening. To say that Collin was unsatisfied with the outcome would be a gross understatement.

The Russian wife exclaimed to her husband, "Damn young people don't know when they've got it good. Millions in Russia are about to be slaughtered in the name of Marxism if Lenin has his way." Sam's father shuffled off to his room, shaking his head at all of them.

Chapter Thirteen
McCarthy Revelation

Wednesday, July 12, 1916
Lisburn, Ireland

*B*reakfast the next morning was a somber and non-communicative affair. The only sounds were the clattering of crockery and the sizzle of bacon in the skillet. Collin poked his head out of the kitchen doorway and spoke more loudly than was necessary in the small room.

"C'mon Kathy, we have to catch that boat to Liverpool in an hour. We've run out of time here. The *Aquitania* leaves Liverpool tomorrow with or without us." He was careful not to look anyone in the eye.

"Hold your horses, Collin. I'm saying goodbye to Morgan," Kathy called out from the parlor. She turned to her newfound sister-in-law who was sitting with her head in her hands on the sofa. "There, there, my dear. Take this hanky for your pretty green eyes. Collin can be such a bother. I was bawling my eyes out because of him a few days ago in this very house. He loves you so much and can't bear to leave you behind now that we've found each other. Don't let us leave in anger."

"I'll come to visit," Morgan keened, as Kathy dabbed at her own eyes.

"Yes, you must, you and Tadgh. Let's plan on it soon."

They both knew that it wouldn't happen, not under the current circumstances anyway. She led a crying Morgan to the front door where Collin and Sam were saying goodbye to the Finlays, Tadgh, and Peader.

Kathy brought Morgan to her husband. "Go on, Collin. Give your sister a big hug and kiss. She's promised to come and visit us soon."

As Collin gave her a hug, he broke down, the two of them crying.

"Remember what we agreed upon last night, dear," Kathy prompted him, still holding hands with Morgan.

"Oh yes," he mumbled, grabbing hold of the locket around his neck. "We agreed that I should break with ancient tradition."

Morgan looked up at her brother through her tears. "What do you mean, Collin?"

"We think that you should have Ma's picture. I took a snap of it with my Brownie to keep for myself. Her picture obviously means a lot to you since it triggered your memories. We had good times with Ma, didn't we?" This shared memory flooded through both of them.

Kathy let go and Morgan held her brother close.

"Oh, Collin, I can never repay you and Kathy for persevering to find me and help me remember. Yes, we had some good times together. I love you, brother!"

"I love you more than you can know," Collin whispered. "It hurts to let you go, after that long search."

"Here," Kathy offered, as she unclasped Collin's locket that was around his neck and removed the small picture wedged into one side.

Morgan gently accepted the small, oval photograph in the palm of her hand, studied it closely, and then kissed it. "This is the best gift you could have given me," she said. "But how can I keep it safe."

Kathy said, "Wait a moment." She pulled a small prayer book from her reticule. "Put it in here, dear. And keep it close to you."

Morgan pressed the photo into the book where it fit perfectly and kissed Kathy on the cheek. "It will mean all the more to me, now." She temporarily slipped the prayer book with its treasure into her skirt pocket. "I will keep and cherish it always. It's all we have to remember her by."

As Kathy closed the locket, she glimpsed tiny squiggles on the locket's interior where the photograph had been, scratches maybe. *How peculiar.* She caught her breath as she snapped the clasp shut and pushed the locket under Collin's shirt. *Probably nothing.* Turning to go, she kissed Morgan goodbye. "I'm glad you two reconciled," she whispered into her sister-in-law's ear

"Time to go," Peader announced, opening the front door and stepping outside, "or you'll miss your boat."

Kathy's heart warmed when she saw Morgan smile for the first time that morning and felt her lingering hug.

"Thank you, for everything," her sister-in-law whispered as she turned to go.

Tadgh had noticed Kathy's expression when she closed the locket, but its significance took him awhile to register. By that time Sam and the O'Donnell couple were out the door, while everyone else followed, with Tadgh some distance back.

"Kathy! The locket! Did you notice anything in the locket?" he called out, just as the O'Donnells had gotten into Mr. Finlay's lorry.

"It was nothing, Tadgh," she called back, just as the lorry door closed.

Everyone waved as Finlay started down Longstone Street. Tadgh sprinted after the vehicle. "Stop!" he yelled at the top of his lungs.

Running after him, Morgan cried out, "Give up, Tadgh. It is over. They're leaving."

Tadgh paid no attention. He pounded his fist on the right rear fender. "Stop!" he yelled again.

The lorry stopped. Finlay jumped out to examine his fender and bellowed, "Are you crazy? You could have been hurt!"

Tadgh rushed past him and opened the passenger door. "Show me your locket, Collin."

"What's this nonsense? We will miss our boat," Collin protested, getting out of the lorry.

Morgan caught up to the group, panting.

"Show me," Tadgh insisted, pulling at the chain around Collin's neck.

"Oh, Collin, do show him so that we can be on our way," Kathy urged, stepping out of the lorry.

Collin clicked open the locket and examined it as they all peered closer.

Kathy spoke first. "See. Nothing but a few scratches."

She tugged at Collin's sleeve, but Tadgh held the locket fast.

"It's a cryptic message, to be sure," Tadgh said, straining to look closer in the morning light.

Collin pulled his arm free of his wife's grip. "What does it say?"

"Not words that I recognize. It appears to be some sort of code. This may be the clue that solves the riddle of our clans. But I need more time and better light. I'm sure Mr. Finlay has a magnifier so that we can decipher these markings."

Morgan said, "Let's return to the house."

Kathy face fell. "But the ship!" Her voice cracked.

Tadgh stared at Collin. "To restore our clans, that's our destiny. What will it be, comrade?"

Collin returned Tadgh's stare, transfixed and conflicted.

Kathy pulled on her husband's arm, her eyes pleading and tearing up. "*You promised!*"

"That you did, lad," Sam added quietly. "Don't forget Mr. Healy's warning. Your time here has expired."

Tadgh pressed his point. "If it's money that's the problem, I have funds for our search, Collin. And then there's Boyle. He's not going to be put off."

Collin wrestled with the decision a few moments more, then turned to his wife. "This delay can't be helped, Kathy. This is our destiny, as Tadgh says, and we are going to meet it. I will contact Mr. Robertson. He will understand why I must continue, and Jack will get us a place on the next troop ship, I'm sure."

Despite Kathy's protests, they all climbed into the lorry, and Finlay turned the vehicle back towards home.

♣ ♣ ♣ ♣

"That's it!" Boyle yelled when Leroy made his report. "The Rock of Cashel must be the 'rock of ages' that they were talking about on the train.'

"What's the grab, boss?" Jackson figured that, at worst, Boyle would just clam up.

Boyle stared him down. He realized that he had made a mistake in judgment. Leroy Jackson was no patsy. Boyle needed his brawn, but the constable would have to be disposed of at some point. If he was lucky, McCarthy would do that for him.

"McCarthy is a German spy, and he has something I want," Boyle divulged, locking eyes with Jackson. He left it like that.

So that's how he wants to play it, Jackson thought. "They got off in Lisburn, but I lost them near the linen mill," he told Boyle. In fact, he had traced them to the Finlay home, but he wasn't going to give that information up.

"You're not holding out on me, are you, Jackson?"

"On the train, I overheard talk that the O'Donnell lad and his wife were going to Liverpool today to catch the troop ship for its return trip to Canada tomorrow. They'd be gone by now."

"We're going to Cashel," Boyle announced abruptly. Damn. *Surely, they would stay if the treasure was at hand.*

Jack Jordan had received an earlier telephone call from Collin when he was at the Nassau Hotel, and he couldn't have been happier to learn that they had found Claire. He was more than eager to meet her again. But Collin's second phone call after the O'Donnells had returned to the Finlay home dashed his hopes.

"We've decided to stay in Ireland for a few more days," Collin announced, turning away from Kathy's disappointed face. "Can you let the *Aquitania* know that we won't be boarding, please?"

"I can take care of that at no cost to you. Any chance you'll be coming my way?"

"I'll have to let you know, Jack. When's the next troop ship to Canada?"

"The *Teutonic* on the twenty-third, leaving from Queenstown, Collin. That is less than two weeks away."

"The delay can't be helped. Thanks for all your assistance, Jack."

Collin and Kathy went upstairs where they could talk privately. When they came back down to the group assembled in the parlor, she announced to all of them, "I'm not upset. I will go along with this as long as we leave on the next boat on the twenty-third. I will hold you to that, Collin O'Donnell."

Morgan hugged Kathy. Sam listened without comment. That would get him home just before school started, but he still felt concerned about Collin risking his career on this ancient set of riddles.

Soon after their discovery, the adventurers were sitting in Finlay's guest bedroom again, excitedly debating the meaning of the new clue that they had found. Collin had convinced them to include Sam in their discussion.

"Read me again what is written in those tiny letters and numbers," Peader asked, pulling out a pen and paper from his pocket.

"*CCTip, BSt, L42, H22, WN164D,*" Tadgh read, using Mr. Finlay's monocle magnifier lens. He sounded completely stumped.

"It is our destiny to solve this riddle," Peader said, as he wrote down the sequence of letters and numbers that Tadgh recited from the inside of Collin's locket.

"Take the picture out of your locket, Tadgh," Kathy said. "Tell us what it says."

"*PPPCCathaoir, BSt, L2284-5, H20, WN99D*"

"That's gibberish," Collin muttered.

Tadgh held the lockets side by side in the light. "Not so, Collin." He whistled. "Well, I'll be damned. We needed the information from both lockets, just like the Clans Pact said. I was right!"

"Right about what, Tadgh?" Peader asked.

"What do these sequences have in common?" Tadgh passed

around the paper with the two sets of characters lined up one above the other across the page.

"BS, L, H, and WN," Morgan answered, scanning the paper, and handing it to Peader.

"Peader, do you remember that I was hesitant when you suggested going to Westminster Abbey to examine *Lil Fáil?*"

Peader looked up from examining the paper. "Yes. So?"

"There is another story about *Lil Fáil*, which now seems related. It has been passed down in the McCarthy Clan over the years, but I thought it was just that, a mythical story, right enough."

"Go on," Morgan urged.

They were captivated while Tadgh told the tale. "So it goes that the great Muskerry Leader, Cormac McCarthy, supplied four thousand men from Munster to aid the forces of Robert the Bruce in his battle against Edward II, who was the English invader at the Battle of Bannockburn in Scotland in 1314. You will remember I told you that Edward I had defeated William Wallace in 1295 and had taken the Stone of Scone to England."

"What does that have to do with these markings, mavourneen?"

"The Clan believed that Wallace, seeing the size of Edward's advancing army, hid the religious relic and substituted a look-alike— sandstone for the true bluestone."

"So they took the wrong stone to London?"

"That's what my ancestors believed, or so my pa told me, Morgan. But anyhow, Robert the Bruce won a great victory that day at Bannockburn and liberated Scotland temporarily from the English. He was a hero for both his own people and for the Irish. I wish he had been here to lead us during the Easter Rising, I must say."

Peader spoke up. "There must be more to this story, comrade. What is it?"

They all leaned forward, close to their leader who was enjoying telling the tale as much as they were hearing it.

"McCarthy legend has it that Robert the Bruce, knowing the Irish lineage of *Lia Fáil*, and as a sign of gratitude for Cormac's pivotal support, cleaved the real *Lia Fáil* in two and gave half to McCarthy to bring back to Ireland."

The group hung on every word.

"The McCarthy Mor Clan leaders zealously guarded and kept this secret. Then one hundred and thirty-three years later, Cormac Laidir MacCarthy, Clan Chieftain, built a castle keep that stands in ruins today. Anyone want to hazard a guess as to which castle this was?" Tadgh knew he was sounding like Lawlor.

"Kilbrittain?" Peader ventured.

"Well, now, comrade. Close, but the wrong Sept."

"Blarney!" Morgan shouted, her hand shooting upward in triumph.

"That's right. Any guesses as to what happened to that half of the *Lia Fáil*?" Tadgh was toying with them now.

When no one responded, Tadgh continued, "McCarthy legend has it that this sacred stone was built into the top of the battlements of Blarney Castle to protect our forefathers. It faces south in the direction from which warring clans or foreign invaders would likely attack, which they did. And now, in our day, in keeping with the ruthless Queen Bess's proclamation, all those who kiss it are given the gift of eloquence."

"It is the Blarney Stone!" Morgan shouted. "How ironic," she laughed.

"There you go, now, but why ironic, my dear sister?"

"It's clever, Collin. Queen Bess criticized the McCarthy chieftain for speaking double talk, calling it Blarney, when all the while Florence and Red Hugh were using Blarney to hide clues that would help defeat her English descendants."

Kathy was a bit more skeptical. "But that's all just a story about the Blarney Stone, surely."

Tadgh folded his arms and smiled before speaking. "Not just a story, but history that the McCarthys believe in whole-heartedly. And it fits with the statements made by Ossain on the final page of the *Colloquy of the Ancients*, doesn't it. Talking stone, gift of the gab."

Tadgh's words were a revelation, and even Kathy was willing to accept his explanation.

Collin was quick to ask, "This is a wonderfully excitin' story. But what does it have to do with these hieroglyphics in our lockets, Tadgh?"

"Well, the story came back to me when I saw the initials BS in Collin's locket."

Morgan couldn't contain herself. "The Blarney Stone! Of course! It ties to the *Book of McCarthaigh Reagh* and back to the Clans Pact."

Collin jumped up and slapped Tadgh on the back, saying, "It would certainly be fittin' that Florence and Red Hugh would use this sacred relic as the cornerstone of their treasure map. No pun intended. It is definitely a 'rock of ages' for all that, hidden in plain sight."

Sam got up and opened the bedroom door. "It doesn't look like we are going to leave today, does it? I'd better alert my father and telegraph Lil."

"I'll call Mr. Healy now," Collin offered, heading toward the open doorway.

Sam's eyebrows arched. "This is all getting too complex. Let's have lunch first, then sort it out."

Kathy, seeing her husband entranced with the figures on the written page, nodded her head, though her stomach churned. She yearned to be with her Liam, but at least she was with her husband once again.

After lunch, Peader assembled the group in the parlor and sat them round the circular table. It was his turn to share information. "I'd like to add more family history. Collin, it all ties together when you realize that St. Columba, an O'Domnaill, like ourselves, exiled himself to Scotland in the sixth century, just sixty-three years after his relative Fergus took *Lia Fáil* there. It is written that Colm Cille, as he was called, performed many of the early crowning ceremonies for the Pict Kings on what would eventually be called this Stone of Scone. So, don't ye see, both Clans are bound to this most sacred relic."

Sam marveled at how well the group was working together to unravel the mystery. Only a week ago he had wondered whether he could salvage a marriage and despaired at the possibility of finding a long-lost sister. Now, here they all were as if they had been blissfully together as a clan for years.

A clap of thunder announced an oncoming storm. Morgan stood up and went to the front window, patting her skirt pocket. "So, the message, 'seek ye the rock of ages', does have a double meaning after all, doesn't it?"

Tadgh crossed the room and brought her back to the group. "That's what we have to figure out. I may have been wrong about the Rock of Cashel, although that seemed to fit the words from the Psalm."

"What did the Clans Pact say about the location of the family treasures, mavourneen?"

Tadgh took out the copy of the pact he had made before leaving Creagh and read, "*each in a place of historical religious significance . . .*" His words trailed away as recognition crept over his face. "Oh, my God, Morgan. The riddle in Collin's locket." Tadgh stared at the piece of paper with the alphanumeric symbols. "That's got to be it."

They all leaned forward, curious to hear what Tadgh had to say. "The CC in Collin's locket. It must stand for Cormac's Chapel, don't ye know, built by my ancestors in 1134. It's the original Gothic church on the Rock of Cashel. The treasure must be on the Rock of Cashel!"

"That's a stretch, I think," Collin commented, standing to take the locket inscriptions sheet from Tadgh's hands. "CC could mean anything, like County Connaught, for example."

Morgan stood up between her partner and her brother and grabbed them by the shoulders, pulling them in together. "But when you combine the clues in both your lockets, the rock of ages,

Lia Fáil, one nation to another, CC and BS in the riddle and place of religious significance connected with the McCarthy clan, it all seems to make sense, doesn't it?"

Peader examined the alphanumeric sequences on Tadgh's written page once more. "If all that is true, then our ancestors did cross-reference these clues in the lockets."

Morgan asked, "What about the rest of the hieroglyphics?"

Sam, who had until now sat quietly in a corner chair smoking his pipe and observing the group, spoke up for the first time. "It seems obvious to me. Since it uses the Blarney Stone, then the L, H, and W refer to the dimensions of the stone."

"And the numbers after the letters could be measurements, either as an addition to the stone dimension or as a multiple of it," Tadgh added, twirling the end of his moustache.

Kathy sat back down on the sofa and flinched as another thunderclap shook the front window. "I have a question, then," she piped up, and all eyes were on her. "What does the D at the end mean?"

"And the letter N?" Tadgh wondered. "If each of these riddles suggests a map, then length and height are obvious. But how does width come in?" He slapped his forehead. "Saints be praised. Any sailor would know this. Any sailor worth his salt, anyway. You know, the angle. And N must refer to the direction north."

Collin stared at him, then at Kathy. "With the D indicating measurement in degrees?"

"Precisely. Now you're thinking," Tadgh nodded.

In the meantime, Morgan had been calculating. "So, from some location in Cormac's Chapel, the McCarthy gold is likely forty-two times L away, one twenty-two times H deep, and at an angle one hundred and sixty-four-times W degrees from north," Morgan offered.

They all sat back down excited by the knowledge that their efforts had paid off. The trail cleverly buried for more than three hundred years was revealed. Now, nothing could prevent them from moving ahead towards the prize that was rightfully theirs.

"Then what does the word "tip" mean?" Sam asked, smoke curling around his head in a cloud like the caterpillar from Alice in Wonderland.

Tadgh scratched his head. "Well now, my friends, it's got to be the starting point in the chapel. I have no idea what that means. Unless we could see it for ourselves."

Peader looked at them all and said aloud what everyone was thinking. "Someone's got to go to Blarney and measure the stone."

Tadgh stood up facing the group and took the lead. "We can't impose further on Mr. Finlay. Since none of us has transportation from here except by train, I am going to call my old colleague Jeffrey Wiggins in Cork to help."

Sitting down beside his wife on the sofa, Collin brightened up and added, "I could call Maureen, my colleague at *The Irish Times*, Tadgh. She has access to a company sedan, and I'm sure that she would be glad to help."

Kathy twirled her hair behind her ear but didn't say a word.

Tadgh held up his hand. "I don't think that is wise, Collin. We wouldn't want the Protestant *Times* getting wind of our adventure, would we now."

Kathy nodded her head in agreement and tugged on Collin's arm. "I think Tadgh's right."

Collin turned to his wife his eyes fixed on hers. "I suppose, but I need to give Maureen the story of finding Claire without telling her where we finally met or what we are doing. Her boss paid for my time here and convinced my boss that I should stay because my search was a good human-interest story."

Sam chimed in. "That reminds me, Collin, my boy. You'd best contact Mr. Robertson at the *Tely* and square things with him. I don't think you should leave it to Healy to tell him. You might also share your story of finding Claire with him. A human-interest story is just as important in Toronto as it is here, lad. And, be sure to tell him that you will be home on the next troop ship. Don't forget what I said about losing your job."

"I'll send Robertson a telegram from Cork, if you will let Kathy and me measure the Blarney Stone. I'd like to see Jack Jordan again and introduce him to you, Kathy."

"I'm sure that he would like to see Morgan again," Kathy chimed in. She had accepted the homebound delay and wanted to see if she was right about Jack's love interest. "She should come with us."

Morgan got up from her chair and hugged Kathy. "And I'd love to see Jack again."

Tadgh had developed confidence in Collin's ability to protect his sister, but he wasn't too keen on Morgan meeting up with Jordan. He thought for a moment before speaking. "All right but remember that Boyle is based out of RIC headquarters in Cork, aroon. Ask Jack to confirm from the district inspector that this devil is out of hospital and back to work. And be careful. He'd recognize you on sight, and he may have mutton chops or the other ruffian watching the Cunard office."

Collin got up and shook Tadgh's hand vigorously. "I'll take very good care of Morgan, Tadgh. You can count on me."

"I know that, Collin. That's not what I'm worried about."

Morgan's green eyes darted to her partner's, eyebrows raised, but she didn't ask the obvious question.

Collin had been studying the hieroglyphics in Tadgh's locket quietly. "What do you think the PPPC stands for?" he asked, unexpectedly.

Peader met his eye. "I've been wondering that myself. I can't think of any place of historical religious significance related to the O'Donnell Clan. The Donegal Abbey comes to mind, but it doesn't have the right initials."

The one suggestion that Kathy offered, checking the Bible for answers, didn't seem to fit.

"I don't think that Pontius Pilate was around when the O'Domnaill Clan was starting up in Ireland, dear," Collin offered, not realizing that she had made her suggestion in jest.

The rest of the group had no ideas.

"That's an adventure for another time, so it is," Peader said, standing up to stretch. "We have enough on our plate."

Tadgh took the lead once more. "Peader and I will go to Cashel and try to determine the tip starting point while you visit Blarney tomorrow. Then we'll meet you on the Rock. Now, Sam, may we impose on your parents to stir us up some lunch?"

Chapter Fourteen
Blarney

Thursday, July 13, 1916
Cork Train Station, Ireland

"There they are, over there," Morgan waved, as she and the O'Donnell couple waited at the Cork train station Thursday, just past noon.

"Good afternoon, Morgan." Jeffrey Wiggins greeted them as he strode over to the threesome. "As requested, I've brought young Aidan. It looks like he's come a long way since his bad-boy days at B&C."

Morgan hugged Tadgh's brother who hugged her back. "Yes, Tadgh and I are quite proud of him."

"And I of you both, Sis. How's the leg?"

"All better now, and you?"

"Fit as a fiddle, Morgan."

"Let me feel, then."

"Always the nurse, that's certain," Aidan said, putting his leg forward for her to examine."

"It seems fine to me, Brother," Morgan said after a gentle prodding of the sealed wound site. You'll live."

Jeffrey broke into the happy reunion. "I'm glad that you survived the Rising, lass. Martin told me of your harrowing escape from Howth."

Morgan kissed him on the cheek and whispered that he should stop talking about the Rising. His rosy face glowed from the exchange and he nodded his understanding. He turned toward the O'Donnells.

"Hello, Collin and Kathy. Friends of Tadgh and Morgan's are friends of mine. My chariot awaits over this way." He took Morgan's hand and led the group to the parked B&C lorry.

"What harrowing escape, sir?" Collin asked, as they reached the vehicle.

"Never you mind, son. I'm given to hyperbole, don't ya know."

Morgan stepped between the two men. "Mr. Wiggin's sea captain Martin Murphy helped us leave Dublin after the Rising. Thank you, Jeffrey. And we're here to tell the tale, so all's well that ends well, eh brother."

Kathy shared an alarmed look with her husband, but Collin let it drop.

En route to Queenstown, Morgan introduced the O'Donnells to Aidan.

"How can I help you all?" the lad asked, having shaken hands with Morgan's brother.

"We're on a grand adventure and you need to be involved," Morgan answered. "We'll fill you in on the way."

Thirty minutes later, the group stood on the pier of the Cunard Ship Line. Jack had been fretting all morning, nervous yet excited at the prospect of seeing Claire again in person. When he saw her coming down the pier, his heart skipped a beat, and he had to concentrate on keeping his bad leg from twitching.

"Is that him?" Kathy asked, referring to the uniformed young man standing upright with a cane by his side.

"I think so." Morgan scanned her memory and remembered a face similar to his. "It all happened so fast."

"I see that you survived the disaster, Claire," Jack said quietly, as they reached him. His heart pounded, and he felt himself take a deep breath.

Morgan reached out and took his outstretched hands in her own. "Jack, is it? I am so glad to meet you again at last. We all just wanted to come by. I never got a chance to thank you for saving me."

"You must have saved yourself, Claire. All I did was direct you to the boats."

"If you hadn't pried me away from the port side passengers, I would have gone down with the ship."

"Terrible tragedy, but at least we're both here now. I hope you have fully recovered your memory despite the amnesia."

"Yes, thanks to my brother and sister-in-law who came all this way to find me. We'd all like to thank you for making contact and arranging their travels."

Kathy rushed forward and shook Jack's hand vigorously. "Yes, our most grateful thanks, Jack. Without you, we would never have found each other."

"Careful, love. Don't hurt the man," Collin warned her. "It means a great deal to all of us."

Jack came to his senses. "Kathy, is it? Where's Sam?"

"With his father in Lisburn, Jack. He sends his regards."

"It was the least I could do I assure you," Jack blushed, trying to hide his nervousness. "Claire, I thought you were so brave that day on the ship." He bit his lip.

"I was in a state of shock, Jack. We all were."

"Most people panicked. But not you."

"And not you, either. I have heard that you have also been searching for me, and I want to thank you for that."

"I was hoping to get to know you better, Claire, much better." Jack could feel his pulse rate accelerate in anticipation of a response.

Morgan looked into his eyes. "I'd like to be your friend, Jack . . . but that's all it *can* be."

Before he could respond, she added, "Jack, I'm going to be married soon to a wonderful Irishman named Tadgh. He's the one who pulled me from the sea and saved me. We talked it over and decided. Tadgh would like you to be a groomsman. Would you accept?"

Jack's first thought was, *crumbs for the invalid,* but he answered, "Congratulations, Claire. I'd be honored. You were the inspiration for me to walk again. And, as you can see, I'm walking. So, thank you for helping me through these last few months." Inside, he was crestfallen, but he squared his shoulders and forced a smile.

"I'm called Morgan now, Jack," she said softly. She explained briefly how Tadgh had given her the name and what it meant to her. "You're a dear lad. Can we be friends?"

Jack wasn't ready to give up his dream, but he said, "Of course, Morgan," so as not to put her off.

"So, there will only be three of you wanting to go back to America on the twenty-third, then?"

"Yes, that's right, since I will be staying in Ireland and I'm soon to be married," Morgan answered, smiling at Collin. Her eyes darkened as she told him the bad news. "I understand that you contacted the RIC in your attempt to find me. Head Constable Boyle is the one, yes? He's a bad man, Jack. We've seen him kill people in cold blood."

Jack was taken aback. "Boyle's gruff, and I wouldn't trust him as far as I could spit, which isn't saying much in my condition. And Collin calls him a murderer. But he does represent law and order, surely."

"Take my word for it, Jack. He's ruthless and only thinking of his own selfish desires. We have something he wants, and he'll stop at nothing to get it." Morgan paused, "Even murder," she whispered hoarsely. "Have you found out where he is?"

"I contacted Inspector Maloney yesterday, knowing you were coming to see me, but I didn't tell him that. He told me that Boyle got himself released from hospital in Tralee, but he was ordered to bed rest at home for at least a month in Cork City to recover from his heart ailment. His condition apparently worsened when someone tried to smother him with a pillow."

Morgan offered, "I wouldn't count on Boyle following those orders, Jack."

The Cunard manager fidgeted with his cane. "He hasn't. Collin knows that Boyle came here and interrogated me with his mousey subordinate a couple of weeks back. He didn't seem sick. You don't need to tell me what a lout he is. Now I worry that Boyle will find a way to come after you because of my actions with the RIC. What can I do to help undo the damage?"

Morgan had an idea. "We think that Boyle has a man who has been following us recently. We need a few days free of him. It would be a big help to us if you could contact Inspector Maloney and tell him you saw us in Cork. It might divert his attention long enough for us to do what we need to do."

"I will see if I can contact him," Jack offered. He aimed to please the girl of his dreams.

"Thank you, Jack. But be careful. This man is very dangerous."

"Do you have the time for tea? I have it here steeping in the office."

"Another time, Jack," Morgan replied, taking and rubbing her hands in his, once again. "We're on a mission out of town this afternoon. But thank you for the offer, my friend."

"Will I see you again, Morgan?"

"We'll be neighbors of a sort, so yes, that would be nice." Morgan leaned in and gave him a hug.

Jack hugged back and held on, the energy of the embrace coursing through his body. The fragrant smell of her hair made him dizzy.

Morgan released her grip. Jack's spine sagged, and the cane dropped from the crook of his arm, so she caught him before he took a tumble.

"Here is your stick, Jack," Collin said, stepping forward as the Cunard manager forced himself to straighten up, taking the cane for support.

"Thank you, Collin. I guess I'm not as sturdy as I used to be," Jack said, lowering his eyes.

Morgan leaned over and kissed him on the cheek. "I think you are doing marvelously, Jack. We'll see you soon."

Jack brought himself to attention once more and raised his eyes to hers. He could see that those green orbs were sympathetic but not glowing with love for him. But sympathy was a start, and it gave him a glimmer of hope.

Constable Simpson notified Boyle just as they were setting up surveillance in Cashel at suppertime. "I checked with headquarters and you have a message from that Cunard agent."

"Damn. What does that cripple want now?"

"He says that he's seen McCarthy and his girl in Queenstown today. He thinks he knows where they might be. So, what do we do now, boss?"

"Jackson, I thought you said they were coming to Cashel."

"That's what they talked about on the train, boss," Leroy snarled back. He wasn't going to take Boyle's treatment for much longer.

"Go to Queenstown immediately. Interrogate Jordan and report back to me. We're staying in Cashel, Simpson. I think that they may have gotten Jordan to lead us away from here."

♣ ♣ ♣ ♣

"Whew. Do you think that we'll ever get to the top?" Morgan asked, after they had climbed ninety steep and narrow worn steps through the battlements of the Blarney Castle ruins.

"Looks like there are only thirty more steps to go," Collin guessed, looking up towards the sky.

Morgan reached ahead, putting her hand on her brother's shoulder.

Looking back down to his sister, he teased, "Let's keep climbing. You're as slow as a snail on a turtle's back."

"I feel as if I'm doing this in full body armor."

"That must have been fun in the old days."

Aidan, who had been bringing up the rear to make sure Morgan didn't fall, called out, "Hurry up. It'll be dark soon enough."

"It is interesting to imagine where each of the wooden floors would have been," Morgan observed once they reached the top, looking down through the interior of the shell of the castle. "Lord

Broghill's forces certainly destroyed a beautiful fortress." She took out the tailor's tape measure that Biddy had loaned them before they left Meenmore. Looking down from the south parapet along the interior of the outside wall, she could see the iron rails that visitors held onto while they bent backwards, head extended over the edge, to kiss the cold gray stone.

"Kind sir, can you tell us which of these embedded rocks they call the Blarney Stone? They all look alike in this wall to me, so they do," Collin asked of the wizened old caretaker who was there to ensure that nobody fell to their death.

"It's that bottom one down there about three feet, where the grab bars circle under," the caretaker explained. "See the flat one that looks different from the rest. You can see how it is holding up the outer parapet section. I hope you don't have a bad back, son. It's a torturous, backwards, heads-down reach with this rock edge pressing into your spine."

"We just need to get its measurements precisely for a university experiment we're doin'," Collin explained as he knelt down facing frontwards towards the hole. "Hey, look down there through the grate. I can see Kathy sitting waiting on that old bench. She looks like an ant from this height." Collin waved but his wife seemed to be dozing.

He bent at the waist, lowering his head, chest, and arms down into the cavity.

"Measurements, please," Morgan reminded him, as Aidan strained to hold his feet to stop him from falling.

"Length, twenty-seven inches," Collin called out. "Height, ten and one-half inches. Lower me farther down so I can measure the width of the stone and parapet."

"If I lower you much more, you'll be joining Kathy sooner than you think," Aidan exclaimed, grunting with the exertion. Morgan lent Tadgh's brother a hand.

"Good, width sixteen inches. Now, pull me up." Before they did, he twisted, arched his neck and head back and kissed the Blarney Stone. "A newspaper man can always use a little more gift of the gab."

After they had pulled Collin up, Morgan announced, "Now it's my turn, brother. I'm going to bend backwards conventionally and kiss the stone. Someday I'm going to write down my adventures for posterity and I can use all the Irish eloquence I can get."

Just then, Kathy happened to look up and saw Morgan dangling upside down a hundred feet above her head. "My dear Claire," she whispered, patting her abdomen, "I think we made a wise choice to wait down here, my baby. Your Auntie Morgan is risking her life again."

Collin helped Morgan stand up. The siblings and Aidan looked southwards towards the lake. Collin commented, "I can see why the attack came from the south. They shelled the castle from Card Hill above the lake, as Tadgh told us."

After the trio walked around the parapet to the northern exposure, Collin pointed to the horizon and said, "It would have been easy for the defenders to escape to the north undetected by doubling back out of the western Kerry exit from the caves down by that thicket."

They started back down the awkward stairs in the deepening dusk, and Morgan mused, "What must this castle have been like all lit up with tapers flickering on its wall tapestries back in the olden days?"

"Much the same as the interior of our ancestor's Donegal Castle, I expect."

"I can't imagine setting fire to my own castle like we were told Red High did, Collin."

"Desperate actions for desperate times, my dear. And we think we have it rough."

The three wound down the outer wall staircase over the castle entrance, and Collin cautioned, "Mind your step or you might fall down that murder hole to your left."

Morgan peered over and her imagination soared. Aidan grabbed her arm as she asked, "That looks right down to the base of the castle. What was it for?"

"They dumped boiling oil or tar down it to maim or kill invaders if they gained access."

Morgan held the handrail on the descent. "We have different visions of the romance of medieval times I guess, brother."

Jackson made good time driving back to Cork. It was midnight when he opened the door to his dingy flat, and after five stouts, he was insensible. But being an ex-military man, he was up early and gone already by five in the morning, guessing that a man pushing himself to regain his health would be an early riser.

Dawn was just breaking Friday morning when he pulled the police lorry to a stop around the corner from the Cunard pier. "I was right," he muttered to himself when he saw the light streaming from the Operations Manager's office. He noticed a few longshoremen working at the other end of the pier. *They won't be a problem unless they come this way.*

Bursting into the office, Jackson saw the nameplate on the invalid's desk.

"Good morning, Mr. Jordan."

"Good morning, sir. I'm sorry, but we don't open until seven thirty."

"I'm not here to book passage, man. I came because you called us."

"I'm confused."

"No uniform today. But I'm RIC."

"Oh, I see. You must work with Head Constable Boyle then. Do you have your badge, sir?"

"Something like that," the constable sneered, ignoring the request for identification. "What's this about seeing the fugitives?"

"They came here yesterday to rebook passage to Canada on the next troop ship. It was the girl from the *Lusitania*, her brother, and his wife," Jordon replied.

"Where was the girl's Irish boyfriend? We were told you saw him too."

"They said that he would arrive when they came for their tickets. I think that they will be here sometime today or tomorrow, so I guess they stayed the night in town."

"Are you damned sure that you're telling me the truth, son?" Jackson's face tightened, his black eyes glared and his sneer deepened.

He saw Jordan shift in his seat.

"Well, yes, of course. Why would I lie about such a simple thing?"

Jackson observed with satisfaction the slight hesitation in the answer and positioned his clenched fists on the manager's desktop. "It's a major offense to lie to a police officer about a murderer. I think that they were here, but you agreed to give us false information to keep us from apprehending them."

With worried eyes, Jordan tried to stand up. Jackson knew that he had guessed correctly.

Before Jordan could respond, Jackson reached over and pulled him up by the collar.

"Now you're going to tell me the truth. Where are they now?"

Jordan tried to squirm away without success. "Like I said, I don't know."

"That's not good enough, son," Jackson hissed, and slapped Jordan's jaw with his other hand hard enough to loosen teeth. "Where are they now?"

Jordan, his face clutched in both hands, spoke in a muffled voice. "If I knew, I'd tell you. But I don't."

The next blow knocked Jordan unconscious.

"I know where they're at, you invalid," the brute snarled. He couldn't believe that the light taps he'd given the boy had knocked him unconscious. "You must be sicker than I thought."

Since he didn't like loose ends, Jackson decided to bring Jordan along with him as an insurance policy. Give one liar to another, that officious bastard Boyle.

Checking the pier for witnesses and finding none, Jackson tucked the inert form under his arm as if Jordan was a rag doll and headed for the lorry. Once there, he tied his prisoner's arms and legs with a stout cord and stuffed him on the floor of the back seat. Surely, Boyle didn't like to leave loose ends either, he reasoned, as he steered the lorry northward toward Cashel.

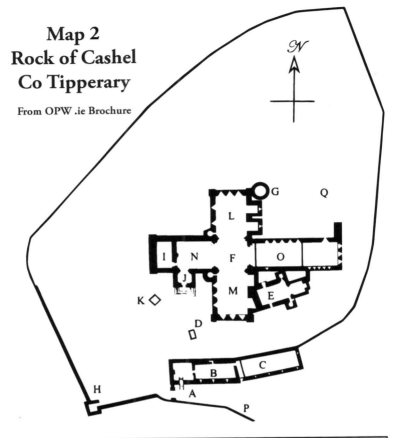

Map 2
Rock of Cashel
Co Tipperary

From OPW .ie Brochure

Table 1. Rock of Cashel Elements - Legend			
Loc'n	**Name**	**Loc'n**	**Name**
A	Entrance	J	Porch
B	Hall of Vicar's Choral	K	Man Size Rock (Ruin)
C	Dormitory of Vicar's Choral	L	Cathedral North Transept
D	St. Patrick's Cross	M	Cathedral South Transept
E	Cormac's Chapel	N	Cathedral Nave
F	Cathedral Tower	O	Cathedral Choir
G	Round Tower	P	Bishop's Walk
H	Enclosing Walls and Corner Tower	Q	Graveyard
I	Bishop's Castle		

Chapter Fifteen
Cormac's Chapel

Friday, July 14, 1916
Cashel, Ireland

*T*wo **pilgrims stepped** off the train in Cashel at noon that Friday. They were plainly dressed, in black cloaks with matching wide brim hats. Their bushy black beards obscured their facial features. Tadgh didn't see mutton chops in plain clothes skulking behind a newspaper, and Simpson didn't recognize his prey.

As they were starting the walk up to the Rock, Peader asked, "When do you expect Wiggins with the others?"

Tadgh checked his watch. "They should meet us at the rendezvous point just after the complex closes at five this afternoon, if all went well. Meanwhile comrade, our job is to try and find the *tip*."

From his perch behind the rock wall, on the 'Path of the Dead'[5.1] between Camas Road and the Rock, Boyle could see them coming from a mile away. Pilgrims were common to this Rock, but these two looked suspicious. *Where were the rest of them?* he wondered, expecting Jackson to be back shortly with news.

He watched the pair as they walked slowly up Bishop's Walk under the fortifications until they disappeared up onto the Rock of Cashel complex two hundred feet above the town. Since there was no sign of Simpson, he decided that they had not come by train. It maddened him to wait for his minions. Then he remembered how patient his mother had been, compared to the fiery intolerance of his father, and that calmed him for the moment.

♣   ♣   ♣   ♣

The two pilgrims entered the historical complex through the south wall near its west end, adjacent to the fifteenth century Hall of the Vicars Choral. There were only a few visitors milling about. Stepping into the inner courtyard, they viewed an old Celtic cross,[5.2] with one subsidiary support piece missing.

"That is the oldest religious relic on this mountain, to be sure," Tadgh said, as they walked the fifty feet to the ancient stone. "This is the High Cross of Cashel, or St. Patrick's Celtic Cross, which is at the focal point on the Rock back in the fifth century. My pa told me about it. That's the place where the saint himself baptized my ancestor, the Munster King Aegnus, in the fifth century, apparently the first king in Ireland to be converted to Christianity."

"Right after your clan moved here from Wales, then, Tadgh?"

"Yes. Pa said that as part of the ceremony, St. Patrick struck the ground with his staff three times. On one of those blows, he hit the King's foot and pierced through it. The stoic King said nothing, thinking that it was a part of the baptism ceremony. From that time on, it is told, my ancestors used the base of St. Patrick's High Cross as the location for crowning all their kings. You can see an image of Jesus on the cross on the west side and what looks like St. Patrick with his staff here on the east side facing the chapel."

Tadgh stepped up onto the flagstone base and reverently touched the worn relief of his patron saint, letting his hand rest on the cold gray stone.

"The way the larger church was built onto Cormac's Chapel is unusual, to say the least," Peader said, as they stepped the few paces to the cathedral ruins after passing by St. Patrick's Cross. "The Chapel is nestled right in the crook of the cathedral diagonally east of the south transept."

"Right enough, lad. It's the history of this sacred place that explains its architecture. The round tower just east of the north transept was the first building on the Rock in about one thousand AD. It protected the *Eoghanachta* forefathers from foreign invaders. That's why its door stands eight feet off the ground. The graveyard lies to its east, where my ancestors could be protected from grave robbers by yeomen in the tower. Come, let's take a look."

Tadgh walked them past the chapel and around the east end of the cathedral to where the ancient tower stood in near the crook of the cathedral east of the north transept.

"An impressive circular structure. It sounds as if you studied this history, my friend."

"My pa brought Aidan and me here when I was twelve, just two years before he was murdered. It is traditional for the McCarthy men to make sure our heritage is passed on generation to generation. By this sentinel tower, he read us one of my great-great-uncle Denis's [4] poems titled, *The Pillar Towers of Ireland*[4.1] to emphasize how sacred this ancient MacCarthaigh fortress is. I memorized a few verses. Let me recite them for you—

> *The pillar towers of Ireland, how wondrously they stand*
> *By the lakes and rushing rivers through the valleys of our land;*
> *In mystic file, through the isle, they lift their heads sublime,*
> *These gray old pillar temples, these conquerors of time!*
>
> *. . . Where blazed the sacred fire, rung out the vesper bell*
> *Where the fugitive found shelter, became the hermit's cell;*
> *And hope hung out its symbol to the innocent and good,*
> *For the cross o'er the moss of the pointed summit stood."*

"That sounds like this tower on this summit and this old cross, Tadgh."

"Aye, Peader, and there's more,

> *There may it stand for ever, while that symbol doth impart*
> *To the mind one glorious vision, or one proud throb to the heart;*

While the breast needeth rest may these gray old temples last,
Bright prophets of the future, as preachers of the past!"

Peader patted the worn rocks, trying to pull himself up to peer into the darkness of the door opening, its oaken door long since disintegrated. "Those are the words of a true Irish storyteller, a poetic *seanachai*, so to speak. He obviously kissed the Blarney Stone as did you, my fine friend."

"Aye. I think I attempted playwriting in Dublin because of Denis's influence. He was a profound poet."

"Prescient, given our little adventure, don't you think, Tadgh?"

"I've been thinking about that ever since we decided to come here, comrade."

Peader looked to the northeast, away from the cathedral ruins. "Speaking of the *'cross o'er the moss of the pointed summit'*, look at all the Irish crosses in the cemetery. So many different designs."

Tadgh gazed out upon his ancestors' resting place. "The names are gone now, obliterated by the rains of time, but my pa showed me several locations, marking my ancestors from eons ago as described to him by his pa before him."

"It's wonderful to have that heritage right here where your Welsh ancestors settled fifteen hundred years ago."

Tadgh slapped his forehead and grabbed Peader by the shoulder. "*Pointed summit*, comrade. Could it be that simple?"

"What?"

"Could it be that the *tip* is the pointed top of the tower? It is the highest pinnacle on the Rock."

"Wouldn't that mean that your uncle knew about the clues to the treasure? That would seem impossible."

Tadgh grimaced. "You're right, Peader. And besides, how would they have climbed to the top to take the measurements? It has to be a hundred feet high."

"And the CC in the riddle presumably refers to the chapel, doesn't it?"

Just to be sure, Peader hoisted Tadgh up through the raised opening of the ancient tower. There was barely enough light to examine the interior and confirm it empty.

"We can return here if we exhaust all the other possibilities," Tadgh said, after Peader let him back down.

"Since your pa brought you here and recited your great-uncle's poetry, do you think that he could have known that the treasure was here on site?"

"No, I don't think so."

"But he knew how important your locket was. Perhaps he figured out the clues as far as we have done but could proceed no further."

"He would have had to be working with Collin's pa, and I never heard him speak the name O'Donnell."

"Yet there is a connection, isn't there. Boyle murdered both men."

Tadgh pounded his fist against the rugged tower wall. "He's killed his last innocent Irishman, Peader. Mark my words, it's his turn, and I'm going to be his executioner." He sucked his scraped knuckles.

"Then we'd better get busy to find the *tip* starting point, Tadgh, before that villain does. I say we investigate CC."

When they reached the southeast entrance of the old gothic-looking chapel, Peader said, "So, where did Cormac come into all of this?"

Tadgh explained. "Cormac MacCarthaigh was a very forward-thinking King at the time after King Brian Boru drove off the Vikings and unified Ireland in the eleventh century. Cormac built the chapel in 1134 to ingratiate himself with the new ruler, as the MacCarthaigh dynasty was being forced to move south to Munster. And it isn't just any old Irish chapel. Along with Clontarf in Dublin, it is the oldest existing Romanesque church in Ireland. You can see the Germanic influence in its two square towers."

"So he built but never used it, himself?"

"That's what I was told. The Catholic Cathedral facing due east was built later in the thirteenth century, long after my Clan moved south to Munster. I can show you if you'd like. It's an aisle-less cruciform design that had a central tower. Quite impressive in its time, I was told."

"What about the west end of the cathedral, Tadgh? Nearer to St. Patrick's Cross. The stonework looks newer than the main structure."

"How observant of you, comrade. In the fifteenth century, Archbishop Richard O'Hedrian built this five-story Bishop's Castle, adding on to this end of the Cathedral. He's also the cleric who built the separate Hall of the Vicars Choral to the south of the cathedral where we came in through the wall."

Tadgh led Peader through the south door of the chapel. Passing over the threshold, they found themselves in a small eighteen by fifty-foot vaulted interior.

"This must have been something in its day," Peader remarked, running his hand over the rough texture of the cool south wall. "Look at the faded frescoes on the ceiling and walls."

"They were almost obliterated in the seventeenth century when Cromwell's forces ordered them whitewashed. As it is, only recently have they been partially uncovered. So if the *tip* clue does lie in one of these frescoes, Cromwell could have inadvertently destroyed the key to the treasure. How's that for irony?"

Peader pointed toward the west wall, "And what's that sarcophagus over there? It must have been an important person to have such ornate carvings."

"They're not sure if it contains the remains of Cormac or his brother Tadgh MacCarthaigh," Tadgh replied, trying unsuccessfully to lift the corner of the box lid to look inside.

"Your namesake, then, my friend?"

"There have been many Tadghs in the McCarthy bloodline, lad."

With the air in the chapel crowded with ghosts of ancient times, Peader turned to Tadgh. "What's the story about the cathedral?"

"One of the bloodiest massacres in Irish history occurred on this hill, indeed in this very cathedral next door." Tadgh paused suddenly, and Peader shivered as if a spirit's cold finger had touched him on the shoulder. "Come with me, Peader."

Tadgh led his comrade out of the chapel and into the cathedral ruins. Standing at the intersection of the south and north transepts, he continued with the story. "About a year after Blarney Castle was besieged by Lord Broghill of the family Boyle, the Irish Confederate army was in retreat northwards. They took a stand here on the Rock of Cashel. Murrough, the Baron of Inchiquin attacked and burned to death all of the villagers and confederate soldiers. Three thousand men, women, and children were killed, roasted on this hill in September 1647, many of them while they sought protection in the sanctity of this Catholic cathedral. That's why he was called Murrough of the Burnings. Good friend of the Boyles, by the way. The attacking forces stripped the cathedral of its valuables. It was just one glaring example in the long list of British atrocities over the ages."

"Could it be that '*Where blazed the sacred fire, rung out the vesper bell. Where the fugitive found shelter, became the hermit's cell,*' was meant to be this very spot?" Peader asked, reaching down to feel the rough stone floor at the center of the ruins.

"There was nothing *sacred* about that fire, lad."

Peader shuddered. "There's quite the checkered history here, Tadgh. Do you think that they attacked Cashel because they knew about the Clans Pact and the clues leading to the McCarthy gold?"

"Well, now." Tadgh scratched his chin. "That's a possibility. Lord Broghill was a Boyle and, as we know, his father, Richard Boyle had been given the *Book of MacCarthaigh* five years earlier by one of his other sons. These were the ancestors of Head Constable Boyle, using similar 'kill the vermin' tactics that he has been using. I can only guess that Boyle wouldn't be trying to kill us if his family had already found the gold. They didn't have the lockets, so they wouldn't have had any trail that we know of to this Rock."

"Unless they trailed the Blarney castle defenders here when they buried the treasure, Tadgh."

"Unlikely, I should think, Peader. We don't know for certain when the treasure was buried. If it happened when Blarney was being besieged, Broghill would have found it then, and Inchiquin would not have been searching for it a year later."

"I can see why your Clan Chieftain Florence would pick this sacred family place to hide the McCarthy treasure when the time came. But you'd think that whoever hid the family wealth would have divulged its location to someone."

"There was a strong Clan bond in those days, Peader. They would have died with the secret intact. Now where is that *tip*?"

"There are a lot of tips around here. The tiptop of one of the two Germanic Towers of Cormac's Chapel, and more besides. And if it was the tiptop of the cathedral roof, it doesn't exist anymore."

"It could also be the tip of any one of the High Crosses out in the graveyard, or even of St. Patrick's Cross for that matter, Peader. One thing, though, it's got to be symbolic. I don't think it would be anything obvious like the tip of the round tower."

"I haven't seen anything that jumps out at me. You?"

"No. Let's keep looking. The answer may be found in the dimensions that Morgan, Collin, and Kathy hopefully have acquired, don't ya know."

"Who the hell do you have there?" Boyle spat when Jackson showed up late that afternoon on the 'Path of the Dead' with a hooded and gagged hostage, who squirmed like a fish on a hook.

"It's that stupid Cunard agent who insisted on lying to me this morning," Jackson muttered, dropping Jack against the wall. "He was the decoy."

"You *idiot*! Did anyone see you? Now they'll trace his disappearance to me. We won't be able to let him go after this."

"What's done is done," Jackson shrugged. He kicked Jordan in the stomach to quiet him and vent his own anger at his boss. "I still think that we will need a hostage before this caper is over, or whatever this is."

Jordan retched and writhed in pain. Boyle pulled out his Webley and knocked him over the head with the butt of the revolver, just once, rendering the Cunard agent senseless. The two officers glared at each other, each scheming how to get rid of the other.

"Go get Simpson at the train station. He's as stupid as you are."

A few hours later, four more pilgrims trudged their way up onto the Rock having left Wiggins at its base to guard the lorry. Morgan outlined the situation to Aidan during the climb.

"Is that what you and Tadgh have been doing all this time? Treasure hunting?"

"You'll find out soon enough, Aidan."

They picked their way around the visitor barricade since it was now after hours.

"There you are, safe and sound, my love," Tadgh exclaimed, when Morgan entered the chapel. The afternoon light streaming in through the cathedral ruins to the tiny window high up on the west Chapel wall caught her rosy cheeks and dimpled chin in its ethereal glow.

"You look just like an angel, standing there, aroon. Don't move." Tadgh crossed to her and took her in his arms, kissing her deep on the mouth.

"I missed you too, my love," she murmured, as she returned his kisses, hugging him with all her might.

Tadgh sniffed the top of her forehead and lingered there, seemingly drinking in the perfume of her hair, she supposed. Morgan wondered whether this sudden public show of affection had anything to do with her having met up with Jack Jordan. Or was it a show for Collin?

Aidan gave his brother a hearty handshake and then hugged Morgan.

"Well, well, brother. You're a sight for these sore eyes. It's past time for you to be involved in our Clans adventure. This is your heritage as well as mine and the rest of our comrades. Welcome to the adventurers."

Aidan was taken aback. "What happened to your obsession with the revolution and killing Boyle, Tadgh?"

"All in good time, brother. First let's find our family treasure so it can be used for the revolution as our ancestors ordained."

Tadgh looked over Morgan's head at Kathy and Collin and asked, "Well, what have you learned?"

Collin hastily retrieved a folded paper from his pocket and read aloud, "L equals twenty-seven inches, W equals sixteen inches, and H equals ten and a half inches."

"Astounding, Collin. Good work," Tadgh replied, "but unless we can find that *tip*, that data is useless. As you can see, there are too many tips around here. We've been searching for hours, and we're stumped."

Tadgh and Peader spent the better part of the next hour walking, pointing, and describing all the tips that they had considered in the complex, to no avail. They were alone in the complex, or so they thought.

Morgan asked suddenly, "What about the Centaur? You must have seen it. The one above the north entrance to the chapel."

"The what?" Tadgh looked up at her with a puzzled expression.

"You know. The half-man, half-beast. The one I saw when I went through the north door of the chapel."

"I'm not following you, aroon."

Peader scoffed at Morgan's suggestion. "You mean the entrance that goes nowhere? The one inaccessible from outside because it's blocked by the south transept and the south wall of the cathedral?"

"Let's look, anyhow," Tadgh countered. "It's at least good as anything you and I've come up with so far today."

They all rushed out of the north entrance into the small, enclosed courtyard and looked back and upwards.

Morgan saw Tadgh's and Peader's shocked expressions. "Really, you men are so observant."

There on the tympanum[5.3] above the five Romanesque arches and columns was the ancient scene of a centaur looking back over his shoulder with bow and arrow in hand, either attacking, or defending itself from a huge, angry lion.

Morgan pointed. "It's as plain as the nose on your face. The tip in question is the *tip* of the centaur's arrow. What better metaphor to use than a man-beast taking his territory back from a ferocious aggressor. Sort of a David and Goliath biblical story. At least that's what I think."

Tadgh saw the symbolism immediately. "Morgan, you're so clever. That's got to be it. Before the cathedral was built, this was the main entrance to the chapel." Changing the subject, he asked, "Did you bring the sextant, Morgan?"

Morgan retrieved her shoulder bag from where she had dropped it in the chapel and handed the instrument to Tadgh, saying, "Wiggins got it for us from Captain Murphy. Why do you need this old sextant on dry land?"

"The third measurement is a compass heading, isn't it?"

Peader was puzzled. "I don't understand the directions if the locket refers to multiples of the Blarney Stone dimensions. Remind me. What is the inscription in Collin's locket, Tadgh?"

McCarthy took a crumpled paper from his pocket and spread it out against the ancient chapel wall. "*CCtip, BSt, L42, H22, WN164D.*" He scribbled on the page with his pencil before adding, "Well, the inscription height is twenty-two. Multiply that by ten and a half inches and you get two hundred and thirty-one inches."

"That would make it a little more than nineteen feet," Morgan announced, having made the division in her head.

"You're a marvel, my love."

"Nurses have to be precise, you know, Tadgh."

"The point of the arrow is about ten feet above ground level. Hoist me up, Collin."

While Tadgh held the end of his cloth tape-measure up to the arrow tip, Morgan read the measurement at the flagstone floor. "Eleven feet, nine inches, to be exact. Then the McCarthy gold should be buried a little more than seven feet deep," she calculated, while Collin eased Tadgh back down.

"That sounds reasonable. L is forty-two. That would mean that the place to start digging should be twenty-seven times forty-two inches away from the point directly under the tympanum in this archway."

"That would make it about ninety-five feet away," Morgan worked out in her head. "But in what direction?"

"According to the locket, the direction should be north sixteen times one hundred and sixty-four degrees clockwise."

They all looked at Morgan for the multiplication. "That doesn't make sense." She grabbed Tadgh's paper and pencil and calculated. A minute later she was scratching her head. "It comes out to two thousand six hundred and twenty-four. That can't be right. There are only three hundred and sixty degrees in a circle, right?"

"That's right, my love." Tadgh thought for a minute. "If they divided it by twelve like we have done for the distances that would be about two hundred degrees, wouldn't it?"

Morgan scratched on the paper. "Two hundred and nineteen to be precise."

They all gathered round Tadgh as he stood under the north chapel doorway and summarized. "All right, adventurers. We are looking for a spot ninety-five feet from here at an angle thirty-nine degrees west of south. Then we dig down seven feet since the land is fairly level here."

Morgan looked where Tadgh was pointing. "Doesn't that direction take us through the corner of the chapel and cathedral?"

"Yes."

"So how would they have measured it, especially under the cover of night? Maybe I was wrong. This location isn't the starting point."

"Your explanation of tip makes so much sense, though, aroon. There has to be something else. Some other clue." Tadgh held the copied inscription page up to the fading light of the enclosed courtyard. "I don't see anything more."

Kathy had been sitting quietly on the sarcophagus and got up to join the group in the yard. "Show me your locket, love."

Collin slipped the necklace over his head and handed it to her. "Tadgh already transcribed the inscription."

"I am just cross-checking, my love." Kathy opened the locket and held the lettering up to the waning light. "This writing is very small, isn't it? Did you bring that magnifying glass, Tadgh?"

"Yes, Sam's father lent it to me." Tadgh took a glass out of his pocket and handed it to her.

Kathy examined the inscription in the locket.

Tadgh was impatient. "There's nothing more there, Kathy."

"A fine job of transcription you did, except—"

"Except what?"

"Did you see the tiny letters after the word 'tip'?"

"What letters? Let me see." Tadgh took the locket and the glass. "Oh, that mark. It just looks like a comma to me."

Morgan took the magnifier and pored over the inscription. After what seemed like a minute, she said, "There are two tiny letters after the word *tip*. I can't make them out."

Kathy reached for the locket. "Let a schoolmarm look at it again."

She turned it to the light and peered through the glass, adjusting its distance from the lettering to maximize the magnification. "I think the letters are SD."

Collin interjected. "Are you sure, darlin'? They're mighty small."

"Yes, I'm sure, my love. I have to decipher my students' terrible scribbly handwriting, don't I?'

Morgan took the glass and squinted through it. "Now that you say it, I can see the letters." She clasped her sister-in-law on the shoulder. "Good work, Kathy, but what, if anything does it mean?"

Tadgh said, "It means that our ancestors buried one last almost indecipherable riddle for those of us who are blessed with Divine intervention to solve. And it took Kathy, an O'Donnell by marriage, to do it." He gave her a big hug. "You helped Collin find us and now this crucial contribution. You're one of us, lass. Thank you for staying."

Kathy tried to hide her smile and said, "Well, I didn't have much choice in that, did I."

Tadgh hugged her even harder.

Peader had been watching the proceedings with interest. "Could it have to do with Saint Dichu? He was the first convert of St. Patrick up north in Ulster, my part of the country in the fifth century."

Morgan thought for a minute. "It must have to do with this Rock of Cashel, and the chapel. What if SD stands for *south door*, which is directly opposite the north one? Florence would have had to use the symbolic tympanum above the north doorway for the starting point, but the measurement has to originate from the opposite south doorway to lead directly out into the open courtyard. Just one more hurdle to put in our way, so he made it almost invisible."

"That's about as obtuse as all the other clues," Tadgh said, moving the group to the southern entrance. "So what if this is the starting point?" With his nautical experience, looking south, he turned roughly forty degrees west and started pacing until he ran into the wall of the Vicar's Choral.

The adventurers had followed his every move.

"Bollocks!" he exclaimed. "I could be off by a couple of feet, but those directions put the treasure right under this thick wall or possibly the floor of the building beyond."

"Wasn't the Hall of the Vicar's Choral here in 1600, Tadgh?"

"Yes, it was, Collin. It was built in the fifteenth century."

"Could they have buried it here, mavourneen?"

Tadgh slowly shook his head. "It would have been very difficult and would have required some demolition which would have attracted the attention of the clergy. No, I don't think so. It would have been a secretive operation by a few trusted men."

"Are you sure of your measurements?"

"Close enough, Aidan."

Morgan sighed audibly. "Maybe I was wrong, and the spear isn't the tip we are looking for."

"But your explanation seemed so fitting, aroon. No, we must still be missing something." Tadgh took out the paper with the inscriptions, went back to Cormac's Chapel and sat down on the sarcophagus. The sun was barely filtering high up through the small western window, illuminating the arched ceiling, which cast an eerie glow on the adventurers below.

Collin looked at his watch. "It'll be dusk soon, Tadgh. We may have to leave for the day."

"I hear you, lad, but there's something in this inscription that we're missing, and I want to figure it out now."

"Let's come back tomorrow, mavourneen. I'm shivering in this damp chapel. Your backside must be frozen from that cold stone seat."

"That's it. That's the word that bothers me. The word 'stone'." Tadgh pointed to some letters on the paper.

"I can't see anything, it's so dark in here with the sunlight fading."

They all walked out through the adjacent south door and Tadgh held the paper up to the dimming sunlight.

Peader pointed at the paper. "It's just the symbol for Blarney Stone, BSt."

"Maybe not, Peader. I thought that the lowercase *t* in *BSt* was part of an abbreviation for the word stone. But what if the *t* has its own meaning that pertains to all the Blarney Stone measurements?"

"What do you mean?"

Tadgh knew he was sounding like Lawlor again. "I seem to recall that there was an ancient Irish name for a nautical measurement that started with *t*. What was it? Trough? No, *troighid*. That's it."

"I remember Pa teaching us that word," Aidan said, craning

forward to examine the cryptic message on the page with a frown. "Does this scribble actually mean something?"

"It's the key to our future, brother and possibly the future of the revolution."

Collin turned to Tadgh. "So, what is its length?"

"Three palm widths or one man's foot. It had to do with the number of times a sailor would wrap the jib line around his hand to hold it fast, I think."

Morgan smiled. "*Now* who holds the font of all knowledge, mavourneen? Give us your hand."

Tadgh held out his palm and Morgan measured with the cloth tape. "My, your hand is wide. Three and a half inches, give or take across your palm."

"You know what they say, aroon, about big hands." He grinned mischievously.

"What, big heart?" she teased.

He grinned back at her.

"Tadgh, not in front of the others."

Collin mused, "I wonder if men were smaller in those days?"

"This is the best measurement that we have, Collin."

"All right, you two," Collin laughed. "If Tadgh is right, then the 't' in the inscription stands for ten and a half inches, give or take. What are the dimensions, if we assume the inscription is in those units, whatever you called them?"

"Troighids. Morgan will calculate that for us, Collin, won't you, aroon."

She took Tadgh's paper and figured the numbers while the others waited in the waning daylight. They could see that she was confused by the wrinkle of her nose and eyes.

"What is it, Sis?"

"Stop me if I'm wrong, Collin. If they measured the Blarney Stone in troighids and the distances here in troighids, wouldn't the multiplication factor be the same as when we measured both in feet and inches?"

"I'm no mathematician, but that sounds right."

"Then the calculations we did previously for length and depth should still be valid. The only thing which will change is the angle measurement. What I've calculated here is that the width of the *Blarney Stone* is a little more than one and a half troighids. Multiplying by one hundred and sixty-four gives an angle of two hundred and fifty degrees. Is that better?"

"Let's see," Tadgh said, walking them back through the chapel north doorway into the enclosed triangular courtyard, Tadgh stepped to the northeast corner where the cathedral and the chapel north Germanic tower walls met. Aligning the sextant horizontally along the south wall of the cathedral, he adjusted the instrument. "Twenty degrees."

"What does that mean?"

"The angle between these two walls is twenty degrees. It means that this wall of Cormac's Chapel, in which the tympanum is located, which is parallel with the chapel's major axis, is two hundred and fifty degrees clockwise from north if the cathedral axis is due east-west, as it should be."

Morgan realized the truth. "That also means that Cormac's Chapel is not just a clue but also a pointer. Tadgh, you said that when this chapel was built, the only other edifices on this hill were the round tower and the High Cross."

"That's right."

"Well then, it seems to me that the chapel was positioned such that the doors are aligned with the round tower and the chapel's main axis points roughly towards St. Patrick's High Cross to the southwest, doesn't it?"

They all rushed to the south door of the chapel where they could see the cross. Directly in line.

Collin threw up his hands in triumph. "Eureka, as Archimedes once said."

Morgan finally voiced their collective conclusion. "Could it be

261

that the treasure is buried under St. Patrick's High Cross?"

Peader repeated Tadgh's earlier history lesson. "The base of which is the spot where St. Patrick baptized the first Irish king and where all the early Eoghanactha MacCarthaigh kings were crowned."

Tadgh muttered, *"And hope hung out its symbol to the innocent and good, For the cross o'er the moss of the pointed summit stood."*

Peader chimed in, "My God, Tadgh. How did he know?"

"What is that all about and who is 'he'?" Morgan asked, turning quickly towards the men.

Tadgh explained about his great uncle's poem regarding pillar towers.

They all stood there, taking in the significance of the moment.

"There you go, now. There's only one way to find out if we're right, friends," Tadgh said.

Morgan stepped back to where the south Germanic tower met the main chapel south wall and looked back along the wall southwest towards St. Patrick's Cross. "If I sight down the south side of the chapel past the door, I can just barely see the Cross past the south transept of the cathedral. See, above the foundation of the cathedral where it necks in?"

"You're right, Morgan. Let's check the length."

After measuring several lengths of the cloth tape-measure they had borrowed from Aunt Biddy, Tadgh and Morgan arrived at the cross. "It's one hundred feet from the chapel door to the base of the cross."

"Since the courtyard is level between here and the chapel, by my calculation the treasure should be about seven and a half feet below us." Tadgh kicked the sand off the large flagstone four feet east of the cross. "We dig here!"

♣ ♣ ♣ ♣

Darcy Boyle snuck back from his hiding position behind the northwest corner of the Bishop's Castle and signaled to his men on the Path of the Dead. He had been dogging McCarthy's group from the shadows throughout their evening of discovery, gloating over the success of his recent cat and mouse *modus operandi*. These vermin were mere pawns in the hands of a chess master. His lifelong goal, handed down to him from his punitive ancestors, was finally coming to fruition. His father had beaten their ancient family mission into him and now, tonight he would reap the reward he so righteously deserved on behalf of all the Boyles.

He tried to erase the recurring vision of his mother pleading with her abusive husband to go easy on their only son. She was always the compassionate one, right up until that horrendous night when his pa got the better of her. He hated that he hadn't tried to defend her, but his father's menacing orders rendered him powerless. Darcy couldn't let her memory cloud his mind tonight when it needed to be so sharp.

After McCarthy found the gold for him, Boyle would torture the O'Donnell boys until they told him what he needed to know. Then, in an historically glorious fashion, he would kill them all off. It was ordained.

Chapter Sixteen
McCarthy Gold

Friday, July 14, 1916
Rock of Cashel, Ireland

*J*ackson circled north through the graveyard, hefting Jordon's body over his shoulder. Simpson silently trailed along after him, burdened with the cans and rope.

Boyle communicated with hand signals when they reached him. Propping Jordan in a sitting position against the north wall of the Bishop's Castle ruins, Jackson joined his boss, peering cautiously around the structure.

"The German spies have discovered something," Boyle whispered, putting his arm out to hold his underling back. "They are going to uncover contraband German arms for their rebel cause. We'll apprehend them after the evidence is in their hands. Did you bring the rope and containers that I had down at the observation point?"

"Simpson brought them. He's back there guarding the hostage."

"Did you take care of the night watchman?"

The sergeant lied through his teeth. "Sleeping like a baby." He had slit the watchman's throat.

"Simpson is an undercover spy for these villains," Boyle hissed, grabbing Jackson's shoulder in a vise grip. "We're going to have to take care of him with the rest."

Jackson knew that was bullshit, but said, "Sure, boss." He knew that he would have to take care of all of them, especially Boyle himself when the time came.

♣ ♣ ♣ ♣

"My God. This must be the place!" Tadgh exclaimed excitedly, looking up at the time-worn image of a monk holding a crozier. "St. Patrick. What better place to hide the treasure, than under the watchful eye of our patron saint?"

"Tadgh, we're six feet east of the High Cross, just off the three-step mount of the base," Collin measured with the tape. "And this is a pretty big piece of ancient-looking flagstone in this pathway."

"It was probably put there to discourage digging in this area. This is where we'll dig," Tadgh instructed. "Morgan, did Jeffrey bring the equipment that I asked for?"

"Yes, he's in the lorry at the base of the Rock."

Collin headed for the south exit. "C'mon Peader. Let's go. We'll have him drive up to the entrance."

Tadgh held them up. "Then have him drive back down into town until we need him. I don't want to attract any attention."

While they were gone, Tadgh examined St. Patrick's High Cross thoroughly. With one of its Latin side supports missing, it was clear that this sacred relic of Christendom had been defaced during the Inchiquin massacre. He noticed a moveable portion of the base. Prying it to the side with his knife, he found a hidden compartment of about one cubic foot inside. Empty. He wondered what might have been hidden there centuries ago.

The O'Donnells returned at that moment with two spades, a shovel, a pail, a crowbar, some rope, a ladder, and four gas torches, all of which distracted Tadgh.

"Let's try and move this flagstone," Tadgh said, so intent on finding the treasure that he let his normal guard down without scouting the perimeter.

Tadgh could see the sun starting to set behind Hore Castle out on the western plain as they began their excavation.

"Come on, boys. Put your backs into it," Morgan urged them as they strained to lift the flagstone up with the crowbar and their bare hands. "We're going to run out of light before long."

"Yeow!" Peader yelled as the large flat stone broke the suction of the earth and flipped up, missing his chin by inches.

"What kind of soil do we have to work with?" Collin asked as Tadgh dug the first shovelful.

"Gravel base, but it looks like sand and clay below," Tadgh replied, examining the dirt he had excavated. "We men should take shifts diggin'."

Morgan broke in, "Let me take a shift, too."

Remembering that she and Aidan were still recovering from gunshot wounds in the leg, Tadgh said, "How about you spell Aidan if his leg starts hurting."

"Fair enough, mavourneen. I'll just keep the surface dirt from falling back into the hole with this shovel."

Tadgh took charge. "All right, you and me then, Aidan, at either end of the hole, spelled by Collin and Peader when we get tired."

In all the excitement, Tadgh had almost forgotten the threat of Boyle and his men. "I forgot to ask. What did you learn about Boyle's whereabouts, lass?"

Morgan told him what Jack had said.

Tadgh hoped that Boyle had not gotten wind that they were at Cashel, although he relished the thought of another opportunity to settle the score with him. "There isn't a thing I wouldn't put past Boyle or Maloney." He stopped digging and turned to Kathy. "Lass, can you stand guard while we dig? Keep a watch for any movement at all."

"All right, but I'm not going to venture out around the grounds in the dark, Tadgh."

"That's fine, stay close. And those who are not digging should also be vigilant in case those RIC goons show up." Tadgh automatically checked that his Luger was still in his trouser pocket before returning to his task. He soon caught up with Morgan.

"We're down about three feet," Collin measured an hour later. "This is startin' to look like a burial site, don't it, now."

"Maybe we'll bury Boyle in it if he shows up," Tadgh wisecracked.

Kathy shuddered. "A chill just ran down my spine."

♣ ♣ ♣ ♣

Boyle heard what McCarthy said and decided to wait behind the Bishop's Castle on the west end of the cathedral until it was dark. Halfway between that ruined structure and the High Cross, he spotted a man-high angular boulder sunken into the grassy area. When the time came, his men would move forward using that rock as a cover. Then they'd be only thirty feet from the excavation.

♣ ♣ ♣ ♣

Just as Tadgh was thinking about asking Collin to light the torches, several localized spotlights popped on, illuminating the High Cross, and the exteriors of both the Chapel and the Cathedral ruins.

"That's convenient," Aidan muttered as he hoisted his next shovelful of dirt out of the hole.

The night progressed. The hole deepened and made the digging that much more arduous. The pit now measured five feet across and six feet in the direction away from the cross at a depth of five feet.

"It's getting bloody hard to see down here," Collin muttered, as he took his turn digging. A hollow thud sounded, as his next shovel dug into the dirt. He felt down with his hand, scraping the soil aside. "I've struck wood. I need light down here, Kathy."

Tadgh peered over the edge, holding his breath as Kathy fumbled to light the torch.

"Logs!" Collin yelled out, as the yellowed beam found the bottom. "There's a raft of logs down here."

"There ye go now. That's a good sign to be sure." Tadgh requested excavation of the logs.

They soon realized that they had been digging a little too far from the High Cross. The roughly six-inch diameter logs ran towards and away to the east from the base of the religious relic. Their eastern ends were located inside the space they had dug. By excavating around and below the ends right up to the cross's base, they were able to provide a grab point on the three central logs.

"Aidan, you try to leverage the middle log up on the side against the others with the crowbar, and we'll try to yank it out horizontally away from the Cross," Tadgh directed, jumping down into the hole.

The task at first seemed futile, but on the fourth try, they moved the log slightly. Kathy and Morgan got up and used a long-handled shovel for leverage opposite Aidan.

"Take it easy, darlin', and let Morgan do that," Collin pleaded, straining on the central log.

On the fifth attempt, it sprang free. The two on either side were easier still.

Collin probed the dirt below the logs. "We're at five and a half feet down now."

At this depth, only he, Aidan and Tadgh had the arm strength to hoist the shovelfuls of dirt up over the lip of the hole. Peader, who had clambered out to give the others room to dig, assisted Morgan in scooping earth back from the edge to prevent it from falling back in.

"I think I may have hit another layer of logs," Tadgh cried out, when his shovel hit another solid obstruction. "Wait a minute. Hand the torch down here."

Clearing away the loose dirt, he bent down with the light and exclaimed, "Damn. It's a chest."

They all let out a yell.

Tadgh took the torch and shone it under the logs. "Easy now, lads—and lasses. This chest is quite worm-eaten below the cracks in its leather cover. We're going to have to remove more logs."

"Why is that?" Collin questioned, rubbing his aching arms.

"Because I've traced the edge of the chest and I think there's a second one next to it," Tadgh replied, trying to keep his excitement under control.

"Now?" Jackson whispered to his boss.

Boyle shook his head. "Let them do all the hard work," he muttered. Boyle was so close to his goal he could taste it.

Jackson kept fingering the Webley on his hip.

Boyle assessed the lights. There was a bright spot on the cross, and the main cathedral ruins were lit, but the Bishop's Castle end and the side of the rock nearest him were in complete darkness. McCarthy's men would be blinded by the light they were in. "You two. Follow me silently. Stay in the dark. We'll move up behind that rock. Then wait for my signal."

They made sure that Jordan could not make noise if he came to by stuffing a rag in his mouth and tying the ends behind his head. They then crossed the open grass to their perch, undetected.

Two more hours passed before the adventurers had dug carefully around the tops and sides of both chests. They now needed the ladder to access the bottom of the pit. It was slow work, using a bucket and rope to haul dirt up from the now roughly six- by eight- foot hole. The chests were sitting at the bottom of an eight-foot-deep excavation.

Tadgh checked his watch; it was one in the morning. He could see the girls and Peader were now exhausted. Morgan was kneading her right thigh, probably a cramp. And they all looked like ragamuffins, their clothes caked with dirt. Collin, on the other hand, looking as dirty as a coal miner, seemed undaunted by the laborious task.

The two round-topped chests were a match, worm-eaten leather covering oaken boxes with somewhat-rusted metal hoop bindings and clasps and partially disintegrated exterior leather straps. Standing thirty inches high, they spanned thirty inches in width and forty-two inches in length. Most significantly, the faded McCarthy red stag crest was burned into the leather of the arched lids.

"Well, now. We have to pass a rope under each end of a chest. Then we should be able to raise it by pulling on the rope, and sliding it up the ladder," Tadgh instructed from the bottom of the pit. It looked to him that the metal hoop bindings were sturdy enough to take the strain.

Thirty minutes later, Tadgh had burrowed under the first chest where the straps were located. He carefully threaded a rope underneath each end and tied them off. Aidan climbed down the ladder to assist him. "Haul away," he yelled up to the O'Donnell boys.

Five minutes full of the sounds of men groaning and ancient leather creaking followed. Tadgh and Aidan pushed the first chest from below as Tadgh struggled up the ladder. The clasps and wooden structure held and eventually the chest landed on level ground. The second one was hoisted out more easily. By two-thirty, both chests were sitting side by side under the eyes of St. Patrick on his cross, visible presumably for the first time since a year before the burning. A huge mound of dirt stood on the south side of the excavation. They had been steadily digging for six and a half hours.

A figure entered the pitch-dark Hall of the Vicar's Choral, pausing to catch his breath after mounting the Rock from the village. The train had been late, making it a long travel day, and he was dog-tired.

Drawn toward the light beyond the courtyard window, he tripped over the pews trying to reach it. Bending down to massage his shin, his thoughts raced. He had a sixth sense for danger and intrigue and right now the hairs on the back of his neck were standing on end. Something electric was happening out there in the light.

Maybe there was good reason why he had been summoned for assistance. He'd heard them talking before they left. A question flooded his mind—where was Boyle?

He wasn't used to missing his commitments and right now things were out of his control. But he wasn't going to let them down, come what may.

Standing up, he could hear the commotion in the courtyard beyond the walls. Reaching the window, he strained to see what was going on in the inner courtyard, his eyes struggling to adjust to the glare from the overhead lights.

Tadgh sat down on the first chest to catch his breath while the others gathered around. Then he stood up and faced his comrades. "Now is the moment of truth, don't ye know. It's the fulfillment of our forefathers' noble plans. We are the generation chosen by God and destiny to recover the treasures of our Clans so that they can be used to fuel our glorious revolution." Tadgh waited for a minute to let his historic words sink in before trying to pick the locks of the first chest.

"Damn, they're rusted shut."

"That chest has been down there for a long time, mavourneen."

"Two hundred and seventy long years," Tadgh spit on his hands and rubbed them together. "Hand me the crowbar, Morgan."

Prying against the metal strap, Tadgh managed to break open one of the clasps, and then the other. With Aidan's assistance, he raised the lid.

Tadgh cried out when he saw the contents.

The raised lid blocked the view of the other adventurers, but they knew from Tadgh's expression that part of the treasure of the McCarthy and the O'Donnell Clans lay before them. And there was one more chest yet to open. Fate would weave the events to come.

Chapter Seventeen
Conflagration

Saturday, July 15, 1916
Rock of Cashel, Ireland

"*N*ow!" **Boyle yelled** to his men as he bounded out from behind the rock, gun drawn.

Tadgh wheeled around and slammed down the lid of the chest. His other hand went for the Luger in his trouser pocket.

"You're all under arrest for espionage and gun running as enemies of the State," Boyle cried as Jackson and Simpson rushed up behind him at the excavation.

Damn, I've been too lax. Tadgh cursed himself,

"I'd drop that weapon if I were you, very slowly, McCarthy," Boyle hissed as he held his Webley to Morgan's temple. "Young McCarthy, get over there by your brother or this fine lass dies."

Aidan swore but moved to be by Tadgh.

Tadgh considered his options quickly. Simpson had a gun to Peader's head and the other henchman held Kathy in his crushing grip, with a gun trained on Collin's forehead twenty feet away. The adventurers were all exhausted from the digging.

He would have to find another way. "All right, Boyle. I'm dropping my gun."

Collin looked like he was going to take a chance but his lightning fists wouldn't be enough from that distance. Tadgh waved him off with his eyes.

"That's wise. Now kick it over my way," Boyle ordered as he pulled on Morgan's hair.

Tadgh obliged begrudgingly. He remembered that his knife was still on the base of the cross but with them all on the other side of the gaping hole he couldn't get to it.

Boyle forced Morgan to her knees while he retrieved and pocketed the Luger, his eyes all the while on the McCarthy brothers, daring them to act. "You boys are expendable now, based on what you have unearthed. I'd just as soon drop you both into that burial hole you just dug."

Jackson lurched towards the chest to take a look, dragging Kathy along with him.

Boyle swiveled his head and brandished his weapon in his underling's direction just long enough to snap, "You do your job, Jackson. Leave that to me." Then he whipped his head around and pointed his revolver back toward the McCarthys.

Tadgh saw that exchange. Then he saw Morgan as she started to struggle to break free of Boyle's grip. He shook his head and said, "No, Morgan." He saw her go limp. *Damn, I should have taken the few seconds to shoot him back in the hospital. I could have killed the guard.*

Jackson hesitated. He desperately wanted to see what was in the chest. Tadgh could see the loathing in the villain's eyes.

Boyle dragged Morgan over to where Simpson was standing, being careful to skirt the edge of the open pit. He tightened the choke hold and trained his gun on Peader.

Flicking his Webley in Tadgh's direction, he snarled, "Get over there with your German leader."

Defiantly, Peader stood his ground. Boyle fired a single shot. Peader gasped, winced in pain, and clapped his hand over his right ear where Boyle's bullet had just grazed it.

"Now!" Boyle barked. "You're expendable, too."

Tadgh said, "Peader, come here." The Irishman obeyed.

"Go on and tie all their hands behind their backs, Simpson. I've all three of these traitors covered."

Simpson obeyed like a cowering dog.

"Now march," Boyle ordered, once their arms were securely bound with rope. You're going to get what's befitting of vermin. Extermination."

Kathy fainted and Jackson threw her over his shoulder with one arm. Collin darted at Jackson even with his wrists tied. The giant RIC officer knocked him to the ground with his free hand.

Simpson was shocked at his boss's plan. "Surely you mean that we are going to run them in, sir."

"I meant what I said, you insubordinate wimp!" Boyle shouted, cuffing his underling on the neck. "Do as you're told!"

♣ ♣ ♣ ♣

The lone figure in the Hall of the Vicar's Choral watched and listened intently as the officers herded their captives north through the entrance porch into the cathedral ruins. One minute later he saw the burly and puny ones return and then disappear around the west end of the Bishop's Castle. He was about to step out of the darkness into the courtyard, when he stopped short. The one they called Jackson returned with a struggling bound and gagged body slung over his shoulder. He turned north and disappeared into the cathedral via the porch. Then the one they called Simpson returned with two petrol cans, one in each hand. He followed Jackson into the ruins.

Scooping up the leader's knife from the base of the Cross, the lone figure followed at a distance. Creeping through the porch opening until he could peer into the Nave and beyond, he saw a horrific sight. Exterior illumination filtering in through the triple lancet window openings high up in the south transept ruins cast a ghoulish glow on the desperate scene under what had been the central tower. The Clans folk were seated back to back in two groups separated by ten feet. McCarthy, a younger version of the Irishman, and Morgan, who Boyle had been holding hostage, were together with the prone, bound body. Morgan had turned sideways and was using her tied hands to pull the rag out of his mouth as he struggled against his bonds.

Collin, Kathy, and Peader were in a separate group under the control of the burly policeman named Jackson.

275

No one spoke until the bound captive, his mouth now free, cried out, "God, Morgan! What's going on here? Last thing I remember I was in my office with that Neanderthal over there."

"I'm sorry that I roped you into this, Jack. Tadgh will get us out of this mess, you'll see."

The lone figure crept closer in the darkness of the Nave until he was positioned opposite the group at the entrance to the circular stairs of the South Transept Tower. Boyle's back was toward him with his gun trained beyond on the leader. The slender constable, Simpson, backed away from the action. Then suddenly he turned on his boss with his revolver aimed at him.

"This has gone far enough. Stop it or I'll shoot you where you stand."

In the flash of an eye, Boyle's free hand swooped around and knocked the gun out of his subordinate's hand. Moments later, Jackson had thrown him down, uncomprehending, with the second group of captives.

"I had been kicking myself that I didn't finish you off in Tralee, McCarthy," Boyle sneered, stooping over to pick up Simpson's Webley. He holstered his own weapon. "But this is much better. Thank you for answering my earlier questions and bringing my birthright to me."

He turned to both groups and continued. "You should all feel privileged. You're going to die in an historically significant manner, just like your ancestors. And I, descendent of Lords Boyle and Broghill, and comrade Inchiquin, will execute you in the same sacrilegious location."

He nodded and Jackson opened the top of one of the cans. Boyle opened the other.

Collin could smell the deadly fluid. He'd grown tired of waiting for Tadgh to act. *Christ Jesus. Not kerosene again. What would*

Sam do?

"But first, I need further information," Boyle hissed. He turned to Collin. "Tell me what I want to know and I won't kill your girlfriend here."

"Don't listen to him!" Tadgh shouted to Collin. "He has to kill us all or be killed himself. And that goes for you too!" he added, shouting in Jackson's direction.

Jackson glared back at him and Collin could see from his eyes that the bastard believed him.

Boyle responded by first dumping kerosene on Tadgh's group, and then throwing the empty can aside. Tadgh dodged sideways, pushing Morgan with him and Aidan instinctively followed his brother's lead. They only got a minor quantity of the fuel on their clothing. But Jack, still bound was soaked with it.

"I don't have the information that you want," Collin snarled back. "If I did, I would tell you to save my wife and unborn child. You've got what you want here, goombah. There's no need to kill us."

Boyle nodded, moving towards the second group, and Jackson doused Kathy with the vile liquid and held up a box of matches so the captives could see them. Looking directly down at Collin, Boyle spat out, "Last chance, lad."

Collin was frantic. He remembered Boyle's words just before he killed his da. "If you let us go, I will take you to the treasure."

"Nice try, but no," Boyle shot back. "Just tell me."

Collin hesitated and then guessed. "It's buried under the dungeon of Donegal Castle."

"You are lying lad. You really don't know, do you?" Boyle concluded.

Jackson pocketed the matches and sloshed kerosene over the rest of them.

Sam knew that he had to act now. Bursting out of the stairway entrance, with a forward underhand throw he sent the knife handle-first along the floor directly toward his protégé's bound hands. In the same movement he lunged at Boyle from behind.

Sensing motion behind him, Boyle whirled around and fired wildly at Sam who dove for cover.

Jackson saw his opportunity and seized it. Bounding forward towards Boyle, he splashed his boss with kerosene, pulling the box of matches from his pocket.

With Boyle distracted, Collin scooped up the knife and gripped it in his fists. Peader rubbed the rope that bound his own wrists against the knife's blade. Freed, he sawed away at Collin's bonds, then Kathy's.

Furious, Boyle turned back to face his henchman. "You bastard." Raising and cocking Simpson's Webley, he aimed to kill.

At that instant, Sam bent low and tackled the rogue head constable at the waist. Boyle's finger tightened on the trigger. The gun went off, its bullet ripping a hole in Jackson's fist and igniting the box of matches it held.

Screaming, the deputy involuntarily fell to his knees. He dropped the kerosene can and flung the box of matches from his injured hand to the floor, where the can's remaining contents spilled.

Fire flared up near Jackson and raced towards the second group. Agonized, he paid it no mind.

Sam lay spread-eagled on top of Boyle, pinning the head constable's wrist to the stone floor so Boyle couldn't shoot. Sam brought Boyle's hand up and smashed it back down. Boyle let go of the revolver, but kneed Sam in the groin, then picked the gun up by the barrel and cracked Sam over the head, rendering him dazed and disoriented.

Boyle sat up and turned back to Jackson.

Collin yelled, "Get up. Run!" to his second group of compatriots as he leapt over to aid Tadgh's group, swiftly slashing their restraints as the flames reached for them.

Morgan and Aidan moved immediately, dragging Jack along. Where the second group had sat only seconds before, Simpson froze in terror. A moment later, flames engulfed the area with Simpson screaming in the middle of it.

Tadgh reacted instantaneously. "Aidan, save him! I'll get Boyle."

♣　♣　♣　♣

Boyle sensed that it was all going wrong. He knew he only had four shots left in Simpson's Webley, but he had his own revolver and McCarthy's pistol.

Recovering his feet from Sam's tackle he saw his henchman get up and charge at him. *First order of business. Kill Jackson.* The first shot stopped Jackson momentarily, but it took the remaining three to bring him down. The burly sergeant teetered sideways and fell into the flaming pool of kerosene previously occupied by Tadgh's group.

The whole central tower area was now a funeral pyre. The screams of both constables were drowned out by the explosion of the kerosene can that Jackson had dropped.

Boyle stepped back a pace to avoid catching on fire. *Second order of business. Kill Tadgh McCarthy.* The smoke from the kerosene fires was billowing inside the ruins and obscuring his line of fire.

♣　♣　♣　♣

Tadgh could see Morgan, still holding Jack's legs where she and Aidan had dragged him. Kathy and Peader huddled together in the North Transept, staying as far as possible away from the fire. Aidan had dashed into the fire to drag Simpson out with one hand and swat fire off himself with the other. He could see him wrapping the constable in his coat to stifle the flames and his screams. Morgan was rushing to help him. But where was Collin?

"You're a dead man, McCarthy," Boyle screamed, with his own

Webley now cocked and ready, as he searched the smoke-filled cathedral for his nemesis. He started shooting wildly, bullets ricocheting off the stone walls of the tower.

"You bastard. You killed my da," Collin yelled as he rushed out of the smoke from the side and caught Boyle off guard. With an uppercut to the jaw he knocked him down. The Webley went flying into the funeral pyre. Boyle tried to get the Luger out of his pocket. Collin wrapped his fingers around the head constable's wrist. The two wrestled for the pistol.

Tadgh could see what was about to happen through the flames. They were twenty feet away on the other side of the pyre. Given Collin's exhausted state, Boyle had gotten the upper hand in the fight and had rolled him over to where he was about to push O'Donnell's kerosene-soaked head into the blaze.

Damn, there's only one thing to do. Leaping with the strength of a gazelle, Tadgh surged through the flames until he reached the two. His clothes were on fire and he could smell the singe of his hair. He batted at his clothing.

Morgan watched in horror as her lover followed up Collin's uppercut with a mighty right cross of his own that knocked the villain down. He dragged him back into the flames with one arm and pushed her brother to safety with the other.

Seeing her betrothed on fire, Morgan dove into the flames herself and yanked him backward, yelling, "Peader, help with Tadgh."

Having come to his senses, Sam held a kerosene-soaked Collin back from jumping into the inferno to save his sister.

Boyle felt his damaged heart artery burst with a knife-like stabbing pain in his chest followed by extreme dizziness. He tried to stand up, but he was overcome with the pain from inside and without. He knelt, cursing in the center of the funeral pyre with his upheld fist clenched. Then realizing he was doomed, with the last of his strength he dove forward, grabbing the fleeing Morgan by the ankles as she pushed Tadgh out towards her cousin. He dragged her body back into the flames yelling, "Maaaaaaaaaa!"

"God, no!" Tadgh cried, squirming to get up as Peader was beating down the flames in his clothing."

Aidan leaped to Morgan's aid, grabbing her outstretched arms to pull her free.

For a moment, Boyle held firm. Then he did something quite unexpected. He let go of Morgan, moaning, "This is for you, Ma. I'm coming." Aidan yanked her clear of the inferno.

With that, Darcy Boyle collapsed, and without uttering another sound, the fire consumed him.

Kathy rushed forward and beat the flames off Morgan's clothing. Miraculously, she had only sustained minor burns since she had initially avoided the kerosene dousing. Peader had stripped the burning clothes off Tadgh in seconds. Tadgh stood there, stark naked. He was staring into the flames to where Boyle had lain, his hair and eyebrows smoking.

The others rushed over and offered pieces of their soaked clothing to cover their leader as the fire burned bright, the stench of burning flesh choking their nostrils.

Recovering from the shock of the last hour, they stood together and watched as the greedy flames died down gradually, having consumed their fuel, human and otherwise. The adventurers were left in the cold, ghoulish glow with the barren stone walls of the ruins rising ominously around them. Shivering, Tadgh wondered how the one villager felt who survived the Inchiquin massacre to tell the tale of this burning cathedral two hundred and sixty-nine years earlier. And if the three thousand were looking down upon them now, would they feel some sense of satisfaction that a descendent of the Murrough of the Burning legacy, of that wicked plundering race, had received justice by fire himself?

♣   ♣   ♣   ♣

"We only have a few hours 'til dawn, dear," Morgan nudged him, breaking his reverie. "We've got to be going before first light."

Tadgh went over and shook Sam's hand. "I'm not going anywhere until I find out how you got here."

It was Kathy's idea, and a bloody good one, to be sure," Sam said, rubbing the back of his head where Boyle had hit him. "She asked me before she left Lisburn to come to Cashel, just in case."

Kathy chimed in. "Two days ago, I decided that Sam should be here with us. I was worried and thought he should remain hidden as a surprise backup in case of trouble. Guerilla warfare tactics I believe, isn't it? Need to know and all that."

Tadgh was surprised. "Heavens, lass, where'd you learn about that?"

"I'm a schoolmarm. We have to know something about just about everything."

Collin gave his wife a squeeze. "I taught her everything she knows, that's certain."

Tadgh winked back. Collin was so much more than a newspaperman. He was an instinctive rebel fighter who could be counted on in dire circumstances. "But, Sam. How . . . ?"

"I came by train and Mr. Wiggins, vowed to silence, picked me up in his B & C lorry earlier tonight. He's waiting down on Rock Road for a signal to come up and get us."

"Well now. You certainly saved us tonight, Sam," Tadgh exclaimed, patting the Canadian on the back. "And that upper cut, Collin. We'd have all been shot and burned without you tonight, to be sure, to be sure."

Collin smiled confidently. All of his demons had now been vanquished. "I'm happy to be a part of this historic adventure Tadgh. I was wrong. At least two Clans are far from dead. There's no doubt of it now!"

Morgan, with her tunic still smoking, worked frantically to resuscitate Simpson. "He's in a state of shock and his heart is erratic. It looks like he has sustained serious burns to more than half his body."

Collin needed no coaxing to tend to Kathy, who was still in a state of shock and anxiety.

Although he felt like he was still on fire, Tadgh took charge again.

"Aidan, take the torch and open the portal gate I noticed just west of the main entrance. Then signal Jeffrey to drive up and in, to St. Patrick's Cross. Peader, please go get the bucket and a shovel. We have some smoldering bones here to bury. And, just as an aside, is anyone curious to see what's really in those chests?"

"I think we need to get out of here," Peader advised, checking his watch.

A short time later, despite her efforts, Morgan, with tears in her eyes, announced, "I couldn't save him. Constable Simpson has passed away."

"You really are a nurse, aren't you Morgan," Jack Jordan finally spoke out. "A kind of Florence Nightingale."

"So we've been told," Collin quipped, showing a strong sense of pride in his long-lost sister. "I was wrong about another thing, Sis. You and Tadgh here were made for each other. If we can endure tonight, then you two can survive anything together. I give you my heartiest approval for your upcomin' nuptials and hope that I can be accepted as your brother and friend, Tadgh."

Just as the first hint of daybreak was peeping over the eastern horizon, the B & C lorry was idling just west of St. Patrick's High Cross, with its precious cargo safely hidden under tarpaulins held down by beer kegs. It took three of the men to lift the heavier of the two chests into the lorry.

"I think that does it," Tadgh announced, setting the large flag-stone back in place and surveying the scene. "Without the tailgate of the lorry we could not have pushed that monstrous pile of dirt and those logs back into the hole in time. At least we have given poor Simpson a burial in a very sacred place. Peader, did you scour the blackened floor of the cathedral with dirt?"

"Taken care of, Tadgh."

"Right you are then. Let's be on our way."

As a final observation of their historic night, Tadgh concluded, "Those two villains got more than they deserve on their way to Hell; to be buried at the foot of our Patron Saint with a true martyr who tried to help us."

"But did you see what Boyle did as his last act on earth, Tadgh?" Morgan asked. "He likely saved my life."

"After he tried desperately to take it, aroon." He grabbed his brother's shoulder. "Aidan saved you. Boyle came to a fitting end."

"And your great uncle's words ring true for me tonight, for certain," Peader said. He recited from recent memory:

> *"Where blazed the sacred fire, rung out the vesper bell*
> *Where the fugitive found shelter, became the hermit's cell;*
> *And hope hung out its symbol to the innocent and good,*
> *For the cross o'er the moss of the pointed summit stood."*

As they started down from the ancient McCarthy Rock of Cashel, Morgan added, "In your vernacular, there ye go now. I think that Saint Patrick was looking after his flock tonight!"

Chapter Eighteen
Tadgh's Clan Gathers

Saturday, July 15, 1916
On the Road to Cork, Ireland

"**W**hat a glorious morning," Morgan exclaimed as they drove back to Cork. Ireland basked in sunlight.

The girls sat up front with Wiggins. Meanwhile, in the bed of the lorry, the men sampled the brew with mugs Jeffrey had brought along.

"I'm glad that we all had a hand in ridding the world of Boyle last night, lads."

Collin replied first. "It can't bring back our kin, Tadgh, but it sure feels good."

"So it was worth it to stay and help us then."

"Abso-bloody-lutely, Tadgh! Even if I do lose my job."

Aidan spoke up. "I remember Mam taught me that '*vengeance is mine, saith the Lord*,' but, in this case I agree with Collin, Brother."

"Jack, I can see that Morgan means a lot to you. She told me how she was an inspiration for your recovery."

"That's true, Tadgh. But last night I saw just how important she is to you too. After what we have been through together, I would be honored and content to be good friends with all of you."

"We're on a dangerous and deadly, yet noble and liberating mission here, Jack."

"After our brush with death, fellows, I'm in a state of shock. I thought that the sinking of the Lusitania was horrific and the ultimate injustice in the Great War. Then I saw how the British Admiralty, Mr. Winston Churchill especially, blamed our dear Captain Will and tried to whitewash their own involvement. Now I can see that there is mayhem and evil all around us here in Ireland. I am sure that you are on the side of justice and freedom and I want to be a part of it, if you'll let me."

"If you'll swear your allegiance and secrecy, Jack, we welcome you to the revolution." Tadgh clapped the newest IRB member on his back. He figured, with the old guard dead and gone, he now had the authority to accept Jack into the fold. They needed new blood.

Collin opened the tap on the keg and filled his mug. "I've got to get Kathy back to Canada as soon as possible, Tadgh. And I have to get back to my job in Toronto if I haven't been fired already. But we'd love to be there for you when you tie the knot with my sister. Any chance you could advance the weddin' date before the twenty-third when the *Teutonic* sails?"

"That's not much time, lad."

"We've got to be on that ship. It gives you roughly a week to prepare. How about it?"

"I didn't tell you all the stories about the High Cross at Cashel," Tadgh confessed, tipping the stout barrel and twisting the tap for another wee drop. "My ancestors believed that if a bachelor and a spinster performed a ritual at its base, it would result in a swift marriage."

"I can only imagine what ritual they were performin'. But surely, what you and my sister did last night would qualify."

"If we can uncover a three-hundred-year-old mystery in one night, then we ought to be able to pull off a wedding in seven days. But I'll have to check with my better half. You know the old adage, 'if the woman's happy then the man's happy'."

They concurred that this was something they all could agree on, as they tapped another small keg in celebration.

By the time that they had reached the Cunard Pier in Queenstown the boys had it all figured out.

"Well then lads. All that remains is for me to convince Morgan," Tadgh announced in a somewhat inebriated tone.

"But I have to convince my ma, don't ye know," Peader chimed in just as Jeffrey stopped at the end of the Cunard pier.

Jack eased himself off the lorry, bending backwards and rubbing his lower spine. "I'll make the arrangements as soon as you both give me the go ahead. Thanks for saving me from those devils."

As Jack walked stiffly toward the front of the vehicle, hoping for a word of encouragement from Morgan, she leaned out the window and called him over.

"Remind us, Jack. When is the next opportunity for Collin, Kathy and their friend Sam to sail to Canada?"

"On the twenty-third from Queenstown, Morgan. Why?"

"I just wondered. I'd be really glad if you would join our cause, Jack."

"I already have."

Then she opened the door, stepped out and kissed him gently on his forehead. "We'll be great friends and compatriots. We already are."

Jack kissed her forehead back. "That's enough," he murmured, making meaningful eye contact and holding her captive in the gaze of his sky-blue eyes. Then he was hobbling off without looking back.

Just after noon, Wiggins dropped them off at home at Creagh.

"Thank you, Jeffrey for all your help this week," Tadgh said, after they all had managed to lug the chests into the secret operations center.

"This is quite a layout my boy," Wiggins remarked, clearly very impressed. "It looks like you have plans for all-out warfare."

"There's been a setback, for certain. But liberation is coming, my friend, to be sure."

"You can count on me, Tadgh," the Beamish & Crawford manager offered.

Tadgh took his hand in a firm grip and said simply, "Thank you, my Beamish boy. I will."

When Tadgh re-entered his home, Morgan was busy showing her relatives its unique features including the curious markings on the circular banister. Tadgh was touched that his beloved had already adopted it as her own. He noted that she stopped short of exposing his hidden genealogy room.

She scrounged up clothes for them all and they took their turns cleaning up and disposing of their kerosene and smoke-imbedded duds.

Fortunately, Aidan had stocked the larder, so Morgan made a hearty soup lunch for them all since they hadn't eaten in more than a day. Then she suggested that they all rest up after their ordeal. She got no arguments. Peader, Aidan and Sam were relegated to cots in the operations center, while Collin and Kathy took the upstairs workroom that Morgan had made up with blankets and pillows on the floor.

Alone in the bathroom at last, Tadgh ran a bath for Morgan.

"I saw some burns when you were buck naked, Tadgh. Get your clothes off." Then she probed the back of his right shoulder. "Does that hurt?"

He winced but said, "Nah, never better."

It reminded her of how he had reacted on that dangerous motorcycle ride home from Cork after he'd been shot through the shoulder. Could that have been more than a year ago? So much had happened. "You're a lucky Irishman, mavourneen, to be sure. There's only one blister area on that shoulder and minor burns on the back of your hands. St. Patrick was looking after you, my love. If there'd been more kerosene on your clothes or if you'd been in that fire a few seconds longer you wouldn't be here right now."

"Wait here a minute." Morgan darted downstairs and reappeared with a bottle of Jameson. Taking a towel, she soaked a corner in the alcohol and then dabbed the burn areas. This time Tadgh didn't flinch, but instead grabbed the bottle and took a mighty swig.

She found the lotion in the cabinet and applied it to his shoulder, then bandaged it carefully.

"All right, my love. You'll live."

Morgan turned towards him as he slowly disrobed her. She was tired but his touch sent shivers up her back.

She stepped into the warm water and slowly sank down. "Would you wash my back?"

"I'm not falling for that again. You're going to pull me in."

"I would never do that, mavourneen."

Luxuriating together in the tub, Morgan sighed. "I can't believe that only twelve hours ago our lives were on the line again. You were so brave, my love. Jumping through that inferno to save my brother and finish off Boyle. You are my hero." She was rubbing his broad chest sensuously.

"Had to be done, don't ya know." Tadgh was thinking of how to broach the subject.

"Tadgh, darling. Kathy and were talking during our ride home this morning. I know that you wanted us to be married on your birthday. But my brother and sister-in-law have to go home before that. What do you think about having our wedding right away so that they can be here?"

If the woman is happy. "That's a bright idea, aroon. But where would we have the ceremony? Your Aunt Biddy is expecting us to be married in Meenmore. Surely Kathy and Collin would leave from Queenstown."

Morgan admitted, "Kathy and I have it all worked out. We're going to convince Peader to bring Aunt Biddy down here."

Great minds think alike. "Wow. Doesn't the next troop ship leave for Canada on the twenty-third? Today's the fifteenth. That only gives us a week. I don't know . . . "

"Please my love?"

"For you, darlin', I would move mountains, or at least the Rock of Cashel."

Delighted, Morgan kissed him long and passionately, and then drew him into her web of ecstasy once more, being careful of his right shoulder.

The next morning, during breakfast, Morgan was particularly cheerful. She winked at Kathy. "Tadgh and I have been talking. We want to have our wedding next Saturday, the twenty-second, so that you all can be there with us. Kathy, would you consent to be my maid of honor?"

"With great pleasure, Sis," she replied, winking back.

The two women giggled with the knowledge that their plan was working. Tadgh shrugged his shoulders to signal mission accomplished to the men.

"Can you ask your ma to come to Queenstown, Peader?"

"There's a telephone at the tailor's shop now. We can but ask."

"I'll call Jack and see what the travel logistics are," Collin offered, knowing the answer already.

"There ye go then. That's sorted," Tadgh said, forking down the last of his eggs. "Today we need to make an inventory of the McCarthy gold treasure." He brandished a dog-eared old tome above his head. "I've been keeping this book of ancient coinage, just in case. Who would like to help me?"

"I can't believe that the McCarthy Clan could have been this wealthy," Morgan marveled as the other five looked on in amazement seven hours later.

Consulting his tally sheet, Tadgh read off, "For the coins, there's two hundred and forty-five Edward IV silver groats, three hundred and twenty-seven three crown groats of Henry VII, five hundred and two Henry VIII Harp groats, five hundred and forty-one English crowns. But strangely, the greatest quantity is six hundred and forty-two *escudo* doubloons from the time of Ferdinand and Isabella, and seven hundred and twelve Spanish eight *reales*, or pieces of eight, from the time of Phillip III of Spain."

"Isn't that the king who provided troops at the Battle of Kinsale?" Peader asked, remembering his research on Red Hugh O'Donnell.

"Yes, I think that's right. It's very interesting that my relatives had that much Spanish money."

"I think that the Spanish coins were used pretty much everywhere because of the pirate trade," Peader remarked, turning one over in his fingers, trying read a date.

"Barbary?"

"Hard to say, Tadgh. They were at war with the Spanish, Italians, any Christians in and around the Mediterranean in those days."

"I think that the most curious find is this small bag of ancient coins. Where did they come from, I wonder?"

Kathy dug one out of the rotting sack. "They look like Yiddish currency from their markings," the schoolmarm remarked. "Now that is strange."

Continuing on, Tadgh read. "In the same chest there are eighteen gold chalices, twelve gold serving plates, thirty-one gold dinner plates, thirty-three sets of silver knives, forks and spoons, and eight golden candelabra. In addition, there are two silver hilted short swords with jeweled pommel, and one crown with emeralds at all six points. I guess this is what they referred to as the McCarthy Gold Plate. I am surprised at the sophistication of all of these treasures. I would have thought that the clansmen would have lived a simpler and cruder existence."

"A thousand years of bartering and plundering from the English and clans from Normandy. I suppose that they would bring out the good silver when the relatives came to call," Morgan offered, somewhat in jest.

"Then there's a ring tiara with gold floral relief with ten ruby and pearl centers, four necklaces of gold, silver or pearls, six similar bracelets or anklets and eight jeweled rings, including one gold claddagh design with what looks like a five-carat diamond in its crown. I particularly like the massive gold one with the McCarthy crest embossed," Tadgh enumerated. "That last one could have been used as a Clan seal."

"Finally, the second chest contains furs wrapped around presumably important family documents. Most of them have been damaged or destroyed by worms and the ravages of time, unfortunately. We'll have to sift through this chest later. There may be some further clues buried inside what's left of those documents."

"But we've already found the McCarthy treasure."

"Yes, but the O'Donnell one is still out there somewhere."

"This is an incredible find, Tadgh," Collin said, hefting the crown with the emeralds onto his head. "You and Aidan are wealthy men now, to be sure."

"Well now, soon-to-be brother. Except for a few of the personal items, all of this is going to be used to help fund our revolution. That was the intent of our ancestors, and I'm going to carry out their wishes. The next time we will fight using guerrilla tactics and our army will need to be well armed for that ballyhoo."

That last comment reminded Tadgh that he needed to check on what happened to Mick Collins after the Rising.

"Can I try the gold tiara on?" Morgan asked enthusiastically, picking it up and settling it over her ears. "It fits."

"You can do better than that, my queen. You can wear it at our wedding."

That afternoon they made the call. Biddy was at her shop sorting a delivery gone wrong.

"Aunt Biddy. This is Morgan. Yes, that's right; your niece Claire and now Morgan. You know that beautiful Celtic ivory satin wedding dress, the medieval-style garment with the mock pearls sewn in under the bodice. Is it still available?"

"Of course, dear. I've already altered it for you. When are you after coming for the weddin'?"

Morgan was hesitant to ask. "That's what I'm calling about. I need to have the wedding down here near Cork. Can you come and bring the dress please?"

"I don't know, dear. It's a long way to go and I'd have to leave the children with my brother now wouldn't I."

"Peader will come and get you on the train if you can manage it. We really want you to be here."

Biddy thought for a minute. "When would this be, Morgan?"

"Peader would come for you on Tuesday by train. The wedding has been moved up to Saturday," Morgan answered, hoping that this information would not cause her aunt to say no.

"This coming Saturday? My, my, dear. What's the hurry?"

"We want Collin and Kathy there and they have to leave on Sunday for Canada."

"I see. I'll have to get back to yourself. Can I talk to Peader?"

"Certainly, he's right here. But first I have another request. Do you have another dress in pink that would complement mine? One that Kathy could wear. She's going to be my maid of honor."

"I guessed as much, niece. That's why I measured her before you all left in such a hurry. And yes, I have just such a dress already picked out for her."

"That's wonderful. Please come, Auntie. Here's Peader."

"Where are we going to have the wedding, dear?" Morgan asked that evening when they were alone. "We obviously can't have it here."

"Now don't get upset, darling. It's a surprise."

"Surely the bride ought to know and organize all the details."

"Well now, lass. Jack has insisted on making all the arrangements in Queenstown in secret. He says that it is his wedding gift to both of us. What I can tell you is that we will be staying in two of the cottages you like so much along the shoreline in Queenstown."

"Who is 'we,' may I ask?" Morgan was drumming her fingers on the bedside table.

"The wedding party and Aunt Biddy."

"What about the police in Queenstown and Cork?"

"As far as I know, the primary RIC police that were after us in Cork were Boyle and his thugs. And we know that they won't bother us anymore. But I don't think that we should go to Dublin any time soon."

"I guess because it's on such short notice."

"Believe me, my dear. You will be delighted. Come over here to me on the bed now, my love. I need you."

Tadgh left with Peader on Monday morning when Jeffrey came to pick them up to take them to the Cork train, saying, "We'll be back to Queenstown on Thursday evening with Peader's ma." Morgan knew that he was going to get the Kerry and ride it home. "Jeffrey will come by on Thursday to collect you four and take you to the cottages."

Three days later just before suppertime, Morgan and Kathy were admiring the view from the cottage patio.

"This is a great place for a wedding. Especially at sunset."

"Yes, Kathy. But I still have no idea where the wedding or the reception will be held. I'm completely in the dark. By the way, where is that brother of mine?"

"He's off with Jack and Sam somewhere contacting Collin's managers at the *Tely* to make sure he doesn't lose his job. But I think that they are up to something."

"That's what I'm afraid of."

"Hello, love," Tadgh called out from inside the cottage. "Look who I have here to see you." He emerged onto the patio with Peader, each ushering Aunt Biddy by an arm.

"Oh dear," Morgan addressed them. "Auntie it's great to see you but you look like you've been on safari in Africa for a week."

"I'm really glad to finally get here, dear. But a bath would be lovely at this point."

She and Kathy showed their aunt to her quarters and promised to have a supper ready for her after she freshened up.

"Thank you. But after supper we will need to have a final fitting on your dresses, don't ye know. And what about shoes and flowers?"

Morgan calmed her saying, "We'll deal with that tomorrow, Auntie."

Later in the evening, Morgan confronted her man. "Okay, darling. This mystery has gone far enough. Please tell me what's going to happen on Saturday."

"We're going to be married, my love." But then he would say no more.

"Did you invite Maurice and Martha?"

"I tried, Morgan, but I'm not sure if they can get away on such short notice, I'm afraid."

Morgan passed a fitful night wondering and waiting At least the beautiful dress fit.

Chapter Nineteen
McCarthy Nuptials

Saturday, July 22, 1916
Queenstown, Ireland

Saturday morning dawned with brilliant sunshine. Collin came in at breakfast and announced with a smile, "The carriage will be here at one pm to pick up the bride, the maid of honor and Aunt Biddy. Please be ready."

"Where are we going, dear?" Kathy asked for the twentieth time.

"My lips are sealed, my love."

Kathy followed him out.

When she returned, Morgan waited with uplifted hands and a quizzical stare.

"He rode off to God knows where," Kathy reported. "He wouldn't say. The men went out to the Pub down by the docks last night, some hangout that Jack recommended. They didn't get back until two in the morning."

"How do you know that?"

"Your brother told me. That's all I could get out of him, in fact. It's a good thing that we three had our own hen party then wasn't it."

Morgan had been amazed at how much Beamish Aunt Biddy could consume and still appear quite normal.

"I guess that they all stayed in the other cottage," Morgan replied, still in the dark.

"Well, if they did, they're gone now," Kathy noted as she looked through the window into the cottage next door.

"We took some control in buying our shoes and flowers and my veil yesterday, didn't we?" Morgan said, still feeling out of the loop. "At least Tadgh gave me the tiara and some other jewelry yesterday to wear to the wedding. It includes a leather thong garter that was tied around the thigh during marriage ceremonies in the middle ages. He made it himself yesterday."

"Something old, I guess, Morgan. Now we just need something borrowed and something blue."

"Well, I am borrowing the tiara, and the necklace he gave me has rough cut sapphires and pearls in it."

"I guess that Tadgh and the boys have thought of everything then."

"Let's get a move on girls," Aunt Biddy boomed out from the kitchen where she cooked breakfast for the other two. "I've heard that pancakes and syrup are good for a hangover."

"So you'll be having plenty, then, I assume."

"There, there, niece. You'll be one to talk then. Here are the first four."

Just then the door knocker clanged. "Is there a bride in here?"

"Deirdre, is that you?" Morgan called joyfully through the door.

"In the flesh, dear," she cried opening the door and stepping into the cottage. "I couldn't let you two get married without being here for you both."

"How did you—"

"Tadgh called me. I took the last train from Dublin last night. I closed my pub up for the next two days."

"I don't suppose that you have a pink dress in that overnight bag you're carrying, do you?"

"As you know, I don't wear dresses in general. But for you I will, and my dress is pink. God awful color, pink."

"And, of course, Tadgh had nothing to do with any of that, right?"

"I cannot tell a lie." Deirdre left it at that.

"That schemer," Morgan fumed, sporting her best mock frown.

Deirdre patted her chest above her heart. "I think that it is very romantic."

After giving Deirdre a big hug and kiss, Morgan introduced her to her entourage.

In unison they all exclaimed, "Welcome to the wedding party."

"You all look so beautiful, don't you now," Aunt Biddy gushed, as they waited just outside the cottage at one o'clock. She, herself, normally dressed in black working clothes, was resplendent in a pale green tweed jumper and skirt to match.

Morgan came over to her and produced a fifteenth century necklace which she fastened around Biddy's neck. The cream-colored pearls matched the ones around her own throat. "There now, you look very elegant, Auntie. Tadgh and I want you to accept this token of our love and appreciation."

"Biddy looked at her reflection in the windowpane and fingered the ancient jewelry fondly. "I really couldn't."

"Hush, now. It was made with you in mind."

"Oh, look," Kathy cried, as the 'carriage' rounded the corner and headed their way.

"There's Jeffrey, driving four chestnut horses from his box front seat. Doesn't he look dapper in his gray morning suit."

The Beamish transportation manager rolled to a stop in front of them. "Your carriage awaits my ladies," he announced, bending at the waist and doffing his felt top hat. "My, don't you all look beautiful, like royalty all dressed up for the Ball. Please step up into my handsome green Clarence coach, my dears."

They loved the beautiful four-passenger four-wheeled closed coach with front and side glass windows. Morgan noticed the scrolled words 'Beamish & Crawford ~ Stout as Ever' on each side. "Aren't the flowers beautiful," Deirdre commented regarding the garlands of white daisies and pink roses that were draped over the back of the front box seat until they almost touched the ground.

Just as Morgan was wondering how she was going to step up with her long bridal dress, Martin Murphy stepped out of the coach, holding out his hand for support.

"Are you the coachman then, Martin?"

"Aye, ma'am among other duties. But I gets a little wobbly when I'm on dry land."

"Oh, I'm starting to love this mystery."

"Up with ye, now. Ye don't want to be late for your own weddin', now do ye?"

As Martin took Morgan's hand to get her situated first with her flowing dress in the carriage, he produced a pink blindfold.

"Tadgh asked me to be sure and put this on you, delicate-like."

"Honestly, Martin. Is this really necessary?"

"Yes ma'am. He'll have my hide if you don't wear it."

"Well, all right then," Morgan giggled, allowing herself to succumb to the intrigue.

"Where are we going?" Kathy asked Martin when they were all seated in the elegant wood trimmed Brougham with its luxurious black leather interior.

"My lips are sealed, lass," the coachman answered as he swung up onto the open box seat with his boss after securing the garland for the trip.

"We've heard that phrase before." The girls all giggled as Jeffrey pointed the carriage northward, heading out of town.

Amazingly enough, Kathy recognized the wedding venue as they finally clopped through the entrance gates two hours later. She was the only one of the bride's party except the bride because they'd been there before, recently.

Jeffrey stopped the carriage at the village and ushered them out onto the grass. "Wait here."

Morgan held her breath. Blindfolded in a carriage wearing her wedding dress for this trip was not her idea of fun.

"Where are we?"

Kathy was deciding whether to tell her or not, when she spied Collin walking out of the trees. She could see that he was dressed in formal attire, sporting a kilt in a Clan O'Donnell tartan of small blue and red checks. An elegant, open-necked, white, starched dress shirt, flowed from under his dapper black waistcoat.

"Good afternoon, ladies. I am here to escort you to the weddin'. Please follow me."

"Collin, is that you? Take this blindfold off at once so I can see my own wedding," Morgan demanded. Her hands went to the silk covering.

Her brother gently restrained her. "Dear Morgan, please don't spoil the surprise. You won't miss your own weddin', I assure you."

He took Morgan's arm lovingly and guided them all through the woods. Morgan could hear the thrushes warbling in the background. Then, as great Irish war pipes started up with the tune of 'Danny Boy', they all stopped. Collin gently removed her blindfold. At first, the brightness overwhelmed her, even though filtered sunlight sifted down through the canopy of oak trees. Gradually her eyes adjusted so that she could take in the scene. To her left, dressed in formal evening attire was Sean O'Casey.

"You wouldn't welch on a promise to let me give the bride away, now would you, lass?"

"Oh no, Sean. I'd love it," Morgan exclaimed, and gave him a big kiss, and her hand.

Fifty feet ahead of her, at the base of the ancient castle keep, stood Jack, Peader, Aidan, and Tadgh, all in a row. Collin rushed ahead to join his mates. They were dressed alike in very similar medieval garments looking very handsome indeed. Peader's kilt and sash were the same pattern as Collin's. Aidan and Tadgh sported McCarthy tartan kilts with larger red, green, and blue squares, and golden strands woven through them. She could see that Aidan was holding the crown with the emerald points. Morgan was startled when Maurice appeared and took Aunt Biddy's arm, leading her down to a wooden bench, located near the wall where Martha was already seated with Sam.

"I see that our whole crew is here," Morgan exclaimed. "How delightful."

Morgan could see that Tadgh also beamed, ear to ear.

Suddenly Captain Martin Murphy popped out from behind a great oak and motioned the women forward. He was dressed in a sea captain's uniform, but he looked more like a pirate captain with his black Wellington boots, flowing swashbuckler's coat and tri-corner hat set jauntily on his head. The front upturn of the hat sported the signature skull and crossbones. First Deirdre, and then Kathy, walked slowly down to the castle and stood to the left of the captain.

"Are you ready, lass, for a lifetime with this scoundrel playwright?" O'Casey asked, adjusting the cant on Morgan's tiara.

"Absolutely! I love him with all my heart."

"Then, what are you waitin' for? Let's go."

The bagpiper switched to the lullaby "When Irish Eyes are Smiling."

As they walked, she grew aware that there were other folks, onlookers, watching them from a distance. Then, as they glided the last few feet, Morgan focused on her man. She thought that she detected tears glistening in his beautiful amber eyes. He looked so happy.

Coming to a stop beside him, she could see that he was mesmerized. "I love you, Morgan. You look so beautiful!"

"You look so handsome, yourself, you mysterious lover. Such medieval highland outfits!"

Tadgh took her hand. "You'll see why later."

"Dearly beloved," the captain began. Morgan noticed that he gingerly held up Tadgh's family Bible.

Morgan was captivated by the moment. She heard Captain Murphy's sermon on the sanctity of marriage and then he asked, "Would you each like to say your vows now?"

Morgan could see that the wedding party was all looking at her, expecting her to go first. Her mind floated on a sea of happiness. She had difficulty in determining how to say what she felt. Finally, she spoke from her heart.

"Since the horrendous sinking of the *Lusitania*, I have gone from having no family, clinging to life on a piece of wood in the sea, to being surrounded by all the friends and family that I have discovered in this amazing journey since. What a wonderful and unexpected outcome for my life so far. I know that the man beside me has been the catalyst and the force behind my transformation. I had prayed throughout the pain and anxiety of my uprooted childhood that I could be reunited with my family. Now, like some magical fairytale, it has come to pass. I am so happy. Tadgh, I love you with all my heart. I will follow you wherever you go in this life and be your soul mate, mother of our children and your nurse if need be again." She paused for effect and then added, ". . . until death do us part."

Tadgh was ready with his vows. "Beloved Morgan, born Claire O'Donnell, I was a soldier without passion or compassion before I met you, to be sure. My life was driven with great purpose, but without love. We were brought together by our Lord's Divine intervention. You have shown me how to love and the joy of companionship that I could never have dreamed of without you. Now, I can only imagine my life with you as my soulmate. Morgan, I love you with all my heart. I will protect you and our family and keep you safe in my arms . . . until death do us part."

"Who has the rings?" the captain asked, laying the Bible carefully on the stone bench beside him, the one Kathy had once sat on.

"Here they are," Aidan said, stepping forward and handing them to Tadgh.

"With this ring, I thee wed," Tadgh spoke out forcefully, as he slipped the sixteenth-century Claddagh ring with the large diamond in the crown at the heart's apex over his love's finger. He was careful to turn it with the point of the heart inwards, signifying that she was now becoming a married woman.

Then Morgan took the massive gold seal ring and placed it on Tadgh's wedding finger. It fit him perfectly. "With this ring, I thee wed."

"I now pronounce you man and wife. You may kiss your bride."

Tadgh gave his bride a heartfelt, prolonged, sensuous kiss.

"And now, my queen, it is time for another important and ancient ceremony," Tadgh said.

"What can be as important as our marriage, mavourneen?"

"Look up. What do you see, aroon?"

It was hard for Morgan to crane her neck backwards that far without her tiara falling off. "I see this shear stone wall of Blarney Castle going up forever. And there's the battlement that protrudes outward at the top," she said. "Collin and I were up there, and Kathy sat on this bench."

"What else do you see, my dear wife?" Tadgh realized that he was starting to sound like Professor Lawlor again.

"I can see a grating right above us, and people way up there are looking down through it," she replied. "What does this have to do with us?"

"We are in a sacred place my love."

"Of course we are. Anywhere a marriage is performed becomes a church."

Martin Murphy stepped forward again with a prepared speech written on a scroll of parchment. He started to read. "Let it be known throughout the realm that a new Ri is to be crowned. Let the stone speak."

At this point Tadgh stepped forward and put out his hand onto the rock wall. A moment later three loud roars from above rocked the tower. Startled, the whole wedding party looked up and the figures on the grate shrugged their elbows while holding their ears.

"*Lia Fáil* has spoken for the first time since Fergus left for Scotland. Hail to the new King MacCarthaigh," Murphy shouted in his swashbuckling tone of voice.

"Here you go, Brother," Aidan said. He placed the ancient crown upon the head of the new Ri.

"Now do you understand, my queen?" Tadgh asked as he and Morgan walked off into the sunlit woods together amidst shouts of approval from the wedding party and other onlookers. "Those other visitors think that these ceremonies were a staged play for their amusement," Morgan marveled.

In reality, the newlyweds knew that the Blarney Stone, a part of the sacred symbol of their ancestors, the Tuatha de Dannan, had awakened after fourteen centuries of silence to proclaim the rightful ruler of the MacCarthaigh Clan.

Little did they know of the stone's true heritage.

Chapter Twenty
New Clans Pact

Saturday, July 22, 1916
Queenstown, Ireland

*J*ack had arranged a private dinner party on the Cunard company yacht in Queenstown Harbour. Now he was observing the interaction of his guests.

"Isn't that a beautiful sight," Kathy exclaimed as the carriage dropped them off pier side just as the sun was setting. "Look at all the colored lights strung everywhere."

Once everyone had arrived from Blarney Castle and boarded, the yacht motored out into the bay.

Jack heralded the newlyweds into the salon with the piper and offered, "Champagne anyone?" After wine and nibbles they sat down to dine.

"Collin, isn't this white linen and real silverware divine?" Kathy marveled, "and the flowers . . . and the lobster . . ."

"It's solid silver, to be precise, my love. Jack had the Cunard wait staff clean the McCarthy utensils, darlin'. See the imprint of the McCarthy stag crest."

Kathy ran her index finger over the indents in the handle of her knife.

After dinner, Aidan, the best man, offered the formal toast.

"When I first met Morgan, I was headed down the road to ruin and probable death because of my attitude after Ma and Pa were murdered, don't ye know. Tadgh had tried to help me over and over, but I wouldn't listen. Morgan, only recently near death from her own horrific circumstances, took me under her wing in more ways than one. Not only did she heal my body, but she touched my soul so that I could banish my guilt feelings about my own tragedy. She accepted me as a valued brother. I've heard it mentioned by others that she, herself, had led a painful childhood, yet had emerged a selfless and fearless caregiver. Well, she surely cared for me in my hour of need. Without her intervention and insight, I would be a mortality statistic today. So, thank you Sis, from the bottom of my reawakened heart."

Turning to the newlyweds, he continued, "The love that you two have openly shared towards one another, and the support you have gladly given to protect each other during dangerous times, has shown me the path for my future. Your guidance for me to get a disciplined schooling has given me some of the tools I will need to be successful along the way. When I heard that Morgan had been called a Florence Nightingale in the past, I realized that both my brother and my new sister have these sterling qualities. So, I want you all to lift your glasses and let's toast to Tadgh and Morgan for their wonderful union and for a long and happy life together."

A teary-eyed Morgan got up and walked over to her new brother-in-law, giving him a bear hug and kiss on the cheek. "You're the best. Who knew you could be so eloquent," she whispered into his ear.

Tadgh replied for both himself and his bride as they exchanged glances. "Thank you, Aidan. Morgan and I are so proud to call you our brother. You've come a long way as have I, since Morgan entered our lives by Divine providence. And we want to thank you all, our best friends and relatives, for joining us on our wedding day. You are all dear to our hearts and to our Cause. I particularly want to thank Peader and Deirdre. Without your support, we would have been captured in Dublin and all of this today could not have happened.

"With regards to our Cause for freedom," he continued, becoming even more passionate, "We are just beginning. The Easter Rising was, in fact, a call to arms, which our Catholic brotherhood chose not to follow, this time. But the ruthless suppression by the British resulting in the martyrdom of our fifteen patriot leaders is awakening Republicans throughout our nation. Next time we will be ready to overthrow the tyrants and win back our native soil. We will be counting on you again when the time comes, don't ye know. The spirit of the Clans is not dead. Padraig Pearse and many others have worked hard to restore our Gaelic way of life. It is now up to us to carry that torch forward. The ceremony to install me as the Clan Chieftain of the McCarthy Clan today was symbolic at best, yet significant. Other Clan leaders can and will rise to follow in our footsteps. Of that you can be sure."

Collin rose to speak. "My wife Kathy and I have been searching to find my long-lost sister for several years at some peril. It had been a great burden to carry since Claire was abducted when under my care many years ago. It is amazing that we found each other after all this time. We want to thank you, Jack, for helping to bring us together. When we first found her, I must admit I selfishly wanted to bring her to our home in Canada, which is a land of great opportunity. I didn't want to lose her again. Now, after our adventures together, I realize that she will be happiest with the love of her life, Tadgh McCarthy, doing everything possible to restore Ireland to its rightful Celtic people. Kathy and I wholeheartedly support your decision, Morgan. We promise to stay connected though we will be an ocean apart."

Sitting at a table with Aunt Biddy, Maurice, Martha and Deirdre, Sam raised his wine glass and silently toasted his protégé. *Here's to you Liam. I've done my best to make amends.* He fervently wished that Lil could have been here with him.

As the evening wore on, Deirdre taught Morgan and Kathy step dancing to the delight of the men.

"Whew," Kathy exclaimed, rubbing her stomach after just a few minutes of this intense exercise." I think that Claire is trying to do these jigs on the inside of my tummy."

Aunt Biddy was overwhelmed with all the ceremony and festivity, but she still had the presence of mind to interrogate Jack on whether the company employees on the liners were unionized. And Peader double teamed him, wanting to know if women employees were being treated fairly. Jack looked around the salon at the happiness of a family reunited and thought to himself, *I'm a lucky man to be considered part of this family. That's enough.*

Tadgh cornered the O'Donnell boys and Aidan later in the evening privately. "You all know that we're only halfway there with the Clans Pact adventure. Collin, you are the O'Donnell Clan leader and we need your support to solve its remaining mysteries."

Peader turned to his comrade and said, "I am going to be very busy starting to teach on Arranmore Island in the fall. So, I won't be available much, although I will be with you in spirit."

"Yes, I know. That's why Collin's participation is so important."

Collin had been thinking about this situation already. "I'm intrigued by this mystery for sure. I want to help with the solution. But I must focus on my life in Toronto where I have responsibilities, not the least of which is my family which appears to be expanding."

"Come on, Brother. You know that you are hooked, aren't ya now?"

"I'll tell you what, Tadgh. If you can get your War of Independence started, I will get my newspaper to assign me over here as a war correspondent."

"Well, fair enough," Tadgh exclaimed clapping him on the shoulder. "I'd better be getting busy then. Speaking of that, I have an idea how you could help."

"From Canada?"

"Yes, that's right. I want to use the coinage, precious plate and some of the jewelry in the McCarthy treasure to buy and deliver weapons for the revolution, just as our forefathers intended."

"How does that involve me?"

"We cannot count on Germany for the support, and it is impossible to get rifles and ammunition from suppliers in Britain. So that leaves America, Collin. The primary rifle of the Allied troops is the Lee-Enfield, which is manufactured in only a few places around the world, including in Philadelphia at Midvale Steel. I found that out when I was with Prince Albert in the Belgium trenches."

"What about Canadian suppliers?"

"The Canadian army apparently gets its weapons from Britain."

"You want me to manage the acquisition and delivery of these rifles to you in Ireland?"

"Yes, Collin. That would require you to commit to support the revolution as well as our Clans Pact adventure. Are you in, lad?"

"After what I saw in post Rising Dublin, Tadgh, just like your citizenry, I am now becoming inclined to favor your revolution. The British are indeed brutal and domineering overlords."

"Our revolution, Collin."

"Yes, our revolution."

Peader chimed in. "You and the British actions have convinced me too that violent armed overthrow of the oppressor will be required."

Surprised at Peader's statement, Tadgh clapped him and Collin on the back, pulling them in with Aidan for a clans hug.

Collin clenched his fists. "I am not sure that I have the connections and skills to pull off such an arms acquisition and delivery Tadgh." He rubbed his forehead. "It would jeopardize my career if I was caught."

"We can't let that happen, Collin. There's a leader of the American Clan na Gael in Philadelphia, named Joseph McGarrity. This group has been funding and leading the push for revolution in Ireland. They spent their funds to try and get German arms for the Rising. I know from experience that he will support us enthusiastically. There is a problem, however. As long as the United States is not a participant in the war in Europe, the arms manufacturer is free to sell guns and ammunition to us if it is done secretly without Britain or Canada's knowledge. But this crucial source will dry up if the United States enters the war as Britain's partner."

Tadgh motioned Jack over to the group. "I've spoken to Jack and he has agreed to organize transport for the weapons from America, haven't you, my friend."

"In my official capacity I cannot involve Cunard in this endeavor. But I have connections, lads, in the freighting business. It's risky in time of war, as you all know. How many rifles are you talking about, Tadgh, and how much ammunition?"

"I don't yet know the value of the treasure but I do know the likely force level that will need weapons. I am hoping there will be enough funds for ten thousand rifles and a million rounds of ammunition. That would be about half the number of the German weapons that were sunk with the *Aud Norge* out there at the narrows to this harbor."

"How much might that cost?"

"I don't know. That's what we have to find out. Maybe a half million pounds."

"Wow. That much."

"Can't we just salvage the ones that are here already?" Aidan asked, pointing out to the harbor entrance.

Jack calculated on his fingers. "I reckon that your needed arms shipment would fill about five train box cars. There is no way that we could salvage that much weaponry under the watchful eyes of the British, even if we could get to it and if it was still serviceable, which it undoubtedly would not be. So no, not feasible."

"That's a huge shipment to deliver in a clandestine manner, Tadgh."

"Yes, I know, Collin. Can you help me brother?"

"I'll give it some thought, Tadgh."

"That's all I ask. Let's not share this with the womenfolk just yet."

Unsheathing his knife, Tadgh pricked his finger and gave the weapon handle first to his new brother-in-law. "A new Clans Pact then, to work together to find the O'Donnell treasure and use all the funds to arm the revolution."

Collin agreed, puncturing his own finger then clasping his ally firmly by the hand.

Jack thought to himself that life takes strange and wonderful turns. Only two weeks earlier he didn't even know if Claire really was alive. Now he was her friend and a partner to a revolution that he hadn't even realized he supported. Now he had a cause, a band of brothers, and a vital purpose in life.

Dusk settled over the Old Head of Kinsale as the *Teutonic* passed by heading out toward the Atlantic as part of the Canada-bound convoy on Sunday evening the twenty-third.

Collin thought it odd to be westbound with just a skeleton troop shipment crew, heading to pick up another six thousand new soldiers destined as fodder for the deadly Western trenches of Belgium and France. One familiar face had greeted them when they boarded, that of Corporal Johnson.

Sam, Collin, and Kathy stood by the starboard rail while taking a tour of the deck after a supper of bullied beef and canned peas on board before sailing. This was not going to be a luxury cruise.

"I could never have imagined the outcome of our trip to Ireland in a million years," Kathy said, holding firm to Collin's hand as the ship rolled gently in the gathering seas. "Finding Claire, I mean Morgan, finding the treasure and almost dying for it and that wondrous marriage and crowning ceremony. Lil isn't going to believe any of it, is she, Sam."

"I'm not sure that I would have believed the Cashel part of your adventure if I hadn't been there to witness it."

"You saved us, Sam, just as you saved me in the earlier warehouse fire. You know that, don't you?"

"We all did our part. Collin, remember. If you hadn't untied me that night so long ago, I couldn't have then come to your assistance now, could I. And Kathy, if you hadn't suggested that I follow you to

Cashel as a backup, then I couldn't have come to your aid. We don't want Lil to fret now, do we, so the tale of our hilltop adventures is best left untold, lass, for now. But we can show her the pictures Collin took of the wedding."

"How are you feeling, darlin'?"

"The rocking of the boat is not bothering me, Collin, only some nausea in the mornings. I think that Claire is in here all right." She padded her stomach and Collin placed his hand over hers at the spot.

"I certainly hope so. It was nice of you to insist that Tadgh and Morgan be her godparents."

"I can't wait to get home to wee Liam. How did Maureen take your story of finding Morgan, my love?"

"She showed it to Mr. Healy and they are going to run it in the paper this Friday. I left out anything that would cause Tadgh, Aunt Biddy, and cousin Peader a problem. I think that Mr. Robertson will also like it. So all's well that ends well, I think."

"As long as you keep your job at the *Tely*, my boy. That remains to be seen."

"I'm not concerned about that, boss. We found Claire and she'll be all right with Tadgh."

"What a turnaround compared to the day we met him, Collin," Kathy said, giving her husband a love tap.

"Going through the fire, literally with him changed my mind, don't ye know. Just as it did back in the warehouse fires with you Sam. How can I ever repay you?"

"You already have, lad, many times over."

Collin gazed off at the lighthouse on the receding Irish coastline. "I am looking forward to getting home, yet I miss Ireland and our new friends and relatives already. I can't help but wonder what my ancestor Red Hugh O'Donnell did with our Clan's fortune back in 1601 before he led his army to that fateful Battle of Kinsale.

At the same time that the *Teutonic* was steaming away from the still-oppressed Emerald Isle, Michael Collins was shouting "C'mon boys" to encourage many of the eighteen hundred Irish inmates of Frongoch Internment Camp in Wales. Conducting an impromptu lesson in guerrilla warfare, he yelled out. "We don't call this the University of Revolution for nothing."

Chapter Twenty-One
Preparing For Battle

Thursday, October 30, 1601
Ballymote, Ireland

Red Hugh O'Donnell, consumed by the urgency to get his army moving south, ignored his twenty-ninth birthday. Dowcra and his British butchers, advancing from Derry and abetted by Red's traitorous cousin Niall O'Donnell had probably already seized Donegal Town. Red had hated to torch his own castle before he headed south for Ballymote, but he couldn't let the enemy occupy his Clan's ancestral stronghold. He worried for the monks and their monastery by the bay. But all this couldn't be helped.

Red prayed to the Lord that Florence had arranged for the disposition of his Clan's wealth as they had agreed secretly when the MacCarthaigh visited Donegal Castle a year earlier. Red had kept his end of the bargain. The O'Donnell treasure was safely buried in a family sacred location in accordance with the talismans and clues that they had prepared together for their joint descendants.

That scurrilous Britisher, George Carew, that the enemy falsely called the Governor of Munster had tricked Florence into meeting under safe conduct protection in Cork City during the summer, and then had him arrested and sent to the Tower of London. Since Florence was the conduit to Phillip III, this had made communications with the supportive Roman Catholic Spanish forces more difficult.

That bastard Carew had also arrested Red's southwestern ally Fitzthomas, the Sugán Earl with the same fate. This would weaken the southern Clans force in the upcoming pitched battle.

Red Hugh's ally, Hugh O'Neill, the remaining clan chieftain

in the north-east had initially held his powder dry during this war. But after Yellow Ford he had thrown in his lot with the O'Donnell. His army would march south separately and link up with Red Hugh before reaching Kinsale. The bond was strong between these two powerful clans since Red Hugh and the O'Neill's daughter Rose had been destined to wed and because the O'Neill sons had escaped imprisonment in the Dublin Castle with Red Hugh back in '92.

Word had come through that the Spanish fleet of 28 ships and 3,300 men under the command of Don Juan del Aguila had arrived and taken control of the provisioner port town of Kinsale south west of Cork City in September. Don Juan had intended to land further north, perhaps in Galway but weather had driven them to Kinsale instead. Unfortunately, the fortifications of this city to hold off a siege were poor. Now they were besieged by the English under their newly appointed and ruthless commander, Lord Mountjoy and they desperately needed the clans. Red hoped that they would gain support from the McCarthy Reagh Clan once they arrived in Munster.

Red's successes with his compatriot northern clans in the evolving Nine-Years War at Clontibret, Tyrell's Pass and Yellow Ford against the superior English forces of the Earl of Essex, Robert Devereux, had been in goodly part a result of engaging the enemy in guerrilla warfare in the mountains. O'Neill had skillfully forged a truce with Devereux in 1599 until an enraged Queen Elizabeth had ordered him home in disgrace. But now, with a more aggressive adversary in Mountjoy, the battle would need to be fought in the plains of Cork County in order to rescue their Spanish allies who had come to defend the Roman Catholic Gaelic Clans.

The O'Donnell knew that Hugh O'Neill was concerned about leaving his northern Ulster lands undefended, but it couldn't be helped. Headstrong and patriotic, Red realized that this was their last stand and he needed all the remaining clans to be united. Fortunately, Hugh O'Neill had been trained in the ways of the British military, so he and his troops were essential to the campaign. A newly committed Knights Hospitaller, Red proclaimed this David and Goliath struggle to be a modern Crusades.

His troops of 3,000 cavalry and 4,000 foot-soldiers assembled in and around the castle and its monastery in Ballymote town on his birthday, which he took as a good sign. But during the war council meeting Red had just concluded in the massive castle courtyard, there was grumbling among the clan leaders. This march south of two hundred and fifty miles in winter through enemy territory was going to be brutal. Even if they survived the ordeal, the condition of the men to battle the English was questionable. But Red Hugh had great faith in God, his Cause, and his countrymen. In the end, they, in turn put their trust in their fervent red-bearded leader despite his young age.

As the chieftains dispersed to inform their men of the plans for the march, Red was left in the courtyard with his twenty-six-year-old brother Rory, his favorite out of his eight siblings. These were brutal times even within the O'Donnell inner circle. In 1590, while Red was being held captive by the English in Dublin castle, Red's mother Ineen Dubh, the second wife of Sir Hugh O'Donnell, had hired Redshank mercenaries from her native Scotland to fight and kill Red's older brother Donnell from another marriage who was favored to become chieftain in order to preserve the Clan leadership for her favorite, Red Hugh.

Rory pulled his brother aside. "Why can't we stay in the mountains and continue guerrilla warfare? We have been so successful, beating back Devereux when he brought 25,000 to Ireland."

"The enemy is already over-running Donegal, as you know, Rory. We need a major victory. Otherwise we will never be rid of the Sassenach."

Red looked around. They were now alone in the 120 by 120 foot-square courtyard with its forty-foot-high walls. He took his broadsword from its scabbard and drew a rough outline of Ireland on the ground. "Fate has brought our Christian allies to our shores.

Would they had landed in Donegal Bay so that we could fight in the mountains, but that was not to be. They are here at Kinsale."[6] Red thrust his sword into ground midway across the southern shore of his drawing. "We cannot let our Spanish allies down, and without them we will not be victorious. Take heart, my brother. The Lord will guide us, and we have *an Cathach* to protect our troops. It has never let us down in my memory. Our own St. Columba ordained it so with our ancestors one thousand and forty years ago."

Being a deeply religious leader, Red Hugh, in truth had concerns. He and Florence had opened the *Cumdach* and removed front and back Psalms from *an Cathach* to point the way for their descendants. He hoped these markers would not be too obtuse for God's chosen ones, and yet would be confounding enough to the Clans enemies should they gain control of the sacred document. He had another nagging feeling. The monks of Kells, at one of St. Columba's sacred monasteries had cautioned Red's ancestors over four hundred years earlier when they completed the *Cumdach*, that it wasn't to be opened and *an Cathach* was not to be altered in accordance with St. Columba's decree back in 561 AD. Would it still protect them during the upcoming battle?

"What role do you have for me then, Brother?"

"I must tell you an ancient story, Rory. Father passed it on to me and you need to hear it in case I am brought to heaven by our Lord in these battles. You must swear silence and allegiance just as I did."

"I so swear. What is it?"

Red strode to the interior north wall of the courtyard where his black Connemara pony pawed the ground. Columba, as Red called him, was a crossbreed between sturdy Andalusian stock that had scrambled ashore when ships of the Spanish Armada were wrecked off the west coast in 1588 with herds of native wild Connemara ponies. This breed was extremely hardy, with tremendous endurance in battle, and Columba had saved Red's life on several occasions. He pulled an apple from his tunic and fed it to his equine partner, stroking his mane while he checked his withers.

Red took a plain tin box from his saddlebags. "Come here, Brother."

Rory obeyed and gave Columba's neck a brush.

Red scanned the interior of the courtyard once again to assure himself that they were still alone. "In this box is a copy I made of an ancient epistle that was entrusted to our ancestral chieftain in 561 in the year of our Lord by our own St. Columba who wrote it. You have been taught about him."

"Yes, Red. He was a prince of the O'Domhnaill Clan who chose the cloth over warrior glory in the sixth century."

"Yes. He gave up the prospect of Clan Chieftain to lead the conversion of our people to Christianity. St. Columba was a great warrior, brother, for Christ and a blessed man to be revered."

"I misspoke. You are right about him."

"He wrote this epistle just before he left for Hy to establish his great monastery there."

"Show me."

"You would not be able to read it, Rory. It is written in the ancient language."

"Greek?"

"Latin."

"What does it say then?"

"It speaks of a gospel given to St. Patrick by God when he showed him purgatory. This gospel apparently chronicles a story of the journey of the Word to our beloved Ireland. This epistle has been passed down chieftain to chieftain and it is to be protected by our clan at all costs. We, the O'Domhniall chieftains are the protectors of the faith and the Irish saints are the protectors of this gospel."

"Saint Patrick and then our own Saint Columba brought Christianity, God's Word, to Ireland. We already know that."

"True, Rory, yet Saint Columba, who knew the contents of the gospel, was adamant that this epistle should be protected by our clan to the death."

"Where is this gospel, itself?"

"That's a mystery that has confounded our ancestors for centuries, Rory. What I was told by father is that our clan fought a battle to gain control of St. Patrick's body after he died in 493. We were successful and the venerated saint was buried in Downpatrick. The gospel was buried with him in a box that was never to be opened."

"So that's where it is then."

"No. I was also told that St. Patrick predicted that a great saint would follow him sixty years hence—St. Columba. I was told that Saint Patrick's body was exhumed in the time of St. Columbia and the gospel was not found afterwards in the empty tomb."

"So, it could be anywhere."

"Yes, that's why it has been so hard to find. Father thought that St. Columba had it. Otherwise why would he have known to write about it in his epistle."

"Fact?"

"No, a family myth, lost in the annals of time."

"If the gospel is lost then why is this epistle so important."

"Our ancestors thought that there are ancient clues in this epistle, which they could not decipher."

"Where is the original epistle and why did you make a copy?"

"It is buried where you helped me hide our clan wealth from the English, lad until we can recover it." Red refrained from telling his brother that he had also hidden the purged Psalms from *an Cathach* with their treasure.

He continued. "It is very fragile and cannot see the light of day. If you and I die in this crucial upcoming battle with the English, then there will be no O'Donnell clan chieftain to carry on the sacred duty to protect this epistle and therefore the gospel. I have decided to get this copy to the only person who should be given that protectorate responsibility in our absence."

"Who?"

"The Grand Master, Fra Alof de Wignacort of the Knights of Malta."

"You mean the head of the Knights Hospitaller?"

"The same."

"You belong now, am I right?"

"Yes, I bought this castle at Ballymote from MacDonagh two years ago for two reasons. The first was needing a stronghold to move to if we had to surrender Donegal to the English. Secondly, Ballymote is a Knights Hospitaller refuge along with the former Knights Templar castle at the lake. In conjunction with the monastery down south at Ardfert where our compatriot Thomas Fitzmaurice still resides, Ballymote provided an escape route for Knights Templar to get to Scotland after the purge of 1307. I believe in their cause, so I joined."

"Is there a connection, Red? Between this story and the one about the gospel, I mean? Is that why you are telling me this?"

"Perceptive of you brother. It is thought by some that the escaping Knights Templar had knowledge of great religious significance based on their time in Jerusalem at the site of Solomon's Temple. They had taken a sacred oath to keep that information secret. I was told by father from his father that at least some of these Templars that passed through Ireland on their way to Scotland around 1310 were looking for this gospel. Our ancestors told them nothing."

"I see now why you want to get this information to the Grand Master then. Is that what you want me to do? Is that why you have confided in me?"

"You remember our cousin Brian MacSweeney from Kilmacrennan? He was here at council."

"Yes, Red. We played with him as children up by Doon Rock where our ancestral chieftains were crowned."

"That's the one. Do you trust him?"

"I don't really know him."

"Well I do, Rory. He saved my life and almost lost his at Yellow Ford."

"As you know, I wasn't there, but I heard you fought bravely."

"I need you with me at Kinsale, so I am going to entrust Brian with the task of getting this copy of the epistle to the Grand Master."

"What of me, then, Brother?"

"If I die in battle and you are spared, then you must become the chieftain of our clan. You would then become the protector of the Faith, Brother, and you know where the original of St. Columba's Epistle is buried. In this case, you must ensure that the Grand Master gets the original in case Brian is unsuccessful. Do you understand?"

"Yes, Red. Of course. You can trust me."

"I wouldn't have told you now before our glorious crusade against the English commences if I didn't already trust you, Brother."

"What about Niall, Red? He courts favor with the English to take over our clan."

Red pounded the wall with his fist and Columba snorted. "Never! He is a slimy toad of a man who must be squashed on sight. A scurrilous traitor to our clan and country."

Unbeknownst to the O'Donnell brothers, the vile Niall, disguised as a gallowglass, had been eavesdropping outside the north wall where he heard some of their conversation through an arrow slit. Chuckling, he slithered back down the path to the town and blended into the throng of warriors who had gathered there. *Dowcra will hear of this after he agrees to my demands. You will both die my cousins and I will be chieftain of all Donegal.*

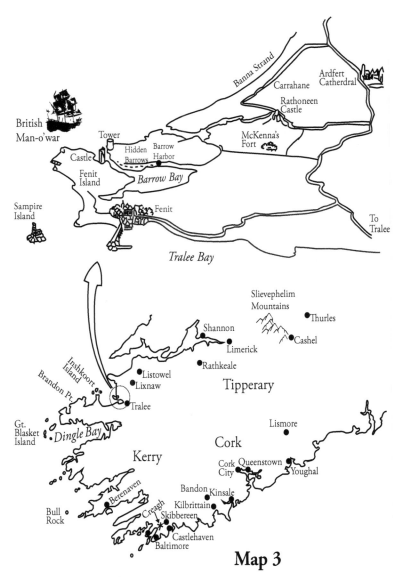

Map 3

Southwest Ireland - 1600 AD

Chapter Twenty-Two
Frozen March

Sunday, November 29, 1601
Holy Cross Church, Near Thurles, Tipperary, Ireland

*R*ory leaned over the pommel of his horse towards his brother. "We've been on the march now for a more than a week, Red. The men are cold and hungry."

Red reined in Columba and dismounted on the stone bridge over the River Suir, just opposite the Holy Cross Church. His brother followed suit.

"God still protects us as St. Patrick ordained with our motto *In hoc signo vinces,—In this sign you will conquer.*" Red raised his battered shield with the red Constantine cross emblazoned on it. And St. Columba's *an Cathach* has never failed us yet. Without the extreme cold through which He froze the bogs, we would still be fifty miles north, brother."

"True, but can we rest, now?"

"Aye, we will celebrate the feast of Saint Andrew tomorrow since the locals support us here. But then we must move on. Don Juan is in desperate need of our warriors."

"I'll alert the chieftains, brother and order the bivouac. What distance is left?"

Red consulted his map "We've come roughly one hundred and fifty miles. If we were to march directly south to Kinsale, it is roughly ninety more miles to go, in four days. But we are to rendezvous with the O'Neill in Bandon west of that port."

"The men will need rest before we engage the heretics."

"We travel through hostile territory from here on, Rory. The villagers here talk about great travesties to the south from that devil George Carew who the invaders call the President of Munster. We need to send a trusted horseman south tomorrow to scout our path. We cannot afford engagement with the English before our forces are united with the O'Neill and the Spanish."

"I recommend the MacDermott. He is swift and tracks well."

"So be it, Rory. Have him ride thirty miles south past Cashel and report back. Meanwhile we will rest. Set up the perimeter and provision the men."

As Rory mounted his horse, Red added, "And send cousin Brian to me. I will be in yon church, praying for our victory."

Red had chosen to come here to Holy Cross on purpose. Its famous church contained a relic of the Holy rood, Jesus' cross, brought to Ireland by the Plantagenet Queen, Isabella of Angoulême around 1233. She was the widow of King John, the benevolent king who created and signed the Magna Carta bill of rights. This became a site of devout Irish pilgrimage in medieval times and a rallying point for the defense of religious freedom and for Irish sovereignty.

Alone, Red venerated the relic. Then he took his knife from its scabbard and touched the ancient wood, then kissed the blade reverently.

Hearing a sound behind him, he whirled around, ready to throw his dagger at the intruder.

"Hold, cousin. 'Tis I, Brian MacSweeney from Kilmacrennan. How may I help you, lord?"

Red clapped his comrade on the shoulder, checked that they were alone and led his cousin to a side cloister. They lit candles for Mother Mary and knelt before the altar.

"I know that you are committed to our fight with the English at Kinsale,[6] but you won't initially be with us there, Brian." Red could see that the man looked crestfallen.

"Have I failed you in any way?"

"Not at all. I have two crucial challenges for you and your men. You will take three *corrughadh* of our best men and head west for Listowel and Ardfert to liberate our ally Thomas Fitzmaurice from the English. Then he and you can join us at Kinsale."

"Aye, lord. That is a march of a hundred miles, about the same as your trek south. After the liberation, we would need to travel another one hundred and fifty miles to join you. I doubt that we would arrive in time or in any condition to join the battle."

"It will take time for the O'Neill to reach us. I don't expect engagement with the enemy until New Years. But you must hurry, cousin."

"What is the strength of Fitzmaurice's men?"

"We don't know. But when he was defeated after a six-day siege of Listowel Castle last November, the enemy, under Charles Wilmot, illegal Governor of Cork, was a thousand foot and fifty horse strong. They may be diluted now because of the Kinsale campaign."

"Are you sure of these facts?"

"Aye, Brian. Thomas escaped with twelve galleys and came to Donegal Bay earlier this year asking for our assistance. He and I are Hospitallers in the faith."

"What is the second task, lord?"

Red turned to face his cousin, gripped his shoulders, and stared into his eyes. "The second task is the most critical of all. I will give you a metal box that you must guard with your life, share with no one until you give it to Fitzmaurice personally. He must have it delivered to the Grand Master of Knights Hospitaller in Malta. This is a matter of the gravest importance. You must not open this box nor let it fall into enemy hands."

"Might I know the contents, Red if I'm to stake my life on it?"

Red stared him down and at that moment decided he could be trusted with the information. "The box contains an ancient epistle of great importance to our Cause from our O'Donnell ancestor, St. Columba."

"I shall guard it with my life, sire and shall deliver it as commanded."

"Good. Now provision your men and prepare to depart after the morrow."

After Brian had left the church, Red Hugh returned to his prayers. He desperately needed God's help for the battles ahead.

By Monday night, his army fed and provisions for the march south laid in during the feast of St. Andrew, Red addressed his troops on the hill north of Holy Cross from the saddle of Columba. "We've just had a scouting report from MacDermott. The well-equipped enemy is encamped just twenty miles south of our position past Cashel, heading this way presumably from Cork. They are three thousand strong, led by that vile George Carew. We have a decision to make."

"Attack," yelled a gallowglass, brandishing his sword above his head.

"Easy, Conor. If we do so and are not victorious, then the English will be successful in splitting our forces before we can unite near Kinsale."

"But they stand in our way."

"Aye. There is another route which God has ordained. But we must be swift. Break camp and we will march tonight."

"Where to, lord?"

"Through Slievephelim Mountains to the west to bypass Carew's troops. They will not believe that we would go there, nor will they follow if they learn our route." Red knew that heading west would get him closer to Thomas Fitzmaurice and potentially more assistance.

Rory mounted his own Connemara pony so he could be seen by the men and spoke up. "For good reason, Red. Those mountains are impassable in winter."

"Our Lord has spoken. He shall provide us safe passage, brother. With *an Cathach*, carried before us by you, Séamus McGroarty, we will be victorious."

Séamus raised the *Cumdach* on its chain around his neck high in the air and shook it violently.

Many of the gallowglass started grumbling, so Red Hugh recited the Twenty-Third Psalm to them. "'…Yea though I walk through the valley of the shadow of death, I will fear no evil…'"

This calmed his men and Red ordered them to action. Then he hailed Rory and Brian to the side as the men dispersed to load up for the march.

"We shall go to the Fitzmaurice town of Rathkeale in Limerick south of the Shannon. It was still not captured by the English when Thomas came to Donegal earlier this year. If we find him there, I shall deliver the box personally."

Red dismounted and stared at his cousin. "In either case, Brian you will follow on to Listowel to liberate Ardfert, Lixnow, Ballykeally and Fenit, and if necessary, take the box with you."

Brian clapped his chest over his heart, leather to leather. "Aye, lord."

"So be it then, lads. Let's get moving."

While Red's troops headed west, MacDermott rode south the next day, Tuesday, November second and hid in Cashel until Carew and his officers arrived. The English commander corralled the town's mayor and other leaders and drove them up into the cathedral on the rock where he interrogated them. The Irish rebel followed and sneaked into the cloisters from which he could overhear the inquisition. Words led to blows, but the town's officials resisted the beatings which left two men dead after claiming truthfully that they had not seen O'Donnell's army.

Carew gathered his five senior officers outside the cathedral and held a war council under the eye of St. Patrick at his cross. MacDermott slid in behind a large rock between the cross and the Bishop's Castle end of the cathedral.

"Should we head north, lord to find O'Donnell's tracks?"

"Dowcra's stooge, Niall O'Donnell reported what he overheard at Ballymote, that O'Donnell planned to come to the Holy Cross at the Feast of St. Andrew as a pilgrimage before advancing on to Kinsale," George Carew said, picking at a loose stone on the base of the cross with his knife, only to find an empty cavity behind it. He turned back to his men. "But this sniveling Irish mongrel cannot be trusted. O'Donnell could have been delayed by weather, but I suspect he has taken a different route to avoid the bogs."

Two riders galloped up Bishop's Walk, dismounted and rushed through the entrance into the courtyard.

Carew swiveled. "What news of O'Donnell, Morton?"

"They were there, sir, in Thurles. The priest denied seeing them, but I found evidence of their bivouac north of town. The fires were recent."

"So the O'Donnell cousin was right. Where are they now?"

"I went back to the town and managed to beat that information out of the blacksmith who shod some of their horses. They're headed west, up into the Slievephelim Mountains."

"That blacksmith must be lying. No military Chieftain would lead his men there in winter. It's impassable."

"I saw evidence of hoofprints heading west, Sir."

Carew had to think a minute.

"I think you had better hear my report, sir," the other scout announced, saluting smartly.

"What is it, Sergeant Carter?"

"O'Neill's march to the east has cut off our supply lines from the Pale and I heard that our main army at Kinsale is now badly afflicted with dysentery and worse. The Spanish are firmly entrenched and we will suffer if the siege is further prolonged. I fear that Mountjoy's slash and burn tactics in Munster were ill-advised, since our army is now without provisions."

"Damn." Carew looked up at the figure of St. Patrick embossed on the ancient cross and snarled before turning back to his officers. "O'Donnell's trying to lure us up into that pass. We're not going to fall into that trap. If he intends to try to scale those hills, his army will be decimated by nature. So be it."

"But if O'Donnell and O'Neill are allowed to join forces, sir?"

"We've been on a wild goose chase, boys. We must return south to Kinsale to support our troops before it's too late. We'll take what supplies we can from here and from Cork on our way." Carew pointed at his junior officer. "I will leave you here, Morton in case O'Donnell doubles back when he finds out we haven't followed him."

Thus decided, Carew and his men strode out of the Rock of Cashel complex, mounted their steeds, and rode off down the Path of the Dead, leaving the town officials cowering in the cathedral looking after their own murdered men.

MacDermott chuckled at this good fortune. Carefully skirting around Carew's withdrawing forces, the advance scout galloped west. Red would hear of this.

The O'Donnell army reached the foothills of the Slievephelim Mountains late Tuesday afternoon, having marched a distance of twenty-five miles. While the men were setting up the bivouac, Red, Rory, and Brian scouted ahead. The temperature had dropped well below freezing but at least the night sky would be clear with a full moon.

Rory patted the left flank of his pony who was laboring on the rocky incline. "The mountains look foreboding, Red. We will lose a lot of our men to the cold, climbing them tomorrow."

"Hold here, lads." Red urged Columba to his right until they were out of sight around the foothill.

Half an hour later he returned. Columba snorted steam clouds into the cold air. "There's a frozen defile three miles north lads, which will reduce the climb from a brutal two thousand to a manageable six hundred feet."

"How wide and long is the pass, Red?"

"I'd say a minimum of fifty yards snaking for what looks like it might be ten miles. I rode a mile into it until I could see over the first ridge."

"The troops will be relieved, Red."

"We are the righteous, Rory." The O'Donnell raised his shield with the red cross of Constantine emblazed on it to God. "Our Lord will provide, and we shall be victorious."

MacDermott caught up to the warriors the following morning when they were just breaking camp to scale the mountains. In his haste to relay the enemy's position and plans, he neglected to pass on one crucial piece of intelligence—that Niall O'Donnell had informed on his clansmen.

Red was pleased that Carew had abandoned his search, yet he wondered if O'Neill, whom he had heard started his march ten days after his own, would encounter Carew's army and be delayed or worse. It couldn't be helped. They were in enemy territory. If only Don Juan had landed at Galway or Donegal.

Two days later, having endured a snowstorm while in the pass, Red had put the Slievephelim Mountains behind them. Although they were tired, with several cases of frostbite, and several pack animals dead, they had accomplished a great feat, like Hannibal crossing the Alps. This bolstered the men's resolve to drive the cursed English from their land.

Skirting Limerick and Askeaton on the Shannon, both of which were under English occupation, Red used local guides to direct them to the Fitzmaurice Castle Matrix stronghold in Rathkeale, twenty miles southwest of Limerick. They arrived just before dark on Friday the fourth. All told they had marched sixty miles since they had left Holy Cross three days earlier.

Thomas Fitzmaurice was not in residence. They were told that he and whatever men he could muster were fighting to retake their lands in Kerry.

"One of our kin has just brought us news from Castletown. The Spanish landed a second force there on the first under Pedro de Zubiaur."

"How large?"

"Six ships and just under a thousand men, I am told, Red Hugh."

"How big is Don Juan del Águila's force, do you know?"

"Around five thousand men before attrition."

"And what of the enemy?"

"The bastard British Commander, Charles Blount, Lord Mountjoy, with the Earl of Thomond and Carew's support had seven thousand men at the start of the siege seven weeks ago. There has been attrition due to cold, sickness and desertion, but we don't know the extent."

Red did a quick calculation in his head. He had managed to retain four thousand foot and three thousand horse. He knew that O'Neill had planned to leave Ulster with about four thousand warriors and with him his trusted Captain Richard Tyrrell with six hundred veterans.

"Our united forces should be approximately eighteen thousand including the Spanish against seven thousand of the English."

"We also heard that the English are planning to send reinforcements, Red."

"Then we must move swiftly. We are to rendezvous with O'Neill at Bandon, west of Kinsale and halfway to Castletown."

"When and how far?"

"Approximately December fifteenth, nine days from now."

"We can march the remaining seventy-five miles easily in that time, brother," Rory offered, counting in his head.

"I want to get there sooner in case O'Neill arrives early and to give our men time to rest before battle."

The next morning, Saturday, December sixth, two armies moved out, the O'Donnells south toward their destiny and trusted Brian with his smaller contingent of three hundred heading west for Listowel twenty-five miles hence. The cousin had the metal box securely in his saddlebags.

Chapter Twenty-Three
Trapped

*L*istowel castle, like Bunratty to its north-east on the north shore of the Shannon, was a large tower house design with four imposing fifty-foot-high bastions connected in a square with heavy curtain walls of the same height. Its arched relief under the battlements stood unique in medieval Ireland. As a testament to the strength of its fortifications, the Fitzmaurices had held out against a twenty-eight-day siege by Sir Charles Wilmot's forces in November 1600 until they finally surrendered, the last Geraldine bastion to resist against Her Majesty Queen Elizabeth's forces in the first Desmond Rebellion. The English summarily executed all of the castle's garrison.

MacSweeney left his forces in a copse of trees five miles east of the town while he scouted out the castle. Situated on a steep bank overlooking the River Feale and the town, the fifteenth century stronghold looked imposing to say the least. Reconnoitering in the town, he learned that Thomas Fitzmaurice had secretly withdrawn toward Fenit Castle prior to the siege, some twenty-five miles south-west. That single tower house castle near Tralee, with its round tower on the other side of the narrow entrance to Barrows Bay, controlled access to the early medieval trade port and educational conduit to the ecclesiastical haven of Ardfert Monastery, just six miles to its north. Queen Elizabeth had granted Fitzmaurice a pardon for his life only. His lands and possessions were forfeit to the crown if captured. Lixnaw castle had already fallen, yet they had so far let Fitzmaurice alone in his smaller Fenit stronghold.

The villagers reported that Wilmot had left an English garrison to guard Listowel castle while he took the bulk of his troops to support his master, the butcher Lord Mountjoy at Kinsale.

Brian saw no immediate advantage to attacking the castle. If successful, he would have to leave a sizeable garrison there himself, diluting his forces. Instead he decided to seek out Fitzmaurice and combine resources with him. After all, Red's orders were to liberate the Clan chieftain and get him the box. Perhaps Thomas would have other plans to retake his territory.

Brian MacSweeney housed his men in the bush near what the locals called McKenna's Fort, an ancient wooden rath two miles south of Ardfert Cathedral on Thursday afternoon the tenth.

"Should we take back Ardfert and Lixnaw or press on south to Fenit Castle in the morrow, my lord?" one of his gallowglass officers called a consapal asked after checking the status of the men in his hundred-man *corraghadh*.

Brian realized that he needed to find Thomas as quickly as possible to deliver the box. "Wherever The Fitzmaurice might be. I will go to mass at the cathedral and find out what I can."

Brian headed into the town of Ardfert on foot and slipped into the cathedral, borrowing a long black priest's cassock from the sacristy. Once he ascertained the clergyman's allegiance to the Clans, he was told that Fitzmaurice had been planning to sail from Barrow Bay to Castlehaven to assist the Clans and the Spanish. Wilmot's forces had descended from Lixnaw and were already occupying the short castle near the Ardfert Cathedral.

"Where is Wilmot?"

"I don't know, sire, but I overheard some of his men mention that his main force is in Tralee. You'd best hurry I should think."

"Who do you trust as a guide for us in this neighborhood, Father?"

"I'd trust young Bradan in the village with my life. He knows his way about, and he hates the English."

The priest sent for the lad while Brian scouted out the enemy. It looked like the short castle was occupied by a dozen soldiers and there were another ten in the local ale house. When Brian returned to the cathedral, he found the priest instructing Bradan on his task.

"What do we know of the English force from Lixnaw?"

"We don't know, sire. There must be more nearby. I overheard them talk in the tavern about apprehending our dear Earl Fitzmaurice. Someone named Mountjoy ordered it, so they said."

"Then we'd best be on our way, Bradan."

Brian thought of borrowing a horse to ride north and determine the force status of the enemy, but it was getting late and there was no telling where they might be.

The sun was setting when Brian and Bradan returned to camp. MacSweeney ordered him fed and then spoke to his *consapals*.

"Let the men rest tonight, no campfire. Double the guard. Wilmot's troops are in the area. We move south to Fenit Castle at dawn."

"Aye, lord."

At the same time that evening, standing in the town square off Princes' Quay in Tralee where his thousand soldiers were bivouacked, Sir Charles Wilmot fumed at his officers. "How did you let four of Fitzmaurice's ships escape from Fenit? Mountjoy sent us here to stop him before he could join up with those devils O'Donnell and O'Neill."

"We interrogated the mayor of Fenit this morning until he broke, sir. The ships slipped out last night from Barrows Bay with three hundred men before we arrived from Kinsale. We sent a scout and two ships are still in Barrow Harbor. One, named *La Rata Santa Maria Encoronada* is flying the earl's colors so he might not have left yet."

"Damn, that was the Spanish Armada ship that was driven ashore by weather in 1588 in Blacksod Bay, Mayo. I remember that Lord Deputy Fitzwilliam reported it had been torched by the Spanish after it was beached."

"Apparently not, sir. The Fitzmaurices must have hidden her from us in some remote cove until now."

"Did the mayor say the earl had left with his four smaller ships?"

"He wouldn't say."

"Why would Fitzmaurice send ships ahead of him."

"We don't know, m'lord."

"How did Fitzmaurice get this army and naval ships? He was confined to his Fenit Tower by the Queen."

"We now know that he visited O'Donnell and O'Neill last summer by ship and the locals here are sympathetic, especially after the Desmond Rebellion."

"Where did this mayor say they were going? Kinsale?"

"We don't know. He expired before we could gain that information."

"Damn. I'll bet they've gone to Castlehaven where the Spanish landed nine days ago. But they'll find five of the six Spanish ships sunk or run ashore in the harbor, won't they lads. Admiral Leveson made quick work of them last Sunday. The Spanish infidels fled for the hills. We'll round them up in due course after we finish off Fitzmaurice's lair and capture him if he's still there. We'll send two of our ships after his fleet at first light and keep three for our attack on Fenit. If we don't get Fitzmaurice at Fenit or Castlehaven, then Leveson will apprehend him if he tries to attack our sea blockade at Kinsale."

"What if Fitzmaurice's fleet returns to Fenit?"

"We'll have captured and razed the castle and be ready for them then. We break camp at six o'clock and attack from land and sea just after dawn, two hours later. Our compatriots from Lixnaw will box them in if they flee north."

♣ ♣ ♣ ♣

Once the camp had settled in for the night, Brian and Bradan headed out on foot again, south through the sands of Carrahane towards Barrow Bay, two miles away.

"The harbor is just over the next knoll, sire. We'll see if Lord Fitzmaurice's ships are still at anchor."

They crept to the ridge just before midnight. The bay was lit only by a sliver moon in the clear, cold sky. Brian saw the harbor on the north shore of the bay and Fenit Castle in the distance, almost a mile to the west on the south shore at the narrow entrance from the sea.

"There are two galleys at anchor but four are gone, sire. They were here yesterday. I'd swear to it. It's not clear then whether Lord Fitzmaurice has already left since the larger ship on the left is flying his colors."

"I believe you lad. The earl came to Donegal last summer in that flagship. I was amazed then that he could have a Spanish galleon and keep it hidden from our enemy."

"I'm told that a Fitzmaurice son died on that ship when it was driven ashore in Mayo during the Spanish Armada invasion, sire."

"What are those other boats at the wharf, Bradan?"

"Fishing boats. They leave each morning for the catch."

"Do they now. Are they ocean worthy? Can they sail to Queenstown for example?"

"Some could, I'd venture, except in a storm. I know old Mc-Namara. His boat could."

"I need to see what's going on at the castle, Bradan."

"Come with me to the tower." The villager turned right and padded down a sheep path on the ridge parallel to the water. Three quarters of a mile west, as they approached the narrow entrance to the bay from Tralee Bay, Brian could see a round tower out on the north point and to the south on the island, across the quarter mile neck of water, he had a better view of Fenit Castle on a spit of land, silent, black and foreboding except for one light in the tower.

Ten minutes later they snuck into the fifteen-foot round tower through its stooped arched entrance into the open enclosure. Climbing the internal spiral staircase, they reached the top with its circular battlement thirty feet above the ground.

Pointing across the water, Brandan explained, "This tower was built by Edmund Fitzmaurice, our tenth Baron of Kerry, sixty-five years ago. It stands on the spot where St. Brendan the Navigator was born in 474. He found the new world you know a thousand years before Columbus. This is sacred land, so it is, and a last possession of Lord Thomas to be protected."

"They've used an iron chain across the narrows from the castle to this tower as a gate for ships."

"For exacting a fee to enter the harbor?"

"Precisely. But it's gone, these five years now."

Brian took his spyglass from his tunic and scanned the castle to the south. "I can see motion in that upper room."

"Those would be Lord Fitzmaurice's quarters, sire."

Brian cursed himself for not bringing the metal box with him, instead having left it wrapped in cloth, safely in his saddlebags in their guarded camp. It would have to be delivered when they met the eighteenth Baron of Kerry later in the day, if he was there.

"Can one of those galleys in the harbor land on the castle side of the bay?"

"No, but the Earl built a deep harbor on the seaward side of the island outside Barrow Bay. They usually ferry men over to the bay harbor in *curraghs* to keep the ships protected here. It's not really an island you know, since it is connected to the mainland on the east with only a tiny river to cross. You can march there with your men."

Brian thought for a moment. Marching around the bay would put them in harm's way from Wilmott if he was attacking from Tralee.

"I want to use those ships to take my men to the island. If we land on the seaward side we will stay out of sight of the eastern approach to the island from Tralee."

"Do your men know how to sail a galley then?"

"We'll figure it out. We marched across Slievephelim in the snow. We can do anything."

"Slievephelim in winter, sire? You don't say."

"All right. Is there any way to travel along the shore from here to the harbor lad, out of sight?"

"There is no shore path, but there are natural barrows."

"Caves you mean. Are there now?"

"Aye, sire. Not known by many. See over there to the left where the north beach meets the cliff a hundred yards hence, near that copse of trees. They are used to smuggle goods to and from ships out here beyond the point, into and out of the fishing harbor."

"By pirates to avoid customs duties?"

"Yes."

"We'd best return to camp, lad. I'll need your help today when we attack Wilmot's forces and defend the castle."

Brian caught only a few winks of sleep. He rose at five o'clock and had his men ready to march by seven-thirty. This would be a good day, a chance to defeat the enemy and to discharge his sacred duty to deliver the box for Red Hugh.

He left one of his corrughadhs of a hundred men at the fort copse to intercept Wilmot's northern forces if they materialized from Lixnaw.

Brian lifted Bradan up onto the back of his horse behind him. The steed could easily handle the load.

Before the two corrughadhs had covered a half a mile, they heard a ship's canon blast.

"On the double men," Brian yelled as he spurred his horse onwards ahead of the column.

Brian and Bradan reached their former observation point above Barrow Bay harbor first. Dawn was breaking over Stack's Mountain to the east on their left.

Brian's two consapals rushed up the backside of the hill with the warriors still on the march behind them.

"My God, we're too late."

An English man-o-war sat squarely in the middle of the bay firing west broadside at Fenit Castle. Its cannon balls blew holes in the eastern side of the tower. Brian had heard that the Elizabethan navy had developed super cannons that could shoot their projectiles a mile and penetrate through both sides of a ship at a hundred yards, but this was the first time he had seen them in action. Frightening.

Through his glass, Brian could plainly see inhabitants of the castle fleeing out of the main entrance. He wondered if one of them could be the Earl.

"Bradan, look through this glass at those people. Do you see Earl Fitzmaurice, lad?"

Bradan took a minute to adjust his sight. No, sire, but I could have missed him."

Brian realized that a good chieftain would stay with his castle until all his subjects were out.

A fire broke out somewhere inside the stronghold and smoke was billowing through the upper windows and arrow slits.

Below them Fitzmaurice's flagship had weighed anchor and was heading out through the narrows at high tide. Since the gun ship was not firing at it, Brian decided that it was manned by English sailors, likely having slipped over from the man-o-war.

He grabbed the glass back and gazed out to his right into Tralee Bay. There were two more English ships guarding the exit of Barrow Bay.

One of the consapals tugged on Brian's shoulder. "Look to the east, my lord."

Brian swiveled, staring into the eastern sun on the horizon. English soldiers were marching up the road from Tralee heading for the north shore of Barrow Bay, likely the harbor. They had reached the east end of the bay, a mile away. He looked southeast, adjusted his glass, and picked up more English mercenaries already coming up onto Fenit Island toward the castle.

"We're being attacked, men."

"How many altogether, Brian?"

"Rough count at least eight hundred, about half on the island. We're in for it, lads."

A horseman from the corrughadh Brian had left at the fort galloped up behind their observation point. He jumped off his lathered steed and announced breathlessly, "Our scout in Ardfert reports that at least three hundred English soldiers are entering Ardfert from the north, sire, likely from Lixnaw, heading south."

Brian MacSweeney didn't like the five to one odds. He made a decision. Fenit Castle was being destroyed and the enemy force was overwhelming. The ship's cannons were a tipping point. There was no reason to try and rescue the tower, only to find Fitzmaurice. If they stayed on this northern point of land and engaged the enemy, they would surely be trapped and annihilated.

But what am I going to do with Red Hugh's precious box? It needs to get to Fitzmaurice. Until then, I am to guard it with my life and cannot let it fall into enemy hands. I need to find out if the earl is still alive and save him if possible.

He could see that the English soldiers on Fenit Island were quickly rounding up the castle's garrison and villagers.

Brian needed a closer observation point to see if he could find Fitzmaurice.

He made another decision. Turning to his two *consapals*, he said, "We must retreat from here. March your men north double time to McKenna's Fort and integrate our force. Attack and destroy the Lixnaw enemy contingent in Ardfert. Then press on north and liberate Lixnaw." He hoped that Wilmot's southern forces would focus on Fenit and not chase the retiring Irish troops. With luck, his men would not be spotted.

"What of you, my lord?"

"I need ten brave volunteers including my son Dermott. We will stay here and provide a diversion if necessary until you have successfully withdrawn."

343

"But my lord?"

"That's my order. I'll join you at Lixnaw. Get moving."

The man-o-war in Barrow Bay had stopped firing at the tower, and instead, shifted starboard. It fired a salvo at the hill above Barrow Harbor chewing up the hillside around MacSweeny and his *consapals*.

"Damn, we've been spotted."

They jumped back down behind their now compromised observation point to where the troops were waiting. One *consapal* barked an order and thirty kerns stepped forward. Brian quickly selected ten of them including eighteen-year-old Dermott and his troops started heading north on a run.

"You men come with me!" Brian yelled, setting off west behind the hill at a trot that his men could keep up with. "Badan, are you still with me?" he said reaching back in the saddle to make sure the lad was still seated squarely.

"Aye sire."

They reached the round tower five minutes later, with what was left of the castle just across the narrow mouth of the bay.

"In here, men. Take up positions on the battlement."

From his perch on the fifteen-foot round battlements, Brian could see the English had corralled the Irish soldiers and women beside the conflagration that until an hour before had been Fenit Castle. "Do you see the Earl, Badan?"

The lad looked through the glass intently. "No, sire. He is not there."

Brian realized that Fitzmaurice could no longer be alive in the burning ruins of his castle. He wouldn't flee, leaving his soldiers to the enemy without him. He was either dead or he had left with his four ships a day earlier.

Brian scanned east and saw that the English soldiers had closed in on their observation point above the harbor.

One of the ships out in Tralee Bay fired a shot that hit the round tower fifteen feet above ground, blowing a hole in the wall below them and taking out two of the stair steps.

"We've been spotted, men. Off the battlements!"

This was getting serious.

As his men scrambled down the inside spiral stairs, Brian stayed on the battlements. He noted that Bradan was still bravely by his side. The English soldiers on the north ridge to the east had seen the hit on the round tower and some were now rushing along the path towards them. Maybe a hundred. They'd be here in five minutes. He could make a run for it, but he would undoubtedly be apprehended.

Fitzmaurice was probably in the castle tower or the English would not have attacked it this morning. He's likely dead. What did Red Hugh say? Fitzmaurice is to get the sacred box to the Grand Master, Hospitallers in Malta. I can't let it fall into enemy hands.

Brian reached into his tunic and withdrew a paper that he sometimes used to diagram attack plans for his consapals. He scribbled the words,

> *Grand Master Hospitaller. There is an ancient epistle of great importance to your cause from St. Columba, being sent to you for protection by Red Hugh O'Donnell via Thomas Fitzmaurice. Alas I cannot fulfill this sacred order because we are being roundly defeated by the English here at Fenit. Search for it my lord. Signed Brian MacSweeney in the year of our Lord, December, 1601.*

Then he folded the paper thrice to hide the words.

The men had assembled in the base of the tower when Brian descended to meet them.

Another cannonball took the top off the tower on the seaward side, raining rubble down onto the kerns. A large fragment just missed striking Brian on the head.

"Get outside, on the north side away from the bay. Quickly."

He ushered them out just as another projectile hit the tower, this time from the man-o-war in Barrow Bay. They were being attacked on both sides.

"Dermott and Bradan come here." Brian took them aside and thrust the folded note into Dermott's hand. Bradan will show you through the barrows." He pointed to the beach. "You must guard this note with your life and deliver it to the Grand Master of the Knights Hospitaller in Malta, son. Do you understand?"

"But how, father?"

Brian rushed to his horse which he had tied to the round tower gate and withdrew the black cassock that he had borrowed. "Wear this, son. Stay out of sight near the harbor until the English leave. Use the galley if they don't take it and search out the old mariner McNamara. Bradan here will help you."

"Aye, father. But I should stay and fight with you."

"This task is much more important, son. Don't let the note fall into the hands of the English infidels."

"I shall not fail you, father." Dermott clapped his father by the shoulders and then reluctantly turned as Bradan pulled him down towards the water.

Brian crossed himself and prayed for Dermott's deliverance as he saw the two safely disappear into the hidden barrows at the east end of the beach.

Returning to the nine men who were guarding the horse, Brian ordered them to flee north to meet up with their compatriots.

They responded in unison "We stay with you, lord."

"So be it. Guard the entrance."

Brian grabbed the metal box from his horse's saddlebags and raced inside the tower. The enemy would descend on them at any moment. Brian found what he was looking for. There in the middle of the floor of the tower was a large flagstone, interlinked with its neighbors. It looked like it had been there for centuries. Brian brushed away the rock debris. He took his sword from its scabbard and begin to wedge it down around the central flagstone. After a minute of probing he finally found a spot where he could pound the sword down below the rock. He pushed outwards as hard as he could on the hilt of the sword, but he couldn't budge the stone.

He poked his head out of the tower and summoned the nearest kern to him.

Once they were inside, he said, "Wedge your sword beside mine. Now push."

Together they managed to dislodge the heavy stone and tilt it on edge.

"You can rejoin your compatriots."

As the kern exited the tower, Brian started digging in the hard ground under the upturned stone with the tip of his sword. Another cannonball rocked the fortification, showering him with rock shards.

Brian didn't notice. He was working with single purpose. A short time later he had a hole big enough to hold the box.

One of the kerns yelled out, "Lord, the enemy is upon us!"

Brian heard swords clanging.

He dropped the box into the hole, pushed most of the dirt back in, and then levered the flagstone down in place. It was slightly off center so he shoved with all his might until it dropped in place.

Brian could hear the screams of agony as soldiers of both sides were being slain.

Quickly he spread the remaining dirt in the far corners of the dark enclosure.

The clanging stopped. From outside the tower he heard a voice call out, "You, coward in there. Your men are dead. Come out and face your maker."

Brian kicked the rock chips back over the central floor area. Not a moment too soon.

Sir Charles Wilmot bent his head momentarily and stepped into the dark tower as three of his soldiers blocked the exit. The only light filtered in through the entrance arch and from the cannonball holes in the stonework above him.

Although he had been forcing Fitzmaurice from his lands over the last year, castle by castle, Wilmot had never met his adversary on the field of battle. As luck would have it, in the dim light, Brian's height and facial features, including burly beard and moustache bore some resemblance to the crude painting of the earl that the English leader had seen in the now-occupied Listowel Castle. Brian's noble uniform devoid of Clan tartan added to the misconception.

Wilmot said, "You are the cowardly leader of this group of vermin. Thomas Fitzmaurice, I presume. Surrender to me, Wilmot, Governor of County Cork, in the name of Her Majesty Queen Elizabeth, ruler of all Ireland."

Brian realized that this deception could give his troops more time to withdraw undetected if these devils believed that his small band of ten had come from Fenit Castle.

"Never! We meet at last, infidel." Brian raised his sword and lunged at his adversary. The Englishman dodged sideways against the inside of the tower, the blade nicking his arm.

"Where is the epistle delivered to you from that traitor Red Hugh O'Donnell?"

Brian couldn't believe his ears. How could he know about that? "What nonsense are you spewing? Are you daft? I have no such document from my ally. You will never defeat us, English dog."

"Take Fitzmaurice," Wilmot cried out, and the three soldiers descended on the Irish warrior and subdued him.

"Where are your ships headed?"

Brian refused to answer.

Wilmot slashed him in the leg with his broadsword and Brian went down in the center of the tower, cursing in Gaelic.

"Where and how many men?"

"English scum."

Wilmot cut him in the side.

Brian still refused to answer. He thought of Jesus on the cross at Calvary having nails in his feet and hands, and a pierced side, and then decided he wasn't worthy to be compared to the Lord. He prayed silently, head down, that Dermott would be able to carry out his mission so that the sacred task that Red Hugh had given him would be fulfilled.

Wilmot had lost all patience. "Hold the earl on his knees."

Then with one swift blow of his sword, Wilmot decapitated brave Brian MacSweeney whose body and head fell on the central flagstone. The blood gushed out of his severed neck and seeped down between the stones, onto the metal box, sealing it forever.

"Come on men. We'll have the man-o-war reduce this tower to ruins and bury that vermin we've just exterminated."

THE END of Book Four
Book Five ***Revolution*** is coming soon!

North America – Historical

John Devoy	Leader of Clan na Gael in America, New York
Dorothy Finlay	Sam and Lil's Younger Daughter
Elizabeth Finlay (Lil)	Sam's Wife
Ernest Finlay	Sam and Lil's Newborn Son
Norah Finlay	Sam and Lil's Older Daughter
Samuel Stevenson Finlay	Artist & Director of Art at Riverdale High School, Toronto
Joseph McGarrity	Leader of Clan na Gael in America, Philadephia
John Ross Robertson	Publisher and Editor-in-Chief, *Toronto Evening Telegram (Tely)*

North America – Fictional

Jim Fletcher	*Toronto Evening Telegram*, News Director, Collin's Boss
Collin O'Donnell	Young Irishman from Toronto
Fiona O'Sullivan	Kathleen's Mother
Kathleen O'Donnell (Kathy)	Young Irish Woman in Toronto, Collin's Wife. (née O'Sullivan)
Liam O'Donnell	Kathy and Collin's Son
Ryan O'Sullivan	Kathleen's Father

Cast of Characters

Europe – Historical

Don Juan del Aguila	Military Leader, Spanish Forces at Kinsale Ireland 1601-2
Herbert Henry Asquith	British Prime Minister during WWI
Augustine Birrell	British Secretary for Ireland
Richard Boyle	Lord Cork, Lismore Castle, British Leader Confederate War, 1640s
Lord Broghill	Roger Boyle, Richard's Son, Laid Siege to Blarney Castle in 1646
Sir George Carew	British Lord Totnes, President of Munster in 1601
Edward Carson	Ulster Unionist Political Leader, Organizer Ulster Volunteers Fought Against Home Rule
Sir Roger Casement	Irish Volunteer, Ambassador to Germany, Recruiter of Irish Brigade
Sir Neville Chamberlain	Chief Inspector, Royal Irish Constabulary (RIC)
Thomas Clarke	Lead Member of Irish Republican Brotherhood (IRB),
	Military Council, Lead Proclamation Signatory
Walter Leonard Cole	Republican, Founder Sinn Fein Organization & Publishing Company, His house at Three Mountjoy Square Used for IRB Meetings

Michael Collins	Member, Irish Volunteers, Joseph Plunkett's Aide in Easter Rising Leader of Prisoners, Frongoch Internment Camp Wales
James Connolly	Head of the Irish Citizens Army (ICA), Dublin Commandant, Military Council, Proclamation Signatory
Oliver Cromwell	English Military and Political Leader, Lord Protector of the British Commonwealth, Conqueror of Irish in 1640s
Sir Henry Dowcra	Governor of Derry after crushing the O'Donnell Irish Clan in 1602
Elizabeth Finlay	(née) Stevenson, John's First Wife, Died before Sam Emigrated
John Finlay	Samuel Finlay's Father, Bleacher at Bessbrook Spinning Company, Lived in Lisburn, Ireland
Riah Finlay	John Finlay's Second Wife, from Russia
Thomas Fitzmaurice	18th Lord Kerry and Baron Lixnaw, Hospitaller, Ally of Red Hugh O'Donnell
James FitzThomas FitzGerald	Sugán Earl of Desmond, Maurice's Ancestor, Captured and Jailed before the Battle of Kinsale
Lovick Friend	British Major General, Commander-in Chief, Ireland during WWI

Lady Gaga	Friend of Nora Perceval, Married to Sir Henry Gore-Booth
Maud Gonne (MacBride)	Irish Revolutionary and Suffragette, Married to John MacBride, Yeats Muse
William Hall (Blinker)	British Captain, Director of British Intelligence, Broke German Code
Lord Hardinge	Lord of Penhurst, Viceroy of India, Head of British Royal, Commission of Inquiry into the Easter Rising, 1916
John Edward Healy	Publisher, *The Irish Times*
John Kearney	Tralee Head District Inspector, RIC
Reverend J.H. Lawlor	Professor of Ecclesiastical Studies, Dublin University Researcher of Ancient Gaelic Documents Including *an Cathach of St. Columba*
Lewis Lord of Kinalmeaky	British Commander, Destroyed Kilbrittain Castle in 1642, Richard Boyle's Son, Delivered *Book of Lismore* to his Father
Florence MacCarthaigh	Clan Chieftain until 1601, Arrested by George Carew before Battle of Kinsale in January 1602
MacCarthaigh Raibhaigh	Lord Finghin, Recipient of the *Book of MacCarthaigh Reagh* at Kilbrittain
Tomas MacCurtain	Head of IRB for Cork, Tadgh's Commanding Officer
Eoin MacNeill	Chief of Staff, Irish Volunteers

Cast of Characters

Agnes Mallin	Wife of Michael Mallin
Constance Markiewicz	Countess, Deputy Commandant Battalion #2, St. Stephen's Green
General Sir Grenfell Maxwell	Commander-in-Chief, British Affairs During and After Rising
McCarthy Mor	Muscry Chieftain, Blarney, Leader Confederate War Rebellion, 1640s
Jacques de Molay	Last Head of the Knights Templar, Burned at the Stake in 1314
Sir Matthew Nathan	British Undersecretary for Ireland
Sean O'Casey	Irish Playwright, Tadgh's Literary Mentor
Brigid O'Donnell	"Biddy," Peader's Mother in Dungloe, Tailor
James O'Donnell	Peader's Father, Seasonal Worker in Scotland
Niall O'Donnell	Red Hugh's traitorous cousin Supported the British to overthrow the Clans
Peader O'Donnell	College Student, Later to be a Revolutionary Leader, "Peadar"
Red Hugh O'Donnell	Last Free Chieftain O'Donnell Clan until 1602, Battle of Kinsale
Rory O'Donnell	1st Earl Tyrconnel, Red Hugh's Younger Brother. Led Flight of the Earls to Europe in 1607.

Cast of Characters

Hugh O'Neill	Clan Chieftain, Northeast Ireland. Compatriot of Red Hugh O'Donnell at the Battle of Kinsale, 1602
Sir Owain	Twelfth Century European Knight, Endured Entrance to Purgatory then Returned to Temple Castle, Now Ghost for Lost Souls There
Padraig Pearse	Lead Member of the IRB and School Master St. Edna's, Military Council, Commandant-General in Easter Rising, Proclamation, Signatory, "President" of the Proclaimed Republic of Ireland
Alexander Perceval	The Hong Kong Taipan, Tea Merchant, Charlotte's Husband's Father, Restored and Expanded Temple House
Ascelin Perceval	Charlotte's Son, Served on the Front during World War I in 1916
Charlotte Perceval	Matron of Temple House, Ballymote, Ireland during WWI
Eleanora Margaret Perceval	"Nora," Ascelin's Wife
Jane Perceval	Matron of Temple House in 1847, Died Helping Hunger Victims
King Phillip III	Catholic King of Spain in 1601, Provided Army to Irish Clans

John Redmond — Irish Nationalist Politician, Organized National Volunteers to Fight for the Allied Cause in WWI, Believed Britain Would Pass Irish Home Rule

John Ross Robertson — Publisher and Editor *Toronto Telegram (Tely)*

Austin Stack — Head of IRB for Tralee

Wolfe Tone — Father of Irish Republicanism and Leader of 1798 Rebellion

Eamon de Valera — Commandant Battalion #3, Boland's Bakery and Mill

Lord Wimborne — Ivor Churchill Guest, British Lord Lieutenant for Ireland

William Butler Yeats — Famous Irish Poet and Pillar of both Irish and British Literary Societies, Co-founder of the Abbey Theatre in Dublin

Europe – Fictional

Darcy Boyle — Head Constable, Royal Irish Constabulatory (RIC), Cork City

Captain Maurice Collis — Fishing Captain, Fenit, Ireland, Descendant of the FitzMaurice Clan, Supporter of Tadgh

Martha Collis — Wife of Maurice Collis

Frank Coltrain — RIC Constable, Tralee, Captured Sir Roger Casement

Deirdre	Owner and Barkeeper of the Temple Bar Pub in Dublin, Ireland
Captain Haig	Captain of the Troop Ship *Aquitania*
Henri and Marg	Neighbors of Sean O'Casey
Henry Hollingsworth	Graduate Student, Working for Professor Lawlor at RIA
Constable Leroy Jackson	Boyle's Burly Subordinate
Constable Jamison	Tralee Constable Killed by Darcy Boyle
Corporal Robert Johnson	Troop Ship Battle Readiness Coordinator
Jack Jordan	Third Bosun's Mate, HMS *Lusitania*, Manager Cunard Operations, Queenstown, Ireland, Looking for Claire
Dean Maloney	District Inspector, RIC Cork
Brian MacSweeney	Red Hugh O'Donnell's cousin Sent to Liberate Fitzmaurice
Aidan McCarthy	Tadgh's Younger Brother, Irish Volunteer
Tadgh McCarthy	Young Irish Revolutionary. Member of Cork IRB, Communications and Transportation Specialist. Fisherman
Morgan McCarthy	Irish Woman Rescued by Tadgh McCarthy, Tadgh's Lover, Partner & Wife

Martin Murphy	Captain of Supply Ships for Beamish & Crawford (B&C) Brewery
Doctor O'Callihan	Hospitaller Doctor at Fenit
Finian O'Donnell	Collin's Father, Murdered in Donegal
Shaina O'Donnell	Collin's Mother, Murdered in Toronto
Maureen O'Sullivan	Journalist for *The Irish Times* Newspaper, Dublin, Ireland
Constable Harry Simpson	Darcy Boyle's Underling, Replacement for Constable Gordon James
Jeffrey Wiggins	Transportation Leader, Beamish & Crawford (B&C) Brewery, Cork City, Ireland, and Tadgh's Colleague at B&C

Historical Background

The purpose of this historical background is to illuminate the historical facts imbedded in Book Four, particularly those associated with the Clans Pact adventure.

In Book Two, *Entente*, I included significant background on the history of World War I and its horrific trench warfare. I did so since this terrible war killed over seventeen million people. Although connected with the Irish fight for freedom, it was not central to the Irish storyline and could therefore not be addressed in overall terms within the novel itself.

I could also have included a thorough account on the Irish Easter Rising of 1916 in the background material in Book Three, *Rising*, but chose not to do so. The treatment of the Rising in ten chapters of that novel, as well as in three chapters regarding the lead-up to the rebellion at the end of Book Two, *Entente*, taken together, provide an accurate description of this pivotal event in Irish history.

At the end of Book Four we step back in time to the preparations for the Battle of Kinsale which took place in January 1602. This subject deserves some mention here, below, as does the convoluted history of the *Book of Mac Carthaigh Riabhach (Lismore)*.

Finally, the Percevals of Temple House near Ballymote have a storied history leading back to Sir Perceval of the Round Table. They and their magnificent manor deserve special mention here since our heroes spend time in Ballymote for reasons yet to be unearthed.

1. The Money Diggers

In the author's note, I provide a brief introduction to the mysteries and exploitation of the illusive search for buried treasure in eastern North America including the wonderful tales of such skullduggery by the famous raconteur Washington Irving. This is in keeping with the story in this novel and the front cover image titled *The Money Diggers* painted by John Quidor. Below are the references for that text,

1.1   https://en.wikipedia.org/wiki/Washington_Irving

1.2   Courtesy of the Brooklyn Museum

1.3   https://morristowngreen.com/2016/10/27/the-morristown-ghost-or-beware-of-ghosts-promising-gifts/

1.4   http://www.mormonhandbook.com/home/joseph-smith-money-digger.html

1.5   https://www.oakislandmoneypit.com/

2. The *Book of Lismore (Book of Mac Carthaigh Riabhach)* *

The fifteenth-century manuscript known as the *Book of Lismore* is so named because it was uncovered during structural modifications of Lismore Castle in 1814. Also included in the walled-up discovery was the Bishop of Lismore's fine crozier.

This crucial compendium document was then determined to have been created for Finghin Mac Carthaigh Riabhach of Cairbre in County Cork, and his wife Caitilin, in approximately 1480 CE. They ruled at Kilbrittain Castle, their ancestral home south-west of Cork City. One hundred and twenty-one years later their descendant, Clan Chieftain Florence MacCarthaigh Reagh left Kilbrittain to visit Sir George Carew and was arrested and sent to the tower of London prior to the Battle of Kinsale. This attribution comes from a scribal note on folio 92R.

At the insistence of Sir George Carew, President of Munster in 1602, Richard Boyle had purchased Sir Walter Raleigh's estates, including Lismore, when the latter gentleman had been executed by Queen Elizabeth. He made Lismore Castle his capital as he proceeded to acquire more land and power. Research shows that Richard Boyle, or Lord Boyle, Baron of Youghal, became the Earl of Cork in 1620.

How then did the *Book of Lismore* get from the MacCarthaigh Reagh Kilbrittain Castle to Lismore some 60 miles northeast? When the Confederate Wars started in 1641, three of Boyle's sons, operating out of Lismore, took up the fight for Protestant England. The MacCarthaigh Reagh (Kilbrittain) and Donagh MacCarthy, 2nd Viscount Muskerry (Blarney) Catholic Clans, were among their sworn Catholic enemies.

The second oldest Boyle brother, Lewis, aged twenty-three and titled 1st Viscount Boyle of Kinalmeaky, led an attack on Kilbrittain Castle in the spring of 1642. He captured the estate of the Mac Carthaigh Reagh, Tadgh's ancestor. Here he found and confiscated the *Book of Mac Carthaigh Riabhach* (Reagh) and sent it, with a letter to his father Richard at Lismore Castle.

In July that year, all three brothers fought under the leadership of Murrough O'Brien, Baron of Inchiquin (later to be called Murrough of the Conflagrations) against a combined Confederate army of six thousand in the major battle of Liscarrol, where Lewis was killed. The British won the battle and thereby retained Cork for the remainder of these wars.

Lewis' oldest brother Richard, already titled 1st Earl of Burlington, also took his title as 2nd Viscount Boyle of Kinalmeaky. A year later, when his father died, young Richard became the 2nd Earl of Cork.

Meanwhile, the third brother, Roger, titled 1st Earl of Orrery and Baron of Broghill (styled Lord Broghill), went on to become a major military foe for the Confederate army.

In July of 1643, with his father very sickly, Roger Boyle defended Lismore Castle from a siege by Confederate forces led by, among others, 2nd Viscount Muskerry (Donagh MacCarthy) whose headquarters was at Blarney Castle, County Cork. We can only speculate that this was, in part, retaliation for the seizure of Kilbrittain Castle the year before.

Perhaps, if truth be known, the attack on Lismore Castle was in part to recover the *Book of Mac Carthaigh Riabhach* (and its hidden Clans Pact). Oh, but here I am mixing fact with fiction. Or am I? Clearly, Richard Boyle hid the book and the crozier by walling it in at that time, likely to keep it safe while the results of the siege were in question. Later in the siege, his son Roger rushed home from England and saved the castle. Lord Boyle died immediately thereafter and Roger (Lord Broghill) left Lismore Castle to wage war against the Confederate army. Had the aged patriarch, Richard, survived, he most likely would have recovered the book from the castle wall after the Confederate Wars were over. (Note: One recent antiquary found a marginal note '1745', which caused him to think the book was not walled up in 1643. But I think this note was likely inserted after 1814, when the elements of these documents were being examined by collectors and others).

Lord Muskerry (Donagh) became the leader of the Confederate army, and as time progressed, took the Royalist side in the English

Civil War. Therefore, when his Blarney Castle was attacked by Lord Broghill in 1646, Donagh was not there.

Oliver Cromwell, Lord Protector of the Commonwealth, arrived in 1649 with an army to dispose of the Irish once and for all, using brutal slash and burn tactics throughout Ireland. Lord Broghill was his staunch ally. Lord Muskerry and his troops fought valiantly but were finally defeated by Lord Broghill at the Battle of Knocknaclashy in 1651. After retiring west into the hills, Donagh MacCarthy and his remaining forces were forced to surrender Ross Castle in 1652. Thus ended the Confederate Wars.

After the *Book of Lismore* was found in the castle walls in 1814, it was given to Dennis O'Flynn, a Cork historian who split it into sections and sold parts of it separately to collectors. He changed the name of the book to Lismore. After 1856, parts of this book were found and reunited at Lismore Castle. The book remained there until 1930, when it was transferred to Chatsworth, the Derbyshire seat of the Duke of Devonshire.

The *Book of Lismore* currently has 198 folios, (42 are missing), which are 14.5 x 10.5 inches. Its condition is acephalous (lacking a head), and lacunose (full of holes or gaps), as a result of O'Flynn's actions. There has been significant research done to assess the original organization and content of this book, including comparing sections with missing leaves to other manuscripts of that era, which might have copied the *Book of Lismore*, or had been copies for that book.

There are two important copies of this manuscript. The first, at the RIA in Dublin, was scribed in 1839 by Eugene O'Curry and collated by John O'Donovan. The second, also at the RIA, was scribed by Joseph Ó Longáin. These copies were available for Professor Hugh Jackson Lawlor to examine in the early twentieth century, even though the original was still at Lismore Castle until 1930.

* References: Wikipedia Sources and www.chatsworth.org/... library/book-of-lismore

The table of contents that had been written down by Professor Lawlor and passed over to Tadgh and Peader is provided below.

Book of Mac Carthaigh Riabhach (Reagh) - Book of Lismore

Table of Contents

1. Preliminaries;
   A History of Israel
2. Lives of the Saints
   (Patrick, Columba, Brigit,
   Senán, Finnian, Finnchua,
   Brénainn, Ciarán)
3. Hagiographical (Saints) Anecdotes
4. Tenga Bithnua
   (Six Days of Creation)
5. Poems
6. Conquests of
   Charlemagne
7. Anecdotes
8. History of the Lombards
9. Marco Polo's Travels
10. Diarmait mac Cerbaill
11. The Book of Rights
12. The Victorious Career of
    Ceallachán of Caiseal
13. Siege of Druim Damhgaire
14. Miscellanea
15. Imthecht na Tromdáimhe
    (Conchobar-cycle)
16. Dialogue of Ancient Men -
    Oisin and Cailte**
    ** last leaf is a faded vellum fragment

Folio 134 v (cropped)

3. Ballymote, Temple House and the Percevals *

Ballymote, a town in county Sligo, some 20 miles south of Sligo Town and 60 miles southwest of Donegal Town, has a rich Irish history.

In 1169, Richard Fitzgilbert de Clare, 2nd Earl of Pembroke (called "Strongbow"), and his army of Norman Knights invaded Ireland. They infiltrated the country and established fortified positions among the clans. Many of them had been to the Crusades and were part of the Knights Templar Order.

The English King Henry II took a strong hand in this Irish "settlement." In 1171 he invaded Ireland and negotiated a settlement with the Normans in return for fealty to the English crown. The Irish church hierarchy also submitted to Henry, believing his intervention would bring greater political stability. Henry "used the church as a vehicle of conquest." He organized the synod of Cashel, at which Irish church practices were brought into line with those of England, and new monastic communities and military orders (such as the Templars) were introduced into Ireland. Through his Norman subjects, Henry oversaw the construction of many castles that would stand the test of time against the native Irish Clans in the centuries to come.

In 1216, the knights built their most westerly European stronghold at Templehouse in County Sligo, four miles north of Ballymote, some say on the ruins of an earlier fortification. As a result of these land grants by Henry II at various locations within Ireland, the Templar estates there were the third most valuable of all the order's holdings. The Templars did not consider themselves as conquerors but rather religious patrons generating funds from these properties to support the Crusades in the Holy Land.

After King Phillipe of France arrested Jacques de Molay and his knights in Paris in October 1307, he and the Pope ordered all kings to arrest the Knights Templar. This included those in Ireland. The Irish knights were arrested, incarcerated in the Castle in Dublin, and subsequently tried in 1310. None of the forty-one witnesses called could find wrongdoing, and the Templars professed their innocence. As a result, they were allowed to live by doing penance.

Their estates were confiscated in 1311 and handed over to Knights Hospitallers, known also as the Knights of the Hospital of St. John of Jerusalem, as confirmed by King Henry II.

At this point, two of these Knights assumed control of the western Irish Templar estates. Thomas FitzMaurice, a Templar recently returned from the Crusades, shifted allegiance in 1307 to become a Knight Hospitaller. He subsequently built the monatery at Ardfert, which would become a great center of ecclesiastical learning in Europe during the Middle Ages. He eventually became the Grand Knight for Ireland. Similarly, another Knight Hospitaller whose name has slipped into antiquity took possession of the Templar Castle on Templehouse Lake, just north of Ballymote.

It is said that they banded together to provide a western route of escape for Knights Templar fleeing to Scotland from persecution. Furthermore, it is said that some of these Knights Templar fought in support of Robert the Bruce at Bannockburn, Scotland, when he took back his country from the English King Edward II in 1314. It is not hard to speculate that some stories regarding what these fleeing Templar Knights may have known of the whereabouts of the Order's hidden treasures, potentially including any saved from Solomon's Temple could have been passed to the Ardfert and/or Ballymote Hospitallers. Further, clues could have been inserted into the now famous *Book of Ballymote* when it was written in the 1400s. Is this why Red High O'Donnell's grandfather procured it back in the early 1500s? Or did Red Hugh just use it for the Clans Pact based upon his own knowledge. But that's a story to unravel in another novel.

Between 1314 and 1600, the castle changed hands several times between the McDonaghs and the O'Haras.

We must draw a distinction between the Templehouse Castle, four miles north of Ballymote, and the keepless Ballymote Castle in the town center. This latter castle was built around 1300, likely by Richard Óg de Burgh, 2nd Earl of Ulster (called "The Red Earl"). It was lost to the O'Connors in 1317, and before the end of the 14th century, fell into the hands of the McDonagh Clan. There is some indication that it was in a dilapidated state up through 1588 when it was sold to Red Hugh O'Donnell for a purported £400 and 300 milk cows.

This is the castle where Red Hugh gathered his forces in the late summer of 1601 before marching south to meet the English near Kinsale. He had burned his castle in Donegal Town to prevent British occupation. It is entirely possible that Red Hugh chose this castle because of its proximity to Templehouse, the Knights Hospitaller, and any possible secret information regarding the disposition of treasures by the retreating Knights Templar.

It is said that Red Hugh entered the Order of the Hospital of St. John of Jerusalem and became a Hospitaller Knight before he marched south to his destiny at the Battle of Kinsale. After the devastating loss there, the Ballymote town castle was surrendered to the British in 1602 likely by Red Hugh's brother Rory.

An abbey had been built in 1442 in Ballymote town by its patron, McDonagh. It was raided and burned at least twice, razing it finally in 1584 in the second raid.

The surname Perceval is synonymous with knighthood and chivalry, starting in the fifth century with Perceval of the Grail, the "Red Knight" of King Arthur's Knights of the Round Table. He was so named because he killed the previous Red Knight of Quinqueroy (Ither of Gavheviez) in combat. The story of his search for the Holy Grail has been told many times, but none is as fascinating—although it is incomplete—as that spun by Cretien de Troyes in Flanders, written about 1150 CE.

Then Ascelin Goval de Perceval defended his castle of Yvery in Normandy in 897, and a few generations later, a Perceval helped to invade England as part of the retinue of William the Conqueror in 1066.

Sir Richard de Perceval, Lord of Stawell settled in Weston on Gordano, England. In the 1191 Irish Expedition of the Crusades, he became the Principal Commander of the Knights Templar under King Richard the Coeur de Lion in the Holy Lands during the battles against the Saracens. There he lost a leg in battle.

Thereafter, thirteen generations of Percevals ruled as Lord of Eastbury at Weston, including Sir Roger de Perceval, who fought and died in King Edward II's army at Bannockburn in 1314, and Sir Walter Perceval, who died fighting in the battle of Cressy in 1349.

In the 16th century, a member of the family was granted land in Ireland as a reward for his services to Queen Elizabeth I for breaking the Armada Code, and his son, George Perceval, married Mary Crofton, heiress to the lands of Temple House, in 1665.

As an aside, John Perceval, First Earl of Egmont, became a close associate of James Oglethorpe, chairman of a committee that in 1730 formed an association later known as the Trustees for the Establishment of the Colony of Georgia in America. King George II approved a charter for the colony in 1732, making Egmont president.

With a short but significant break in the 19th century, the Percevals have owned the one- thousand-acre property with its Templar castle just north of Ballymote and have lived there ever since. They rebuilt the old castle and lived there until 1760, when they built a new home for the family nearby, leaving the servants to occupy the castle.

The present manor house dates to 1825, when Colonel Alexander Perceval moved a little way up the hill and embarked on building a new house in classical style with room once more for family and retinue together. This was his country seat and family home, the colonel having an honourable post in London as Sergeant at Arms in the House of Lords, while his wife Jane remained in Sligo to rear their large family.

At a time when many of the owners of Ireland's demesnes lived in splendor in faraway London and extracted crippling rents from their unfortunate tenants, the Percevals distinguished themselves by their concern for the welfare of their poorer neighbours—a noble sentiment that was to end in tragedy. Jane Perceval customarily visited the workers and tenantry with gifts of food and medicine. She died in the winter of 1847 of "famine fever," the fate of many of those good people who had gone to the assistance of the starving peasantry. Her large portrait may be seen in the family home's dining room. A touching letter from her at that time offers reminders for those around her "not to neglect the tenant families between my death and my funeral."

The death of her husband, eleven years later, forced the son and heir to sell the entire property because of the new inheritance tax. The new owners from Essex had a very different view of their duties and became notorious for evicting many families. Then things took a remarkable turn for the better. Christopher L'Estrange, agent and a brother-in-law of the late colonel, reacted positively to a suggestion made by some of the dispossessed families to invite Jane's third son Alexander to buy the estate back.

As was the usual practice of the time, younger sons left home to seek their fortunes elsewhere as the estates were passed on, undivided, to the eldest. Alexander, a barrister, had gone to Shanghai and then to Hong Kong, where he made a more than ordinary fortune in the tea trade and became the first chairman of the Chamber of Commerce in that city. Not only did he buy back the ancestral home, he also paid for a number of the evicted families to return from Britain and America, and he rebuilt their houses.

The big house created by his father did not seem big enough, so in 1862, Alexander began work to transform it. He built a seven-bay entrance front at right angles to the original building, which had five bays and now forms the side elevation. This explains all sorts of intriguing irregularities in the building that stands there now. Hidden from the house by trees, a palatial coach house and stable yard were constructed, and on the south front, a terraced garden was added.

Alexander, whose portrait hangs above the dining room fireplace, is known affectionately as "The Chinaman." He died in 1866, a poorer but probably happier man, knowing he had spent his fortune on undertakings that provided employment and a measure of security for an unknown number of local people.

A remarkable revival of times long gone came to pass when his son Alec married the girl next door, Charlotte O'Hara. The O'Hara chieftains, onetime owners of Temple House lands, had been ousted in the 16th century by the Crown, and this marriage signified a happy return of their descendants. Charlotte, indeed, became more than the lady of the manor. Her husband died in 1887, only two years after the birth of their son Ascelin. For the next thirty years, she was the mistress of the demesne, seeing it through a stirring period in Irish history, from the times of Parnell and English rule, to the Easter Rising of 1916 and the birth of independence, the Lands Acts giving the tenants right of tenure.

As an aside, Charlotte's great-grandfather, General Charles O'Hara is best remembered in U.S history as the British Officer who substituted for Lieutenant General Lord Charles Cornwallis at the surrender of the British Army at Yorktown, Virginia, in October 1781.

Charlotte would tell you the story of Sir Owain, the medieval knight who sought penance by surviving a night in the pit of St. Patrick's Purgatory in Donegal in 1153 **. He traveled from continental Europe through Ballymote and stayed on at the Templar lands, where he met and fell in love with a local maiden after his ordeal. He was saddened when, out of duty, he left her there to return to his homeland, never to return while still alive. They say that his ghost on horseback appears at night in the Templar Castle ruins of Temple House to visitors who are troubled about losses in their own lives, just before a revelation of their circumstances.

Ascelin's wife Eleanora Margaret, called "Nora," lived with Charlotte while her husband fought in WWI, during which time he rose to the rank of major. Interestingly enough, Nora did have a good friend called Lady Gaga (no relation to the U.S. celebrity as far as I know).

In 1920, during the Irish War of Independence, the house was attacked twice by the IRA, the second incursion seriously injuring

Nora. Sandy Perceval, father of the current owner of Temple House, kindly offered the following family reflection on the first incident: "There was a staff of eleven women and five men in the house at that time. Nora met the attacking rebels after they pushed past the butler who then stood behind her. The first raid was from nearby, and when asked what they wanted, Nora was told, 'Ma'am, we have been sent for arms'. She replied that all the guns except for her husband's and the Gamekeeper's were in the barracks. 'We know, Ma'am,' the leader said. 'We waited until we saw the major leave for Lurganboy [45 miles away] for the day. Is there anything you could suggest that we might take instead?' Nora piled their open arms with old swords and pikes off the gallery wall, and as they left, the leader took her open handbag off the hall table and closed it before handing it back saying, 'Ma'am, you should never leave your handbag open like that as it could be a temptation to someone'."

Since 2004, this important ninety-seven-room historical demesne, now a charming country retreat for guests, has been owned and operated by Roderick Perceval, who grew up there. He and his charming wife Helena have restored the manor to its former glory, now some three hundred fifty-three years after George Perceval and Mary Crofton settled there in the 1660s.

It's a wonderful place to visit and stay for a bit.

* References: Wikipedia Sources, Temple House website www.templehouse.ie and Perceval Family Members)

** This tale of Owain's journey is the *Tractatus de Purga-torio Sancti Patricii* by H. of Sawtrey. This narrative became a very popular document in medieval Europe and spurred on the pilgrimages to this sacred spot over the centuries. Here we are on firm historical ground, at least in the origins and transmission of the narrative, because the text exists, and its genesis can be reconstructed from contemporary ecclesiastical sources, even if they are not always precise.

Ninty-seven Room Temple House Demesne, on a 1,000-Acre Estate, built in 1825 by the Perceval Family, Adjacent to the 13th Century Knights Templar Castle Ruins.
Courtesy of Roderick and Helena Perceval

Ruins of 13th Century Knights Templar Castle built in 1216. Westernmost European Property of the K.T. Transferred to Knights Hospitallers in 1311. Occupied by Percevals 1665-1760.
Courtesy of Roderick and Helena Percevel

Dining Room of Temple House, Sligo. Picture of Jane Perceval over the sideboard. Picture of Alexander Perceval, the Hong Kong Taipan "Chinaman," over the Fireplace.
Courtesy of Roderick and Helena Perceval.

Main Staircase of Temple House, Sligo, as seen from the Upstairs Hallway. Ancestral Paintings line the walls.
Courtesy of Roderick and Helena Perceval

4. Poems of Denis Florence MacCarthy

Denis Florence MacCarthy *, a prolific Irish poet, translator and biographer, was born in Lower O'Connell Street in 1817, and died in Dublin in 1882. During his life, he lived in Dublin, continental Europe, and London. In 1846 he was called to the Irish bar, but never practiced law.

He was a prolific translator, notably of Pedro Calderón de la Barca, the Spanish Shakespeare, and he edited notable poetic compendia such as *The Poets and Dramatists of Ireland* and *The Book of Irish Ballads*. He greatly admired Percy Bysshe Shelley and published *Shelley's Early Life* while living in London.

Denis's own *Ballads, Poems and Lyrics* was published in 1850. Two of his poems with excerpts quoted in the novel are included below in their entirety. A third poem was included in the historical background section of *Entente: The Irish Clans: Book Two*.

4.1 The "Pillar Towers of Ireland" by Denis Florence MacCarthy

The pillar towers of Ireland, how wondrously they stand
By the lakes and rushing rivers through the valleys of our land;
In mystic file, through the isle, they lift their heads sublime,
These gray old pillar temples, these conquerors of time!

Beside these gray old pillars, how perishing and weak
The Roman's arch of triumph, and the temple of the Greek,
And the gold domes of Byzantium, and the pointed Gothic spires,
All are gone, one by one, but the temples of our sires!

The column, with its capital, is level with the dust,
And the proud halls of the mighty and the calm homes of the just;
For the proudest works of man, as certainly, but slower,
Pass like the grass at the sharp scythe of the mower!

375

But the grass grows again when in majesty and mirth,
On the wing of the spring, comes the Goddess of the Earth;
But for man in this world no springtide e'er returns
To the labours of his hands or the ashes of his urns!

Two favourites hath Time—the pyramids of Nile,
And the old mystic temples of our own dear isle;
As the breeze o'er the seas, where the halcyon has its nest,
Thus Time o'er Egypt's tombs and the temples of the West!

The names of their founders have vanished in the gloom,
Like the dry branch in the fire or the body in the tomb;
But to-day, in the ray, their shadows still they cast—
These temples of forgotten gods—these relics of the past!

Around these walls have wandered the Briton and the Dane—
The captives of Armorica, the cavaliers of Spain—
Phœnician and Milesian, and the plundering Norman Peers—
And the swordsmen of brave Brian, and the chiefs of later years!

How many different rites have these gray old temples known!
To the mind what dreams are written in these chronicles of stone!
What terror and what error, what gleams of love and truth,
Have flashed from these walls since the world was in its youth?

Here blazed the sacred fire, and, when the sun was gone,
As a star from afar to the traveller it shone;
And the warm blood of the victim have these gray old temples drunk,
And the death-song of the druid and the matin of the monk.

Here was placed the holy chalice that held the sacred wine,
And the gold cross from the altar, and the relics from the shrine,
And the mitre shining brighter with its diamonds than the East,
And the crosier of the pontiff and the vestments of the priest.

Where blazed the sacred fire, rung out the vesper bell,
Where the fugitive found shelter, became the hermit's cell;
And hope hung out its symbol to the innocent and good,
For the cross o'er the moss of the pointed summit stood.

There may it stand for ever, while that symbol doth impart
To the mind one glorious vision, or one proud throb to the heart;
While the breast needeth rest may these gray old temples last,
Bright prophets of the future, as preachers of the past!

4.2 "A Mystery" by Denis Florence MacCarthy

They are dying! they are dying! where the golden corn is growing,
They are dying! they are dying! where the crowded herds are lowing;
They are gasping for existence where the streams of life are flowing,
And they perish of the plague where the breeze of health is blowing!

> *God of Justice! God of Power!*
> *Do we dream? Can it be?*
> *In this land, at this hour,*
> *With the blossom on the tree,*
> *In the gladsome month of May,*
> *When the young lambs play,*
> *When Nature looks around*
> *On her waking children now,*
> *The seed within the ground,*
> *The bud upon the bough?*
> *Is it right, is it fair,*
> *That we perish of despair*
> *In this land, on this soil,*
> *Where our destiny is set,*
> *Which we cultured with our toil,*
> *And watered with our sweat?*

We have ploughed, we have sown
But the crop was not our own;
We have reaped, but harpy hands
Swept the harvest from our lands;
We were perishing for food,
When, lo! in pitying mood,
Our kindly rulers gave
The fat fluid of the slave,
While our corn filled the manger
Of the war-horse of the stranger!

God of Mercy! must this last?
Is this land preordained
For the present and the past,
And the future, to be chained,
To be ravaged, to be drained,
To be robbed, to be spoiled,
To be hushed, to be whipt,
Its soaring pinions clipt,
And its every effort foiled?

Do our numbers multiply
But to perish and to die?
Is this all our destiny below,
That our bodies, as they rot,
May fertilise the spot
Where the harvests of the stranger grow?

If this be, indeed, our fate,
Far, far better now, though late,
That we seek some other land and try some other zone;
The coldest, bleakest shore
Will surely yield us more
Than the store-house of the stranger that we dare not call our own.

378

Kindly brothers of the West,
Who from Liberty's full breast
Have fed us, who are orphans, beneath a step-dame's frown,
Behold our happy state,
And weep your wretched fate
That you share not in the splendours of our empire and our crown!

Kindly brothers of the East,
Thou great tiara'd priest,
Thou sanctified Rienzi of Rome and of the earth--
Or thou who bear'st control
Over golden Istambol,
Who felt for our misfortunes and helped us in our dearth,

Turn here your wondering eyes,
Call your wisest of the wise,
Your Muftis and your ministers, your men of deepest lore;
Let the sagest of your sages
Ope our island's mystic pages,
And explain unto your Highness the wonders of our shore.

A fruitful teeming soil,
Where the patient peasants toil
Beneath the summer's sun and the watery winter sky--
Where they tend the golden grain
Till it bends upon the plain,
Then reap it for the stranger, and turn aside to die.

Where they watch their flocks increase,
And store the snowy fleece,
Till they send it to their masters to be woven o'er the waves;
Where, having sent their meat
For the foreigner to eat,
Their mission is fulfilled, and they creep into their graves.

'Tis for this they are dying where the golden corn is growing,
'Tis for this they are dying where the crowded herds are lowing,
'Tis for this they are dying where the streams of life are flowing,
And they perish of the plague where the breeze of health is blowing.

* (Reference: Wikipedia Sources and http://www.gutenberg.org/ebooks/author/4460)

5. The Rock of Cashel

The Eoghanachta Clan emigrated from Wales to Cashel Ireland in the 5th century, CE. There on the high rock they raised a Celtic cross to St. Patrick on the spot where he first baptized their ancestral Chieftain. They erected a Celtic round tower to defend against their enemies, foreign and domestic and to protect their buried ancestors. They ruled there until 1,000 CE when they were conquered by the forces of Brian Boru as he integrated the Irish in their fight to rid Ireland of the Vikings.

They moved south and occupied much of Munster and Kerry in the southwest of Ireland. There they became known as the Mac-Carthaigh Clan, building twenty-six castles in southwestern Ireland including Kilbrittain and Blarney.

In 1134, as a sign of goodwill, the MacCarthaigh Chieftain Cormac built a chapel on his old territory, the Rock of Cashel, to appease the descendants of Brian Boru. Centuries later, the cathedral was built, along with the adjoining Bishop's Castle and his Vicar's Choral, to house his priests.

During the rebellious Confederate Wars of 1642–1652, English forces under the offspring of Richard Boyle, Lismore Castle attacked and defeated MacCarthaigh forces at Kilbrittain (1642) and McCarthy Mor forces at Blarney (1646).

As the murderous English pushed their enemy northward, slashing and burning the villages and countryside as they went, the rebels took a stand on the Rock of Cashel. Murrough, the Baron of Inchiquin and strong ally of the Boyles, attacked and burned to death all of the villagers and confederate soldiers. Three thousand men, women, and children were killed, roasted on this hill in September 1647, many of them while they sought protection in the sanctity of this Catholic cathedral. That's why he was called Murrough of the Conflagrations. The attacking forces stripped the cathedral of its valuables and destroyed much of it.

Now the magnificent and historic Rock of Cashel is operated by the Office of Public Works, Ireland.

Rock of Cashel
(Images Courtesy of the Office of Public Works, Ireland)

Aerial View
(From OPW.ie Rock of Cashel Brochure)

St. Patrick's High Cross
Looking Northwest from Vicar's Choral
(S. F. Archer Photo)

Tympanum Over North Door of Cormac's Chapel
(Photo OPW.ie Rock of Cashel Brochure)

6. The Pivotal Battle of Kinsale, January 1602

In the last ten years of the 1500s, the English were gaining ground in Ireland, having suppressed the Rebellion in Kerry in the 1580s. From their stronghold of Dublin (The Pale), they advanced west in the south, strengthening a second stronghold in Cork City.

A fierce campaign by England, named the Nine Years War, ensued in the hills of Ireland from 1593 to 1602. The Clans won decisive victories at the Battle of Belleek in 1593, led by northeastern Clan Chieftain Hugh O'Neill and at the Battle of Yellow Ford in 1598, led by the northwestern Clan Chieftain Red Hugh O'Donnell.

In 1599, Queen Elizabeth sent her favorite earl, Robert Devereux, to Ireland with an army of over 17,000 soldiers to conquer the Clans once and for all. The Second Earl of Essex had great trouble with these northern clans, who fought successfully in the hill country. Losing the fight to disease and his Irish enemy, Devereux formed an ill-fated treaty with The O'Neill and headed home to England.

The queen was furious that he had come home without her approval and with his tail between his legs. Devereux, feeling betrayed, formed a pact with King James of Scotland and then led a coup attempt on Elizabeth. This was summarily squashed, and Devereux was arrested and finally beheaded at the Tower of London in 1602.

Meanwhile, Elizabeth sent stronger warriors to Ireland in the name of George Carew to Munster, George Wilmot to Kerry, and Henry Dowcra to attack Derry in the central north between the O'Donnell and the O'Neill forces. Carew and Dowcra had fought successfully under Devereux in the attack on Cadiz, Spain, in 1596.

Carew was skillful and deviously cunning in negotiating with the McCarthy Clans in the south, while Dowcra eventually captured Derry in 1601 with the help of Red Hugh's traitorous cousin Niall O'Donnell who mistakenly expected to be named Clan Chieftain after the English conquered Ireland.

At that moment, Clan Chieftains Florence McCarthy (Kilbrittain) and Red Hugh O'Donnell (Donegal) plotted to bring the Catholic Spanish, (still incensed after the defeat of their attacking Spanish armada) to their aid against the Protestant English. Florence was the emissary to Spanish King Philip III.

In the summer of 1601, having organized for the Spanish to come to Ireland, Florence was tricked into visiting Carew in Cork. He was immediately arrested and sent to the Tower of London where he was incarcerated until 1620.

When Derry fell to the English in late summer, Red Hugh realized that he and O'Neill needed to combine forces. They needed to reach their Spanish ally's army that was unfortunately planning to land at a southern Ireland location instead of at a more favorable northwestern port.

He burned his own castle stronghold in Donegal Town to keep the English from using it and headed south into Sligo to the castle of Ballymote which he had cunningly purchased three years earlier. There, in October 1601, Red Hugh and his brother Rory amassed his army of 4,000 gallowglass soldiers and 3,000 horse soldiers.

The Spanish landed at Kinsale, the Irish provisioners town on the south coast west of Cork City on September 23, 1601. In the 16th century, this town had sprung up as the furthest-west northern European port before the dangerous voyage to the New World.

Unfortunately a critical portion of the 6,000 man Spanish force had turned back due to bad weather, so their commander, Don Juan del Águila, arrived in Kinsale with only 4,000 men and without much of their munitions.

The English were quick to send forces led by Charles Blount, Lord Mountjoy, the newly assigned Lord Deputy of Ireland, from the Pale to Kinsale to lay siege to the town and the Spanish, hemming them in against the Celtic Sea. Of the 12,000 English forces who initially surrounded the port, only 7,500 remained by the time of the battle in January 1602, due to attrition from winter illnesses brought on by lack of supplies.

Hugh O'Neill initially was reluctant to march south, preferring to stay within his own territory to defend against the English. But Red Hugh convinced him that the remaining Clans needed to band together, joined with the Spanish, in a last-ditch effort to rid their country of the invading infidels.

While O'Neill led his forces south down an easterly path, cutting off supplies between the Pale and the English army at Kinsale, Red Hugh accompanied by his ally Richard Tyrell marched south through the winter blizzards, fortunately across unusually frozen bogs. He arrived in Thurles at the site of Holy Cross Church with the Holy Rood (Piece of the Cross of Jesus) at the feast of St. Andrew on November 30.

There he split his forces with a small contingent being sent west to liberate his compatriot, Thomas FitzMaurice, whose lands had been captured by the English under the leadership of George Wilmot a year earlier. His hope was that FitzMaurice could muster an army to aid in the cause at Kinsale.

Then Red Hugh headed south to a rendezvous point at Bandon, west of Kinsale and halfway to Castlehaven. He estimated that the combined Irish army would be eighteen thousand plus the Spaniards and by his intelligence, the British army numbered only seven thousand. Good odds.

In December 1601, a secondary Spanish force of seven ships with 2,000 men led by Pedro de Zubiaur, which had been diverted from Aquila's fleet by weather, landed at Castlehaven, west of Kinsale. They were quickly dispatched by the English navy under the leadership of Admiral Richard Leveson.

Battle of Kinsale – January 3, 1602

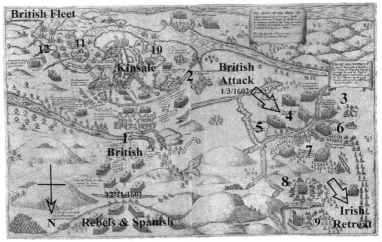

Table 2: The Seige and Battle of Kinsale Map Legend

1	Lord Deputy Mountjoy's Camp	7	Tyrrell's Irish Forces
2	Earl of Thomond's Camp	8	O'Donnell's Irish Forces
3	Cavalry Attack on the Irish	9	Don Juan del Aguila's Spanish Forces
4	Henry Power's Squadron Volant	10	George Carew's Siege Forces
5	St John's Regiment	11	Castlepark
6	O'Neill's Irish Forces	12	Ringcurran Castle

O'Neill controlled the ridge and intended to fight for it, with support from Aguila, O'Donnell, and Tyrell on multiple sides. Del Águila, the Spanish commander, was an experienced soldier and put up a fierce defense. Due to poor communications, neither of his allies showed signs of movement, so O'Neill ordered a retreat into the marshes, hoping to mire the English cavalry in the soft land. In the end, the Irish were overpowered by the English cavalry, who charged through O'Neill's men, and prevented a flanking maneuver by O'Donnell.

The tactics showed that the Irish infantry were poorly trained for pitched battle in formation against a well drilled professional army. It also showed that the English cavalry techniques using the lance, were superior when compared to the Irish method of no stirrup and overhead spear throwing.

The Irish army left the field in some disorder while the supporting Spanish army now led by Ocampo tried to hold up the English charge and the ensuing massacre of the Irish. Most of the Irish fled back to Ulster, though a few remained to continue the war with O'Sullivan Beare and Dermot Maol MacCarthy Reagh.

As described in the historical background section of *Searchers: The Irish Clans, Book One*, Red Hugh and Rory O'Donnell survived the battle. Red Hugh sailed immediately for Spain in an attempt to recruit more Spanish forces from Philip III's units to fight the English, while Rory led the remnants of their army back to northern Ulster.

One of the English generals and President of Munster in the south, Sir George Carew, sent James Blake, a spy, after Red Hugh to poison him. Within the year the Clan Chieftain was dead in Spain and there was no more assistance forthcoming from that country.

Within five years, the Clan leaders in the north were forced to flee Ireland or be captured and executed. Rory O'Donnell and his family were a main part of the flight of the Earls to the European continent in 1607. Rory went to Rome and met with the Pope. Then he died mysteriously in the Roman port of Ostia.

Niall was eventually incarcerated after an abortive uprising in Derry (now Londonderry) was quelled by the English in 1608, and he and his son died in prison.

With that, the English had taken over Ireland from the native Irish, and they planted their own nobility into the castles and lands of the Irish Clans.

About the Author

Stephen in his office
with original artwork by Mr. Norman Tealing

Stephen Finlay Archer
was brought up in the Beaches, Toronto, Canada. His mother is Dot in
the novels and his Irish grandfather is Samuel Stevenson Finlay, an artist
of some renoun.

Following acquisition of a Masters of Science degree from the
University of Toronto, Stephen spent thirty-five years as an aerospace
engineering manager, working initially in Canada and mainly in the
United States. He directed satellite systems design, implementation,
launch, and mission programs with the U.S. Navy and with NASA/
NOAA, among others.

Upon retirement, Stephen completed courses in short story and
novel writing with the Long Ridge Writers Group in Connecticut. He is
a member of Writers Unlimited Group in California Gold Country and
the North-American Historical Novel Society.

Stephen can be reached at   or via his website at
stephenarcher@earthlink.net   *www.stephenfinlayarcher.com*

Made in the USA
Lexington, KY
03 December 2019